Paul Stuar          l, England
in 1972.      D0766926      ovel, and
accompani              able at his
official website at www.paulstuartkemp.com.

As an English writer, he has managed to resist the mainstream American influence, and casts dark tales throughout major British cities such as London and Liverpool.

Paul Stuart Kemp lives in Berkshire, England.

also by Paul Stuart Kemp

# EDEN

## PAUL STUART KEMP

decapita

Published in Great Britain in 2004 by
Decapita Publishing
PO BOX 3802
Bracknell RG12 7XT

Email: mail@paulstuartkemp.com
Website: www.paulstuartkemp.com

Cover artwork by Fabrice Lavollay
Illustrations by Paul Stuart Kemp

Photograph of author by Helen Priest

The Author asserts the moral right to be
identified as the author of this work

ISBN 0 9538215 6 0

Set in Meridien

Printed and bound in Great Britain by
Decapita Publishing
PO BOX 3802
Bracknell RG12 7XT

# EDEN

# CONTENTS

## PART SIX
## ADVENTURES IN A NEW WORLD

## PART SEVEN
## PASSION AND WARFARE

# PROLOGUE

It is a freezing night, but the cold is refreshing compared to the humidity of the life I have lived. Life, can it even be called such? An existence, that seems closer.

I have existed.

I can see the frost already beginning to glisten across the back of my hand as I sit here and look out over the valley floor.

I made my home here in the mountains just a handful of years ago, in my home land, away from both mortals and vampires, away from the oppressions and desires of both, a place where I could chart the years I had passed.

Did anyone even miss me?

That is hard to tell. I had no need of them anyway, and, I suspected, I would never want for their company again. But for them to miss me? Who knows? That is another story, I fear.

I may have had impacts on the lives of others, I may have drifted through others without casting so much as a ripple on their imaginations. That notion is irrelevant now. I left them all behind me, and I intended to live here alone. But things have changed, circumstances beyond my influence.

The dreams started many months ago, strange vivid dreams about my husband. I saw him alive, witnessed him digging himself out of his earthy grave, his flesh-torn hands clawing at the dirt and rock that had kept him buried, scrabbling towards the night air that would see his resurrection.

My husband, you see, is dead, my husband of over two hundred years. I know he is dead, because I killed him myself. His desire to walk the earth has returned and therefore I must return to find him, to rekindle our vows and retain what we had once shared.

There is a wind gusting over the ridge now, I can feel the freezing cold of the ice it has blown over to get here, but it does not chill my body. It has kept others from coming here, and because of that I have tolerated it. But I will leave it now, to return to the land of the mortal, the land of warmth and agreed society, to find my husband Carlos and tell him that his sins have finally been absolved.

I have had no desire to tell of my memories, no desire to recount my decision to leave what had once been my home, no desire to even tell of how I came to leave that home, and travel a vast divide to a place so very alien to me. It had been a time lived, a journey travelled, but for my future, I saw nothing. It was uncharted, unlived, and that in itself gave a clearer perspective.

I thought one day I would tell it all. And I think that perhaps that time has now come. My name is Catherine Calleh and I am a Faraoh, one of the last few remaining of a decimated tribe of BloodGods, and I have existed for over a thousand years. My husband has awakened and become reborn, and I must leave my home of ice and desolation, and travel back across the divide to find him.

# PART ONE

# ECHOES OF A DEAD MAN

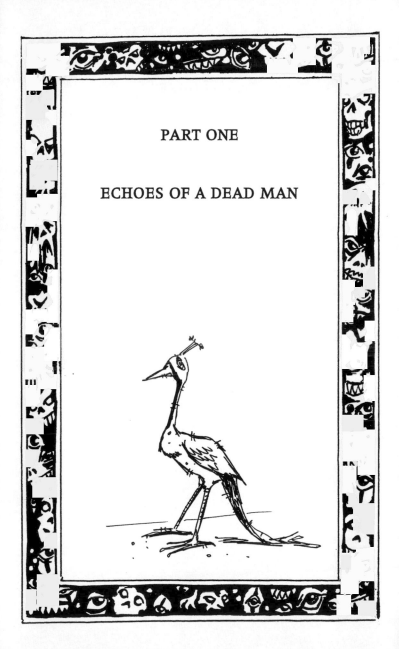

## ONE

## RESIDENT

The thud came dull and heavy against the wall. Her eyes shot open, water spilling over the edge of the bathtub as she lurched forward. But there was nothing there. Nothing she could see anyway.

With her heart hammering sharply in her chest, Romy Birch found herself staring hard out of the bathroom, through the door that still stood ajar, and into her bedroom. But nothing moved there either. No one fleeting past the doorway.

The house returned to its previous smothering silence, and inside its clinging depths her mind conjured depravities regarding the maker of the noise. She was alone in the house, and after her divorce it was gonna stay that way for a good long while yet.

Had she locked the front door?

Had she locked the back?

Her heart ticked over rapidly as her head went through the checklist.

Maybe she had imagined it. Yeah, that was possible. Maybe it had seemed louder than it had really been because she'd been dozing in the tub. Maybe it had come from next door, or maybe some local kids had thrown something up at the front of the house. A football maybe. Or a Frisbee - did kids still play with those things?

She was aware that her heart was still thudding against her ribs, pounding noticeably against the silence of the house. Romy took a few deep breaths as she placed a hand against her chest.

Sitting upright in her hot bath, meringues of delicately scented bubbles clinging to her reddened skin, ears pricked and desperately aware of just how vulnerable she was at the moment, she listened to the heavy quiet. But no further noise came. The house remained silent. A car drove quietly by outside in the street. A garden bird was singing close by. But that was all.

She lay back slowly in the bath once again and let the hot water creep back up and over her body, allowing the level to glance her chin and the bubbles her nose, but kept her eyes open and watching for a while.

It wasn't an old house. In fact it was part of a relatively new estate. Maybe it was just one of those things, she thought. A pipe in the attic or something. It had been unlived in for a while after all.

The sound didn't come again, its memory ultimately fading in her head, and Romy soaked for maybe quarter of an hour more before reaching for the soap.

After stepping out of the bath and drying herself with one of the new fluffy towels she'd treated herself to, she dried a patch of steam away on the mirror with it and studied herself. Her face was pretty, she thought, small but attractive. It was like her body in many ways and she wasn't displeased with either of them. In her teens she'd thought her nose too upright, too small, but former boyfriends had liked it, and Andrew had called it cute. With her face flushed from her bath it didn't even look like it needed make-up.

She turned her head from side to side, observing her complexion and bone structure more closely. Then, reasonably satisfied with herself, she towel-dried her dark hair roughly before brushing it out, and then pushed it back behind her ears before returning to the bedroom.

Rummaging through her chest of drawers, she found an old pair of jogging bottoms and a t-shirt, the one with BB King cradling Lucille on the front, and pulled them on before wandering back downstairs.

Back in the living room, Romy pushed some of the packing boxes away from the sofa before collapsing down onto it. She closed her eyes and luxuriated in the fact that this was her house now, and hers alone. The divorce from Andrew had been settled in April and her new house bought in July, but after three months of chasing paperwork between the estate agent and her solicitor and back again she had finally moved in.

She reached for one of the two remaining beers sitting on the coffee table. The chill had gone out of it while she'd been in the bath but she didn't care, and slipped the cap off the bottle with the opener before taking a long draw on it.

The beer was good, and welcome too, and Romy took several long swallows before sliding back into the billowing cushions of her sofa. She looked around her new living room, familiarizing herself with each new angle and wall socket. A smile crept across her lips, partly from the alcohol finding its way into her system, but mostly from the knowledge that she was finally out of a shit relationship and back into a world that she could run herself properly.

The survey of the house had uncovered some odd details, though, about which her solicitor had cautioned her, primarily pertaining to extensive refurbishment to what the previous owners had used as a dining room, and specifically relating to an unauthorised excavation which had led to an entirely new floor being laid right down to the foundation. Such details had made other potential buyers wary, it seemed, but at twenty thousand pounds below market value the house had suited her post divorce resources precisely. Better a house than a flat, Romy had said, also thrilled at all the extra space she would have to herself.

Her first night under a roof which was solely hers had so far been bliss. She'd dined on delivered pizza washed down with half a four pack of nicely-chilled bottled beers, and now she'd had her bath she was intent on finishing off the other two.

She'd spent most of the afternoon unpacking and sorting boxes, and with tiredness now competing with beer to close her eyes, she half-listened to the muted sounds of cars passing outside in the street as her muscles wound slowly down. It was six o'clock, and sleep must have stolen her quickly, for when she opened her eyes again the sky outside the curtainless window was dark and the room around her, cloaked in absolute blackness, seemed alien and clinging.

Her bladder was crippling, the need to urinate suddenly her only priority. Romy blinked several times, attempting to locate landmarks in the room, but none of them made any sense. A bright halo from a streetlamp outside reflected across the flat screen of her television, but that was it.

Romy pushed herself out of the sofa, her muscles as well as her bladder complaining from the movement. Warily she made her way forward with arms outstretched towards the darker silhouette of the open door, its shape gradually appearing out of the gloom as her sight made small efforts to help her navigate the route ahead.

She swiped blindly at the wall with the flat of her hand until her fingers fell upon the light switch. The room filled instantly with stark white light from the central unshaded bulb, the excess glow spilling out into the hallway and through the opposite open doorway into what the previous owners had used as the dining room, illuminating also the newly laid concrete floor where once an impromptu trench had been dug with a pick and a shovel.

Romy turned back to face the living room, her bladder still bloated and painful, and realised as she did so that her fingers were trembling with unease. With the light now on, the window reflected the room back at her like an ebony mirror, including the sight of her staring back at herself from the open doorway. She needed curtains, her mind thought stupidly, even as she pressed a hand to her screaming bladder again. She'd have to go shopping for some tomorrow.

She hurried along the hallway to the downstairs toilet and urinated for a long time, glad of the relief as her pee splashed down into the pan. Her head swam a little from both the beer and the unintentional sleep, and she held her head in her hands as she watched the shapes swirl behind her eyelids.

With her bladder empty and placated, she glanced at her watch as she emerged from the toilet. It was almost nine thirty. Despite her brief sleep, and probably in spite of the beers she'd drunk earlier, she felt tired, her muscles aching painfully as though she'd been marched across a hot desert all day without rest, yet it still felt too early to go to bed just yet.

Romy wandered back along the dark hallway, pushing her fingers through her hair, found the hall light switch, and turned that on too. She stopped halfway to the kitchen and turned back to step into the dining room, studying its shadows from the light that spilled in from the hallway. It already felt like the rooms had chosen their own purpose, despite the fact that the only fireplace in the house stood in this room and seemed better suited to a cosy living room than a dining room. Not even the cards she'd had through the post welcoming her to her new house seemed comfortable sitting in here on the mantelpiece.

Romy switched on the dining room light to see better and gazed around the room, her sight drawn almost immediately to the new patch of concrete spread out in front of the fireplace. Her mind conjured images of people digging, pickaxes and shovels leaning against the wallpaper, buckets of rubble scattered around and waiting for an imaginary skip outside.

She tried to imagine them in her mind as sane people, doing something so very logical and natural as digging a hole inside their own home. But as the invented people turned to look at her, their eyes suddenly glared white with lunacy, and toothless maws cackled terrifying curses at her.

Romy tried to stifle the shudder before it even came, chastising herself for allowing her imagination to try and scare her on her very first night alone - it was sick, that's what it was - but she left the light on anyway as she hurried back out of the dining room and along the hallway to the kitchen.

She'd been married to Andrew for only two years, yet she'd lived with him for four years prior to that. Before her relationship with him she'd shared a flat with her best friend from university, which had been residential, and had gone straight there from living with her parents. And it occurred to her now, as she sorted through boxes marked 'kitchen', that she had never lived on her own in her life. It suddenly seemed both thrilling and somehow long overdue, the sudden shock of independence dispelling the trepidation of being alone. Perhaps this was her time for adventure, she thought. Maybe this could spark something new and exciting in her life.

Yet even as she unpacked her blue patterned mugs from their travel blankets of bubble wrap, Romy struggled to keep the images of the former owners of the house from crawling into her imagination. She'd not spoken to anyone since the removal men had left at two o'clock that afternoon. And that was a first for her. The telephone was still packed away in a box somewhere. After the kettle was located, she noted, that would definitely be next on the list.

With her six blue patterned mugs sitting on the

worktop in front of a pile of torn bubble wrap, and the kettle found and plugged in, she wrung her hands through her hair as she realised she still needed to find both the coffee jar and the sugar. Plus she knew for a fact that she had no milk, and she wasn't about to drive to the local shops at this hour on her own.

The idea of coffee was out, she didn't want anything else to eat, and she couldn't be bothered to sit through anything on tv just for the sake of staying up, so Romy systematically set about checking the front and back doors, and making sure that all the downstairs windows were closed and locked.

The house was thick with smothering silence again with neither the tv on nor any music playing, but she made a point, as she walked back into the dining room, of humming loudly to herself, dispelling the heavy quiet if only in that room.

The windows were still locked tight, but she hesitated momentarily at the mantelpiece, staring down at the patch of newly laid concrete in front of the fireplace. She pleaded with her imagination not to kick off again - that was the last thing she needed before going to bed on her own - but her ears ignored her and instead delivered into her head the muted but unmistakable sound of something groaning beneath the floor at her feet.

The sound crawled inside her head like spiders across naked skin, and she shuddered with physical fear and loathing. She willed herself to stop listening, willed herself to just move away from the mantelpiece and go upstairs to bed. But the groaning continued like someone buried alive beneath her feet, and she was powerless to leave before it had spoken to her.

"Stop it," she suddenly cried to herself, pinching her skin and forcing herself away from the fireplace and the newly-laid concrete spread out before it. "Don't give me nightmares on my first night, for God's sake."

Romy hurried to the door now as she switched off the lights, glancing only briefly into the living room before hurrying quickly along the hallway as the darkness chased the hairs on the back of her neck.

She left the landing light on but slammed the bedroom door behind her, hunting through her chest of drawers and some of her packing boxes for anything heavy that she could leave beside the bed. Choices were few, and she knew you couldn't exactly belt a ghost with a hair-dryer even if you wanted to, but she felt better with it sitting on her bedside cabinet just the same.

She undressed cautiously - her ears still straining to pick out anything supernatural from downstairs in the dining room, her mind praying that they wouldn't - and slipped beneath the covers with her heart yammering wildly in her chest.

As she reached and turned out the light, she lay motionless for a while just listening to the sound of her blood pumping in her ears, deafening against the suffocating silence of the house. A car passed by out in the street - a snatch of normality, thank God - but it also helped to highlight the fact that assistance, should she need it, was still a long way away.

Pulling the covers up tight under her chin, she forced her eyes closed against the darkness of the room, and prayed that sleep would claim her quickly before the ground upon which the house was built offered up any more groans or laments, or whatever made those groans or laments crawled up out of the earth.

## TWO

## AIR IN THE PIPES

S unlight blazed. With neither curtains nor blinds to shield the bright dawn, the bedroom shone with glorious hues of yellow and gold. Romy rolled out from beneath the duvet to look up through the window at a completely cloudless blue sky. Birds wheeled past in formation, chasing an insect breakfast. She inhaled deeply, content with the new dawn, and exhaled noisily to the world.

Stretching out her limbs beneath the covers, Romy luxuriated in the comfort of her new beginning as a single woman. Cardboard boxes still littered the bedroom, as they did downstairs in the kitchen, dining and living rooms. There was plenty to be done but no desperate hurry in which to do any of it. The day was bright and dry. She didn't have to go back to work until the following week. She stretched out again, feeling the muscles tightening the length of her legs, and then she closed her eyes and dozed once again.

A slow rhythmic thumping jerked her instantly back to consciousness. Her eyes open wide, Romy lay perfectly still, clutching the duvet with both fists. The sound was muted, distant yet somehow close. It was coming from inside the house but from somewhere outside the room.

Her eyes rose to the ceiling, her ears filtering out every other sound except for the subtle gentle thumping above her head. It was as if somebody was up in the attic, treading carefully from one joist to another, the full length of the house.

She dry swallowed, lying stricken, listening.

The sound faded, and then disappeared altogether, as though the stranger in the attic had reached the end of the building only to discover that there was nowhere else to go.

The house fell once more to silence.

Romy began to breathe again, slow measured breaths, concentrating on filling each lung with equal volumes of oxygen, calming her panicking heart.

With the house quiet once again - save for the occasional car that passed outside in the street, and the intermittent birdsong in the hedgerows and decorative trees that lined the road - Romy attempted to make sense of both the thumping as well as the thud from the previous evening.

It wasn't an old house, but it had stood empty for a long time. She reasoned that neither the water nor the electricity or gas had been connected during that time. The utility companies had all set everything in motion for the same day, the day of her moving. It made sense that standing water in pipes may have become filled with pockets of air that would take time to work their way out. It sounded likely. Hell, it sounded logical.

She tried to recall similar problems in the flat she and Andrew had first moved into, or the house they had bought shortly before they were married. But DIY jobs had been Andrew's forte. She'd cleaned. He'd fixed. It had been a simple deal from the start.

The notion leapt into her head that maybe she should call him, ask him if thumps and thuds and groans were to be expected in houses that had stood empty for a long time. But she chased the thought away almost immediately, physically dispelled it with a double wave of her hands, before she pushed back the duvet and slung her legs out over the side. Standing up, almost in defiance of her former (and presumably still current) dependence upon him, she marched through into the bathroom to brush her teeth and wash herself for the new day.

Dressed in jeans and a clean white t-shirt, Romy went downstairs to the kitchen, her thoughts gaining even more clarity as she hunted for her purse. If there had been air still stuck in the water pipes, she thought, it would make perfect sense for them to become disturbed at such a time in the morning if the central heating or hot water tank had a timer set for that time.

Even as she made her way out through the front door to her car, Romy cursed herself again for her initial reaction of running to Andrew with the first problem her house had thrown at her. As she reversed out of the driveway, she glanced back at the house, and for just a fraction of a second she was certain that she saw a dark and awkward shape, but nothing human-shaped, staring back at her from the shadows behind the dining room window.

Her mind lurched, but she swallowed it down, dismissing what she was sure she had just seen. Yet it played on her mind, as she drove away from the house, like impatient fingers drumming on the edge of a desk.

It was expected that she should have jitters - hell, it was probably normal - it was the first time she had ever lived on her own, after all. Once she was settled, she promised herself, with new curtains and cushions and candles, it would feel more like her home and she would be able to relax properly.

Romy didn't venture to the nearest shopping centre, but instead drove to where she had shopped for the last four years, a place that was more familiar, a place where she was more comfortable and would get more done. She forgot all about the thumps and the thuds and the shadowy shapes in the dining room as she made her way round, and concentrated instead on loading her credit card with as much as she dared (new lamps, a long brightly coloured rug, at least a dozen differently scented candles, some glassware for the kitchen, and an assortment of furniture that would be delivered sometime within the next six weeks).

The trip was like therapy, garnished with a special treat of an expensive lunch at the posh café she'd always wanted to try but had never dared. The prawn and avocado was not cheap but it was beyond divinity, as was the lobster and squid terrine, but she returned home with her car laden with her purchases, as well as a week's groceries, happier than when she had left.

The dining room window was devoid of any monsters when she pulled into the driveway, and nothing hideous leapt out at her from the bushes or surprised her as she brought in her lamps and candles and began arranging them neatly in the corners of rooms. Luckily the previous owners had left curtain poles behind so it was a relatively easy task for her to feed the tag-topped curtains onto them. And what a difference her cream Habitat curtains made. The house seemed warmer, cosier, and more importantly, like her own.

At four o'clock in the afternoon, with the last of the accessories placed and the food put away in the fridge and the cupboards, Romy sank down into her cream leather sofa, kicked off her boots, and spread her bare feet across her new brightly-coloured rug. And boy, did it feel good.

# THREE

## SO IT BEGINS ANEW

It was whilst she was measuring for new carpet in the dining room that Romy first noticed the crack in the new patch of concrete. It could have been there when she'd first viewed the property in June, she couldn't recall, but there was still a crack a good four inches long making its way across the floor in front of the fireplace.

It was little more than a hairline spider-crawl, but that wasn't the point. Shoddy workmanship was shoddy workmanship, and she began to wonder about any other shortcuts the builders may have tried their luck with. The house may have been twenty grand shy of its expected market value, but the last thing she needed was a lemon with a patched hole underneath it.

It seemed like such a trivial thing - Andrew probably wouldn't have given it a second thought and been quite happy to lay carpet over the top of it - but this was her house, damn it, and she was trying to make it perfect, and this had given the whole affair a note of impending doom. Maybe once the new carpet was laid and she could no longer see the crack she'd feel better, she thought. Out of sight, out of mind. That kind of thing. So with the measurements of the room noted down on the back of an envelope, she slipped it into her handbag ready to pop it into the carpet fitters when she was next out.

What rattled Romy more than first seeing the crack, however, was when she went into the dining room later that afternoon with a couple of scented candles for the mantelpiece, and saw that what had earlier been four inches was now six.

She stood and stared down at it, candles still in hand. Had it grown? Was the house falling down around her? Had her solicitor been right to advise caution? Was this the first sign?

She chastened herself, foolishly perhaps, for not having measured the crack earlier when she'd first seen it. Then she'd know for sure. It seemed pointless to measure it now, it was too late, but the dread that now began to circulate in the pit of her stomach was what if the crack grew another two inches by teatime? What if grew to a foot or more by morning? And more to the point, what exactly was forcing the crack open?

Romy set the candles down on the mantelpiece and hurried out of the room, rifling through the sparsely-filled drawers in the kitchen for the tape measure she knew she'd put there only hours before. But it wasn't there and just where she had put it after measuring the room earlier for carpet she now had no idea.

She stood and stopped for a second, trying to focus her memory.

It wasn't in any of the kitchen drawers.

She checked her handbag. The envelope with the dimensions of the dining room was in there but not the tape measure itself.

Romy hurried through into the living room as panic began to set in. What if the crack was growing bigger still while she was searching fruitlessly for the tool with which to measure it? She knew she hadn't been in the living room all day yet she still poked through every open box and behind every plant pot and candle.

Eventually she stood up, exasperated, and pushed her hair back behind her ears as she stared out through the living room window at the overgrown garden. There was a small pond back there somewhere, ripe with frogs apparently, but she couldn't see it past all the long grass and rioting shrubs.

Then she mentally struck her forehead with one hand, echoed it physically with an open palm to emphasis her stupidity, and dashed back through into the kitchen, snatching up a felt-tip pen from the second drawer down.

Back once again in the dining room, Romy knelt down and scrawled over the coarse surface of the concrete floor until thick visible lines marked each end of the crack. Then she sat back on her heels to study her handiwork, content that not even the marks could spread out across the floor along with the crack. Then, pushing herself back up onto her feet, Romy pushed the felt-tip pen into the back pocket of her jeans and left it at that.

# FOUR

## IT WILL GET IN, ONE WAY OR ANOTHER

Romy checked the crack twice before she went to bed and again in the morning when she came downstairs, and was glad on all three occasions that it had not crept beyond the marks she had drawn across the concrete floor.

The carpet was due to arrive within a week, once she was back at work, so she had to take an extra day's holiday in order to let the carpet fitters in. But once the carpet was down and laid, the difference was staggering.

Romy never gave the crack another thought once it was covered and concealed from sight, so wonderful was her new beige carpet. It was clean and elegant and set the room off better than she had ever imagined when she'd chosen it in the shop. Once the table and chairs were delivered, she thought to herself, along with the rest of the furniture she'd ordered, she would feel comfortable enough to have her friends and family over to celebrate her new place properly. Even as it currently stood she wouldn't be quite so embarrassed. She'd been particular enough about them not helping or seeing the house until she was ready to have them see it. But when they did, they wouldn't be able to say another negative word about her divorce from

Andrew or about her not being able to cope without him.

But they'd not known the half of it, had they? Only Romy, Andrew and the other women he'd slept with knew the real truth. And even those other women, Romy suspected, had not known about her. It had been a secret kept from everyone else, but unlike Andrew's promises never to stray again, it was the only thing that had been maintained.

He'd told her that he'd always been faithful before their marriage, and only afterwards had he felt suffocated. She still wasn't sure whether she believed that or not, and to a certain degree it neither mattered nor made much of a difference any more. She still had some feelings for him - they'd shared six years together, how could they not? - but there was a hurt where none had been before and that would take a long time, if ever, to fade away.

So maybe it was that hurt that she attributed the first of her nightmares to. She was not a psychiatrist so she could only interpret things as best she could. But to see a vast ugly monster, misshapen and twisted, crawling up out of a pit towards her could surely be explained as very little else.

Her nightmare had been vivid, scary, and she had sat bolt upright in bed, soaked with sweat and shaking. She had woken in the early hours of the morning, the utter blackness of the room still swathed with echoes of the monster reaching for her, and Romy had flailed disorientated with her arms in front of her.

She'd dispelled most of the darkness of the room by grabbing at the lamp beside the bed, the weak low wattage bulb illuminating most of the bedroom but managing to create eerie shadows that seemed to bloat and bulge with living breath.

Romy had sat upright for a few moments just waiting for the dream to disperse from her head and for reality to filter back in. Her skin had been freezing where her sweat-soaked nightie had clung to her, raising gooseflesh all across her body as she'd shuddered.

"Get a grip," Romy had muttered to the empty room, more to breathe life into the dead silence of the house than anything else.

But her voice had disappeared, sucked into the ill-lit murk of the room with neither trace nor echo.

She'd swallowed, and then hauled the duvet, half-hanging off the edge of the bed, back into place. She'd waited a moment more, and then slid her legs out from underneath and trotted through into the bathroom to splash water onto her face.

Romy had studied her reflection as rivulets of water skipped down her face and into the basin. Her eyes had seemed so stark and weary, almost as though they were not even hers, as though she was somehow looking back at herself through someone else's eyes. Her skin had prickled again as another shiver had come.

Slipping her nightie up and over her head, she'd rubbed her cold damp skin briskly with a towel before hurrying back through into the bedroom where she'd slipped on a clean t-shirt, an old grey Bruce Springsteen tour shirt she'd bought when she and her friends had seen him live at the Milton Keynes Bowl in '93. Climbing back into bed, she'd found the bottom sheet soaked through, and cursed aloud into the silent room as she'd pulled back the duvet and stripped off the sheet. It was the only one she'd had, so she had been forced to sleep on top of the mattress, hauling the duvet up and back over herself, and had begun cursing the nightmare afresh.

She'd been loathe to turn off the lamp, and had laid for a few moments just gazing around the room, studying the packing boxes and the old furniture she'd claimed from the marriage, studying the shadows behind each of them in case anything was lurking there and staring back at her. Nothing had been, of course, but her heart had still yammered, and her innards had still itched, and ultimately she'd had to reach down and switch off the light.

"Get a grip," she'd muttered again to the darkness, realising as she'd done so that maybe if there had been something in the room with her, it might just have taken her up on the offer.

So Romy had laid motionless, too petrified to even close her eyes, her sight barely able to penetrate the murk above her to even make sense of where the wall met the ceiling.

But sleep was keen to have her back in its embrace, and she descended quickly down into its arms that lay open and waiting. But the return was more peaceful, the matrimonial monster kept, for the moment, at bay. And Romy was allowed a restful slumber for at least a handful of hours until the following dawn.

# FIVE

## AS IN DREAMS, SO IN LIFE

The dream couldn't have been more prophetic. Andrew turned up the following morning, Saturday morning, just before eleven. Romy stared at him as he stood on her doorstep, not even attempting to return the tentative smile he wore. She watched as he retrieved a bouquet of flowers wrapped in lavender-patterned paper from behind his back.

"For you," he said. "For your new place."

"How did you know where I was? No, let me guess. Mum."

"In one."

Romy made no gesture to either take the flowers or allow him over the threshold. She didn't want him in, didn't want any trace of him anywhere in her house. Maybe there were still echoes of his monster scratching around inside her head or under her skin, she didn't know, and maybe her initial reaction may have been different had she not dreamt about him or his grotesquery, but she was suddenly defiant and stood her ground against him.

"What do you want?" she asked, stone-faced.

"Come on, Ro," he said, his bouquet faltering in his hand. "I know we've had some shit but we can still be civil, can't we?"

"I got shit, you got laid, remember?"

Her words came out curt and she liked them. She wondered why they'd not come out like that more often when they might have actually done some good.

Andrew's smile slunk away like a scolded dog. He did seem genuinely hurt. And she hated herself even as she relented and took a step sideways and consented to his coming in with a brief nod of her head.

He smiled with shamed gratitude, and Romy closed the door after him.

She followed him into the kitchen and saw that he'd set the flowers down on the countertop and was already gazing around the room as though he was a potential buyer. She half expected him to start sucking air in through his teeth and pointing out where repairs or renovations might be needed. But he just looked, full circle, until his eyes came back once again to look at her.

"So," he started, "how have you been?"

"I see," she countered, folding her arms. "It's going to be small talk, is it?"

"What is?"

"Just came round to shoot the breeze, did we? I didn't think you'd be up and about at this time of day. I thought you'd still have some slut wrapped round your waist."

The words came thick and fast, gaining momentum as each one slipped from her tongue. A rush of adrenaline came with them, hand in hand with all the hurt and all the negative emotions that she'd been forced to sit through and stifle for the last year. They had the desired effect, though. Andrew stood motionless, chastened, and simply stared at her in utter disbelief. Her former lapse of compassion at the door had taken full retreat, and she was now ready to give out a whole lot more.

"This is my house, Andrew," she stormed, "and not somewhere you can just turn up when you feel like it. If you want to see me - and God knows why, seeing as how you didn't much want to when we were married - then I suggest you call first and make a fucking appointment."

The F word shocked even her. It wasn't a word she used often or even liked to hear, but it came out just the same, directed as hard at him as any weapon ever could be.

Still he gazed, part open-mouthed and part wide-eyed, and for a moment she thought he would just stand there in her new kitchen and never say another word.

Romy noticed she was breathing hard, puffed out as though she had just run a marathon, a two year marathon on an uphill route. But her head felt lighter for it, more livid, like a raging fire, but somehow still under control. Maybe more in control.

"That said," she went on, her voice and tone calming, almost comically so, as she composed herself. "What is it that you came here for?"

Andrew paused before answering, uncertain, thoughts flickering visibly behind his eyes.

"I think anything I could possibly think of to say now," he said, "is going to be a bit of a come down, isn't it?"

That was another of his traits, a sense of humour with a matching time and wit that could force the edges of her mouth into a smirk even when she didn't want them to. She'd adored him for it so many times in the past, but now it grated. It was old, irksome. But the smile came just the same, right on cue, and he was standing directly in front of her to witness it.

Romy felt the dominant stance she'd just made crumble like the blocks of an ancient ruin. Andrew had made a comfortable position for himself out of an uncomfortable situation yet again.

"I guess it's kind of awkward," he went on, somehow finding the words when he'd just admitted to them being elusive.

Maybe they'd been rehearsed in advance, Romy thought. Or maybe he was just good at bullshitting the second it was required. God knew he'd had the practice.

"It's about Terri," he went on, then stopped as if that was explanation enough.

Romy stared.

Clearly it wasn't.

"I'm not sure if her name ever came up," Andrew said, wandering to his gift of flowers and toying with the lavender-patterned paper with his fingertips. "She was someone I met when we, you know, had our differences."

"I recall it was only you who had our differences, Andrew."

Her arms had become uncrossed during their exchange, but she crossed them again now as she stared at him. Painful thorns had already formed inside her chest and were steadily growing. Their needle-points hurt, jabbing at her delicate innards, but she wasn't about to show it on her face for him.

"Well, the thing is," he told her, glancing up

now from the flowers to look at her, (don't show him the hurt, she demanded of herself, don't you dare), "is that we want to get married."

The thorns congealed into one single ice-cold spike of steel and speared her right through the heart.

Her throat was sandpaper. Tears welled before she could turn away. And the sob came before she could cloak it with her hands.

"You bastard," she gasped, her words barely audible as they croaked across a throat drier and more painful than any desert floor.

Romy turned away from him then, her hands clasped to her face as she stumbled away, out through the nearest door and into the hallway. Tears skipped down her cheeks, she felt them go, her chest stricken as though it had been seized by some almighty fist. He was watching all this, damn it, she thought, and she hated herself perhaps more than him for that. He'd done it to her again, hadn't he? The bastard had smiled his way in one more time and speared her through the heart.

She heard him say her name, his voice still in the kitchen. She was thankful that at least he was not coming after her. She couldn't bear that, couldn't bear to have him desecrate another room of her house. He'd already poisoned the front door, the hallway and the kitchen. What more did he want?

Romy continued on through the house, her face awash with tears and snot, her feet stumbling and graceless, past the doors to the living room and the dining room, until she came to a halt at the foot of the stairs that led up to the bedrooms.

Romy stood at the end of the hallway, sobbing

into her hands like a schoolgirl with her first broken heart. He'd done it again. That's what kept rattling around inside her head. The bastard had done it to her yet again.

She'd not heard the front door shut behind him and she presumed that he was still waiting for her to come back, maybe still dumbfounded by her inability to be reasonable about his fucking around. But she would never go back in there, not until he was out of the house and gone. She had no other choice but to retreat even further into her own home. So outstretching one hand to the balustrade to steady her ascent, Romy climbed the staircase to the first floor landing.

Sunlight shone in through the upstairs windows, oblivious to her pain. It seemed so wrong that she should feel so bad when all the rest of the world appeared to be so glorious and content.

She stumbled through into the master bedroom and collapsed onto the bed, wringing her hair with her hands as the tears continued to come. She thought about the spare bed that she and Andrew had kept in their guest room. They'd never slept in that bed themselves, but she wondered now (as the image of him with another woman, maybe this Terri to whom he was already betrothed, raced into her head), whether they had fucked on it like animals when she had not been home.

She wept face down into the pillow, concealing her heaving sobs from both Andrew downstairs and the rest of the house that somehow seemed to be watching her. She didn't even want the bricks to see her so utterly reduced.

She cried until her eyes stung, until her throat

threatened to seize up entirely, until her stomach knotted so painfully that she thought it would never right itself again.

Romy couldn't recall stopping crying. Or even falling asleep. When she lifted her head again the pillow was damp and stained with mascara, the room dark, and the windows through which the sunlight had earlier been so bright were now soulless panes with which to frame the night.

Her bladder ached and it was an effort to push herself off the bed, so tired and aching were her muscles. She pushed her hair behind her ears as she stumbled through into the bathroom, glancing out at the road with sleep-beleaguered eyes as she passed the undrawn curtains. She started as she saw a figure there, standing motionless on the pavement and staring up at the front of the house.

A sudden cold fingertip of unease tapped Romy inside her chest. The hairs on her neck bristled. The figure was dressed from head to foot in black, and stood mostly unlit by the wash of the yellow streetlamps. It was impossible to see any features, anything that might aid recognition, but it was clear that it was not Andrew. The stranger was definitely a woman.

Perhaps it was this Terri.

The thought burned like acid in the pit of her stomach, and she tried to think it away, but it was persistent.

Perhaps she'd come to see Andrew's ex-wife, her mind thought, come to make either peace or war. Whichever was easier to draw. Placated smiles or blood.

Romy stood as still as her observer, her chest

thumping madly.

Surely the stranger couldn't see her, Romy thought. Surely it was impossible to see someone in an unlit upstairs bedroom from outside in the street.

Romy swallowed. Her bladder reminded her with a renewed ache that it was in danger of folding in on itself. She pressed a hand to it but couldn't turn away from the stranger still standing there. Romy tried to make something out, anything, any small detail about the strange woman staring up at her house, but her eyes could make out nothing.

Then it became something of a sick game.

Who would turn away first?

Who was the weaker?

Again her bladder tweaked, painfully so, and Romy instantly lost the game. She moved away from the window, quickly, and hurried through into the bathroom to pee. She kept the light off, urinating in the darkness before zipping up her jeans and feeling her way back into the bedroom.

She approached the window cautiously and from a distance, as though afraid that the glass might shatter inwards under the weight of the woman's intense scrutiny and slash her face with lethal shards.

Romy craned her neck to see out into the street an inch at a time, realising even as she did so how ridiculous her behaviour was. It was her house, for God's sake. The stranger outside in the street was the one being obtrusive.

She moved closer until the front garden came into view, then the driveway, then the pavement. But it seemed that having won the game, the stranger had tired and moved on. The pavement was now empty once again.

Romy stepped closer to the window and now studied the empty road with more confidence, but there was nothing moving in any direction, nothing at all. Lights burned in the windows of the other houses, but she could see no one about. The street had returned to quiet once again. The woman had gone.

## SIX

## RELENTLESS

When she went downstairs, she found Andrew gone. His flowers too, for which she was glad. The memory of the woman outside the house remained uncomfortable in her head, however, as she wandered through into the kitchen to find something to put into her growling stomach.

Had it been Terri come to check out the opposition, she wondered? She did seem the likeliest suspect. Who else would come to stare up at a house and not even knock at the front door? That said something about Andrew's new woman at least. Spineless. What a complementary trait to go along with starting a relationship with a married man. At least they'd not had kids. What a mess that would have been.

Romy pulled some cold produce out of the fridge - meats and cheese, some pickles and a jar of green olives - and set them down on the counter. From one cupboard she retrieved a box of crackers, and from another a plate, and then set about making herself a decent snack. She wasn't in the mood to cook. It was too late, her hunger too severe to wait. She just wanted to satisfy it quickly, collapse in front of the tv and drift away from all the shit of the real world.

Wandering out of the kitchen with her plate of food and a large glass of red wine, she hesitated as she reached the living room door. There was a sound coming from somewhere, a strange kind of humming sound, like a low whine of something electrical.

She stood, head cocked, filtering out the noise from the silence of the house. She took a step into the living room, switched on the light with the hand that held her wine glass, and then walked further into the room to put the glass and the plate down on the coffee table before going back into the hallway to listen again.

It almost sounded like the hum of a generator, which first made her panic thinking that there might be an electrical problem somewhere. But the meter was out in the porch, and she hadn't heard anything when she'd been in the kitchen where she would have been closer to it and the sound more prominent.

Then she inclined her head towards the dining room. She didn't know why her skin prickled when she did so, but hairs bristled all over her body as her fears were confirmed. The sound was definitely coming from inside.

She reached a hesitant hand inside the room to switch on the light before she took a step across the threshold. When she did so, the sound grew louder still. Now with more information to work with, her hearing defined the sound as irregular, building and falling like something organic, something living, something breathing, less like the buzzing whine from some kind of turbine and more like the deep low groan from some kind of -

She wanted to punch herself before the word even sprang into her head. Gooseflesh came right on the back of the shiver as the word 'monster' declared itself in all its glory, etched in bold and italicised.

"That's good, Romy," she forced herself to say out loud, saying anything to drown out the groaning that still ebbed and flowed from under the floor, even if it was only for a second. "Scare yourself witless, you stupid bitch. What a fucking treat."

It seemed to do the trick though. In the aftermath of her spoken words, the room fell back to silence as if shunned.

She stood listening, hugging herself with shaking arms, but it was true. The deep low groan had gone.

Romy waited only a few moments, long enough to take one steady look around the room, and then she stepped out, slowly but bravely, and switched off the light from the safety of the hallway. Then she returned to the living room, whereupon she turned on the tv and turned the volume up a little louder than was usual.

The meats and the cheese went down well, as did the olives and the crackers. She forced herself to eat steadily with measured bites as though nothing was wrong, but when she got to the wine she couldn't stop herself downing it in one go.

After the first glass Romy returned to the kitchen to fetch the bottle, which described the contents as light and easy-going. The dining room remained in silence when she passed it, and nothing untoward happened throughout the rest of the evening as she finished off the wine and watched tv until late. When she went to bed and slept again, however, that was when the dreams started up again. And this time they decided to step things up a notch.

# SEVEN

## BLACK, THE COLOUR OF IT ALL

The ground gaped, a chasm sucking her towards its bottomless depths, and from its maw crawled the repulsive beast. Misshapen and awkwardly moulded, like a rough sketch in clay hacked by an amateur sculptor, not even its eyes sat level as they stared at her from its pit. Its jagged mouth hung open, the hinges that joined the lower jaw to the skull barely up to the task of allowing it to utter words. Yet speak it did, and the monster from below grated several words out of the darkness towards her.

"I know... what it was like," it groaned.

In the nightmare Romy was stood in her hallway, staring into the dining room which had become a vast echoing cavern. Water dripped into unseen pools. Black movements crawled across the high ceiling and across the walls. She was naked, her hair now jet black and long and flowing down towards the small of her back. It was unutterably cold, her breath fogging in front of her, her exposed skin sharp with freezing pain.

"I know..." the beast went on, struggling to climb to its full height, "because I... have been him."

It seemed insane to be watching this thing attempt to clamber closer to her, hauling its ugly frame across the bare rock, especially from the vantage point of her own hallway, but Romy stood without flight, listening to the groaning ill-formed words as they tumbled from its grating jaws.

"He... hurt you," it said, acrid fluid dripping from lips that could not contain the spittle, "so I hurt him. I have done... this for you."

Romy wanted to ask so many things but words eluded her. Her sight was drawn, however, past the monster and into the impenetrable darkness beyond it. Something moved there, something other than the swarming shapes that crawled across the rock, but she could not discern it. It wanted to be seen. It yearned for her recognition. Yet it remained beyond her ability.

Then a glimmer of light, tiny, a sparkle of something reflected in an eyeball, the light from the hallway in which she stood.

Romy took a step towards the edge of the cavern. It seemed to reach for her in turn, pulling her towards it. The monster wanted her here with it, just as it had claimed the owner of the eye. She struggled to see what it was, this creature that lurked trapped in the darkness, shackled and restrained, but she somehow already knew. But if the owner of this eye was Andrew, then the beast could not be him. The beast was something else.

Her sight returned to the monster that had managed several ghastly steps towards her. Its hideous mouth cracked into a grin of mismatched teeth, some white and sharp like those of a keen wolf, others blunted and yellowed like those of a dead dog.

Romy shrank back from its attention.

"All this..." it said again, "I have done for you."

And then it reached for her, irregular limbs that stretched from shoulders too misshapen to have been anything designed by God.

Romy stumbled away from it and felt a wall hard at her back, sealing her retreat. She shot a look back. The doorway had gone, severing her from the hallway on the other side of it. She looked back to see the monster shuffling towards her, its arms still outstretched, yearning for her love.

Then a scream, a cry of anguish loosed from the blackness of the cavern behind it.

It shattered the blackness.

And the dream crumbled with it.

2

Romy's eyes opened.

The blackness remained but the monster had gone, defeated by reality. Her eyes blinked rapidly, dispelling the echoes of its gruesome face, as she sought out familiar shapes in her bedroom. They didn't come readily in the darkness, but she found enough clues to make sense of them.

Her heart was busy, her skin and nightclothes soaked with sweat. She sat up and pushed her hair back out of her face and found that it was her own, no longer black and long.

Slipping her legs out from beneath the duvet, she stumbled through into the bathroom with one hand pressed against her head. This had to stop, she told herself. She couldn't wake from nightmares every night. She didn't have enough t-shirts or nighties to sleep in for a start.

After emptying her bladder, Romy returned to the bedroom. She paused halfway and went to the window, tugging back the curtain an inch to look out at the street outside. Reality was still there, still normal. Until a movement snatched her attention from below, straight down at the front of the house. The woman was back.

She pushed her head nearer to the glass and looked straight down. There was no mistaking it. A figure was walking away from the front of her house.

Romy swallowed as a sudden panic washed over her. She tugged the curtain closed in case the stranger should see her, then tugged it straight back as she told herself that this was her house, damn it, and she'd look at someone on her property if she fucking chose to.

Romy studied the woman leaving the front garden, suddenly outraged by her impudence, and even thought about banging on the window. But then the woman stopped, turned, and then stared right up at her.

Romy's flesh turned to ice.

The full moon high overhead cast a glimmering silver wash over everything below, and by its light Romy now saw the woman's face revealed. It was a moon all its own, stark and white like a china mask, with eyes that swallowed her scrutiny into two black bottomless pools. She was dressed in swathes of black from head to foot, as she had been the previous night, but Romy now observed that she possessed long black hair, hair that stretched down to the small of her back, just like the hair that she had worn in her dream as she'd stood before the beast in its pit.

The game had returned too. They stared at each other for what seemed like an hour, the woman daring her to turn away first, her glare fierce and unfaltering. Romy tried to tell herself again that this was her house, damn it, but this time there was no commitment in her outrage, no will to bang against the window.

Her fingers shook, her heart skipping like something fragile and brittle inside a chest that seemed barely stronger than a thin wire birdcage. She tugged the curtain closed as her body lurched with dread, severing the sight of the woman outside. Relief flooded swiftly, despite the knowledge that the woman was still out there, watching from her front garden.

Romy took a step away from the window, her fingers trembling at her lips. She forced herself to return to bed, but her mind was manic. The whole situation was insane. If this was Terri, Andrew's new woman, then what was she doing coming to her house in the middle of the night and staring into her house through the dining room window? Her fear was strong, but her anger suddenly came stronger.

Romy slipped out of bed once again and crossed the room in three strides, stepping back up to the window and tugging back the curtain. She gazed down into her front garden, ready to bang on the glass and shout down at her. But the strange woman dressed all in black had gone.

Romy stood there panting, scrutinising her garden and then the pavement and then the rest of the street. But the woman had simply vanished. Romy pulled the curtains closed once more, straightened them neatly, and returned to bed with the frail hope that she would not see her near her house again.

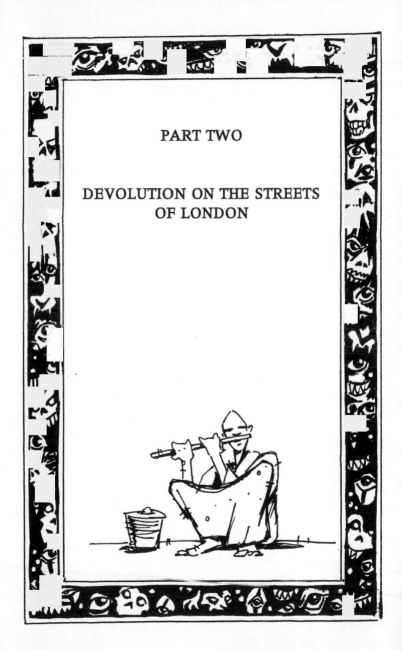

PART TWO

DEVOLUTION ON THE STREETS
OF LONDON

# ONE

## WELCOME TO LONDON

The vampire watched the two girls standing outside Kings Cross Station. It was a cold night but neither one of them was dressed sufficiently warm enough. The blonde girl was thin. He could see how blue her skin was becoming. He watched as she hugged herself as she paced beside the dark-haired girl, clouds of breath visible in front of her, gooseflesh raised on her exposed forearms. She wore a black miniskirt over black and white striped leggings, and a thin t-shirt beneath an orange body warmer that exposed her waist. Her belly-button was pierced, he could see the glint of the fake diamond that glittered weakly there, and he wondered how taut her skin really was down there, how resilient it would be against his hands, his teeth.

He knew it would not take long for the two girls to be separated. A car pulled up beside them as he watched, the vampire noting the brief exchange between the driver and the two prostitutes from the depths of the shadows across the street. He watched the dark-haired girl climb into the passenger seat, and then the car as it sped away from the kerb. The thin blonde girl wandered back to where she had been standing before, and it was to her that the vampire now returned his attention once again.

Despite his hunger he was swift, and crossed the street towards the girl before she had even noticed his approach. She was startled, and jumped at his proximity.

Now he was close to her, he could see that he had been mistaken in thinking that she was pretty. Dark skin hung beneath her bloodshot eyes like bad makeup. Her skin was not just pale for a white girl and turning shades of blue with the cold, but it seemed almost a sickly yellow colour beneath the sallow illumination emanating from the train station streetlights. Her hair was dishevelled and dirty, and he could now smell the rank odour of stale sweat and old semen. He stared at her, attempting to parade himself like a human client and smile in order to coax her away from the light where they might be seen. But he just couldn't manage it. He didn't want to manage it.

"You want some action?" the girl asked bluntly.

She had no smile for him either, and kept her arms folded in front of her in a pitiful attempt to keep some warmth in them. She shook from the cold, her teeth visibly chattering.

"I think I do," the vampire replied slowly.

His eyes roved across her body, taking in her small breasts, her narrow hips. If he did want some of the action she thought she was offering, she would snap so very easily.

"But not here," he added quickly.

"Of course not here," she snapped. "Your place. I'll do the lot for forty quid. In advance."

She seemed defiant, so very far from a professional used to arousing her customers.

"My place is fine," the vampire said, "but we

should go quickly, you look so cold."

"No fucking wonder, it's freezing out here. Where's your car?"

The vampire studied her. He could see the haze behind her eyes.

This would be swift.

"Just around the corner," he explained, coaxing her away from the front of the station.

It was past one o'clock in the morning. There would be no commuters at this time of night, no do-gooders or policemen, but there were still eyes on the street that could bring him harm.

Even when they had turned the corner where the streetlamps were less garish, the two of them were still visible to anyone who might be watching. As they passed an alleyway, however, the vampire took hold of her wrist and hauled her in one sharp movement into its unlit depths.

A scream rose in her throat as she fought to keep her feet, but the vampire forced his fingers deep into her mouth before it found the air. She gagged as his hand filled her mouth, but with his other arm holding her tight against his body, he sank his teeth deep into the arch of her neck and broke the surface of her skin. Blood spilled instantly and he sucked hard, drinking voraciously and clamping her contorting body tightly to him, ignoring the pain in his knuckles as she involuntarily bit down upon them.

The blood was bad but it was at least blood. He had not fed in over a week. The skulkers that scoured the city were cunning and organised, and had killed so many of his kind already. Humans killing vampires, it was a sickening reality, like foxes killing the hounds, maggots devouring the crows.

His stomach lurched as it rejected the meal – he had smelt the disease of drug abuse in her before he had led her away, the heroin that befouled her arteries, but he had been so very hungry and she so very desperate, and so easy a prey.

Even now she was clasping at life, her fingernails clawing at his arm, her teeth breaking the skin of his fingers to the bone. But he would kill her. He would finish her and leave her filthy corpse in the gutter where it belonged. He'd never asked her name. It hadn't mattered before, and it didn't matter now.

Nausea suddenly overtook him and he pulled away from her, letting her slack body drop onto the wet ground with a dull slap. Her body still kicked and jerked with the memories of what had once passed through it, but she was gone – or as close to it that it made little difference.

The vampire glared down at her as he struggled to keep in his stomach the poisoned blood that he knew would make him ill for the next few days. But better to be ill than hungry and weak, and after a few nights he would be strong enough to find something more worthwhile, fresh veins from some mortal that did not work off the streets.

The girl was young, perhaps twenty years old, certainly no older, and even in the semi-darkness of the alleyway he could see the needle marks in the crook of her elbow, the scabs and permanent holes that he had failed to see earlier. Perhaps that was another reason why she hugged her own arms, to keep her customers from seeing her addiction.

With a growing curiosity, he moved her body

warmer to one side with the toe of his boot and lifted up her t-shirt to study her breasts. They were indeed small, the nipples bullet-hard and erect, but they were wasted like the thin flesh around her stomach and hips. Maybe it was because of the poison, he had no idea, and nor did he care. Her legs, too, now that he glanced down at them beneath her miniskirt and striped leggings, were thin and bony, awkwardly splayed from where she had fallen, and he wondered how someone could get so sick from self-induced abuse and still not stop.

The poison in his stomach was already burning in his veins, and he questioned the sense in keeping the meal down. His head was already growing blurred, his thoughts becoming disjointed, disconnecting from one another like parched kindling snapping and popping in a catching fire.

A panic suddenly gripped him as he felt a tug inside his head, as though something was attempting to snatch his sanity away, like the only life preserver on a sinking ship that was being wrenched just beyond his grasp.

He bent double and forced himself to vomit, heaving the foul blood back up out of his body and onto the filthy ground beside the dead girl. It spattered across her as it came. He wanted it out of him. He wanted it gone.

Slowly he staggered away, weaker than he had been before, blood still dripping from his lips and teeth, his hand outstretched towards the wall in case he should stumble. He cursed the girl, cursed the drugs that riddled this godforsaken city, and prayed that he might find something else soon before his strength left him altogether.

# TWO

## THE VAMPIRE CATHERINE CALLEH

The sound of glass breaking outside snagged the vampire's attention and she went to the window to glance down into the lamp lit street. Two youths had broken into a car parked below and were now attempting to steal either it or its contents. She could see one of their legs flailing as they struggled with something inside, but she turned away from both the window and the disturbance and walked back into the centre of the living room of the first floor flat to think some more.

It seemed strange for her to walk these same London streets that had been her home for over a century, after having returned to Kar'mi'shah and found it desolate and in ruins. She'd needed to take refuge in the mountains, to be alone and think through the events of her life, the deaths and the deals, the propaganda and the betrayals. She'd been a Goddess in Kar'mi'shah, a powerful deity worshipped by the populace of the city, a being worthy of praise for the blessings she had performed, the help she had offered to lesser mortals. But that had all changed in a single night when the world she had known had been torn apart by an unfathomable monster, a hellish demon whose only purpose was to destroy and devour them. The world of the gods had been decimated that night, and she, along with what few gods had discovered the same means of escape, had found herself on Earth, a strange and unnatural world where gods were only worshipped in books not in flesh.

She'd found herself shunned and then chased for her life by ignorant barbaric tribes those hundred or more years ago, so that all she could do was hide and take whatever life she could find in order to sustain herself. It had been pitiful at first, and perhaps it was because of that that she had soon begun to kill their number out of spite and vengeance, instead of answering their desires for bountiful lands. It was shortly after that too that she had begun to find pleasure in their misery, joy in their suffering, until those that had sought the death of the blasphemer had begun to beg for their own deaths, if only to quench the suffering that she had gleefully imposed upon them.

Catherine stood in the darkness of the room, her long black hair falling to her waist, her black clothes blending with the unlit room. She stood motionless, nothing about her moving, her eyes staring only ahead as her mind turned over events of importance, filtering out those with none.

She had visited Camden a couple of nights ago in the middle of a torrential downpour and had been surprised at how empty the streets had been: not of humans, no (for they still bustled as fruitlessly as ever, the poor and the ill-guided), but of her own kind.

She'd stood on the bridge as people had dashed from doorway to doorway, their heads covered by umbrellas and newspapers, but she had seen no vampires.

She'd turned as two people had dashed along the pavement towards her, a man and a woman, arm in arm, both approximately two decades into their lives. They'd been drinking. Catherine had smelt the heady stench of alcohol on their breaths even from such a distance, seeping through the pores of their rain-glistened skin. They'd laughed together as their feet had splashed through the deep puddles, soaking their shoes and jeans. And yet as they'd approached her, they'd both stared wide-eyed as they'd taken in the sight of this solitary female dressed all in black, standing perfectly still in the downpour, nothing about her in motion but for her hair that whipped sideways in the fitful wind.

Their smiles had dropped, uncertain about this strange woman, and they had hurried on past, glancing only briefly over their shoulders as if afraid she might follow after them. But Catherine had remained where she was, and had searched the darkest shadows of Camden High Street one last time, hoping to find a vampire who had chosen to stay behind to watch the mortals of the night. But she'd found none.

Surely, she reasoned as she now stood in the flat, not all of them had returned home. Kar'mi'shah had prospered in the years in which Alexia had brought rebirth to the province, but that was not everything to all vampires. Some had found their own rebirth here in this city, finding worshippers in desperate souls, in the homeless and the lost, those beaten by fathers or husbands, or those just looking for something beyond their banal existence. The vampire had become revered in some circles. He had become not godlike, but something else entirely. He had become reinvented.

But all her spies and contacts had gone. She stood in the middle of the living room, her eyes closed now against the darkness, her feet beside the body of the owner of the flat, and studied the thousands of images that filled her head as though she was leafing through the yellowed pages of an old photograph album.

The city seemed hollow and somehow empty. She felt alone, something she had not felt in a very long time, even on the ice fields of Akhahsus, and she loathed the void that had taken its hateful place inside her.

There used to be vampires in this city, that was the fact that pained her, as the late night sounds of the city fought to find their way into her head. They had not all been from the same tribe, and wars had raged between them for as long as anyone could remember, but at least they'd been there. Now there was nothing. It was as though they had all made the decision to abandon London and start afresh somewhere else, but where that somewhere was she did not know. They can't all have returned to Kar'mi'shah, she tried to reason, they can't all have found the way home.

And what of Carlos? That was the reason for her return to this dominion. She had visited the site of his grave only to find a vast sprawling housing estate raised in its place. She had stood and watched the house that stood atop it, listening to the echoes of his screams, the cries in the wake of his ascension. But they were just echoes, memories of what had once been. He was indeed gone now. But where? His home was Seville, might he have returned there?

Might she have to travel south through Europe to find him? She had no idea, but knew that she only wanted to be at his side again.

The sound of sickness stole her attention suddenly, of retching somewhere close-by, and returning to the window her eyes tracked instantly to the spot. Several hundred yards further along the street from where the two youths had now abandoned the vehicle, a figure stood doubled over, vomiting onto the pavement at his feet, one hand outstretched against black railings to steady himself. Ordinarily she would not have even given him so much attention, but there was something about him, maybe something in the way he stood, or what he was actually throwing up.

Catherine left the flat quickly and hurried down the stairs and out into the street. Crossing the road to where he still stood hunched, she came to a halt just yards in front of him. His nausea was violent, his hands shaking as he tried to force whatever was inside him up and out of his body, and even though the wind tried to snatch it away, Catherine could still smell the stench of soured blood and wondered whether this individual had ruptured something inside himself, or whether he was a vampire struggling to keep down his meal. The smell should have attracted her to him, the tang of lifeblood, but it only sickened her. It was wrong, that blood. It smelt poisonous to her, and it was only then that she realised that this man was definitely not human but vampire, and that the blood that he was expelling was not his own but was indeed someone else's.

She took hold of him suddenly, despite her disgust, unbalancing him and forcing him back hard against the black iron railings that fronted the apartment buildings. His face was beyond pale, his eyes sunken and dull, and Catherine released him immediately, revolted by both her contact and her proximity.

"Who are you?" she demanded of him.

"Does it matter?" he replied, covering what had become of his face with his arms, shielding it from both the night and her scrutiny of him.

"Where are the others like you? What has become of them?"

"There's no one."

"Tell me, damn you. Where are they?"

The other vampire gagged suddenly, and heaved another thick mouthful of bad blood up and over himself. He struggled to wipe it from his dowdy clothes, and Catherine watched with loathing until he was able to continue.

"They heard of a prophet who spoke of their home and went in search of him. He showed them the doorway and they stepped through."

"All of them?"

"Those desperate enough to believe in the words of a mortal," the vampire said to her. "Some thought he was a skulker, come to trick us into oblivion. Nobody who stepped through ever returned."

"You were not born in Kar'mi'shah," Catherine stated bluntly.

The other vampire shook his head. His hair, rank and rotten, hung across his spoiled face like weed in a stagnant pond.

"And what of you?" Catherine demanded again. "What has turned you into something so pitiful?"

71

His eyes found her now as he finally looked fully up at her, and she could see how terrible they were, sunken and spoilt, mirrors for the diseases that he carried.

"I've collected the plague," he murmured, "the human infection that flows through their veins. It is like a poison that burns inside me. I try to feed but I am always weak. I can only prey on their helpless and most desperate, and that only serves to make me worse."

"You repulse even me," she spat, and then turned and left him, retreating back to the flat of the man upon whom she had fed earlier that night.

She heard his protestations as she made her way back across the street, but she was interested in none of them. She hated this place, hated what she had once loved, and that burned inside her more violently than his disease.

But at least he had told her that not all of them had gone. At least some had feared to trust this prophet and had remained behind, news which, although delivered by so filthy a messenger, at least offered her some hope. She no longer knew what went on in this city. She had been away for only a handful of years, and yet so much had already changed, so many faces gone, so many allegiances turned to nothing.

Catherine thought about the plague that some of these creatures carried in their veins as she made her way back into the flat and closed the door behind her, wondering about the sickness that had started bringing disease to her own kind. She suddenly felt disgusted by them all, every single mortal human, and loathed to touch a single individual, even as she stared down at the corpse upon which she had sated her own hunger only hours before. She remembered how she had gouged a man several nights ago with her hand for no other reason than apathy. She'd been wandering along a busy street, and her proximity amongst so many people had made her skin crawl. She'd simply forced her hand into him, feeling her fingers penetrate through his clothes and into the hot wet meat of his innards. She'd seen his knees buckle, his eyes roll up into his head as he'd half-turned, and had then watched him drop beneath the mass of people that followed. A clamour had risen behind her, voices raised, shouts and cries for help harrying the air, but she had already been whisked along with those humans around her, and she never saw that dead human male again.

She'd felt his blood on her skin, and she now wiped the memory of it from her in a kind of desperate panic. She hated them, hated them all, and always had. But now she could do little but search the city street by filthy street, and all because of her dreams of Carlos and his ascension from the grave. She hated everything in the entire vermin-filled metropolis in which she had been forced to return, and she now knew she could still do little to accelerate her departure out of it.

# THREE

## THE VAMPIRE ANTOINETTE DE BRUGE

From the edge of Chelsea Bridge, Antoinette could see all the way along The Embankment. It was night, the sky cloudless above her head, the reflection of the full moon glittering like slivers of winking silver across the turbulent surface of the Thames. A cool breeze blew out of the summer night, bringing on its back a myriad of juxtaposed smells, roses and diesel fumes, seafood and fresh blood.

Antoinette sniffed suddenly at the wind like a dog snagged by an unexpected scent. Someone had an open wound somewhere close by, and the sickly sweet aroma played across her senses like an intoxicating liquor. Her eyes flickered closed with delirium. She had not tasted fresh blood for seven days, but tonight she would feed.

She scanned the pedestrians strolling beside the river with eyes like those of a hawk, sharp and focussed - filtering out the weak from the strong, the lone stray from the healthy pack - while her nose luxuriated in the tang of freshly drawn blood.

Couples walked hand in hand, joggers darting between them in shorts of bright yellow lycra. Dog-walkers took their pets for their last constitutional. Businessmen walked the last stretch home. Nightclubbers in short dresses and cheap gold jewellery took to the streets for the start of a drunken night out, caterwauled by council workers repairing a faulty streetlamp. So many people, so many veins, and all of them pumping with the rich hot fluid that would keep her alive.

The skulkers had been close, though, that was all she could think, and closer than was comfortable. She'd managed to keep ahead of them since she'd left the body of the man from the nightclub in the alleyway behind the cinema further along the street. She'd slit his throat and barely pressed her tongue against the wound before they'd pounced upon her. Three men with clubs and knives had appeared from out of the shadows with nothing but her destruction on their minds. She'd managed to use the darkness to her advantage and escape them before receiving a single blow. She had been weak, and to have stood and fought them in such a state would have been impossible.

But it was getting more and more difficult to stay even one step ahead of them, to keep an ear to the ground, or to trust other sources that were already stretched paper-thin across the sprawling grimy metropolis of London.

One night a week ago she had been foolish. She had allowed a taxi driver to sweep her home with him after the streets had grown quiet in the early hours of the morning.

She had ridden up front with him, had even allowed him to press his sweaty hands across the flesh of her thighs, pushing them up towards her sex. She had allowed him that because to have denied him then would have been to deny herself his blood.

She'd known she could have killed him there and then in his cab, but it was safer to feed off the streets, away from prying eyes. Safer to feed inside, always safer behind locked doors.

But it had been a trap. In hindsight the clues had been obvious. She knew that now. But then? She had been hungry, hungrier than she had felt in a long time, and she had been stupid.

Inside the taxi driver's flat in Clapham waited four skulkers. As soon as the door had closed behind her, it had been locked and double bolted.

She had killed that skulker instantly, breaking his neck with a single sharp blow to the front of his throat. But she had not been quick enough to unbolt the door and flee. She had been grabbed by too many hands and hauled back away from it. She'd struggled but the wire was already being wrapped tight around her wrists, cutting into her flesh like razors. She remembered thrashing like some wild animal, something she had not done in a very long time, but it had shaken her free of all but one of her assailants, and had at least afforded her an accurate look at the rest of the flat in the handful of seconds that she had won.

The windows to the main room had been secured with metal bars fixed from the inside, the front door she could now see had heavy bolts drawn top and bottom. Whatever doors ran off from the living room were hidden by tall wardrobes, and it was clear in those few snatched moments that the vampire killers had prepared themselves well for this moment. Maybe it was even a commonly-used trap. The din of shouting voices hammered her attention back, and she lurched to find two of the skulkers and the taxi driver coming back at her, the skulkers with a blanket stretched between them, the driver with a baseball bat.

Antoinette retreated quickly, the third skulker still standing behind her, still clasping with gloved hands the length of wire that tore and bit into her wrists. She felt his weight lift beneath her strength, and she forced him back hard into the wall.

She heard his bones crack and grinned with glee, grinned too at the faces of the remaining three before her, hesitant now that their accomplice had dropped down onto his knees. But with her hands still bound hard and tight behind her, she had trouble even facing them.

She checked the windows once again. The bars were screwed into the brickwork. Even if she'd had her hands free she might not be able to rip them free, but like this she was trapped for certain.

Her eyes flickered back as the taxi driver threw himself at her, the baseball bat swinging down out of the air. Antoinette ducked swiftly but the bat found her shoulder, breaking the bone with a loud crack and bringing a searing pain that thumped at the point of the injury. Stumbling down onto one knee as nausea turned her stomach over, she fought to clear the unexpected agony as the second blow came.

The world went black for a few seconds as the impact battered her skull. But when her eyes re-opened, the skulkers were descending upon her with their blanket, disorientating her and smothering her thrashing limbs.

Over and over the bat found her body, each blow bludgeoning her limbs and bringing agonising pain. She was screaming, thrashing with her legs and her head until her foot found one of the skulkers. She yanked at his leg, and felt the weight of his body tumble. It must have knocked the second skulker sideways for the blanket lifted suddenly from her and she managed to find strength enough to haul herself upright. The taxi driver stared down at her with incredulous eyes, wondering how this being could still be alive. And then she lunged at him, sinking her teeth deep into the meat of his chest and tearing at it.

The flesh came away inside the ripping threads of his shirt, hot rich blood coating her tongue and throat as it pulsed out over them both. She took partial pleasure in it as it gifted her a shock of energy and revenge, forcing her to her feet before throwing herself on towards the door. She heard the deafening din of their shouts and screams at her back as she ran, but even that was shattered as she hurled herself at the front door with what little strength she had left.

The wood cracked and splintered as the door broke in two, Antoinette landing in a twisted heap on the other side. She lifted her head, thumping with injuries and running with blood, to find the skulkers already coming after her. But she had escaped their safe room and was back in the real world.

The landing window was only yards away, unhindered by any metal bars, and before they could reach for her and drag her back inside to finish her, she was up and off towards it.

With no bars protecting it, the glass shattered into tiny glinting darts as her weight tumbled through it. Three storeys up, she found herself plummeting towards the hard ground. But what did it matter what was below? Better broken bones and fleeting pain than death at the hands of mortals.

There were trees below, however, a line of thin conifers that at least partially broke her fall. But with her arms still bound at her back with piercing wire and no hands with which to protect herself, their branches scratched at her face and throat, drawing blood swiftly inside razored nicks, until she tumbled out of their boughs and landed hard on the pavement beneath.

Her thoughts were thick and slow like gallons of black oil as her eyes struggled to open to the darkness of the ill-lit street. Agony shot across her face and shoulders, her mouth running with blood and grit, but already there were raised voices from somewhere nearby – the skulkers already running to finish the job – and so she had to force energy into her limbs, and haul herself into the darkest shadows of the night before she was found.

Anyone could have done her harm in the state she had been in, battered and still bound at the wrists, but the night offered at least some refuge, and she slipped into its welcoming depths as swiftly as she could.

A vampire that haunted the arches of Chelsea Bridge had freed her from her shackles that night, and she had indeed been grateful. That had been a week ago. Her wounds had mostly healed, the visible ones at least, but six nights rest had done their job, and she was ready to hunt once more.

Her shoulders still ached and she could still trace the last of the lines of scar tissue across her cheek and chin, but in a few more nights even they would be gone.

She'd felt ashamed of offering herself to another vampire in such a state, especially beaten so badly at the hands of human skulkers, but this other vampire had felt neither pity nor amusement, but had simply tended to her as much as she had required and then left.

But he was not here this night. Did he even still frequent this place beside the Thames, or had she just stumbled upon him as he had hunted?

She had no idea, and they had barely conversed that night. She had waited at the bridge for an hour already tonight, and she'd reasoned in her head a hundred times that perhaps he knew she was there and chose not to show himself this second time. She recalled how he had seemed to simply uncloak the night from around him, as if the darkness was a cowl for him to wear when he so chose. Antoinette looked around her again, but he was not here, or if he was, she could not detect his presence.

The sweet scent of blood on the air caught her attention once again as the gentle breeze lifted it to her nostrils. Her eyes flickered closed with pleasure and hunger as she inhaled it slowly, its tang caressing the back of her tongue with its heady bliss. Her eyes opened, focussed and sharp, and surveyed the mortals still passing along the embankment, hoping to find the owner of the sweet wound, not caring if she had to open it wider for herself.

The dog-walkers had moved on, the joggers too, but new ones had arrived to take their place in the popular walkway across the water from Battersea Park. The council workmen were finishing up their emergency repair, packing away tools into battered plastic boxes, winding up rolls of cable. Their muscles were strong but layered with stale fat. Experience taught her that the flesh would be tough too, the blood tainted from bad diets. The joggers would make a better meal, neat tight flesh, thin blood pumping eagerly through veins ripe for puncturing. She'd fed on the healthy before and fed well, but that was not for her tonight.

Antoinette continued to search the busy pavement, her keen unblinking eyes searching the pedestrians that made their way beneath the insipid yellow streetlamps like those of an owl surveying a buffet of field mice. Two lovers sat on a bench looking out over the glittering river, their hands locked together, fingers entwined, and she wondered briefly about killing them both. How romantic that would be, to die in each other's arms, and be together for all eternity.

Her mind wandered back to the vampire who'd looked down upon her those seven nights before with such compassion. She'd imagined so much, wondered about the possibilities, but that was not for her either. She'd been in love as a mortal, a century and more ago, and had been cherished by vampires since. But not for a decade had she been with another vampire, and although she knew of others in the city she had come to call home, she would not visit that tricky domain of love again.

A black cab pulled up at the kerb less than a hundred yards away, the sight startling her with memories of the skulkers. It was innocent enough, she suspected, as she watched a city gent climb out of the back and close the door after him. Even as the cab pulled back out into the flow of traffic,

Antoinette could see that he was no vampire killer. But still the tremors continued in her body, even once the cab had turned the corner and was out of sight, and she felt ashamed that so small a group of mortals could have such a lasting effect upon her.

Her mind was busy once again with renewed fears, and Antoinette left Chelsea Bridge and made her way through the walkers and joggers, all of them blissfully unaware of the killer that walked amongst them.

The breeze lifted her hair from her forehead as she walked. She barely cast an eye across the glittering surface of the surging river, but instead kept her gaze mostly at the pavement as her thoughts whirled inside her head.

A hundred and more years she had been a vampire, and she had seen more than most. So how had she managed to virtually hand those skulkers a free ticket to destroy her? She should have known better than that, should've known what plans these mortals could devise to try and even the odds that were stacked so desperately against them.

How could she be sure that she'd recognise those signs again?

How could she be sure that those same skulkers from whom she had managed to escape were not still watching her, were not still following her even now? She glanced behind her more swiftly than any mortal could notice, an unnatural motion that afforded her a peripheral vision of the walkers at her back as well as of those across the street. Nobody seemed to pay her any heed, no one visible to her scrutiny anyway. There were those that could hide themselves effectively, those that had learned from vampires themselves in exchange for worldly goods or even immunity. There were even vampires that hunted their own kind. It was a dangerous time. But that last week? She had failed in her duty to protect herself, but had thankfully escaped with rational fears for the future. They had taught her a good lesson. But they would not congratulate themselves for that.

A young man stood leaning against the railings looking out over the river. She could see his hair, light in colour and long enough to move beneath the caress of the breeze. Although he wore a tan leather jacket, she could sense by his stature the firmness of his muscles, the fitness of his body, the taut flesh of his throat stretched tantalising as he bent his head. There were fewer pedestrians along this stretch of the embankment, and Antoinette made her way towards him now, focussing out the din and the fumes of the cars passing by, focussing in the pulsing heartbeat of this man, the scent of his skin, his ignorance of her proximity.

She could bend over him and puncture his flesh and feed before anyone even noticed, she thought. No one would give any heed to what they would recognise as a lover's kiss, the woman behind the man, pressing kisses of love against the neck of her beloved. And with the weight of his blood in her belly she could flee back into the darkest of the night's shadows leaving him slumped across the railings where she had found him, with no repercussions until someone discovered the corpse the following daybreak with the morning's weight of passing commuters.

But as she closed within inches of him he lifted his head. Was it some motion that she had caused, some movement that had alerted him to his dispatcher? And if so, what?

Her mind reeled as she saw his face. Her feet faltered and would carry her no more. Her teeth, which had already lengthened in her jaw, froze, and all desire to destroy this man went from her head.

It was his eyes that halted her, wide and blue, and she felt herself drowning as they regarded her. She seemed to swim helplessly for a few moments, disorientated by this mere mortal.

The two of them stared at one another, he with curiosity at this stranger almost touching him, she with emotions that both enraptured and disorientated her. But when he smiled at her, a delicate smile encased inside his curiosity, she thought she would lose consciousness.

She could smell the blood in him, could hear and feel the pulse of his heart, yet the desire to feed had drained almost instantly out of her. Even when he spoke, and she could not be sure what he had actually said to her, she felt weak inside, weaker than she'd felt after the skulkers had beaten her.

She knew she was still staring at him but she couldn't help it. A palette of thoughts swirled insanely inside her head like a modern canvas, and she was unable to make sense of any one of them. He spoke again, the smile still on his lips, and she realised he had asked her name.

"Antoinette De Bruge," she replied, her eyes still transfixed by his.

"What a stunning name," he said to her, his voice breathless, genuine, his smile still enrapturing her.

"And yours?" she asked, sanity sweeping over

her like an ocean over rocks.

"Nothing nearly so wonderful," he said, that smile of his breaking just as magnificently into a grin. "It's Stevie."

She knew he was no vampire, but what did that suddenly matter? She knew this was flirting, a petty act played out by mortals for cheap eroticism before their brief lives were snuffed out, but she didn't care. She'd promised herself so much, to abstain from such ludicrous notions, to feed and then retreat back into the shadows, but here he was, still looking at her, still smiling.

A thought surged into her head to bludgeon the rest that swirled unchecked there – kill him now and be done with all this nonsense. But how could she kill him? She could never destroy this beautiful Stevie.

"It's a bit late for you to be out walking here alone, isn't it?" he asked.

His voice shook her from her conflict, and in her hesitation to reply, he added:

"You are alone, are you?"

"Yes," she told him, attempting to reclaim some of her former calm. "I'm taking the night air. That's all. There's no harm in that."

"I had to get out of the flat too. I was going stir-crazy," he told her. "I've been working too much lately. I need to spend more time doing this."

"Talking to strangers?"

He smiled again. A laugh reverberated in his throat but didn't make it as far as his lips.

"No, this," he waved his hand down at the Thames. "I love this river. I should spend more time here. Especially on nights like this."

Antoinette watched him closely as he spoke, confirming the firm muscle of his torso through his white t-shirt, the way his jeans hugged his legs. Then her eyes fell upon his neck, the flesh she had expected to puncture, to press her lips against and then drink. But not tonight, she promised. Not ever. He did not deserve that.

"Do you want to go and get a coffee or something?"

His question caught her off guard. This was flirting, but with growing consequences. Did he not realise she was a vampire? Did he not know that she was over a hundred and fifty years old? Did he not think to ask about how she fed only after the sun went down? Perhaps she should tell him. Perhaps she should explain how she butchered his kind in order to drink from them.

But to tell that would be to lose his company, and she found herself accepting his invitation, found herself walking beside him along the embankment beneath the huge pale moon, the breeze bringing scents of roses and diesel fumes to them in an awkward marriage of delicate scent and grey poison. Antoinette knew the insanity of it, the two of them together, but what did one night matter? They could drink coffee and talk about the city and then they would never see each other again. She would leave him to go on his way. She would see to that.

# FOUR

## UNION AND REUNION

S tevie was waiting for her by Chelsea Bridge the following night. Antoinette saw him from the other side of the river, his hair lifted on the wind that blew off the Thames, his eyes searching along both directions of the Embankment.

It was a dark night, overcast with the threat of heavy rain, but Antoinette saw him clearly. He, on the other hand, would have no chance of viewing her, so fragile was his human vision.

She knew the insanity of the situation, the frailty of his mortality that would never last, and the repulsion that he would have for her once he discovered the legacy she had been born into. And she would die before she saw that repulsion upon his beautiful face.

She'd not made plans to see him, in fact she'd been defiant at the end of the previous evening, telling him that she had enjoyed his company but that nothing would come of it.

She'd left him miserable, disappearing into the shadowed haunts of London swiftly so that he would not see the grief their parting had caused. His face had been hurtful enough to see, the pain that creased it, the look of excised love. But she'd needed to leave him, needed to end something that she should never have started. If only she'd been able to kill him before he'd turned round. But then how could she deprive the world of something so handsome?

It hurt her to see him looking for her. She could see the need on his face, the longing in his eyes, and realised that she had put it there. How could she not go to him? The futility of it pained her - she was a vampire, he a vessel of blood, and that was all there was to it.

She could so easily remove herself from her vantage point at the opposite end of Chelsea Bridge, and yet her feet refused to transport her. She reasoned that she could make it clear to him again, explain that nothing would come of it, and try to dispel some of the loss that would come. Maybe it would dispel some of her own.

Her foot moved as this last thought formed, taking a step across the bridge towards him.

The rain clouds had stolen the moon, robbing the night of its luminescence, but she estimated that it was somewhere close to midnight. There was still traffic on the bridge, joining other traffic that was light on the roads ahead of her. Antoinette concealed herself so that she moved unseen, even under the brightness of the lights that flooded the bridge, and arrived beside Stevie without him seeing her first. She studied him briefly as his eyes still searched the night for her, and she almost felt her dead heart skip in her chest. She wanted him then, more than she had the previous night, if only to comfort him and put right the whole mess that she had so foolishly initiated.

She spoke his name gently beside him and saw

him jump at her sudden proximity. A smile came swiftly to his lips to match her own, however, and she felt a spreading warmth flood through her that only feeding could attempt to match.

"I didn't think you'd come," Stevie said to her.

"I shouldn't have."

"But you did."

He smiled at her again, and she wanted then to kiss him, to press her lips against his and feel the heat of his body against hers. But he was a man, a mortal, and that was all. He was a vessel...

"I came to wait for you," he confessed. "I didn't know if last night was a chance meeting, or whether you walked this way often. So I just came down hoping to find you, to try to explain to you that what happened last night wasn't just a passing attraction –"

"It was a conversation over coffee, Stevie, and that was all."

"No," he said, shaking his head. "You felt something for me. I felt it too. Tell me I'm wrong."

Antoinette stared at his lips as he spoke. The colour of them was intoxicating, blissful. And then, as she looked up into his eyes, the weight of his words seemed to restrain her defence and haul her emotions up into her throat as if to choke her.

"We need to talk," he said more quietly now.

"No," Antoinette said defiantly. "We need to be naked and entwined around each other."

His face froze, his eyes stark and wide, but then the understanding flooded visibly into both his face and his groin.

They went back to his place in Hammersmith, an apartment in a converted three storey Victorian

89

terraced house, the exterior of which stood coated heavily with the black pollution of city fumes. It was bright inside, however, from both the decoration as well as the illumination, and Antoinette coaxed Stevie out of its harshness and through into his bedroom where a small lamp beside his bed cast a gentle glow across them both.

Antoinette took hold of his face in her hands and felt the warmth of his skin against her fingertips, before she pressed her lips against his and relished their heat.

She could almost taste his blood, separated from her tongue by only the frailest of skin layers. But she was not here to feed, only to give herself over to pleasure and be filled by this most beautiful of men.

She let her arms fall away from him and allowed Stevie to undress her, watching as his fingers pulled away her blouse to expose her small but rounded breasts. Her stare lingered as he bowed his face to them, taking them into his mouth with hot kisses that made her eyelids flicker heavily. Her head fell back as she felt his hands beneath her long skirt, stroking the insides of her thighs as they roved higher towards her sex. She'd dreamt of this moment throughout the previous day, imagining his lips where his fingers now strayed, planted between her legs, his tongue stimulating her utterly, and she had worn no underwear, hoping secretly that this night might happen. She wanted herself to be seduced.

Antoinette fell backwards onto the bed and allowed him full access to her body. Her legs parted as Stevie pushed her skirt up to her waist, and as he bowed his head down towards her exposed vagina, she arched her back up towards him as the first

90

waves of pleasure coursed through her body.

She grasped his hair in both fists as his tongue glanced slickly and eagerly across her clitoris. Her eyes rolled up into their sockets, her head a swirling void of elation, and it surprised her at just how quickly and easily he could bring such rapture.

Lifting his head up with her hands still clenched inside his hair, she sat up with her blouse still open and her skirt still bunched around her waist and began clawing Stevie's clothes away, hauling his shirt up over his head before tearing at the buckle and zipper at the front of his jeans.

His cock was erect and huge in her hands, pumped hard with blood, its head the colour of beetroot. Stevie groaned loudly as she mauled it, forcing his foreskin up and down thickly, but she wanted to have it in her hands first before he pushed it inside her, wanted to see it and study its exquisite shape.

Stevie knelt on the bed in front of her with his arms at his side as Antoinette began to pump him with her hand. She studied his foreskin as it stretched tight and then wrinkled in her fist, exposing and then concealing the livid purple, fascinated by the veins that stood out so starkly, and wondering how they could be so brutal in colour and yet remain unbroken by her forceful motions. She knew she was starting to hurt him, but there was something about the livid purple of those veins, the ferociousness of the colour, and the heat held firmly in her fist.

Stevie groaned again, his face flickering with pain, and for a moment she thought he was going to either pull out of her grasp or just take hold of her hand altogether. It had gone far enough, and after pushing a kiss down over the very end of his penis, Antoinette let him go and rolled over onto her belly. She felt his hands grasp her buttocks then, kneading them as hard as she had worked him, and she squirmed beneath his force. She lifted her hips towards him to allow him entry, and wondered why his cock had not even touched her. She realised that his hands had left her too, and tried to make sense of it. Perhaps he was having problems. Perhaps he'd delved into the cupboard beside the bed upon which his lamp sat looking for a condom. She hoped he hadn't come yet.

Then she lifted her head and craned it round, looking for him.

He was still kneeling on the bed, his cock still wonderfully erect and bruised with colour, but his head was hanging back as though frozen in a moment of ecstasy. Her position was awkward, straining to look right behind her, but then she realised that his expression was not one of pleasure, but of surprise, of alarm. Something had stained his neck, as though he had just cut himself shaving. But that was crazy, that was insane. Then her eyes flickered towards the dark space just above his exposed neck. A face hovered there, unseen at first in the half-light, but Antoinette saw it now, saw it as the vampire allowed herself now to be seen.

"Catherine," Antoinette whispered, her throat barely able to feed her voice.

The other vampire simply stared down at her with utter contempt, and for a moment Antoinette feared that she would kill her too.

Stevie was already dead, she could see the

blankness in his eyes that had rolled up into his skull. There was no saving him, and her loss was held only momentarily by the threat to her own life.

Catherine Calleh let the body of the human male fall sideways onto the bed so that she could have a full look at the vampire slut lying half-naked and bared before her.

Antoinette could feel the hatred buzzing in the air between them like electricity, could feel the disgust in that stare that threatened her very life. But only when she thought she was safe, at least temporarily, did she dare pull her blouse back around herself to cover her breasts and ease her skirt down to conceal her nakedness.

Antoinette climbed warily off the bed then and glanced down at Stevie's body. He was dead, his body still convulsing with the echoes of life. And yet his cock was still rigid, still defiant to the last.

"Once a whore..." Catherine seethed finally, her lips motionless, her black eyes furious and sharp.

"What do you want?" Antoinette managed to say.

"I followed you from the bridge. I watched your profanity."

"You didn't have to kill him."

"I did what you should have done. Look at you, coming here and doing the things that you did –"

"Maybe if you had learnt a few of those tricks you wouldn't have lost Carlos." It was a cheap shot, she knew, but Catherine had killed her Stevie.

Antoinette expected her to fly at her then, to tear her limb from limb, but she remained where she was. Catherine had sired her many years ago, and in return for the gift of everlasting life, Antoinette had tempted and then stolen her husband away from her side. She'd known how vicious Catherine could be, and had known how stupid it was to try and seduce her Carlos. That was why she had fled after their affair, knowing that to be found was to be tortured or murdered. Or both. That had been many decades ago. But at long last, she had been found.

"I'm surprised it's taken you this long to find me."

"Don't flatter yourself," Catherine spat. "I've not been looking for you. I only saw you by accident. But now I find you still whoring, I wonder why I never chose to destroy you before."

Her words were fierce but Antoinette tried to show she was at least a match for her, standing her ground with words she knew were tougher than she could back up.

"Why didn't you just kill me at the bridge? Why wait until now?"

"Oh, my intention was not to kill you," Catherine said to her. "I want to know where my Carlos is."

Antoinette stared at her.

"I haven't seen Carlos."

Catherine's eyes narrowed almost imperceptibly, but Antoinette saw them, and saw the fury in them and realised the dangerous game she was playing.

"I left and never returned," Antoinette explained.

"Carlos was dead," Catherine told her. "I know, because I killed him myself."

Antoinette opened her mouth to speak but Catherine cut her short.

"I've dreamt that he has risen from the grave that I dug for him. I returned to find that a whole new community has been built there. I found his grave empty, and only echoes of his bones that I'd stripped of flesh left behind."

Antoinette glanced over her shoulder and saw that the bedroom door was closed. She was sure she had left it open in her urgency to be fucked by the human male. Catherine must have closed it after her, probably fixed it shut somehow too. Not that she would make it that far anyway.

"Where is he, Antoinette?"

The younger vampire shook her head.

"I don't know, I haven't seen him."

"Who else would want him?" Catherine growled. "He couldn't rise by himself, not the way I left him."

She was seething again, her voice spit-flecked with rage.

"Did you excavate his grave? Did you take his body? The solitary female who lives there now could not have done it? She is clean, ignorant."

Antoinette took a stumbling step back towards the door, locked or not, but it was already too late. Catherine flew at her across the room like a savage beast, a vast swathe of black that seemed to scythe the very air in two. Antoinette felt something pierce her spine as she turned to run, and the sight of Stevie's bedroom flickered into blackness as a stab of icy cold penetrated her torso. She heard Catherine scream as though she was already deep inside her head, and as the torture commenced, she wondered whether the deceit all those years ago had been worth it.

# FIVE

## REFLECTIONS

The vampire Catherine Calleh returned to the place on the Embankment where she had watched Antoinette's sordid submission to the human male, and watched the turbulent flow of the Thames, the great river that surged through the heart of the city. She had wanted to kill her then, to put an end to the disgust that she felt, but she had wanted to question her about Carlos first. It had been rage from seeing her debase herself with the mortal that had forced her to torture Antoinette, rather than the fury that she'd once harboured, but she did not regret the impulsiveness of her assault upon the younger vampire, and what was done was done. The punishment had been right.

Although she believed what Antoinette had told her (that she had not seen him since their affair), Catherine knew that she would have to track her husband down now by other means. The city was huge, and those she had once known within its sprawling limits were gone. She was alone, apart from Antoinette, and she would not be visiting her again. Their brief reunion was over as far as she was concerned.

As Catherine watched the river surge beneath the bridge upon which she now stood, her mind returned to the history of her and her future husband's chance meeting.

She had first met him in Seville when the city had been small, nothing like the size it had come to grow to over the centuries he had been away, and not nearly so grand. He had been tall and handsome, with a full mane of long black hair, and she had watched him break horses deep into the night in a corral at the rear of his family's villa. Maybe it had been the vista of mountains that reminded her of her own home, or the sweet aromas from the groves of oranges and almonds that drifted down the slopes on the back of the Mediterranean breezes, but she had fallen for him then, a mortal man, and taken him for her own.

They had exchanged blood beneath a pearlescent moon, there in the corral as the horses beat their hooves against the hard-packed dirt. He had seemed enchanted by the stranger come down from the hill to watch him, and they had talked as the moon rose higher in the sky and the stars panned across the heavens. He had offered himself to her then and she had drunk from him, feeling his rich blood on her tongue, an act which had aroused her in a way she had never felt before or since.

Catherine had opened a vein in her wrist then and pressed it against his lips, coaxing him to drink from her like a mother coaxing an infant to her breast.

Carlos had been weak at first, gagging as the first of her blood had found his throat. But as his body began to accept the potency of what flowed through her, so he became stronger, drinking from her vein like a desert dweller at an oasis.

She'd had to force him away from her in the end, tugging his head back from her with his wonderful black hair clasped in her fist. She'd found herself giving herself over to him, surrendering to him in a growing state of erotic submission. His eyes had stared up at her as her blood ran down his chin and throat, somewhere between that half-fed infant snatched away from his mother's milk, and the lover chastened partway through seduction.

They had left that night without any word to his family and travelled north until dawn, waiting out the following day's lethal sunlight in a shepherd's hut. Catherine had killed the family that they'd found inside, a mother and three children, and used them to strengthen Carlos' already weakening body over the coming days while the shepherd remained up in the mountains with his flock. She herself needed to replenish the blood that Carlos had drained from her, needed to fortify her muscles for the journey ahead. Carlos's family would come looking for him, of that there could be no doubt, and until he had sufficient strength to leave the region, they were forced to remain hidden away in the isolated shack.

They lived well after that, the two of them, as husband and wife. Carlos learned well and became a strong and swift hunter, but his audacity sometimes became a problem. He would take mortals from the street in open view, rather than seducing them out of a crowd or from unlit boulevards. They were immortal and they were infinitely stronger than their prey, but a mob was dangerous, potentially lethal, and could do them massive harm. Catherine had tried to make Carlos see this over and over, but there seemed to be something hard-headed about him, a bullish arrogance or defiance, maybe even a desire to test the everlasting life she had bestowed upon him. But to belittle him in such petty ways was not to remember him as she did. She had loved him utterly to the point of devotion. They had travelled everywhere together, rarely leaving each other's sight.

They'd spent much of the nineteenth century in the northern provinces of Spain, heading finally into France to taste the ever-flourishing culture and hedonism of a burgeoning country, and to taste the richer blood of the famed aristocracy. Existence had been good back then, a life worth living.

Catherine grinned to herself as she stood beside the surging Thames, her mind recalling the grand balls and banquets she and Carlos had once invaded, the opulent palaces they had stolen into, to dance away the night with fine music, the likes of which they had rarely heard of before in the rural towns they had usually frequented. Were they not a king and queen of a higher order? Did they not deserve to tread the floors of lesser mortal royalty? And they were wise to feed from their guests too, not from their hosts - an unruly mob in a town square was one thing, but an organised garrison of paid guards was quite another.

Antoinette De Bruge had been a servant girl in a palace near Versailles. There had been something innocent and virginal about her, and Carlos had commented how rewarding a subservient minor might be to them. Catherine had suspected then that maybe Carlos had begun to grown weary of his immortality, and maybe longed for either something new or for an end to it entirely. He still had a passion for both her and the lives they led, and also a vivacity for killing, but a kind of tedium had slowly begun to crawl into the way he spoke and behaved, like a tapeworm burrowing slowly but surely into a man's flesh, and this simple servant girl had been put upon the table as a possible solution.

Catherine could not imagine living without her beloved Carlos, especially after the opulence and grandeur they had come to expect. So and after much discussion, they did indeed choose to bring this third member into their family.

That this insignificant and worthless girl might ultimately seduce her husband hadn't entered her mind for a single moment, but she had followed the youthful-looking servant down into the kitchens, seduced her outside with talk of lost dreams and everlasting adventure, and took her into her embrace amongst the manicured gardens beneath the fall of the bright moon.

Nobody would have missed a servant girl from below stairs, but they all left France shortly afterwards anyway in 1870 when France declared war on Prussia and invading German armies brought desperation and a fear of strangers to the streets.

There was easy prey on the streets, sufficient for a new vampire to learn her skills as a hunter, but the people of Versailles were growing thin and weak as the war quickly took its toll. Catherine had thought how ridiculous it was for these mortals, already cursed by such a short lifespan, to desire to shorten it still.

But the threat to themselves was growing, day by day and rapidly, whole armies and artillery

100

destroying places that had once been safe and wonderful. There were even difficult times as they then tried to leave the country, for the German army possessed a stranglehold on every route and every town in France. Yet somehow they managed to smuggle themselves aboard a vehicle to Normandy, and together the three of them crossed a turbulent Channel to another province called England.

They missed the world they had left, the opulent world of the richer classes, for which the war had been little more than a distraction to their banquets and celebrations. Kent, on the other hand, they found cold and disagreeable, and despised it intensely from the outset. But with few choices left to them they persisted, and together they headed north again to a crowded bustling metropolis called London, and found once again the lifestyle they had grown to love in France.

But it was different - not better or worse - just different, and the three of them came to enjoy their time almost equally. Perhaps it was then that Catherine first noticed how the servant girl was taking too keen an interest in social living, and less in subservience. Perhaps it was then that Catherine should have set things straight. Hindsight had a tendency to burn like acid sometimes.

They lost themselves inside the new movements of music and art (husband, wife and servant), for it seemed to change everything around them, and they kept close inside the wealthy circles of the West End. But Antoinette had clearly been clever enough to disguise the intent she'd had for Carlos, at least when the three of them had been together. If Catherine had suspected anything, she knew she would have destroyed that whoring immortal there and then.

The night of the seduction came just a handful of years before the turn of the new century. Carlos had become enraptured by the new music of a young composer named Claude Debussy, and sought to listen to his performances at every opportunity. It was something that Catherine could not find a similar taste for, but one for which Antoinette could. The two of them would go together while Catherine wandered alone along the banks of the Thames, but never once did she think what might be occurring. Only when Carlos returned alone one morning less than an hour before sunrise did she learn the truth.

He confessed to Catherine how he and Antoinette had consummated a growing passion for each other, and it was that night that Catherine had lost herself to rage. She destroyed the apartment they had shared and lashed out at him with all her anger. He tried to defend himself, but slowed by liquor and spent love, he could not match Catherine's speed or fury. She did not break his bones, but kept his body intact as she fought, sinking her teeth into him and drinking from his veins, tearing his flesh from his bones and devouring it as though his infidelity had somehow reduced her to little more than a base wild animal.

She'd taken what was left of her husband's bloodless corpse and buried it on waste ground in the poorer suburbs that skirted the city, well away from the delights he had revelled in. She went out to search for Antoinette after that, but she never found her, never even discovered a single clue about her sudden and wise disappearance.

Catherine had never regretted killing her beloved Carlos, and, until recently, had never desired to visit his grave. Only in dreams had she seen him, memories conjured from a love once cherished, fleeting images distorted and altered by time's separation.

Until she had dreamt of his ascension.

That had changed things.

She'd needed to return to this world, needed to find his grave once again, needed to cradle his face in her hands.

His rebirth had initiated the resurrection of their union. True, he had done the most terrible disservice to her, and she had given his crime the only punishment it had deserved. But now he had risen from the very grave she had dug for him with her bare hands over a century ago. With that grave now empty, there was no longer any path for her to follow to find him. She was lost in a place that had once been called her home. Yet the return to England was not all wasted. She had found her husband's seducer Antoinette, the insignificant servant girl of Versailles, and had at last dealt with her in a manner that befitted her. That, in itself, had been reason enough to stand once again upon England's soil. And that had brought the grin to the face of the vampire.

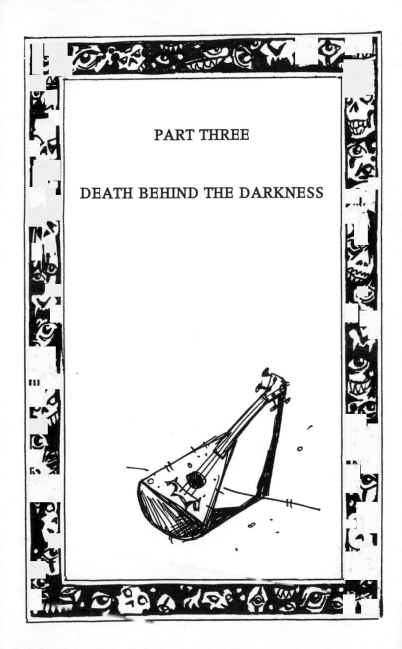

# PART THREE

# DEATH BEHIND THE DARKNESS

# ONE

## MESSENGER

Jenner Hoard stood beneath a dimly lit archway inside Jar's Nightclub and watched the dancers on the floor. He was human, and so were they (as far as he could tell anyway). The vampires had not made an appearance yet.

He'd taken it upon himself to tell them that Kar'mi'shah existed once again, that their home-world was just a door away. Some listened with interest, wondering how a mere mortal could know of such a hallowed and lost place, while others simply saw him as food come to place itself at their feet. But he'd learned to defend himself, learned some neat tricks in the ways of dealing with vampires. Plus he now carried a handgun big enough to floor some of the biggest while he ran for his life.

As he wandered inside the darkest hollows of the club taking slow draws from his bottle of beer, he wondered just how many vampires he'd actually directed to the hotel in Kensington. It wasn't much of a portal, a shabby run-down building with more rats in the basement than guests in the rooms above, but that was what made it so special. It was the gateway to a revered place hidden in the heart of shit, tucked away from eyes that did not need to see it, shrouded by fume-blackened buildings and litter-strewn streets. He'd been a saviour to many, but only to those for whom Kar'mi'shah had been a home. For the others, for those made undead here in the world that he knew, it was nothing, which made him nothing but a hot meal, a blood bank come looking to die.

A man and a woman stood talking at the crowded bar, but there was something about the man that held Jenner's eye. He was too sober, his vision too clear, too focussed on the young woman into whose ear he was speaking.

She, rather than laughing at her beau's words, looked stern, as though he was talking deeply about the world, about souls lost in a society that didn't care.

Jenner knew how some vampires worked, knew the tricks they used to seduce their prey, maybe even to convince them into thinking that their lives weren't worth the effort of keeping. Everyone feels lonely at some point in their life, everyone feels disconnected from the rest of society. But the funny thing, Jenner thought as he watched them both, was how people managed to feel so apart at the same time.

Jenner watched as the two of them started away from the bar, neither of them with faces swamped with bliss at the promise of passion in each other's arms.

Jenner drained his beer and set the bottle down on the table behind him, but when he looked back he'd lost sight of them already in the busy crowd of the club.

He started towards the exit, his eyes searching for them both. Then he found them, already close to the top of the stairs which led down to the street.

They'd covered ground quickly, eager to be out of sight, and Jenner had to force his way through the throng of bodies. He heard shouts at his back, from people whose drinks he'd spilled (he even felt someone punch him in the back), but he had no time, a life was at stake, and he continued on at a run.

At the top of the stairs he looked down to find them gone. A bouncer stood just inside the door, and when Jenner got outside onto the pavement, two more stood talking. Jenner scanned the street in both directions but there was no longer any sign of them.

He approached the two bouncers out on the pavement and asked if they'd seen the couple who had just left the club. They stared at him as though he was shit, looking him up and down. One of them said no, the other didn't even answer him, and then they turned their backs and carried on with their conversation. Jenner felt his anger rise up in him, at the arrogance and ignorance of this pair of muscle-clad idiots. Someone was going to die tonight, and soon, but he knew that he could not explain that to them, could not explain that to anyone. Time and rationality prevented any explanation.

He scanned the pavement afresh and although there were plenty of people still walking the streets, some of them shouting and singing, he could not find the couple who had just left the club.

He started off regardless, hurrying down the street, hoping that he had at least picked the right direction, but he knew in the pit of his stomach that it was already too late. Vampires knew the streets better than he did, knew the deepest shadows, knew how to disappear. The vampire at the bar could have taken her anywhere: to a car, an alleyway, back to a hotel room or apartment.

Jenner stopped at a junction and gazed along the length of each road.

London was huge.

And he'd already lost them.

Jenner returned despondent to his flat in Hammersmith. He'd seen it so many times – people killed and drained of their blood – but it was worse, sometimes, not to see it; to be so close to saving someone but fail, that was the kicker. How do you tell someone that the person that they've just taken for their lover is a vampire? That was a skill he had not yet discovered. Better to separate them quickly and deal with them one on one, than to have a three-way debate.

He pulled his gun from the holster under his armpit and set it down on the kitchen counter before reaching for the bottle of vodka that stood beside the kettle. His hand froze momentarily on the glass as his eyes flickered closed. The alcohol helped sometimes, but other times made things worse. It was painful working alone, painful being separated from his beloved Emma. She was a very long way away now, and she was different: she was one of them now and she had her own life to lead. He'd not seen her in almost a year, not since he'd made the decision to return to London and help the vampires return to Kar'mi'shah.

He lifted his hand from the vodka bottle and instead took up of the kettle. Dregs swilled at the bottom and he went to the sink to fill it, pulling the coffee jar down from one of the cupboards as he switched on the kettle and waited for it to boil.

He pulled his cigarettes from his jacket pocket and lit one, leaning against the counter as he watched the blue smoke curl gently in front of him, bright embers crackling noticeably in the silence of the flat as he drew on it, the tobacco fading quickly to frail ash.

Jenner pushed his free hand through his hair and cursed.

If he'd been quicker, the woman from the nightclub might still be alive.

"Fuck," he shouted into the silent kitchen, and stormed through into the living room, leaving the kettle to boil unattended behind him.

He slumped onto the sofa and gazed out through the undrawn curtains at the buildings across the street. Some of the rooms were still lit, even at this hour. He could see movement through the blinds of one, a woman by the shape of the silhouette, and she looked to be alone. Of the others, there was no sign of life. But London was such a sprawling metropolis that it was impossible to know what secrets and depravities went unknown and unchecked behind locked and bolted doors.

Jenner sat motionless as he gazed out through the window, his cigarette balanced in his fingers, smoke rising unhindered for several inches before curling into thin circles and dispersing.

His life had been a tough journey, and sometimes it felt like a rite of passage, a test for something grander that he might someday hope to uncover along the way. But nothing had shown itself to him so far, no glimmer of hope that one day this might all be over.

He'd been a thief and he'd been convicted for it. He'd peddled blood to vampires and seen the ruin of another world. He'd seen his girlfriend dead only to see her rise again. And he'd seen monsters, the kind that should belong only in the nightmares of the insane. Now he was a messenger, and that was it.

There was a doorway home for some of these monsters, and most of them just wanted the chance to return, even if that chance was being offered by a human mortal. It had once seemed like a decent trade-off, but now he was not so sure. It had been a hard fight at first, explaining to the skulkers of the city that the vampires living in London should not be destroyed, for there was a far grander scheme waiting for them if only they knew the right path to tread. But the skulkers wanted only their destruction, of course, and lately Jenner had found himself siding with them. He'd seen too much death, and too many vampires who knew nothing of Kar'mi'shah. Surely, he'd reasoned, anyone who wanted to go home had already done so. Whatever was left were the vermin that needed to be gotten off their streets and exterminated. For the sake of their own kind if nothing else.

And yet he was caught up in the middle, wasn't he? He was a human, and yet his girlfriend (his ex-girlfriend) was a vampire, worshipped as a goddess in another realm. Where were his allegiances? What was he supposed to be doing?

Did he even need to side with anyone?

Couldn't he just continue as he was?

No, it had gone as far as it could. He'd known that for a while, perhaps known it all along. No one gave a shit what he did, not any more. Had they ever?

Jenner pushed himself to his feet and went back through into the kitchen, making the coffee that he knew he'd need.

He drank it quickly there in the kitchen and then left the flat, hurrying down to the street and along the pavement to where he'd parked his car. The clock on the dashboard read 2:48 AM, but time did not have the same importance for him as it did for normal people. As a thief he'd loved the cloak that night could offer, as a pusher it had concealed both himself and those that he had delivered to. But it was also the best time to find the predators of London, as well as those that hunted them, and as he turned the key in the ignition and pulled away from the kerb, he knew exactly where he would find them.

## TWO

## THOSE THAT WATCH THE NIGHT

At Regents Park Jenner stopped and looked through the railings at the expanse of darkness beyond. How many bodies had the police retrieved from in there over the past year alone, he thought to himself? It was literally a picnic area for vampires, a place where that very darkness shrouded their actions, where they could lure their victims and not be seen as they fed. Or so they thought.

Jenner drove slowly around the perimeter. It was after three am and the roads were ghostly quiet, empty even of early-morning pedestrians (or which there were usually at least a handful), scared to walk or even drive this route because of the regular stories that took up space in the Evening Standard: 'Another Dead Body Found In The Park'.

He turned a corner and saw a dark transit van parked halfway along the street. There were few cars parked here, and Jenner pulled up at the side of the road a discreet distance from the van. He walked the remaining yards.

The whole place was deadly silent - no cars or late night music, no voices coming from open windows or drunken shouts from obscured terraces – and it seemed as though everyone had universally decided to leave this place to whatever death now haunted this once beloved park.

Of course that meant it was ideal for others, those humans who thrived after the sun went down, both the hunters and the vigilantes. Jenner tapped lightly on the driver's side door, the window tinted to near black. He could make out no movement from inside but he knew the layout, the skulkers sitting inside watching the movements within the park. The door clicked open and a face appeared at the gap. It wasn't Rocket, but one of the newer recruits from his mob, a weasly little character with the apt clan name of Ferret. He was short and gaunt, his build light and his cheeks sunken, and his eyes glimmered sharply with incessant movement. He narrowed them at Jenner and asked him what he wanted.

"Is Rocket here?" Jenner wanted to know.

Ferret had obviously heard the stories about him, a man that was neither a hunter nor a protector of vampires, and he could clearly not make his mind up about him. Jenner didn't give a shit one way or the other what he thought. He'd known Rocket a long time and could only really be bothered discussing things with him.

"He's here," Ferret relented under the weight of the visitor's stare, and slid back across the seat to allow Jenner access to climb inside.

Jenner found Rocket sitting in the back, looking out through the van's tinted side windows, a pair of night-vision binoculars held up in front of him. He didn't look round when Jenner clambered through into the back, but kept up his vigil, gazing out into the black unlit depths of Regents Park.

"What brings you out this way?" Rocket asked

115

him, his voice monotonous, distant.

"The usual..."

Rocket glanced round at him now, his face slack and weary.

"Coming round to our side, are you?"

"I didn't say that."

"Face it, Jenner, you've got to pick a side. If you carry on sitting on the fence, all you're going to end up with is piles."

Jenner glanced across at Remus, the third skulker, who was sitting in the corner of the van at the back. He was holding a machete in one hand, polishing it slowly with a cloth he held in the other, his cold eyes glaring back at him.

"I lost another one tonight," Jenner said finally, turning back to Rocket who had resumed his sweep of the park. "I felt sure I was going to make it –"

"But he gave you the slip?" Rocket finished. "How long is this going to go on for? I've told you there's a place for you here. You're good on the street, we both know that. Come and fight for the good guys, Jen. Make a difference."

Ferret suddenly appeared from the front of the van, his face flushed with excitement.

"There's a fucking vamp coming this way, boss. Up the street. Eleven o'clock."

Rocket pressed his face against the side window and tried to stare ahead, but before he could say anything, Ferret had the van door open and was whooping up the street.

"Shit," Rocket cried, as he hauled open the van's sliding door, and all three of them dashed out in pursuit of the fledgling skulker who had already covered some considerable distance.

It was clear that Ferret was not about to listen to anyone's pleas to stop, and was already approaching the couple in full flight. Jenner could see something clasped in his hand, a huge knife that threatened to supersede Remus' machete, and hoped that this was indeed a vampire he was about to slaughter and not an innocent human male.

He'd never liked Ferret, Jenner thought as he ran. He'd never liked his thoughtless impetuousness, his slimy attitude, or his bulging eyes that seemed to grope across his flesh like a sex offender's hands on a victim.

The couple had seen him and stumbled apart, the girl clutching her mouth and staggering against the railings, the man starting to stand his ground but then turning and fleeing. Jenner and the other two skulkers were fifty yards behind, and it remained that distance as Ferret gave chase to the man he'd already deemed a vampire.

Along the pavement they ran, Ferret just yards behind the man, whooping at the top of his voice, his knife still clasped high above his head.

They turned a corner up ahead, and it took a handful of agonising seconds for Jenner and the other two skulkers to reach it and turn it themselves. When they did, however, neither Ferret nor the fleeing man were anywhere to be seen.

Jenner turned in circles while the two skulkers wandered into the road, gazing in all directions, sucking in air through bared teeth. But the street was deserted. Even Ferret's wailing had died to nothing, leaving the air as silent as it had been before.

Then their eyes ultimately fell upon the railings that circumscribed the park and realised that the vampire, if that was indeed what he was, must have chosen to fight in a realm in which he held the advantage.

Rocket yelled the skulker's name as he clambered up and over the railings, dashing off into the blackness as Remus and Jenner climbed after him. The three of them searched as they listened, but the park was deathly still, and it seemed a futile hunt. But when a shrill whistle split the night in two behind them they turned to see Ferret silhouetted against the brightness of the lamp lit street, his knife held high above his head like a victorious warrior's sword.

"What the hell happened?" Rocket demanded when they reached him.

"Another of the undead slain, thank you very much."

"He was a vampire?"

"Until I sliced off his head," Ferret exclaimed, whooping again as he spun full circle on his heel, a maniacal grin creasing his sallow face in two.

Jenner exchanged glances with Rocket, but Ferret was already sprinting back towards the railings, whooping into the night as he went. It seemed they both had their doubts about him, but Rocket had explained to him before about the inherent difficulties of recruiting. You couldn't just place an ad in the paper, he'd said, but then he'd gone right ahead and done just that, and found both Remus and Ferret within the week.

Jenner followed the skulkers back to the railings, wondering as he walked whether there was a decapitated human body left lying somewhere in the dark, or just the fragmented dusty remains of what had once been a vampire left to blow across the park once the breeze picked up again.

# THREE

## THE RACE TO FIND A NEW WORLD

Ferret sat up front gazing out at the street, alone, his eyes busy in middle distance. Rocket and the interloper were still talking in the back of the van, Remus still brooding with them. Ferret knew they didn't trust him and he didn't care. He'd seen things that would make them shit, and not just vampires either. They knew nothing about death, or life, or who deserved either.

He knew things too, secrets that they'd never know about. There was a door somewhere, a door to another world. He'd overheard two vampires talking about it just a couple of weeks ago, whispering in secret in an unlit alleyway. They hadn't given away it's actual location, which was the fucking pain in the arse, but he'd sat squashed and cramped in that filthy wheelie bin for well over an hour until they'd tired with the young girl, waiting to see if they would.

But he'd remained quiet while they'd killed her, confined inside that filthy bin amongst the rotting food and putrefying liquids as they'd talked of visiting a lush and verdant land where they would be gods once again. He'd heard them taking turns drinking from her, heard her moans and her last gasps for breath, while he'd listened to their plans of resurrection. But they had not divulged the whereabouts of this secret doorway.

Ferret played his fingertips across the edge of his knife as he reminisced once again about that night, his mind trying to recall details that he knew he hadn't heard. Their words played over and over inside his head like a scratched record, skipping back and forth until their meaning turned to nonsense, to gibberish that just made his thoughts ache.

He'd stayed where he was even after they had finished, his head too busy with the promise of bliss in a fresh new underworld, and his sense of self preservation knowing that two vampires with blood already on their lips would rip him apart before he'd set one foot on the ground.

He'd hoped that tonight might have gifted him a chance to put right that elusive moment, to fill in the blanks of where that doorway actually lay. He'd seen that couple and he'd wanted the vampire all to himself. Rocket never quizzed any of them anyway. All he wanted was for them to be dead and despatched out of London.

But he knew different. He knew now that they held secrets, and he'd chased one into the park and caught him. Only it hadn't been a vampire that he had cornered and stuck with his knife at all, oh no. It had been a man, a worthless man that had pissed himself openly like a petrified sheep.

His knife was well used to niggers and queers, and he'd fed it to more than he could care to remember. His fingertips scratched across the tip of his knife as the memory brought a grin. The man in the park had been white with one wound already pulsing blood that came hot and thick. But what was one more dead man in a city that didn't give a shit about anything? The man had been shaking like he had hypothermia, but he never let out so much as a whimper as Ferret had stuck him over and over until he collapsed onto the ground dead.

He'd sat amongst the wet shit of the man's body for a few moments after that, wondering whether there really was another world out there, a world where vampires really could rise to become gods.

He had glanced back over his shoulder when he'd heard the vampire-lover Jenner Hoard and Rocket searching for him amongst the bushes. He'd wiped the blade on the man's suit and hurried away, skirting the others deftly in order to appear behind them, away from where the man lay dead.

There were some secrets going on between those two anyway, Ferret knew. They were in deep discussion now in the back of the van, with voices low and huddled, avoiding his scrutiny, as though they were a old fucking married couple. Maybe they were both queers too. Maybe one of them had been plugging the other's arsehole for years. The thought sickened him. His nose curled, his fingers tightening around the handle of his knife as he thought about sticking it in one or both of them.

He didn't know what they were talking about, and even if it was about him he'd didn't much care. There was a world lying hidden out there somewhere, that's all he knew, and if there was one thing he was certain about, it was that he was going to be the first human to find it and step through.

The last gang he'd been a part of had had nothing on their agenda except butchering anyone who wasn't white, a semi-organised group of nazis with some real head-stompers amongst them. But two of their leaders had gotten arrested for murder and were doing some serious long years in prison, the rest of the pussies having swiftly ducked their heads shortly afterwards and gone into hiding. The gang was over now, extinct, but he was still kicking. And he'd found himself another gang, hadn't he? Maybe not niggers but something else that was causing problems. He still had his knife and he still had his hatreds, and both burned under his skin like firebrands. He'd been hired to kill again by Rocket and that was fine by him. The cleansing of a city and all the other doctrines Rocket and his skulkers were fixated upon were fine, but they came in a poor second behind the first commandment according to the master race.

There was a whole new world waiting to be found, a whole new world crying out to have a pioneer of genocide. Jews, blacks and faggots had been well documented, but that was all old hat. This was something else entirely. A new world order.

He already had some secret investigations of his own to follow up on. He had a meeting lined up with a couple of brothers from Brazil come daybreak, and they'd seemed pretty interested about what he'd already discovered for himself, and had promised him something special the next time they met. That meeting was less than three hours away, and his skin was already crawling with the promise of what secrets were going to be revealed. His grin came again as he played his fingertips across the knife he knew so well, its metal already cleansed of the blood it had spilt less than thirty minutes before.

# FOUR

## LOOSE LIPS

Jenner woke with the phone ringing in the living room. His head was pounding, a dull ache nagging behind his eyes, and he glanced at the clock beside him through heavy slits and saw that it was just after twelve. He cursed whoever was calling him. His number was ex-directory and he gave it to no one except those in the hidden underworld that operated after the sun went down.

The bedroom was dark because of the boards and black cloth that he'd made permanent over the window, and he stumbled out of the room and down the narrow hallway to the living room where the phone continued to ring. He recoiled from the bright midday sunlight that streamed in through the tall living room window as he entered, and he shielded his eyes with one hand against the curtains that were never drawn as he reached to pick up the phone with the other.

"This had better be good," he rasped, his throat as dry as the undisturbed dust on every surface in the flat.

"Jenner, its Rocket," came the voice on the other end. "We've got a problem."

"At this time of day?"

"Not with a vampire. It's Ferret."

"What about him?"

"He's dead."

Jenner stood for a moment in silence, the dull ache thumping behind his eyes, as the skulker's words took a while to make sense.

"Blood loss?" he said at last.

"No," Rocket told him. "This was murder, and nothing that a vampire would do either. This was done by human hands. I think you should come and see."

"When?"

"What about now?"

When there was silence, Rocket went on:

"Don't tell me you were sleeping? What, you need a good eight hours sleep like some nancy boy? Grab a couple of hours when you can like the rest of us. This city never sleeps."

"Where are you?" Jenner asked.

"Same place he was found. Knightsbridge."

Jenner put the phone down with a head busy with distorted images: Ferret lying dead in a pool of his own blood, a murderer carrying a gun or a knife, vampires watching from a corner huddled with glee, pleased that a human had been killed by one of his own.

The city had taken yet another dark turn.

There had once been a black and white, a time when good and bad had stood on opposite sides of the fence, but since he had been dragged down into the bloody underworld that guttered beneath the accepted face of decent society, it had dissolved rapidly into sickening shades of grey. And sometimes even those shades seemed somehow inadequate.

Where did he fit into all this? Why was he even

125

still alive? He made no difference, not really, not in the real world, not in the human world. He'd lost his girlfriend and his home, he'd lost everyone he'd ever known, and now he tried to fool himself on a day to day basis that he was a messenger, a saviour for those vampires who still searched for their one true home. But it was bullshit, all of it. They were killers, and the people with whom he shared a race were killers. In the end, he realised with a shallow shake of his head, everything ended up dead and rotted.

He went back through into the bedroom and dressed, pulling on a t-shirt and jeans and grabbing his leather jacket from the chair beside his bed, before heading out of his flat and down to his car parked a couple of hundred yards further down the street.

The traffic was busy, lunchtime snarls at every junction and every traffic light, and it took him nearly an hour to reach Knightsbridge. He pulled into Rutland Gardens and crossed the street, heading back the way he'd come, looking for Rocket.

He found the skulker standing on the pavement, a solitary motionless man amongst a surging throng of pedestrians, smoking a cigarette and staring into middle distance. He looked round as Jenner approached, but his face was as blank as a mannequin's.

He didn't say a word, but just dragged on his cigarette with fingers that trembled. The skulker had seen some evil deeds in his life, the same as he, but he was visibly shaken, disturbed by the death of one of his own. Rocket inclined his head towards one of the big office buildings behind him, and then together they made their way round to the back to where a line of wheelie bins stood. Sprawled between two of them was Ferret, or rather what was left of him.

His body had been worked over plenty, that much was obvious from the start, but this wasn't a street crime by any stretch of the imagination. The feeling that Ferret had stumbled into some far greater scheme couldn't easily be gotten away from, but what was worse was the feeling that crawled into Jenner's gut that he'd somehow managed to drag the lot of them into it as well.

His mouth had been sown up, and a note stitched to his cheek with the same black thread for those who found him to read. All the note said, was: Loose lips, sink ships. Back off.

Jenner looked back round for Rocket, but he'd wandered several yards away. He went over to him and found that he'd lit another cigarette and was holding it to his lips with hands that were shaking even more than they had been out on the main street.

"I've seen some shit in my time," he said, his voice wavering, "but this is different. A fucking human did this to him. For Christ's sake, Jen, how the fuck does that happen?"

"How do you know it was a human who killed him?" Jenner asked, but both of them already knew it was the truth. They'd both seen what vampires were capable of, even in the deepest fits of rage, and this was unlike anything that they had ever witnessed before. This had been planned. This had precision written all over it. A vampire wouldn't waste his time with anything so elaborate on a mortal man.

"He was twenty four," Rocket went on. "Twenty fucking four. And someone does this to him. He might have been off his head, but he didn't deserve this."

"Maybe he was on to something."

"On to what, Jenner? We kill vampires. You'd think other humans would be glad."

"Maybe this was another kind of cult."

"Like what?"

Silence fell between them again, and then Jenner tried again:

"You're sure this wasn't a vampire?" he said, but he knew it was a hopeless argument.

"Come on, Jen," Rocket exclaimed. "Have you ever seen a vampire do anything like this?"

Jenner waited a moment and then shook his head. He didn't really know Ferret, and on the few occasions he had met him, he hadn't liked him. But that didn't matter. This act was frightening. It had been a warning, but a warning for what neither of them knew. And that was the scariest part of all. They'd been told to back off, but back off from what?

"What was Ferret up to?" Jenner asked. "Was he talking about anything?"

Rocket stared at him, and then shook his head.

"Only killing vampires. He was dubious when he first replied to the ad, I think he thought it was some new kind of racial army. But after the facts about what we do sank in and he got his first kill, he turned a bit gung ho overnight, and all he talked about after that was killing more of them. I think I got a buzz out of it because killing wasn't just talked about but keenly encouraged. And because what we do isn't exactly covered in the tabloids, it's not exactly illegal either. I think that appealed most of all. He wasn't the most saintly wretch I've ever met, but then this job calls for someone a bit... mental."

Jenner glanced back to where Ferret's body still lay amongst the wheelie bins, and to where his lips had been sewn together with black thread, the wounds now encrusted with dried and blackened blood.

"They're warning us to stop talking about something –"

"Well I'm not stopping what I'm doing," Rocket spat. "I'm going to carry on tracking and killing vampires until there isn't a single fucking one left in my town."

"I don't think the note-writer's got a problem with that," Jenner said to him. "I think it's Ferret. I think he's been up to something we don't know about, maybe something in his history before he even became a skulker, and these people think we're all in on it."

Rocket stared at him as he struggled to draw deeply on his cigarette. The embers glimmered brightly. It seemed he didn't know what to say any more than Jenner. Eventually Jenner asked what was going to happen to Ferret's body.

"Don't worry about it," Rocket said, dismissing the issue, "we'll move it. I don't need the police asking any fucking questions right about now."

Jenner nodded and then turned as if to leave.

"Don't be worrying needlessly," he said quietly over his shoulder. "There's nothing you could've done."

"I recruited him, Jenner. I brought him into this."

"Not this far, Rocket. This he did on his own."

# FIVE

## LOST

The sight of Ferret murdered and disfigured had disturbed Jenner greatly. He'd hadn't liked him, but the boy hadn't deserved that.

There was an evil on the streets that he had been trying to help, guiding them away from his home and back to their own, vampires that fed only to survive, and yet continued to kill his own kind, human men and women. Some of these vampires desired more than a banal existence and had prospered, but others sought only death in the inferior race they called mortals. But what had happened to Ferret was something else entirely. He had been killed by human hands, not vampire, and seemingly as a warning to Rocket and the other skulkers around the city, and possibly himself as well.

Jenner had chosen to play this dangerous game since he'd first unwittingly trafficked blood for them in unlit alleyways and sordid back streets a few years ago. His girlfriend had been claimed by them and he'd been sucked in yet further. But now he didn't see the point in continuing any more. He was making no progress. People were still dying. And for what? For what it always came down to in the end – personal gain and desire.

He glanced up and watched the handful of pedestrians hurrying past on both sides of the street, struggling with umbrellas against the onslaught of wind and rain, collars turned up against the cold. Any one of them could be next to die, just as any one of them could be a vampire moving swiftly to despatch their prey.

Nobody cared, that was the truth of it. He'd always claimed that he did care, that he struggled against insurmountable odds every day and night to try and make that difference. It had taken over his life – fuck, who was he kidding, it was his life! But now? Now things had changed. Now there were no longer two sides in the war. There were dissidents hiding amongst the ranks on both sides, bounty hunters and selfish mutineers whose only concerns were money and a guaranteed future in the game.

He glanced at his watch. With the dark heavy skies night had come early, and yet it was only five thirty. The undead had probably already left their haunts in search of desperate humans. The foul night would only make their killing more easy: less visibility for the hunted, greater camouflage for the hunter.

Jenner pushed his hands up over his face and then up through his soaked mop of hair. He knew he couldn't just leave people to die, not even the ignorant or the foolhardy. The rain was coming down hard, spearing the sheets of puddles that reached across the pavements and roads, but he stepped out from under the grimy shop awning regardless and headed back out into the downpour.

He couldn't be bothered to drive any more. He'd leave his car in Knightsbridge and pick it up later.

Tonight he'd travel the dismal tunnels of the Underground.

Jenner hurried down the escalator and stepped onto the busy tube amid the throng of commuters, crushed inside a brightly-lit packed Circle Line carriage, elbows whacking him as the train rumbled clumsily away from the station. Everyone wore blank expressions and stared either at their feet or out through the windows which only looked out onto the black unlit tunnel walls, a mirror for their voyeurism, observing the other passengers around them. Sometimes he envied them for that, to be faceless and miserable and be ignorant of the real world around them. To go back to ignorance, he thought as the train rocked from side to side, would be bliss.

Jenner rode the train until the carriages began to hold less and less people and the seats freed up. He glanced at his watch and saw that two hours had passed, whereupon he decided to get off at the next station and monitor another line.

In some ways he missed the thrill of approaching the watchful killers armed only with news of a doorway home, but he also knew that that thrill had long since gone. He'd seen too much shit to worry about the whims or desires of either people or vampires.

He felt tired, that was the truth of it, exhausted by endless journeys around the metropolis, searching, chasing, negotiating, fighting. Why did he even give a fuck anymore? That was the question that got to him more than any other.

The tube juddered to a halt at the Oxford Street platform and Jenner clambered out, his head thumping with turbulent thoughts. The platform was still relatively busy, more commuters travelling home after the insane rush hour period, some perhaps venturing out for the night to a loved one or to some social event. But not one of them appeared to be a Bloodgod looking for a way home.

In the white-tiled pedestrian tunnels he could hear the dissonant echo of a busker amongst the din of echoing footsteps, his mumbled voice awkward and eerie over the dirge of his acoustic guitar. As the tunnel bore round to the right Jenner saw him, a dishevelled man that could have been anywhere between forty or seventy so foul were his clothes and long beard. His battered guitar showed little wood veneer through its covering of worn stickers and badges, and in front of him was a simple green checked cap littered with a scattering of silver and copper change.

Jenner halted in front of him as he dug in his pockets, retrieving what little change he had, and dropped it into the man's hat. The old man nodded as he continued to croon, barely holding his gaze but looking at every other pedestrian that hurried by.

"How's business tonight?" Jenner asked.

But the man just nodded and continued with his song, again not wishing to hold Jenner's eye.

"You haven't seen anything strange along this way tonight?" Jenner went on. "No one hassled, no one followed closely by –"

"Fuck off, mate, eh?" the busker suddenly blurted, his fingers stopping suddenly on his guitar and sending the tunnel into a harsh silence in the sudden absence of his music. "Can't you see I'm trying to earn a fucking crust here?"

Jenner stared at him, the old man's eyes glaring, his teeth yellow and bared.

"Thanks for your change and all that, mate. But go on, fuck off, eh?"

He started up his song again as if nothing had happened, his eyes once again trying to catch the attention of passers-by, and Jenner found himself leaving the old bastard to it.

He wanted to look back at him over his shoulder before the corner took him out of sight, so incredulous was he by what the old man had just said to him, but he fought it with a shake of his head; he didn't need another scowl from some cunt off the street; not now, not ever.

Wandering along the mindless halls and tunnels of the Underground at Paddington, Jenner struggled to put the old busker out of his head, but his words continued to rattle around inside, aggravating him. He could still find no trace of vampires, just an endless throng of people drowned by the night's downpour.

He began to wonder whether they had perhaps all gone: either listened to the directions he had been giving them, or else killed by skulkers.

There used to be so many more than this, an endless line of killers watching and waiting, examining those in need of hope or salvation and coaxing them away to some better place, a place of shadow or salvation where their despair or sins might be redeemed through the simple act of submission. Jenner had seen it too, this act of feeding, had interrupted vampires as they'd drunk from their victims, some of them struggling, others consenting. But now the city seemed full of nobody else but people, simple ignorant human beings going about their mundane and ignorant little lives. And all this time he'd been trying to save them.

He climbed aboard a train heading northbound. He had no idea where it was going and he didn't much care. It didn't seem to matter much anymore where he went, the view was exactly the same. All of it darkness and despair.

He'd thought many times of returning to Kar'mi'shah, to find Emma, the girl who had once been his girlfriend but who had since become a Goddess. The last time they had spoken had been inside a temple that had been built for her, a vast stone pyramid in which the women of the ruined city had already begun to bring offerings for her, asking for her protection from the encroaching desert.

It still seemed impossible to believe how she had once been a vacuous socialite living out of her daddy's wallet. She had come so very far - which seemed an odd statement, but a fair one – and yet if anything, it served to highlight just how far he hadn't come: he was still walking the streets in search of something better, and yet he had found it, another world with possibilities, with dreams as yet undreamt. But he had left it behind in order to return to the only place he had ever lived, a filthy city crammed with rude and superficial people who would never return the benevolence and good intentions he had come back bearing. And now he was sitting aboard a train that rocked and lurched from side to side still in the heart of it all, and still wondering why?

Jenner stepped off the train at the next station,

his head mired with a grisly black soup that the city had put there, and stood for a few moments just staring into middle distance. He felt lost, abandoned, as though everyone else had moved on and left him behind in some kind of sordid limbo.

His apathy was dangerous, he knew, given the numerous enemies that he had in the city, which was probably why he never saw the attack coming. The platform was emptying, but still populated, yet she flew at him anyway, taking hold of his throat within a heartbeat and sending them both to the ground.

"I should kill you now," she hissed into his face, her long black hair flowing down across his face just inches beneath hers.

She had both hands around his throat now, claws scratching at his frail skin, and he could feel the blood thumping thickly inside his arteries as she forced them closed inside his neck. She would have his blood too, he had no doubt about that as he struggled beneath her colossal grasp, and would bathe in it until every inch of her pale skin was slick with it.

But Jenner managed to take hold of his knife and tug it from its scabbard, despite the awkwardness of her weight upon him, and pushed it up and into her body in one jagged but swift motion.

His sight was already coming in snatches because of the hold she had upon his throat, but he saw her expression falter as she felt something at her side, a sharp pain where none had been before, and he saw her also glance downward to see his hand pressed hard against her flank, before registering the handle of the knife he clasped inside it.

The smell of blood rose into the air around them as she recoiled from him, her grip around his neck dissolving as the vampire realised that the smell of blood was her own. She looked down into the eyes of the mortal who had wounded her, and Jenner saw that they were now wide with shock.

The vampire released her grip altogether and then crawled back away from him, examining with incredulity the wound that this mortal had somehow managed to inflict upon her. Jenner watched as she pressed her hands to her side, sickened and furious that they came away bloody. She had underestimated him.

Jenner waited until his vision was more certain before he attempted to find his feet. Once he had done so, and they were standing face to face, both of them clutching their injuries, he realised that he knew her. He recognised her, and although he had not seen her in a long time, he could not put a name to her. He knew that they had exchanged threats before, that memory was clear, but they had never fought. Not like this. And not until now.

"So I finally meet the prophet," the vampire seethed, her hand still clasped to her flank.

Jenner said nothing, just held one hand to the bruises at his throat, and his other on the knife still dripping her blood at his side in case she came at him again. He remembered her, from before, when his whole world had first been turned upside down. Now his memory struggled to name her, even though her face had been burned there.

"You're the one who has been emptying this city," she hissed, "sending vampires back to Kar'mi'shah."

"I would think you'd be grateful."

The vampire stared at him for a moment, as though her thoughts were divided on the issue. Her eyes burned with a livid fury, and Jenner was certain she still desired to kill him, but there was something between them, a history they both shared. They'd both known Montague, the dealer who had trafficked the blood of her immortal ancestors. They'd both stood before the threshold that led to Kar'mi'shah. And it was then that her name clicked inside his head like a light switch, and he voiced it before he was even aware of his doing so.

"Catherine Calleh," he murmured.

His words were like a gentle breath on the air between them, and the vampire stared at him, her eyes narrowing with an even greater wrath.

"You did not even know who I was until now?" she spat.

"I remembered... but not fully."

"Your mortal life might be forgettable, but mine should never be."

As Jenner stood staring at her a cold wind suddenly gusted along the tunnel, declaring the approach of the next train before the rumble of the carriages even came to his ears. He glanced past the vampire to see that a dozen or more people were standing on the platform, watching them intently with apprehensive concern, the assaulted woman, the attacker with the knife still in his hand. Jenner saw one of them clutching a mobile phone to their ear.

"Why are you here?" he asked her at last, if only to hasten them away from the platform and the authorities that would soon be on their way.

She glared at him, hatred still burning in her eyes, her lips pressed thin and tight. But she had to relent, she had to answer his question.

"I am lost in this city because you have emptied it," she finally murmured. "I... I need your help."

"With what?" Jenner wanted to know.

The vampire stared at him for a few moments more, as if to ask him anything would mean to negate her existence. Finally she spoke, but with words that seemed to have burned inside her like acid before they had even been voiced.

"I cannot find my husband without the vampires of the city, without the network of eyes that had been in place before. With all the vampires gone, there is no one who knows this city better than you. You must help me find him, so I place my only hope at your feet."

She clearly wanted her words to undo her utterly and be done with it, so vehemently did she loathe him. But death did not visit her, and the human male only returned her livid stare. But at least he did not mock her. At least he received her words with good grace.

"Then we should get out of here," he said to her, his voice almost rational, the motions of his arms attempting to coax her away from the platform.

"You know where Carlos might be?"

Jenner glanced back at the woman who still held her mobile phone, and who still stared at them with horror upon her face.

"No," he said, "but I think trouble might be coming."

## SIX

## MOMENTUM

The last time Jenner had seen the vampire Catherine Calleh - the one Montague had dubbed the most vicious vampire he had ever encountered - had been in a room in a dirty hotel at the threshold to another world. She had since returned only to attack him with words of his death upon her lips like acrid spittle. Now she stood in the living room of his flat, her hair thick with the night's rain and dripping on his carpet. He knew the ramifications of what he had done, inviting a vampire into his home - indeed the most vicious of vampires - but what was perhaps more insane was that she refused the least civil of tones with him and he accepted it all as par for the course.

Jenner had gone through into the bathroom to relieve his bladder, but returned with both a towel for her and what passed for a first aid kit, an old ice cream box with little more than a few bandages and some antiseptic. She scowled at him as he offered them to her, refusing both.

"I have no need for those," Catherine said. "The rain is nothing more than an inconvenience, as too was your paltry attack upon me."

Jenner set the first aid box down on the coffee table, and then began drying his own hair with the towel.

140

"Please yourself," he said dismissively, turning his back on her and wandering through into the kitchen. "I don't suppose you want a coffee then either?"

Jenner turned to see her already filling the doorway behind him, and lost his smirk. She was dangerous, he knew, and would be on him again before he could redraw his knife. She knew what he had now, and where he kept it. Drawing his gun took longer. That was not an option.

"You said you could help me," the vampire said, her face pale and perfect like that of a white china doll, shrouded by her glistening black hair. She was beautiful, of that there was no doubt, but the intent behind her seething words stole any comfort her beauty might have given him.

"You said that once you found your husband you would leave," Jenner said to her, his words sounding almost like a feeble effort of defence.

"I abide by my promises," she told him. "Find him and I will leave this miserable place."

Jenner set his wet towel down on the counter, and turned back to look at her. She did not move, and although he had seen many vampires, most had been in flight. Catherine stood before him motionless, however, not a single movement in her expression. She did not blink or look away, she always kept her eyes fixed upon him, and moved her lips only when she spoke. Her hands remained still at her sides throughout their exchange, and not even her long black cloak moved around her, her hair hanging straight down under the weight of the rain, the only movement droplets of moisture that trickled and dripped from the thickened ends.

"I'll need some time," he finally said to her.

"For what?"

"I need to ask around."

"For what?" she said again. "I thought you claimed to know everything about us."

"I don't know everything," Jenner explained. "But you'll need to tell me more about your husband."

"His name is Carlos and he has risen from his grave. That is all you need to know."

Jenner stared at her.

Could vampires rise from the grave?

He hadn't known that before.

Suddenly a million questions began to skip through his head as he watched the vampire glare at him. Under what circumstances could they rise? If they were not killed in a certain way? If not killed or buried on hallowed ground? Could those already killed rise again? And if so, how soon?

"You do not need to know the history of his death, nor of his ascension," Catherine said to him, as if she had been studying the turmoil inside his skull. "You need only inform me of his whereabouts, and this brief union between us will be at an end."

Jenner left her in his flat while he went back out into the night. The rain had begun to let up a little, the downpour replaced by a clinging drizzle. His head felt like it had been shaken, his thoughts tumbling in disarray like the flakes of white in a snow-shaker. He felt like he was back at the beginning of the game again, only with the rules now changed, and he had to catch up quick to all the other players or be left behind and ejected.

It had all seemed black and white at the start,

humans and vampires, innocents and killers, and with his life rammed hard into the centre of them both there had been nothing but a sea of miserable grey. To have taken his own life would have been to witness nothing, and somehow the pain and the anguish was worth more than nothingness. But now the lethargy of his existence had been upended, forcing him to pay attention once again, and it was that, he guessed, that he didn't like. He'd wanted an end to all this for so very long, and at times he'd thought he had been close. But now he'd been shoved right back to the very beginning, to learn once again, only this time he didn't think it was worth it.

He was on his way to see Rocket, the only man who perhaps knew more about the secret heart of London than he did, but he suddenly pulled up at the side of the road and hung his head in his hands.

Why was he doing this, he asked himself?

Who even cared?

He dragged his fingers through his hair, clenching them into fists and pulling at his scalp until it hurt. His life was a fucking mess as it was, why was he making it worse by doing the run-around for a vampire? And one that promised his murder with every other breath at that.

He sat there for a while just listening to the sound of the engine idling, staring out through the windscreen as the wipers continued to sweep the settling raindrops away with their monotonous rhythm, his eyes seeing nothing.

Everything was grey and miserable and rotten. He could see himself sitting amongst it all, motionless, just like the vampire who had stood

143

motionless in his flat, as the grey slowly rose up around him, ready to smother him whole. A notion entered his head that perhaps he was ready to die at last, that it was time for it all to come to an end for him.

It was bleak, and under other circumstances it might have been sick, but now it felt like the right thought to have inside his head, and a kind of dull peace began to spread through him, as though perhaps he had finally found the zenith of his existence after all this time searching.

Jenner put the car back into gear and pulled away from the kerb, joining the flow of traffic that relentlessly flowed throughout the city.

He didn't know where he was going, not really, but he made a right hand turn at the end of the street, away from Regent's Park, away from Rocket and the other skulkers, and away from the life he had lived for what now seemed an eternity.

He suspected that his brain knew a long time before he did, but it took about an hour's directionless driving for him to realise just where he was going. He didn't look for the map in the glove compartment in order to find the correct or the quickest route, or particularly pay much attention to the road signs that might deliver him there more readily. There was no speed involved in getting to his destination, not when he realised that perhaps this trip had been delayed for weeks or even months.

He drove the streets and turned the corners in the same kind of melancholy, pulling up at the lights, patiently waiting while other drivers cut lanes, until he arrived once again in the familiar street and pulled up outside the grim hotel that concealed the gateway to Kar'mi'shah. It was where he needed to be, that's all he could think, and if the end was indeed close and death did indeed desire to pull him into its embrace, then better to die in the arms of the woman he loved, than to pass away shivering and alone in the gutter of a freezing street.

# PART FOUR

# HONOUR AMONG THIEVES

# ONE

## THE RACE TO THE PRIZE

Rio Barros thumbed through the thick wad of banknotes in the wallet, roughly calculating the amount, and imagined how good they would look in his wallet. But he was not here for petty theft. Lawson wanted much more than that. He wanted religious documents, artefacts, or any one of a hundred different kinds of evidence of a new world he claimed existed. But this was London, not Samarkand or Narnia. Just what in God's name did he expect to find here? A holy book? A map?

The house on Hill Rise was the home of Richard Lazenby-Hunter, a wealthy stockbroker that ran a team of yuppies in the city. He was renowned for his quick turnover of staff. He would bring them in, train them quickly, have them dealing hard, and then burn them out usually inside the same year. A high percentage of them became alcoholics, others addicted to the drugs that they needed to keep the fast pace going. But they were handsomely rewarded for the deals they made - in money at least. Nobody complained of the treatment, and there were always newcomers ready to take over from those that couldn't cut it; a six figure salary in exchange for running themselves into the ground.

Rio placed the wallet back on the antique

bureau. Lawson gave strict instructions to those he paid: take anything that might lead to Kar'mi'shah and nothing else.

Lazenby was in the shower in the en-suite and would not be long, so Rio swept swiftly around the spacious bedroom, his fingers in every drawer and behind every painting, his eyes scanning everything that he opened or overturned. But there were no hidden safes or briefcases in the opulent bedroom, no caches or golden-edged envelopes secreted away. Just silk shirts and imported underwear belonging to a very rich city broker.

There was a huge reward for the man who found the location of the door, ten million pounds first prize for confirmation of the route to the new world. That kind of cash brought bounty hunters of all kinds from every corner of the globe, but not everyone revelled in the competition. Runts like that lowlife Ferret had needed to be taught some respect, told how it was going to be, just like the rest of his after-dark gang. They weren't officially on Lawson's payroll, as far as he knew, but it would be one of those kinds of lucky fucks that stumbled onto something that Lawson was looking for.

The mirror above the bed swung suddenly on a hinge as he played his fingers behind it, and a smile spread across his face as he saw the gun-metal grey façade of a safe behind it. In the en-suite, he heard the sound of the shower dying and then Lazenby's footsteps slapping across the tiles.

Rio placed the magnetic side of his listening device against the safe and pressed the ear-piece into his ear, listening intently and with utter focus as he then turned the dial back and forth systematically to release the tumblers.

He loved the old men of the upper classes: always kept with the tried and tested rules of security. Rarely did they go for anything new; it was always the Rolls Royce in front of the stately home, the mistress at Royal Ascot, and the 'three to the left, two to the right' tumbler safes.

Lazenby began singing in the bathroom as the safe door swung open. Rio's eyes widened as he observed the stacks of used banknotes, the velvet-lined jewellery boxes, letters bound with red wax and purple ribbon, and a series of brown paper scrolls bound with leather thongs. Funny how the law-abiding never get to see this kind of stuff, Rio thought to himself as he retrieved the filthy-looking scrolls. Taking valuables was straight theft, and Lawson would have him murdered for something so petty, and sealed letters were either political or material worthy of blackmail. His only interest was satisfying Lawson's crazy whims, an obsession which granted him a sizeable weekly wage for his efforts. So slipping the scrolls into the pack around his waist, Rio resealed the safe and set the mirror back, darting back across the room and out into the unlit hallway as Richard Lazenby-Hunter stepped back through into his bedroom, drying his receding hair with a towel, and blissfully unaware that such a professional thief had even dared to set foot upon his property.

It had started to rain outside, and Cortez Barros was waiting for him in the car, the engine already running. He grinned as his younger brother climbed into the passenger seat, and pulled away from the kerb before the door was closed.

"Where the fuck were you?" Rio snapped, glaring at him.

"While you were playing peek-a-boo with the fossil in the shower, I was down in the kitchen gathering information for the boss."

"I got some scrolls from his safe above the bed."

"Have a word," Cortez scoffed. "The real booty is always in the busiest room of the house."

Rio scowled at him. He had the scrolls, and they looked real old, but Cortez had an infuriating knack of not only being right most of the time, but also being smug about it too.

"Show me what you got," Rio said to him.

"You show me first," Cortez retorted.

They turned a corner onto the main road that would take them most of the way towards Westminster. It was the heart of British politics and ironically the centre of its dark underground movement too. The public face and the secret hidden agenda, living almost in unison beneath the noses of the ignorant common man. It probably made the bosses piss themselves with glee.

Rio retrieved the scrolls from the pack around his waist and slid the brown leather thong down from the first. Unrolling it, he switched on the internal car light and began to attempt to read the scratchy penmanship.

It was difficult to decipher the tiny handwriting with the motion of the car, and he could see Cortez leaning over as he drove, but it was clear that the document recorded information about the excavation of a tomb in South East Asia.

He glanced up and saw a smirk on Cortez's face, his eyebrow raised, but thankfully he didn't say a word. Perhaps he knew that if he had, Rio would have punched him, hard, and that would have led to yet another pointless fist-fight between them.

Cortez was the older of the two brothers by four years, and had a considerable weight advantage too. Rio was quick, but Cortez had the weight to put behind his blows. It was never wise to initiate a fight, but it usually cleared the air between them in a dispute. This time, however, there was no dispute, just that smug expression that Rio had been staring at all his life.

"So what was in the kitchen?" Rio asked him finally, resisting the urge to add any childish insult to the question.

If his brother had indeed found something worthy of Lawson's bounty, he didn't want to miss out on their agreed twenty percent runner-up prize.

Cortez inclined his head towards the back seat of the car and Rio followed his gaze. But all he could see there was a diary, and a modern-looking diary at that.

Rio looked back at his brother.

"There are entries in there in a language I've never even seen before," Cortez told him. "I'm going to take it to Victoria and have her cast an eye over it."

"At the National History?"

"Sure."

"You're just going to walk in there and ask her to translate it?"

Cortez stared at him, his face suddenly stern.

"What's your problem?"

"I'll tell you what the problem is," Rio snapped, jabbing a thumb backwards in the direction of the diary. "If that thing does say where the doorway is, she's not exactly going to tell us, now is she? Not with a ten million pound price tag on that kind of information."

"She probably doesn't even know about any of this."

"Yeah, right. Lawson would never think of approaching archaeological experts first, would he? Much better to come straight to a couple of Brazilian smugglers, eh?"

Cortez stared out of the windscreen in silence after that, his forehead furrowed in deep concentration. Rio could see his teeth clenched in his head.

"If the language is alien, or whatever the fuck it is that Lawson's after," Cortez suddenly said, "she won't be able to recognise it and sell it out from under us."

"So what's the fucking point in taking it to her in the first place?"

Cortez smacked his fist against the steering wheel. Rio could see his teeth bared now and decided to keep quiet for a while, or at least let his brother mull it over for a bit.

Someone had to be able to decipher foreign languages in this city and not be on Lawson's payroll, he thought, there just had to be. London was a sprawling metropolis with just about every kind of sage and mystic under the sun hidden away in its depths.

Then he mentally slapped himself on the head. Why were they even worrying about it? Lawson just wanted documentation. He hadn't specified what language that documentation had to be in, just that he wanted it.

The notion was tenuous, sure, but Lawson could always find his own translators. But as Rio was about to tell his brother his idea, Cortez suddenly pulled up sharply at the side of the road, both of them lurching forward in their seats as the tyres grappled for adhesion, and turned to look at him.

"We need to make a copy," he said.

Rio stared at him for a moment, his head reeling.

"And then what?"

"Victoria can have the copy and we'll have the original. When it comes down to it, Lawson will know that we found it first."

Rio raised an eyebrow. He wasn't sure about the genius of this new plan at all.

"Or better still," Cortez went on with a conspiratorial grin, "we'll divide the text up into parts and hand them out to different people. Then the individual translation will make no sense without the other parts."

"But you're talking about a language that possibly never even originated in this world. How the hell are you going to find that many people to decipher it? You'll be lucky if Vicky doesn't just laugh in your face."

The furrow came back to Cortez's brow as they both sat silently in the car, the night's rain steadily beating its rhythm upon the roof of the car, and Rio saw the frustration sweep over his brother. He tried to placate him quickly with his own idea, telling him that it would be far easier just to hand over the diary, as it was, to Lawson. Cortez seemed to actually think through the merits of this as he pulled away from the kerb and continued on through the streets of

London. Then he murmured his disapproval.

"I think this diary might be legit," he said, "so I don't think it'd be wise to get shot of it just yet."

"So what do you suggest?"

"No one knows we've got it," Cortez told him, "so it ain't gonna make too much difference what we do with it just yet. I think we should hang on to it, for now at least, and have a proper nose through it."

"But we don't know what it says."

"We might be able to make some sense of something. I didn't have time to have a decent look through it back there. But I clocked the foreign language and a handful of rough sketches and that was enough for me. I say we take our time. One vote for that. What about you?"

Rio chewed his lip. It seemed unnecessarily reckless.

He glanced across at his brother, who glanced back at him as he did so. There was a familiar glint in his eye, a glint that usually meant 'if someone's willing to pay a lot of money for something, then it's fair to expect that something is worth a damn sight more'.

"I don't know how you get me to agree with your stupid ideas," he said at last, "but scratch me up a second vote."

# TWO

## GREED

Rio lay on his bed and thumbed through the diary while Cortez was in the shower. He had a beer in one hand and a cigarette in the hand he was turning the pages with. Cortez had yelled at him when he'd lit up, telling him that he'd burn the whole fucking book to nothing. Rio had conceded, waited until his brother was in the shower, and then lit up again.

The hotel room was small but practical, two single beds keeping tensions high as it denied the two brothers any personal space. The bathroom was en-suite, of course, and light and steam spilled through the semi-open door in equal measure.

It was a modern diary for fuck's sake. How the hell could it hold the secrets of a lost world? The scrolls he'd found in the safe were old, not centuries old, but older than the diary that looked like it had been bought from Rymans six months ago.

He idly flicked through the pages, dragging on his cigarette periodically when he stopped to study a sketch scrawled roughly with pen and ink. There was one depicting a pyramid, and beside it what looked more like a doodle than anything else, a bare-chested man with the head of a crocodile. Rio shook his head dismissively, took another draw on his cigarette, and

157

went back to flipping pages.

The incident with the boy called Ferret still troubled him. Not for how they'd gone about it, no, because they'd done far worse in their time. But stitching his lips had seemed a step too far. And that had been another of his brother's less intelligent ideas.

Rio glanced over the top of the diary at the bathroom door. Cortez had turned off the shower. Rio could see the edge of a white towel as Cortez began to dry himself. He'd probably be another half hour yet the way he preened himself in the mirror.

The kid had a mouth on him, though, a dangerous mouth that didn't know when to keep closed. It was obvious that he'd heard some stories somewhere and was looking for personal gain. There were some good secrets hiding under the surface of London, secrets pertaining to this Kar'mi'shah that Lawson was so obsessed over, and to have someone blurting those secrets out so openly was not on. So they'd arranged a meeting, a back alley in Knightsbridge, and the boy had swooped on it like a barn owl on a rat.

They'd beaten him first, laying down the law before filtering out what he knew from what he thought he knew. As it turned out it wasn't very much. And to be blunt, he had nothing but a half-heard conversation.

But Cortez wasn't having it. Ten million was a lot to lose to a slimy kid and his nocturnal mates, so they'd finished the job and dumped his body behind some refuse bins. It was only afterwards, when they'd been drinking in a nearby pub, that Cortez suddenly declared that a dead body amounted to nothing. No one would know what that meant, and police involvement was not exactly what they needed at the moment.

So they'd returned to their hotel room, scrawled a quick note, grabbed the sewing kit from the complimentary welcome basket, and then returned to Knightsbridge.

The body had remained undisturbed. It had been Cortez's original plan to sew the note to Ferret's clothing somewhere. But staring down at the pale boy that they'd beaten to death only hours earlier had brought something bad out in his brother, worse than the indifference with which he had first punched him.

There had almost been a glint in Cortez's eyes as Rio had watched him slip the needle through the boy's top lip. Rio had gone to say something, and then stopped, and then hissed at him, asking him just what the fuck he was doing.

"Shut up," Cortez had hissed back. "When the others find him like this, and they will, it'll fuck 'em up and ensure they'll be no police involvement all in one go."

Rio had thought at the time that his brother's bared teeth had been because of effort or anger. Now he began to wonder whether it hadn't just been a grin.

"What are you doing?" Cortez suddenly cried from the bathroom.

Rio jumped, his eyes immediately over the top of the diary. Cortez was still in the bathroom, lost in steam, but his detached voice still carried weight.

He stabbed his cigarette out in the ashtray beside his bed and waved the smoke away with his hand.

"Nothing," he called back.

"Don't be fucking with that diary," Cortez went on, his face suddenly appearing at the doorway. "I told you I wanted to study it later. I don't want you fucking it up. Why don't you look at you scrolls," he added with a smirk, "I'm sure they'll be full of useful information."

He disappeared back into the bathroom after that, closing the door after him. Rio took the book back up and flicked through a few more pages.

The language looked more like gibberish than anything else. Most were words that made no sense to him, but others were pictures strung together, like hieroglyphics that the Ancient Egyptians used to use. It went hand in hand with the sketch of the pyramid on the other page, and it was then that Rio began to wonder whether his brother's cockiness was about to bite him in the arse.

A smile crept into the edge of his mouth as he turned a few more pages. It was starting to make sense now. The diary now began to look like a modern notebook that someone had used to research one or more of the temples in Egypt, maybe Karnak or Giza. Maybe the language was Egyptian and note the alien language Lawson was hoping to find, or maybe something else.

Rio turned and set the diary back down on the cabinet between the two beds, content that he had learned the truth of his brother's oh-so-valuable find. He was sure it was interesting to someone, but it was not exactly what they were after. He just hoped he'd be there when a scientist deciphered the text so that he could see that smug expression smacked off his brother's face.

## THREE

## NO EXPERT

B ut Cortez didn't take it to a scientist. After his shower he took a beer from the mini-fridge, lit up one of his rank cigars, made himself comfortable on his bed with his pillow behind him, and then proceeded to leaf delicately through the pages of the diary.

Rio studied him, but silently, as his brother did exactly what he had yelled at him not to do. Maybe he was doing it on purpose, Rio didn't know, but he didn't much care now that he was certain that the diary held only research about an archaeological dig somewhere on this planet.

Cortez murmured something that took his approval, nodding his head as if he was actually following anything of what had been written. Rio turned away and wandered to the window to look out at the street.

The sky was dark and overcast, the high buildings on both sides of the street lit brightly by streetlamps and other illuminations. The road was still busy with cars, the footpaths likewise with pedestrians. London always seemed busy, no matter what hour it was. He'd heard that every period in Man's history could be found at some location or other in London, the only city in the world that could boast such an accomplishment. He'd thought it preposterous at first, but later when he'd given the notion some time, he'd reckoned that it probably was true.

Cortez murmured again behind him, but he fought the urge to look round. There was no way his brother would be able to read anything anywhere in that book. He wasn't a scientist. He was a thief and a smuggler, the same as he.

Rio forced his attention back to the street outside the window. London was a city of contrasts, even down to the small things. Even the street outside their hotel was ancient yet modern, filthy yet clean, bright but dark. And just about anything could be going on at any one time, benevolent or depraved. Sometimes, since they'd first arrived here, he'd felt totally in control, safe as a thief and smuggler could feel. But other times he'd felt afraid, a seemingly irrational fear of unlit alleyways and old winding thoroughfares. London had its history all right, and while some of it was clearly worthy of praise and recognition, other incidents were surely begged to disappear. The city had a murderous heart, the old cobbled streets having gorged on the blood of its human victims in decades past, and threatening to heave it back up should anyone dare to seek them out.

Sometimes the shadows seemed to have eyes, other times tranquillity and calm. It was a paradox that shifted from doorway to doorway, alleyway to alleyway. No two were ever the same, and there seemed to be no justification to his fear.

Cortez spoke this time behind him.

"Yes, of course," he said. "That makes sense."

Rio had turned before he was even aware of it. His brother had his cigar in the hand he was turning the pages with, smoke curling in great grey whips as he nodded vehemently at the diary, forehead stern with deep concentration.

"You ain't got a fucking clue what's in there," Rio snapped, his tolerance finally evaporated.

Cortez looked up. He looked like he'd genuinely been interrupted from deep thoughts.

It took a few seconds for what Rio had said to filter through whatever had been engrossing him, and then a wave of rage broke over his face.

"What the fuck did you say to me?"

Rio swallowed, but stood his ground.

"That's book's gibberish. There's no way you're following what's going on in there."

"Why? Because you don't?"

"You ain't no scientist."

"And neither are you, but at least I'm giving it a go."

The two brothers stared at each other for a moment, until Cortez spun the book round and showed the pages he'd been studying to him.

"These pictures show a doorway," Cortez told him, "a portal, if you like. It's this that's of such great importance."

"Yeah, so?"

"So that's what so valuable. That's what Lawson wants to get his hands on."

"Yeah, so?" Rio said again.

Anger flickered across his brother's face again.

"So wherever the portal is, that land is going to beyond price."

"Unless Lawson can buy it before anyone

163

knows just what they're selling."

"Exactly."

"So where is this portal?" Rio wanted to know, stepping away from the window and approaching his brother.

Cortez shifted uncomfortably on the bed, then he sucked on his huge cigar. He pulled the diary back into his lap and riffled through the pages, searching for one in particular.

"Cortez?" Rio asked.

"Hold on."

"You have found something useful," Rio went on, "something like where this portal can be found?"

Cortez continued to search through the book. Then he stopped and traced his finger very carefully along the lines that had been written.

"The Regency Hotel in Kensington," Cortez said, his words deliberate as he spoke.

"What about the Regency Hotel in Kensington?"

"I don't know, but it mentions Room 31 as well. I think we should go there and have a look."

"What the hell for?" Rio exclaimed. "What's so special about it?"

"Well for one thing," Cortez told him, "it's the only thing in this damned book that's written in English."

# FOUR

## WHAT HAPPENED ON THE WAY
## TO THE REGENCY

There was less traffic on the roads than when Rio had watched it from the window, but still far from quiet. Vans, already dented from previous accidents and collisions, cut lanes and overtook other vehicles. BMWs and Mercedes sped through red lights. Cyclists ignored them altogether and wobbled across treacherous junctions. The night was crazy for traffic, yet no one else seemed much to notice.

The overcast sky had begun to drop its freight, heavy bulbs of rain that spattered the tarmac and concrete, soaking them instantly. Puddles formed swiftly, swilling across the road in washes that sprayed up in great waves as the cars and vans pushed through them. It was a foul night, and a cold blustery wind gusted in to makes things worse.

They drove mostly in silence, both of them lost in thought. Cortez drove, his knuckles pale as he gripped the wheel tightly. He sat forward, glaring out through the windscreen, headlights and streetlamps blurring the road ahead as they made a kaleidoscope out of the dazzling rain. Rio held the diary in his hands. He'd not opened it since Cortez had entrusted him with it.

Suddenly a motorcycle overtook them, the roar of its engine and its proximity making Cortez jump. A fan of spray trailed the rider, his red tail-light a bright arc.

"Fucking sod," Cortez cried, shaking his hand after the motorcyclist.

Rio grunted an acknowledgement beside him.

Then, when two black vans pulled out in front of them from a side road, forcing Cortez to swerve violently, it seemed almost normal behaviour for the city's idiotic drivers.

Luckily there was a long gap in the traffic in the other lane. The car's tyres snatched at traction on the slick road, but there was little to be had. Cortez wrenched at the steering wheel, fighting the slide, but the car clipped the kerb on the other side of the road before he managed to swerve back into his own lane, narrowly missing a traffic island.

"Jesus," Rio cried, gazing into the wing mirror on his side of the car. "You should've beeped him."

"Like I had fucking time to do that."

Rio gazed across at his brother. He was sweating and breathing hard, still sitting forward, uncomfortable in his seat.

"Fucking arsehole," he muttered.

A loud 'ping' made them both jump in their seats again.

Rio hunched down in his seat.

"What the fuck was that?" he cried, taking hold of the dashboard as he stared round the inside of the car.

"Like I would know," Cortez said.

Then a second 'ping' came. Then a third.

"That's a fucking bullet," Cortez screamed this

time, ducking down in his seat.

He snatched hold of the rear view mirror and angled it swiftly so that he could see out through the rear window.

"What's going on?" Rio yelled.

"They're fucking shooting at us," Cortez yelled back, his eyes glued to the rear view mirror.

"Lose them, for Christ's sake."

"What do you think... I'm gonna try and do?"

Cortez suddenly steered hard into the next turning, wrenching the wheel with all his strength and hanging on as the tyres slid across the wet road. The car slithered on the greasy road, the rain dazzling as it continued to pour down, and they mounted a footpath before bringing the car back onto the road.

But the drivers of the two vehicles behind them were good, and took the turn better than Cortez had done and managed to close the distance between them. Bullets ricocheted off the bodywork of the car again, one shattering the glass of Rio's side mirror, others landing solidly in the metal.

"Get us out of here," Rio screamed, cramming himself down into the foot-well as Cortez snaked violently down the street.

Suddenly one of the vans appeared beside them, careening to stay level on the slippery road. Oncoming cars blared their horns, swerving to avoid the collision.

Then the van veered hard into them.

Cortez lost control of the steering wheel only briefly as it spun in his hands, but it was enough to force them off the road, across the pavement and into a shop-front, the window shattering with a colossal din of tumbling shards.

Glass rained down all around them, glinting and chinking in through the windscreen that had blown outwards. Luckily Cortez had managed to keep the engine running, had somehow managed to get the car into reverse, and was now backing out onto the street with the tyres spinning wildly.

Rio lifted his head to catch a glimpse of any sign of hope. But gunmen had already emerged from the second black van that had screeched to a halt behind them, and had opened fire upon them once again.

Rio slid back down into the foot-well as Cortez ducked out of the line of fire, the car reversing blindly and at speed back up the street in the direction they'd just come as bullets streaked in through the smashed windows. As the bullets ceased and the shouting gunmen ran back to their van, Cortez hauled on the steering wheel and spun the car around, pushing the gear-stick into first and flooring the accelerator once again.

With one tyre blown from the impact and another from bullet holes, the car lurched and bucked dangerously along the street. Cortez wrestled with it as best he could, but they both knew that they'd have to ditch it and make a run for it. It would not be long before the gunmen, the number of whom they could only guess at, were once more on their trail.

Cortez yelled across at his brother only moments before he slid the car to a jerking halt at the entrance to an unlit alleyway.

"We'll have to split up," he cried. "We'll rendezvous later."

"Where?" Rio wanted to know, as he

shouldered his way out of the battered door. "We don't know how long they've been following us. And we can't exactly go back to where we've been staying either, can we? They must have bugged us somehow."

Cortez rounded the car. Rio thought he was going to check on his brother's well-being, or convince him that everything was going to be alright. But instead he just snatched the diary out of his hands.

"Then we'll head for the Regency Hotel," he told him, clutching the diary under his jacket, out of the rain. Then he added with a grin: "If we're gonna get killed for something, we may as well see it first. And then he turned and dashed headlong into the dark thoroughfare without another word.

# FIVE

## BROTHERS PARTED

The rain was coming down harder than ever. His clothes were soaked and clung to his skin like ice, prickling his skin with a cruel chill and restricting his movements as though he was wrapped in cling film.

The streetlamps blurred into swirling haloes of glittering light inside the rain that swept down from the black skies in gusting sheets, the spears of raindrops themselves lit up like myriad shards of glass. The pavements were deep with puddles and strewn with litter, both spilling over into gutters already clogged with discarded burger cartons and old drinks cans, some of them caught up and floating away in the filthy fast-flowing rivers of rainwater. But Rio knew there was no time to wait out the storm. Cortez was waiting in the hotel for him, and there were gunmen loose and after them.

Turning a corner, the heights of the Regency suddenly loomed before him in all its unlikely glory out of the maze of dark London streets. Was this where the showdown would be, Rio thought as the wind whipped a flurry of rain hard into his face, a diesel fume-covered building in the heart of Kensington?

Rio crossed the quiet street, certain that no one

was following, and entered through the revolving door, glad to at least be out of the filthy night. He wasn't sure what he had expected to find inside, but something, surely, more opulent than this.

It seemed more like a flop-house than a hotel. The wallpapers that might once have been grand, hung soiled with peeling corners. The carpets were threadbare beneath his feet in well-worn routes from the main entrance to the two tarnished lifts. A middle-aged man with several days growth of beard sat in a chair behind what passed for a reception desk, his head thrown back as he dozed open-mouthed. And a spill of newspapers that had presumably once been stacked neatly, covered part of the floor beside the two lift doors.

Apart from the name of the hotel, the only other legible phrase on the pages of the diary had been Room 31. Rio stepped into the lift and waited with apprehension until the metal doors clanked slowly closed and the lift began to creak into motion.

Rio glanced around the metal box, curling his nose at the stench of stale urine as he spied the suspicious puddle on the floor, as he rode the lift up to the fourth floor. He tugged his cigarettes from his jacket pocket as the lift bucked past the first level and took one out, lighting it as he watched the dull orange bulbs illuminate the floor numbers weakly, the third bulb missing altogether.

The lift reached the fourth floor and the doors shuddered slowly open, as though there was an old man somewhere hauling them open on the end of a length of weathered rope, and Rio stepped out into the corridor and looked cautiously in both directions, drawing deeply on his cigarette as he did so. The hotel was eerily silent, the smoke curling around him like the ghosts of coiling snakes as he exhaled. Both directions seemed empty.

He started off to the right, guided only by the room numbers on the battered doors along the passage, wallpaper brown with nicotine peeling from walls, as the same stench of stale urine soured the air.

He found the door to Room 31 and knocked twice, hissing his brother's name at the jamb. But there was no sound from the other side - no footsteps across a foul carpet, no TV, not even a cough.

Rio knocked again, inclining his head towards the door, listening intently. But there was nothing, just the same hollow silence like the rest of the hotel. Cautiously he grasped the handle, his cigarette trembling between lips as dry as old bones. He turned it - it was unlocked - then he entered the room.

It was a mess inside, not in a way that looked as if it had been turned over, just in a similar state to the rest of the hotel. The room was lit by a single bare bulb that hung from a ceiling browned by cigarette smoke, and speckled with fly-shit. It looked as if someone had at least been here, and very recently. Rio smelled smoke too, and not cigarettes either, but cigars, the same foul-smelling cigars that Cortez managed to suck his way through. Then he saw a glass ashtray sitting on a cabinet beside the bed, the remnants of a cigar still smoking as proof. But it was clear, just from what he had seen in those first few moments, that the room had been abandoned, and quickly.

Rio stepped fully into the room and closed the door behind him. He took the cigarette from his lips as he put his head through the door of the adjoining bathroom, but Cortez was no longer here.

Rio scanned the room, his head whirling, wondering where the hell his brother was and just what he was going to do now. This was the only discernible location in that damned diary that Cortez had stolen, the reason they had been run off the road and shot at, the reason they were still being chased, and Cortez was nowhere to be seen.

Perhaps he'd sniffed the gunmen that were already on their trail. Perhaps they'd already got him. But Rio was certain that they had lost them in the narrow thoroughfares of London. And besides, he reasoned, how would they know that this was where they were even headed?

He stepped across the room to the window to think, tugging the stained curtain back and looking out into the filthy night.

The rain seemed to be coming down even harder outside, he could see the pattern made as each drop hit the flooded street, the swirls and the gusts that harried the downpour across London. There was no one about, he was glad to see, at least no pedestrians, no one stupid enough to walk anywhere on such a night. But then he saw two men scurrying across the street from the other side, and as he looked down to try and find where they had come from, he saw one of the two black vans, its front grill smashed, parked at the kerb further up the street.

Rio swallowed hard, and turned and stabbed his cigarette out in the ashtray beside the bed. He needed to think. But there was no time. As he went to leave the room, however, he noticed something on the inside of the door. It looked like a letter A that had been scratched into the wood, with two vertical lines dropping down from it. Rio stared at it, his fingers inches from the handle, his heart thudding hard inside his chest, his legs screaming at him to get out of the hotel before the two gunmen found him. But he knew that somehow this was a message from Cortez, and that it was meant for him. But what the fuck did it mean?

Images of the black van parked out in the street pounded inside his head as he stared at the roughly-scrawled marks. But this was an urgent message from Cortez, surely.

His hand grasped the handle now, itching to pull open the door and carry him back over the threshold. But this was something important, a message meant for him that explained the abandoned room.

And then it struck him.

It wasn't a letter A after all.

It was an arrow pointing up. Cortez had fled to the roof.

Rio raced out of the room and back down the corridor, and guessing that the two gunmen would most likely be covering the lifts, decided that the stairs would be both quicker and less likely to deliver him straight into their hands.

After locating the door, which was unmarked and tucked away at the far end of the corridor, he climbed them two at a time, hauling himself up the banister, before reaching the access door to the roof. It wouldn't readily open, but as he put his weight to it and the door flew wide, a scrap of paper that had been lying on the top step was sucked out into the foulness of the night.

Staggering out into the darkness, he had to lift his arms up over his face as the storm harried the roof with its violent barrage of torrential rain. He turned in circles across the slick surface, his feet kicking through the deep puddles that had accumulated as he searched hopelessly for his brother.

The howling wind gusted the rain into his face making it difficult to see, but the roof was surprisingly open and it was clear that if Cortez had come up here, then he had already left. It was then that Rio saw the white scrap of paper that had blown off the top of the stairs, clinging to the low wall that skirted the roof. His heart sank as he saw it. Had Cortez left word after all, a note that would explain everything?

Rio started towards it. But then, as he saw the other tall buildings of Kensington around him, he slowed his pace. His senses blurred, his head went light as vertigo overtook him, and he cursed the weakness of his body for giving him such an irrational fear.

He stopped, staring down at the note that clung to the brickwork from the rain that soaked it, as the storm threatened to unbalance him and drag him over the edge.

The wind was no longer snatching at the paper. It was saturated and stuck fast, but it was blustery up here, blustery enough to swirl the rain into harsh dervishes, and surely blustery enough to whip that note right off the roof (and him along with it), if he got too close.

Rio knelt down, his eyes clenched half-shut out of terror of the edge he knew he had to go near, shivering from the furious cold and the shame of being halted by so ridiculous a phobia. There were gunmen coming for him, for God's sake, gunmen who had perhaps already found his brother, but he would rather face them now than retrieve this note from the edge of the hotel roof. If those men could see him now, Rio thought to himself, prostrate and crawling through deep freezing puddles, they would laugh until they shat. But on he went, crawling on his hands and knees across the coarse flattop, on towards his brother's note.

The wind suddenly gusted, snatching up a corner of the white sheet, and Rio stiffened. Don't blow away now, he prayed inside his head, don't let me be this close to the edge and lose you now.

But the note was stuck firmly to the brickwork, the corner flapping madly like the wing of a wounded bird.

When he was within reach, he stretched forward and carefully peeled it away with his fingertips, the note so wet that it began to come apart with soggy fibrous threads. His eyes flickered between the note and the edge of the building - he could see hundreds of windows dropping down towards the street below, he could feel the wind gusting up the side of the hotel, snatching at his wet hair. He shuddered as he reached further forward, the storm seeming to unbalance him and pull him towards the edge as he took hold of the note more firmly, not even looking at it until he had crawled steadily back away from the edge to a safe distance. Then, as he unballed the note from his shaking fist, he stared at it in horror to find that the weather had all but blurred Cortez's briskly-scrawled words into a soft blue watercolour wash. His note had gone.

All Rio could do was sit and stare at it as the rain continued to batter him in gusting sheets. The gunmen were still coming. In his head he could hear their footsteps already on the stairs. Perhaps they had already gotten Cortez. This blurred sheet of paper was not even proof of his safety, that he had gotten this far away. Hell, it was proof of nothing. There wasn't even evidence that Cortez had even written it.

Rio snatched a frantic look behind him to the doorway that still stood open, but at the moment it was empty, and still remained quiet. He clenched his eyes once again, but this time in despair. He felt the rain running in rivulets across his scalp and down over his face. He felt the cold chill that had already soaked his clothes permeate through his skin and into his bones. He could feel the icy approach of death coming for him, either with bullets or with hypothermia, it didn't really matter that much now. His brother had gone, and he had no idea where he could be. He had no idea where he could even go now. If gunmen could find and track them hours after stealing Lazenby's secret diary, then they would be able to find and track them anywhere and at any time. There were secret eyes everywhere. He couldn't go back to their hotel room, that would be suicide, and now he was trapped on a roof with no way back down. Except over the edge.

He opened his eyes again and stared straight ahead. Through the swirling rain he could see the edge looming like the horizon of a new world. How easy would it be to just throw himself over, he thought? How simple to just stand up now, close his eyes, and walk forward until there was no more roof beneath his feet?

He swallowed hard and glanced down again at the note that may or may not have been written by Cortez, or may or may not have even been a note. There had been no questions answered tonight, he thought, about a new world or indeed any other, and to die now would solve nothing. Better to frustrate the men that sought him, as well as whoever had put them after him and his brother in the first place, than to give them so easy a gift. So he turned away from the edge, stepped back through the rooftop door, and hurried down into the dry stale air of the flop-house hotel once again.

# SIX

## CONSORTIUM

It had been a busy night already, and yet the night was still far from over. Lawson sat across the table from the others, the meeting with the consortium having been called quickly, watching who would speak first. There were furtive glances from everyone present, none of them knowing exactly what was going on, or what was likely to happen, but soon the words would be flowing like the blood that had already been spilled in order to have gotten this far.

There were seven of them in total, seven members with enough accumulated wealth to pull this unprecedented venture off. It lessened ownership, of course - how could it not? - but there would be councillors to bribe, members of parliament to be bought, businessmen to be blackmailed and disgraced; and for those that would not make way for the biggest venture in the history of mankind, murders to be planned and executed.

Of all the members of the consortium, the one who took Lawson's breath away was Sabastine. He was a real vampire, a true god of Kar'mi'shah, and the one who had first started Lawson's pilgrimage to find this new world he had spoken of. Other men would have scoffed at his stories, but Lawson had seen things in his life that most men had not, and

Sabastine's doctrines had turned him into a believer. Sabastine had not known of the portal home, but had not desired to learn of its location either. He'd found a better home in Europe, he'd said, particularly in England where he had used his immortality to accumulate and secure immense funds and possessions over the centuries he had resided here. He owned countless properties and vast expanses of land all over the country, and had influenced many treaties and laws over those centuries. Like the other seven members of the consortium, he desired the monetary benefits of owning a doorway to another world. But unlike the other members, he did not desire to actually step across the threshold himself.

Frederick Kramer, on the other hand, had earned his money in the media, from television mostly, but also from tabloid newspapers and magazines, with his PaceNet News Group empire. He had been there at the start of the Internet boom too, and had added millions to his already monstrous stockpile. He was also famous for spending his money lavishly, even now at the age of seventy two, but there was only so much he could buy before boredom and depression set in.

When Lawson had first met him, he was gambling not only in casinos and racetracks around the world, but also on the lives of prostitutes he'd take back to hotel rooms with his hangers-on, sick bizarre games he'd play with them with the promises of fortunes or death. Lawson managed to convince him that there was something far greater than money, something unique in Mankind's history, something that would change the past, the present and the future. Such temptation (proved with evidence Lawson had collected since his first meeting with Sabastine), enticed the multi-millionaire out of his downward decadent spiral, and brought a gleam back into the old man's eyes. He sat opposite Lawson now at the grand table, two of his bodyguards standing behind him just out of the light cast by the lamps hanging over the centre of the table, those bright eyes watching the other six with a barely concealed glee.

Candice Rhodes was not well known, except in society circles. She wasn't famous, she had no influential connections, no family money, and she offered no dirt on anyone. What she did have, however, was a beautiful face, beautiful enough to trap the hearts of probably every prince and eligible bachelor around the globe. Most had fought for her, some had died for her, but they had all at some point entertained every notion imaginable in order to have her by their side.

Candice had made a handsome living from that face, allowing herself to be bought incredible luxuries and gifts, to be a walking jewellery box adorned with diamonds and gold, and all of it in exchange for an affair that could last only moments of her life. She sat at the table now, smiling across at Sabastine, a black wide-brimmed hat perched at an elegant angle, its veil cast across her stunning blue eyes. But Sabastine merely regarded her, his ebony eyes simply returning her stare. Did she even know that he was a vampire? Lawson suspected not, suspected that none of them other than himself knew the truth about the most mysterious member of their association. Her life to him was fleeting, her

181

beauty more so. What could she offer him that he did not already possess? Indeed, what else was there for him, Lawson wondered, except to keep amassing what he already owned in abundance?

David Embers was a businessman, a consultant in the city that could demand high fees for his experience and knowledge. It was not certain whether he had gathered his fortune any way other than legally, and to a certain extent it did not matter, but Embers was a boon to the consortium, bringing a working knowledge of how the big boys played, and, more importantly, how they could fall.

Cecil Lovegrove was born from money, an aristocrat who had nothing better to do with his family's wealth than to force it into ventures where he might be able to at least buy a little respect for himself. To be fair he had shown several times a desire to want more from life, a longing for a better world, but Lawson had grown up working class, he'd known what it was like to go without, and for the rich classes to complain of their lot gripped his shit every time he heard it.

Lawson disliked Lovegrove intensely for his poor-little-rich-kid attitude, but showed it in no other way than his curt manner with him. There was no need to rock the boat because of superficial differences, and Lovegrove was bringing a sizeable sum and influence with him. They were all here for the same reason, to see another sky and own a part of the journey that would take his fellow man to see it.

Yvette Moore was somewhat of a mystery, however. Lawson had come upon her in a casino in Mayfair, watching her winning big at the roulette

182

wheel but seeming indifferent or even melancholy about the growing stack of chips that was rapidly accumulating in front of her. He had watched her for an hour or more, spellbound not only by her young beauty but also by the lack of enjoyment her skill at the wheel was bringing her. He'd joined her at the table and initiated conversation with her, finding out later in the evening how the money she won would only distract her from the monotony of life for a short spell.

Lawson had offered her the chance at something grander that night, had managed to convince her that he too searched for an end to the tedium. By the end of the night they had formed an understanding based upon his ideas and promises. So young and attractive was she (and perhaps there was something close to helplessness in her large blue eyes that enraptured him), that he would have longed to have taken her to bed. But so important was the journey that he knew existed somewhere in London, that to offer her the chance to walk upon the shores of another land would bring a far greater bliss.

He looked at her now across the table, her eyes cast down at her hands in front of her, and wanted only to see her smile. She knew she was here for some grand scheme, but he guessed that he was not the only man who had tried to offer her that.

But he would succeed where others had taken failure to their graves. He had more to set before her than any other man ever could. He had a world to offer, an end to the only life she had ever known, and tonight he would make good on that promise he had made to her.

As for himself, the last and final member of the

consortium, what was his story? Well, he was just a thief. He had stolen his money, embezzled it from banks and international traders, drained vast accounts using hired computer hackers, kidnapped the rich and famous alike and demanded huge ransoms. He had employed everyone at one time or another, from burglars to hitmen, assassins to pickpockets. Anything to accumulate the amount of money necessary for such a massive operation. Anything other than working for it.

It couldn't be earned or worked for anyway, money, not the amount that was needed for this venture. Anyone would agree with that. But it had brought him to where he was now, one of seven men and women about to own the greatest wonder of the world, a doorway to a province other than the one they knew, a realm of the unknown and unknowable. It had turned a criminal into a businessman, made a scoundrel honourable, and he was going to live this new life better than his last.

The portal had at last been found, the fabled gateway to Kar'mi'shah, and he wanted the gears of forward momentum to turn swiftly.

Funds had already been pooled from each of them, but they would need so much more to survive. Their interests were already being looked after by a team of lawyers headed by a man named Victor Nash. He was present in the room but he did not sit at the table. Instead he stood in the shadows at the back of the room, away from the light cast down onto the table by the overhanging lamps. He was not a member of the consortium, but just another one of its paid runners. He had no place at the table.

"I think I should be the one to bring the first

glimpses of this new world to the masses." It was Frederick Kramer who spoke first, and he leant across the table, the skin of his wrists sallow and sagging as it appeared from the sleeves of his silver-grey suit.

"No complaints here," Candice said, her smile infectious. "You boys can have all the publicity you want. I just want to see something new, something better than all this."

Kramer smiled back at her, showing her a full set of immaculate white teeth, the old man proud that they were still his own.

"I want no limelight," Sabastine said to them all. "And as I've already made clear to Lawson, I do not desire to step through the portal either."

"Then why don't you explain to us why the hell you want to be a part of this in the first place?" Kramer exclaimed.

Sabastine shot him an icy glare. Only Lawson knew that Sabastine was a vampire, but not even he knew his true intentions. How could he? They were nothing but passing beings to him, mortals he'd called them, things that would soon be dust and may never have even been.

Sabastine wanted to tell this old fossil that he did not want to go to this brave new world because he'd already been there; he'd been born there, made a vampire and a god there. The lure of material wealth had been too great on Earth, and more specifically in England where he'd had devotion pledged by the fathers of upper class wealthy families, and he still desired nothing more than to accumulate it. So he kept his silence; it would be easy to find another wealthy man with millions to invest

185

in the project (a man unhappy in his money and still seeking more who would give it all up for just a single glance of a brand new sky), but Kramer's media empire was ideal. He would not destroy him yet for so foolish a trait as insolence.

"Mr Nash will be distributing offers for the buildings and land that surround the Regency," Lawson said to them, addressing them all as one now. "And he has told me that some should readily accept given the current economic state."

"Twice the current market value is quite a pull," Kramer agreed with disdain. "But negotiating from a lower figure would have saved us millions."

"It doesn't matter," Lawson explained. "Costs are irrelevant at the moment. The money is unimportant to us, we have it in abundance. What we don't have is the ownership of the properties and the land beneath both the Regency and what immediately surrounds it."

Kramer folded his arms and glared at him. He knew what Lawson said was right, but to give away money unnecessarily just didn't sit well with him.

"Only a handful will accept."

It was Sabastine who spoke, sitting back, away from the heated conversation. "Most will simply reject the offer out of hand."

Lawson glanced across at Victor Nash, and indicated for him to step forward.

Nash approached the table, a wallet of papers in his hands. He tried to show a professional face but it was clear he was nervous. As successful and highly paid as he was, he had never been in charge of anything like this before. To make any errors, he knew, would result in more than just his dismissal from the post.

"We feel confident that the majority of businesses and landowners will act favourably to a high offer. A high price in London will help swallow costs of their relocation."

"And what about the ones who don't want to sell or move?" Kramer interjected. "The ones who already have plenty of money. What about them?"

"Council land will be the most difficult," Nash went on. "There will be a lot of political and legislative barriers regarding sale of the land, to the point where it may just be impossible."

The lawyer finished talking to a dead silence. He could feel the weight of their eyes pressing against him like a physical force. He swallowed hard, his throat dry. A sweat broke on his brow and trickled. He didn't wipe it away.

"Persevere with the ones who may think this is some kind of joke," Lawson explained to him, "and persuade them that we are earnest in our intentions. To those who say they would never sell, offer them three times the market value."

"And the others?"

"Find out who looks after what and bring me a list of names - directors, councillors, chief executives, members of parliament. All of them."

"And what if we still can't buy it all?" Kramer interjected.

"Then I'll send some of my lads round to break a few skulls."

## SEVEN

## INTERROGATION

The meeting had gone about as well as Lawson could have expected, given the speed at which the information about the diary had travelled. Since he'd laid his hands on the pages (or more accurately the translation of those pages), which gave the location of the portal to Kar'mi'shah, an unlikely place in a near-derelict hotel in Kensington, events had progressed surprisingly smoothly.

Sabastine was not the only vampire he had met in his life, and not the only one who had been born in Kar'mi'shah either, although it had been the chance meeting with Sabastine that had started this quest that had dominated his life ever since. No, this other vampire had been an ancient creature by the name of Eisha Piel, and she had translated the document for him in exchange for two young lads he'd had literally pulled off the street. He hadn't stayed to watch her feed, but he had heard the screams as he'd left her flat.

The Brazilian thief Cortez Barros was still holed up back at his mansion house. He'd not had a chance to question him about why he hadn't handed over the diary directly to him instead of trying to follow its instructions for his own purposes. The thief's brother had so far eluded him, but London was not that big a city given the number of men who worked for him. He'd turn up sooner or later, especially when he found out where his big brother was being held.

Lawson sat in the back of his Mercedes as Jimmy drove him home. It was getting close to three in the morning and he was tired. His eyes ached as he looked out through the tinted windows at the grim yellow-lit streets, imagining the people tucked away inside their tiny homes, ignorant of what was to come to the dreary mundane world that they knew and despised.

The gateway to paradise was nearly in his grasp, and as much as he wanted to go there now, to step through and feel the soil of another dominion beneath his feet, he knew that it would destroy all the plans that he had for it. And he had plans for his Eden in abundance. Better to wait, he thought, until he could have it all.

He wasn't sure that he entirely trusted anyone in the consortium, but he figured that it was reasonable to assume that it was just his nature as a thief.

He wasn't certain just what the socialite Candy Rhodes was looking for. After a life spent trying to get out of the poverty she'd grown up in, he figured that she was perhaps attempting to claim something otherworldly for herself, something entirely beyond wealth, he had no idea. He couldn't see her as an adventurer, and he sure as hell couldn't see her as a pioneer.

David Embers was a businessman, on the other hand, a true entrepreneur if ever there was one, and for him to be a part of the greatest acquisition in the history of mankind seemed nothing short of reasonable.

Lovegrove, however, was a lazy toff, no question, and as much as Lawson would love to deny him access to such a wonderful opportunity, he knew the man's influence could not be underestimated.

Yvette Moore? He had no idea about her whatsoever, but he knew that her face was just waiting to smile, and he wanted to be there when it came.

Kramer was easy. In his head, Lawson could see the old bastard just wanting to experience as much as could before he succumbed to death, the only deal his money couldn't buy him out of.

But Sabastine? He was something entirely different. He couldn't figure him out at all. To invest so heavily in something he seemed so laid back about. He seemed content to take a back seat, indeed he showed no interest whatsoever in using the portal itself.

Lawson knew that Sabastine had come from Kar'mi'shah, it was his true home after all, which made it doubly confusing as to why he would not want to return. Even the hardest of men have a fondness for home. He wasn't exactly expecting the vampire to get all teary eyed about a return trip, but to not even desire to set foot there was something that just wouldn't sit right with him.

He, on the other hand, could barely wait to see what lay on the other side. So many ideas wanted to plant themselves in his head and take root, waiting to blossom and fulfil all his fantasies and dreams, and he tried hard to keep them at bay; he so desperately wanted to see Kar'mi'shah with open eyes and without preconceptions. He didn't even want to visualise what he'd see. The sky could be green for all he knew, or there might be two suns in the sky, or hell, no suns at all. It was a world of vampires, he knew that much at least, and so dangerous a notion was that that he frequently attempted to disregard it. He could feel his heart thudding more quickly in his chest as his very thoughts began to speed up. He settled back in the soft leather upholstery and took several deep breaths, attempting to empty his mind of excitable thoughts.

He felt like a kid let loose in a toy shop, unable to decide which toys to drag off the shelves first, petrified in case his greed might destroy the whole adventure altogether and send him home with nothing. That was the law of the sod, and he'd been burned by it before.

The Mercedes pulled up at the gates of his house, and he watched from the back as they rolled slowly open. Jimmy hadn't said a word the whole journey, which was something he liked about the kid. He knew when to speak, which wasn't often, and when not to ask questions. He knew his place, a bottom rung monkey who Lawson could see climbing pretty damn quickly. Jimmy pulled the car up at the front door and still kept himself to himself. He didn't even turn around.

"Cheers, Jimmy," Lawson said to him, as he opened the door and climbed out. "You drive real good."

"Thank you, sir."

He felt like tipping him. It seemed crazy in his head, but it wasn't often that one of his employees acted so perfectly without instruction, despite the large sums of money he doled out to them like confetti at a wedding.

Inside he found Rodrigues and Patten eating his food in the kitchen. They stood up as Lawson entered, Rodrigues wiping chicken grease hastily from his face with a paper towel.

"Where's Cortez?" Lawson demanded.

"Downstairs where you left him," Rodrigues replied guiltily, setting his chicken leg down on one of the huge plates in front of him.

"Has he told you anything?"

"Nothing yet. We were waiting for you to return."

"You two come with me then," Lawson told them both, and headed to the door beneath the stairs that led down to the basement.

Cortez Barros was down there and tied to a chair, exactly where Lawson had left him. He wasn't gagged - who would hear him scream anyway? - but he looked up at Lawson now with wide eyes as he hurriedly descended the stairs.

"I did good by you, Mr Lawson," Cortez started, as soon as he was within conversation distance. "I found the diary. I was on my way here to give it to you."

"I was told a very different story, and the way I figure it, judging by the route they said you were taking, you were headed to find out for yourself just what was in that book."

"We were just making sure that the book was useful. We thought it was about an expedition to Egypt that some scientist had written about digging up pyramids. We couldn't read any of it."

"It seems like you managed to read just about enough of it to go to the Regency Hotel."

"That's all we could read."

Lawson began to circle him, his prisoner struggling to turn his head to follow sight of him. It all seemed very reasonable behaviour, a man tied up in a basement, paid thugs, espionage. He'd come a long way.

"And what about that museum bitch?" Lawson suddenly went on. "Or don't you think I know about her either?"

"She knows ancient languages. That's her shit."

"That diary wasn't the first thing you'd planned on taking to her either, was it?"

Cortez stared at him. He swallowed painfully. The ropes were burning the skin at his wrists.

"You've put a few artefacts her way, haven't you?"

"We just thought that it was better that way. You know, trying not to waste your time. The other things were no good. Not for you, anyway."

"And the fact that the young Victoria Hamilton has been building quite an enviable file, a file the likes of which I myself have been paying lots of money to acquire, doesn't faze you at all?"

"I... I didn't know."

"She told us that much anyway," Lawson walked a circle around the Brazilian in the opposite direction, disorientating him.

Cortez tried to keep eye contact, expecting that there might be a blow coming, but it hurt his neck, made the ropes at his wrists burn more.

"Where exactly is your brother?" Lawson asked lightly.

"You don't know?"

"If I did, I wouldn't be asking, now would I?"

Cortez took a breath. Lawson could see that his mind was working quickly, and saw his eyes flickering as he sought his best reply.

"It doesn't matter too much whether you tell me or not," Lawson said to him. "I have people looking for him. I just thought you could save me some time."

"Come on, man," Cortez pleaded. "I got you the damn information you wanted. Why are you doing this? And what do you want with my brother?"

Lawson grabbed hold of the other thief by his throat, squeezing it hard.

"Because you were trying to figure out the location for yourself, you sneaky little shit, that's why."

"No, man," he choked. "You got it wrong. We just wanted to make sure we got you the right information. We just wanted the reward money you were offering. You offered some good dough, man. We just wanted that, I swear."

Lawson squeezed just that bit harder until he could see the thief's eyes begin to bulge, and then he let him go, turning his back on him and putting his hands on his hips.

"Fuck, Cortez, I don't know whether to let you go or fill you full of holes."

He turned to look back at him again now, staring hard at the man as he struggled to get his breath back.

"I'm grateful for you two boys finding me that diary, I really am, but I just can't get this image out of my head of you two owning the deeds to that there hotel and dancing the night away in a fountain of money. All I can see at the moment is you two taking the piss out of me and it grips my shit."

"No, Mr Lawson," Cortez gasped. "we weren't doing anything like that. We were going to bring you the diary all along. We just wanted it verified, that's all."

"By an expert."

Cortez nodded as vigorously as he could, given his bondage.

"An expert that's never seen that language in her life. So far as you knew anyway."

Cortez stopped nodding, his eyes wide. It was clear that he didn't have a fucking clue what was going on anymore.

"I'll tell you what I'll do then," Lawson said to him, going down on his haunches in front of him. "I might need some work doing, and your brother might be the perfect candidate."

An uneasy silence hung between them for a while.

"Seems reasonable," Cortez finally said slowly.

"The payment would be you walking out of here."

Cortez studied him carefully.

"How am I going to let him know –"

"- if I don't let you go first? Don't worry, I'll get word to him. And if he doesn't do good by me, you'll have him to blame for it."

"Have him to blame for what?"

Lawson winked at him, and then got up and turned away from him, taking his two voiceless associates with him and leaving Cortez alone in the ill-lit basement once again.

## EIGHT

## WHAT NASH SAID

Lawson spoke to Victor Nash on the telephone a few days later and was glad to hear that two companies had received the consortium's offer of two times the market value offer favourably. Nash also gave him the bad news that he'd had a reply from a planning officer of the local authority saying that under no circumstances would the land be sold. There were still several businesses that he was waiting to hear back from, plus one that had told him to stop calling.

Lawson took the list of names Nash had prepared for him, the decision-makers and the executives, but instructed Nash to keep badgering them anyway. Three times market value might budge some of the hungry ones, but he knew that some would just never move.

"Put some cash under some people's noses," Lawson said to him. "You've got some sneaky little shits on your team, make it clear that I want some councillors on my side, a few members of parliament too. If anything comes down to a vote and we don't win it, I'm going to want to know why. Is that clear?"

"Yes, Mr Lawson."

"Good. That money's not just sitting in our account to make interest. Spend it on whatever you have to."

"Yes, Mr Lawson," Nash said again.

When he replaced the receiver, Lawson picked it back up almost immediately and called Rodrigues.

"Any word from Rio Barros yet?"

"Not yet."

"Then try harder. I need to talk to him about running a few errands."

## NINE

## ERRAND BOY

He guessed that it was a note from whoever had tried to kill them, but never for one moment did he think that that person was Lawson. Rio had seen the envelope speared over one of the spikes of the railings that ran up to the front door of their hotel building, and after thinking that it might be a trap, reasoned that it was not much of one, and had crossed the street to pick it up.

It was a brief note from Rodrigues, another Brazilian that Lawson had put on his payroll, and it stuck in his throat how little patriotism there was any more in the world, especially beneath their green and yellow flag. 'Come and see Lawson or your brother gets it', was all Rodrigues had written in his untidy scrawl. Rio realised he was grinding his teeth as he read and reread the note, his hatred filling for the total lack of respect his so-called countryman had for either him or his brother. Money talked, but it also kicked like a fucking mule.

It had surprised him to find their hired car exactly where they had ditched it. It had been raided in the time it had sat there unlocked, some passing punk kid stealing anything of theirs that they'd left behind (his brother's cigars, maps and papers out of the glove box, a pack of condoms with two left inside), plus someone had stuck a large orange sticker on the side window saying that their abandoned car was scheduled to be removed. The car was perforated with bullet holes, heavily dented as though it had been joy-ridden by the same wanker who had stolen their stuff, and the engine didn't sound right when he started it up. But although it probably would have been at least partly serviceable, the car sported three flat tyres, and so he had been forced to abandon it for good and go find himself a taxi. It wasn't exactly discreet travelling but he didn't exactly have much choice.

It was December and it was dark. He arrived outside the black gates of Lawson's mansion home at six o'clock, the taxi pulling up at the kerb on the opposite side of the street. A freezing wind had been gusting all day, but since the sun had gone down it had gotten a whole lot colder.

He pulled his coat around himself as he climbed out of the taxi, instructing the driver to wait for him as the wind tried to snatch everything away including his words, and strode across the street to the gates where one of Lawson's guards was waiting. He knew the guards were all armed and paid well enough not to have a conscience about shooting anyone who asked for it, and he stepped through the gates, his arms raised shoulder-high as the gates rolled slowly open, and allowed the guard to search him. But he was clean; it would have been stupid to bring his gun here tonight, anyway, despite how much he'd wanted to. Who knows, he thought to himself as the guard roughly frisked him, if he'd had enough money to bribe his security, he might have been able to take out Rodrigues as well as Lawson.

But that was for another night. The life of his brother was at stake, and that took precedent.

Luckily it wasn't Rodrigues who took him up to Lawson's study, but Patten, a huge bullish numbskull who'd spent time on the boxing circuit. His nose was wide and his ears were dishevelled, his hands hanging from the end of his thick arms like shovels, and he looked a lot like a gorilla who'd been forced inside an expensive suit (which probably wasn't that far from the truth). Neither of them said a word to each other as they climbed the stairs, and once Patten had knocked on Lawson's door and Rio had been summoned inside, Patten waited just outside, his hands folded in front of him.

"Don't say a damn word," Lawson said immediately after Rio closed the door behind him. "I know what questions you've got and I know you'd sure as hell like to take a swing at me."

"I'd like to do a lot more than that."

"But that ain't going to happen tonight, because unless you've got a death wish, you ain't packing nothing more than sour acid in your gut. Am I right?"

"Yeah," Rio spat. "You're right."

Lawson offered the Brazilian a seat but Rio just shook his head, telling him that he preferred to stand, and that the sooner he was away from him the better.

"Please yourself," Lawson said to him, leaning back in his chair. "Why don't we get straight down to business. I need you to go and persuade a few people to sell me their land. Some have been helpful so far, others not so. I've arranged for you to meet up with some lawyers, suits that will be handing out briefcases full of cash."

"And you want me to be the muscle behind the pound sign."

"That's the general idea. The more honourable of the elected might need to be shown the full benefits of a higher wage."

"And how will I manage that without facing prison time for assault?"

"Just imagine their faces are mine," Lawson said with a humourless grin.

"Then I'll kick their fucking faces in."


Rio stormed out of Lawson's house cursing his name, his teeth grinding with rage once again. He had the name of one of Lawson's lawmen, plus the address where he was to meet him. He knew that the sooner he got his business done with the officials that Lawson wanted to bribe or intimidate, the sooner he and his brother would be gone, maybe back to Brazil and away from the whole fucking mess. But he took Lawson at his word, despite how much he wanted to kill him, and despite the reward money that neither he nor his brother would ever receive for finding that diary.

He should've been more forceful with Cortez about taking it straight to Lawson, he knew that now, just as he knew that he should've told his brother not to interfere with these big players and just to drive it over.

But Cortez wouldn't have it, would he? No, his head had come up with all these big ideas about not getting ripped off. Hell, Lawson had paid them both well up until now. The reward money was nothing to him, why would he have ripped them off? Rio slammed his fist into the palm of his other hand as he stormed across the street to where the taxi still waited, and swore out loud into the night. The driver spun round startled, clocked that it was his passenger, and then turned back swiftly to start the engine. They could be sitting on a fucking beach right now, Rio raged inside his head, if Cortez hadn't gone off on one of his stupid fucking ideas.

Rio clambered into the car and slammed the door hard after him. He sat there for a few minutes just staring ahead as the driver waited quietly for new directions, feeling the pain in his jaws from where he'd ground his teeth together, and the ache in his hands from where his fists had been clenched. He hated Lawson, hated this whole fucking business, and now he couldn't even walk away from it.

When he glanced up he saw the driver's eyes returning his gaze in the rear view mirror. Rio stared at him for a few moments without uttering a word, as the thoughts continued to rage inside his head. Then he relented, reached for the scrap of paper with the lawyer's address on it, and then handed it over to the taxi driver.

"Take me here," he said.

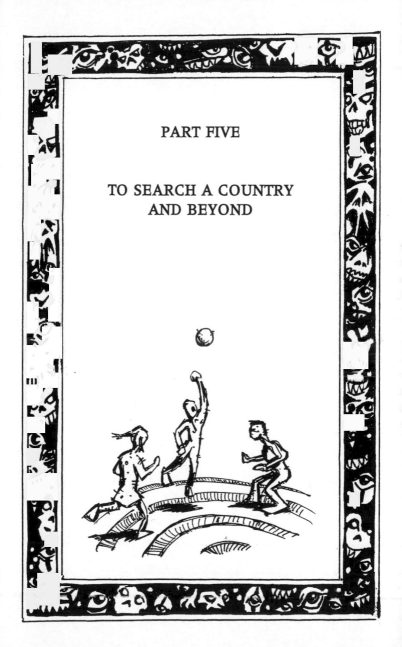

PART FIVE

TO SEARCH A COUNTRY
AND BEYOND

# ONE

## LEFT ALONE WITH THE NIGHTMARES

Catherine had waited in the thief's flat until dawn without hearing any word from him. With the onset of sunrise, she'd ventured into his bedroom to sleep out the day and learnt that his window had been secured efficiently against the harmful light. Why he had done this she could only guess, and presumed that he offered vampires some kind of halfway house to add to his list of services to the immortal community. But his secret life was of no interest to her, she told herself, and she was glad to at least have a sealed chamber away from the day.

Her dreams had begun to grow more vivid and graphic since her husband's ascension, witnessing images of tortures and agonies inflicted upon the very young and the very old alike. While she had performed some of the deeds she saw by her own hands, and were therefore of little distress to her, the images had not been created by her own mind and she took no pleasure in seeing them.

Even though she was not averse to committing some of these witnessed atrocities when circumstances desired them, the dreams were becoming more and more painful to accept; more so when they came day after day, every time she closed her eyes for restful sleep.

Carlos was putting them there, of that certainty there was no doubt in her mind, but what concerned her more was the fact that his mind was clearly out of control; his thoughts had become derailed, and some form of lusting insanity had surely taken up residence inside his skull.

During her fitful sleep that first day, Catherine had dreamt of hooded torturers and their arsenal of needle-pointed instruments, some surgically clean, others rusted to bitter barbs. Their victims had bled from sliced and butchered wounds, their screams piercing the scarlet of their blood with livid colours all their own – sharp blues shot through with electric yellows, browns and purples glistening like burnished shit and bruises – as the thump of their sewn-together hearts pounded inside her head and chest, booming like a single heavy drum that beat the rhythm of their unhurried executions.

Her eyes had shot open to the black room, echoes of her dream still contorting in the corners of the unlit chamber, shadows and figures writhing in desperate agony from the touch of the torturer's tools.

They'd reached for her, their ethereal fingers clawing at her from the echoes of her dream world, tendrils and filaments of their uncertain matter entwined inside the shadows of the room that she knew were real.

They'd faded as she'd lain there - their twisting bodies becoming less solid, the shadows of the conscious world stealing what strength they had possessed behind the vampire's eyes – but not before they'd whispered the message that their master had sent them to bear:

*come find me...*

*my life is agony...*

Then they'd disappeared entirely, their delicate filaments finally snuffed out and erased, and she had been left once again to lie alone in a silent flat in the heart of London.

It had not been the first time his night children had visited her, but it had been the first time they had spoken to her. It chilled her to think what he might be capable of, or what forces had begun to grow and evolve out of him. She needed to find him, needed to know the truth and be with him once again, to tend to his madness and comfort him where he belonged, at her breast and by her side.

Her desire for him was unconditional. They'd lived and loved so many lifetimes, and little had changed. But she was still not with him, still could not find him, and she felt helpless as she remained alone in the darkness of Jenner Hoard's sealed bedroom.

She waited for the human thief all that day and night, but he did not come back. She waited the following day and night and still he did not return. On the third day, she realised he would not be coming back to his flat at all, and so she left it, never to return.

It was painful on the streets knowing no one, and she wandered them alone that third night. She'd fed early on - seizing a young woman as she'd jogged along the Embankment beside the Thames, devouring her swiftly, and discarding the corpse over the side into surging waters that were eager to claim her utterly - and then spent the remaining hours watching the black river surge beneath the cold glowering sky. The freezing wind snatched fitfully at her hair but the certainty of what she would have to do snatched at her more. Despite how much she tried to ignore it, she had to relent in the end. She had to find Antoinette once again.

# TWO

## WE HAVE ONLY EACH OTHER NOW

S he found her in the gutter, not two streets from the apartment building inside which Catherine had exacted her revenge. Antoinette had healed little, if any, and looked more like a wraith than a vampire, her flesh torn and hanging in filthy scraps like delicate veils, her face scarred and open as though to let the wind pass effortlessly through. But Catherine felt no pity for her, no remorse for the deeds she had performed. She had done what she had done, and that was all.

Lying amongst refuse that had been dumped and piled at the side of the road, Antoinette seemed no more than rubbish herself, flotsam discarded just like anything else deemed unwanted and left to rot. Her black eyes barely opened when Catherine stood before her. The gleam had gone from them, the sparkle extinguished. She would seduce no one again.

"I have use for you," Catherine said to her. "Get up."

Antoinette said nothing, made no indication that she had even heard her, and remained in her foetal position amongst the rubbish. A truck thundered past, splashing spray across the wet road in spiralling dervishes. The streetlamps illuminated the coiling mist like a kaleidoscope.

Antoinette shivered.

"I said get up. I spared you your life, now it's time to repay my favour."

"You call what you left me life?" Antoinette uttered almost imperceptibly, her face still pressed against the cold rotting matter spilled from torn plastic sacks. "I have nothing now. I may as well be a ghost."

"Your self pity is of no interest. Get up and come with me. We need to leave this city."

"What are you walking about? I don't have to do anything for you."

"You will travel with me."

"Where?"

"South. To Spain."

"For what?"

"For Carlos."

Antoinette said nothing for a while.

Then she simply said: "Leave me alone."

Catherine stared at her for a good long while, the wretch indifferent to the cars that rushed by just inches from her huddled body. She would end up as landfill along with the rest of the rubbish, Catherine knew, and suspected also that this was probably what Antoinette desired most, to be dumped in a world of darkness where she might slowly rot and decay over time, partners with whatever she had been buried along with. But Catherine knew that she could not travel alone to Spain. The wraith vampire was far from ideal but better than nothing, and nothing was all she had right now.

"Come with me," Catherine persevered, her tone almost reasonable now, "and I will give you purpose again. I don't desire to hurt you anymore. That part is done. Forgotten."

"I don't care what you desire. And what you have done will never be forgotten. Do you hear me? Never."

Catherine reached down suddenly and took hold of the rags Antoinette was still dressed in and began to haul her gently out of the refuse. Antoinette, although disfigured and mutilated, was still quick, and lashed out in retaliation.

Her jagged nails found Catherine's face and cut four deep furrows, tracks of blood rising quickly inside of each. Catherine shrieked with rage, recoiled for a moment and then came back at her, yanking at Antoinette's body hard enough to snap it in two.

But she faltered before she did so. She kept the other vampire off-balance, her hold on her still immense.

"I do not want this," Catherine threatened. "I have need of you. Don't make me finish you."

Antoinette hung from her sire's grasp like a puppet, at an awkward angle and not able to make another profitable attack could she even get a chance.

She glared at her, her veins suddenly charged with venom and renewed fury. But this was not the time for revenge, only further pain.

"Why do you need me?" she wanted to know.

"You know how unsafe it is for a vampire to travel between countries, especially across seas, and especially alone. I need another pair of eyes, another set of senses. There is no one else in London, no other vampires to converse with. We are alone, you and I, in this lunatic mortal world. We have only each other now."

Antoinette glared at her.

"Where do we go?" she asked quietly.

"Firstly," Catherine told her, "we go to Dover."

# THREE

## AT THE HARBOUR

It seemed that Catherine Calleh possessed plentiful skills when it came to bringing pain and misery, but next to nothing when it came to the practical skills required with obtaining satisfactory transportation. Antoinette pondered this certainty, wondering whether her sire travelled everywhere on foot because of this ignorance, as she looked for a suitable car to steal.

The night was cold and bleak. Catherine had stripped Antoinette almost naked in Steve's apartment before she'd begun her tortures, removing her clothes before removing her skin, stripping her 'more naked than any whore deserved to be'.

She'd broken her right hand because 'she had held his cock with it'. She had ripped out her cunt because 'his lips had tasted it'. And she had scratched raw every place of flesh that Carlos may have found pleasure in: breasts and buttocks but most of all her face.

When Catherine was done and had left, Antoinette had lain there pleading for death. But immortality was a cruel beast, and she had waited in degrading agony for hours before it seemed certain that she would live.

She'd found a blanket to wrap herself in, and

then staggered outside with only the intention of the approaching dawn undoing her into oblivion.

But she had been too slow. The torturous night had expired, the following day too, and she would have to wait out the lengthy hours of the subsequent night before the next day's sunlight might destroy her.

She had lingered a while as thoughts of revenge began to take seed in her mind – why should she give Catherine the satisfaction of pitiful suicide? – but ultimately the fleshless agony of living each minute was too great, and she had staggered out once more to greet her fate beneath the sun.

Yet Catherine had found her again, hadn't she. She was now to prolong her suffering. And her previous thoughts of revenge clawed their way out of her slough of torment.

The back window broke easily. Inside was the long winter coat she had seen, and Antoinette dragged it over her painful body and drew the hood up over her bloodied face before climbing into the driver's seat. She watched as Catherine hesitantly repeated the movement, unsure even of the simple act of sitting inside a car, and wondered again at how such a scholar of the underworld could be so uneducated of the real world.

Antoinette started the engine with neither key nor tools, another trick she'd learned from her time spent in London. The motions were awkward and painful with the bones of her right hand broken, but they were already mending, bone fragments melding whole once again. Her fingers were disfigured, so badly had Catherine smashed them, and Antoinette guessed they would always remain so, curled and twisted like a crow's claw.

With the engine revving, she put the car into gear and pulled away from the kerb. She was glad of the coat's hood, it shielded Catherine's attention of her. Antoinette did want her to see what she had done to her, even though Catherine made no further mention of her disfigurement, or even registered how broken she felt. So they drove in silence, heading only south towards the coast.

They ended up, however, not in Dover, but in a small town called Cove, at three thirty in the morning. Every light, apart from the dozen or so streetlamps that burned weakly along the short promenade, was out. The town was silent, every soul asleep.

The harbour was small, and only one fishing boat bobbed at the quayside, the yellow light of occupancy spilling across the choppy surface of the sea. They parked beside the harbour wall, extinguished the lights, and moved towards the boat as a stiff salt-laden wind gusted off the sea.

The sky was heavy with swiftly-moving cloud, a bright full moon gilding the edges of the clouds with pearlescent white, beaming like a searchlight whenever it broke through the cloudbanks and illuminating everything with its silver-white wash. Eerie shadows played amongst lobster pots and buoys stacked along the harbour wall. There were two fishermen on board the fishing boat, one old the other young, busy with crates of silver-flanked fish that glistened in the moonlight, hauling them to one side of the boat ready to be unloaded.

The name of the boat, painted in black upon the white peeling hull, read *The Shanty*. Antoinette knew her part in this and slid down silently onto the deck. She approached the older of the two fishermen and took hold of his yellow life-jacket with her left hand, tugging back her hood with her right to reveal her face.

The old man was startled by the contact, a yelp slipping from his throat. He reeled at the sight of her face, his eyes as wide and white at the full moon overhead. His mouth gaped, the yelp stricken, and nothing else came out except a strangled choking breath.

"Take us to France," was all Antoinette said.

But the old man just stared in her grasp.

She heard the young man yell now, and she looked up to observe him dashing across the many obstacles strewn across the small deck towards her. But the moon must have caught her face for as she turned her head to look at him, it fixed him to the boards where he stood.

He staggered as though suddenly drunk, clutching at a stack of crates in order to keep himself upright as the boat rocked beneath his feet, but his gaze refused to leave the horror of the wraith that had visited his boat.

So cruelly butchered was she that she must have appeared to them like a sea-hag risen out of the waters to claim their souls. But she was not a creature of fable. She did not desire their souls, only their vessel and their seamanship, and with the younger of the two fisherman stricken, she turned back to the old man still powerless in her grasp.

"I want you to take us to France," she demanded again. "Do you understand?"

The old man continued to stare at her, his eyes

(like his hair billowed by the wind off the sea), as stark and white as the moon overhead. Then slowly he began to nod under the weight of her intense scrutiny and proximity. This was a nightmare that wasn't going away.

Only when Catherine stepped down into the boat did the two fishermen see the second demon for the first time, her pale expressionless face appearing out of the murk and eerie shadows like a haunted mask, a stark white moon of her own, and their fear doubled.

The younger man stumbled back and tumbled to the ground amongst his nets. And there he stayed as the old man buckled. He tried to escape now but Antoinette held him fast.

"You will take us now," she said. "And before sunrise."

The old man nodded again, hesitantly, terrified, unable to take his eyes off this second creature of the night. He seemed to know that neither of these two women, if they could be called that, were human.

Antoinette released him then, and watched him scurry towards the cabin where he fumbled to start the boat's engine. She turned to see the younger man still lying amongst his nets. He stared back, his hands clenched nervously to inadequate fists inside them.

"Untie the boat," Antoinette said.

Like a slave unable to do anything except what was instructed of him, the younger of the two fishermen struggled to find his feet and then worked his round to the other side of the boat where the huge weathered ropes held the boat at quay, keeping always his front to the two unnatural creatures that stood motionless and studying his every movement.

"Don't try and run," Antoinette warned.

Her words were quiet and measured, but he heard everything she said over the gusting of the cold sea wind as clearly as if they were both inside a small quiet room.

He nodded and slipped the ropes up and off the black steel posts anchored to the harbour wall. Then the boat was riding the waves unfettered and drifting.

Suddenly the engine guttered and then took. It idled badly for a moment or two, and then the revs increased and the boat lurched forward towards the entrance to the harbour.

The waves were already choppy, the boat bucking from side to side as the fishermen took them away from solid land, and away from England. The harbour wall grew smaller behind them as the engine rumbled and the boat rocked steadily on.

They passed the thick boundary bulwark.

The wind gusted.

Then they were out in the open sea.

# FOUR

## WHAT HAPPENED ON THE SHANTY

The journey across The Channel did not seem like a journey at all, but time spent lost inside a vindictive maelstrom. The boat rocked on all sides and rose and pitched upon the building turbulent waves like a fly trapped inside a bottle, shaken hard by an ever inquisitive child. The moon emerged periodically from behind the fast-moving clouds to observe their progress, but sought to illuminate only the surging surface of the sea and the frosted-white wash behind them. Everything else was black and faceless. There was nothing but open sea. No land for endless hours.

Catherine sat inside the small timber cabin with the two fishermen, its interior sparsely furnished with worn and weathered benches and instruments, while Antoinette stood at the rear of the boat, her left hand clasping part of the net winch for support, and watched the motions of the trailing wash. She could see the wounds upon her body clear enough, but with no reflection she had no idea what horror her once beautiful face now showed, only what her fingertips could feel in the furrows and tears of her open wounds.

The evidence of her distressing disfigurement was echoed in how the two fishermen had received her. That had hurt almost as much as the torture. She had spent a lifetime and more worshipped by men because of her innocent beauty. That had been her greatest gift, the reason for her swift despatch of mortals, and her only hope for a prosperous future when times went bad. It was who she was. Now she was a beast, a thing of nightmares, and she had already seen the worst of it in the eyes of the two mortals upon this very boat.

She glanced over her shoulder and saw Catherine sitting inside the shelter of the cabin, the two fishermen beyond her huddled at the wheel, their backs to her to avoid her relentless scrutiny. She hated her, hated everything about her, but knew that there was some truth in what she had said on the streets of London: they were alone, the two of them, and they would indeed need to rely on each other if they were to find a renewed place of safety somewhere. Whether that was in her own homeland of France, or Catherine's ultimate destination of Spain (or even Kar'mi'shah), Antoinette had no idea. But London was dead to her now, as dead as her Stevie who still remained murdered on the floor of his own flat, and had nothing left to offer her anymore but memories of heartache and despair.

She turned back to watch the white trail of hissing foam folding in upon itself behind the boat, the sting of the salt in the air pricking her nose even as it burned inside her open wounds. But her focus was far beyond surface pain.

A mind could get lost inside that churning foam, she was thinking, enough so that the body floundered and toppled, headlong into the icy sea, seconds before that body shut down from the savage cold. Would that cold even kill her? Probably not. There would surely just be more pain to tolerate, more agonies to suffer until she was retrieved from the waters.

Antoinette clung to the net winch with her left hand more tightly. She would not fall. Neither would Catherine, she thought. The pain would be manageable for her, and the retaliation would be insurmountable. Later, she thought. It would have to come much later.

The small fishing boat bobbed and bucked across the swelling English Channel without incident as each hour passed. The banks of gilt-edged clouds began to part and disperse, and the huge glowing moon appeared between them to illuminate the surface of the sea in huge great slabs of dappled white, but revealed only half-whispered promises of land. Filaments of yellow light glimmered weakly on the crest of the horizon like the now-visible stars overhead, a hope that land might sometime be reached, but with many fathoms of cruel sea still beneath their feet, that promise seemed tenuous and fragile.

Dawn crept cautiously across the edges of the night as the sky began to lighten, the coastline of France solidifying out of the uncertain murk of the darkness. There were still hours of travel left and it was uncertain that they would reach land safely and find somewhere to wait out the following day before the sun broke the horizon. Antoinette resisted leaving her solitary vigil at the back of the boat, but her own existence demanded it as well as Catherine's. The other vampire had clearly also noted the sky's brightening for she had already made plans for the day's duration.

Upon her word the older fisherman cut the engine, leaving the boat to drift in silence but for the smack of the waves against the boards of the hull. Catherine then ordered him down into the small galley beneath, while the younger stayed up top to keep watch, with instructions that the old man would be murdered if anything untoward was attempted.

The younger fisherman protested with hesitancy, saying that he would try nothing and would do whatever was asked of him as long as they promised to leave his father alone. So with the two vampires secured below deck and away from the approaching dawn, The Shanty bobbed alone on the surface of the sea, a stone's throw from the coast of France, to wait out the day.

The galley was cramped and dirty, the air putrid with the sourness of stale fish. Lit only by two small portholes, one of either side of the tiny space, they were easily and swiftly covered by heavy tarpaulins that had been stowed inside the cupboards of the kitchenette. Catherine even extinguished the oil lamp as soon as the old man took it down and lit it, with instructions that they would all sit in darkness until sunset.

She told Antoinette to watch him while she slept upon one of the bunks at the far end, but it seemed certain that he was beyond brave heroics anyway. But she did as Catherine demanded, and sat with him until her sire was asleep, and then moved further along the galley closer to where she lay.

Antoinette examined the galley only briefly in the darkness, but confirmed that there was nothing significant with which to attack her, nothing that would tip the balance of the conflict in her favour. She was still deeply injured, after all, too badly disfigured to fight her one on one (could she ever hope or dare to fight her one on one?). She had lost miserably in Stevie's flat. Just how well did she think she could fare in her current state?

Her revenge would not come yet, that much was clear, but there was time aplenty. They were immortal. She had an eternity to wait for the right moment. But it would come, oh yes, and it would be sweet.

# FIVE

## UPON FRENCH SHORES

Sunset was called with the young fisherman's fists upon the galley's hatch. Antoinette unbolted the small doorway and climbed back up into the cabin. The sky was heavy with rain clouds, the wind gusting across the sea with no small amount of fury. The waves still slapped the sides of the boat like the hands of giants, the air still livid with salt. Catherine appeared behind her, took one look at the sky, and then commanded that the engine be restarted and they finally head for shore. The young fisherman hurried to obey her orders, his eye hesitant to leave the galley's hatch where his father had still not yet appeared.

The engine guttered and rumbled as it had done in Cove's harbour, but then roared to life as he feathered the throttle forward. They would be on land in two hours, he told them, but there would be questions asked about an English fishing boat landing in a French harbour. Catherine said nothing to this, but simply glared at him from behind her white unflinching mask.

Antoinette took to standing at the front of the boat this time, watching the coastline growing ever larger. This was where she had been born, a home she had not seen in several decades. It would have changed, of course, just as London had changed. But she had lived through the transformations of England. To see France altered after so long away would be difficult to comprehend. She braced herself for whatever miracles she would see along the way.

"Steer away from the port," Catherine suddenly told the fisherman.

"What?"

"The port you're heading towards. Steer away from it."

"But why?"

"We need to go somewhere discreet, somewhere quiet. Any unpopulated beach you can find."

The fisherman stared at her for a while but her gaze was impenetrable. She would not be argued with, the matter would not be discussed.

His eyes returned to the galley hatch from which his father had still not emerged. He wanted to ask after him but he dared not. Maybe they had put him to strange duties. They concealed themselves from daylight scrutiny after all. What other abnormalities might these creatures consider rational?

He steered the boat away from the well-lit port and focussed on a stretch of low dark shoreline. As they grew steadily closer, so it seemed ideal for his two passengers: there were no buildings of any kind for a mile in either direction, no lights burning at any window, no streetlamps.

As they came within a few hundred yards, he could make out in the dull grey light that the shore was made up of endless dunes facing out to sea. He put his hand to the throttle to slow the engine before the hull grounded, but as he moved so he felt Catherine's icy grip upon his. He flashed a glance towards her but it was already too late. She loomed out of the murk of the cabin, her mask of white splitting in two as fangs sprang open like a trap to consume him.

Before he could even struggle he felt his shoulders seized by some massive force – surely not her arms – and then intense agony seared at his neck. His shirt ran wet, a smell so sickly sweet (it reminded him of childhood treats) rose thickly around him, and he felt his legs buckle beneath him. But he was buoyed up, so strong was the clamp-like hold around his torso, and he did not drop. His legs carried no weight and yet he hung suspended as the woman gorged at the crook of his neck.

He gasped aloud, clutching weakly with his fists only once before his eyes rolled up into his skull. Then his consciousness slipped as blackness rushed in like water through the side of a ship, and Catherine dropped him lifeless to the deck, dead before The Shanty had even run aground on the hissing shingle of the French coast.

"Someone will find the boat," Antoinette warned, as they climbed over the edge of the boat and dropped waist-deep into the freezing sea.

Waves slapped against them as they waded through the thick tide, up onto the beach, but Catherine didn't reply. There was no one in sight in either direction, no lights lit along the desolate shore. Their clothes were soaked from the waist down and clung to them like icy sheets, restricting their movements and paining their numbed bodies.

"You should have left him to sail back. We

226

shouldn't have murder on our trail. Not yet."

"It was you that killed the old man," Catherine retorted now.

"I needed to feed."

And that ended the conversation.

They climbed the slope of the pebble beach towards the ridge, the headwind that gusted over the top of it chilling their soaked clothes even more, and looked down across an expanse of nothingness. Lights designated a population some miles beyond, and it was towards this that they now trekked. It would be a few miles walk across uncomfortable terrain, but they would at least arrive unseen and anonymous.

The weight of fresh blood in Antoinette's stomach had been gratefully welcomed, her strength returning swiftly to her in warming waves. Their journey would be long, their unrelenting vigilance necessary, and to be weak with deprived senses would leave them vulnerable to a great many things. She knew first-hand the skulkers that watched the streets of London, and she would be foolish indeed to think that France did not have its counterpart, not just on the streets of major cities, but anywhere that vampires had designated safe places to feed and grow strong.

As they walked across the uneven terrain, the wind harrying them with every step, Antoinette dared to turn her mind to fancy, and wondered if they might return to the mansion houses they had frequented a century and more ago, perhaps even to the house inside which she had lived as a mortal, the house where Catherine and Carlos had first encountered her and made her what she was. Maybe the family still owned it, or maybe they had been driven out or lost their fortune as had so many families at that time of war and revolt. It would matter little. To see the house and wander its grounds again would satisfy only a passing whim. The building would have rotted over time as she had remained the same (with the exception of what Catherine had done to her), but to visit the past might bring some pleasure with it.

The only part of Catherine's agenda that Antoinette had been allowed to know was her compulsion to find her husband once again. To view old haunts had surely not entered her head. What would be the point anyway? Would Carlos be sentimental about his past enough to return there himself? Probably not, was the answer.

With no shelter across the expanse of shingle, the wind gusted strong and cold, whipping their hair to snakes and forcing ice shards through their slowly-drying clothes. Neither of them spoke – what, indeed, was there to say? – until they approached the outskirts of the town, and even then it was only practical. Transport was a must, Antoinette would be expected to steal another car, and as they found the first tarmac road which headed into the small town, Antoinette studied the first vehicles they came upon.

They could not afford to be choosy. If the coastguard or the police, or hell even a passing dog-walker, came upon the boat and the drained bodies inside, the streets would be thick with authorities. Their journey would be over, or at least inconvenienced, before it had even begun.

She settled quickly upon a fairly new Peugeot, and after smashing the rear window and clambering inside, Antoinette set about starting the engine as she had done so before. Once again Catherine was wary about climbing inside. She seemed to view at as something far beyond alien. But once seated and relatively settled, and with the engine fired and revving, the two vampires stole away into the night in their unlikely transportation.

The road signs were all for small coastal towns Antoinette had never heard of before, so she tried to head south as best as she could. Only after twenty minutes of silence did Catherine offer any kind of guidance to Antoinette's blind driving.

"Head East," was all she said.

"What for?"

"We should go to Paris first."

Antoinette stared at her as the car hurtled down the narrow country roads.

"What for?" she asked again.

"It was where we spent many wonderful years, before you came, before everything went wrong."

## SIX

## TO SEARCH A CITY, A COUNTRY

Catherine led Antoinette through boulevards lined with tall three storey terraced houses that seemed to hang over the narrow thoroughfares, until they came to a stone archway that led through to the Rue du Lac. The houses here were older but stood just as tall and oppressive, their black timber frames and white rendered facades describing a period almost long forgotten. They were stacked one after the other, terraced on both sides, the cobbled passage that ran between them suitable only for the single horse-drawn carriages they had been designed for. No cars were parked along its length and no pedestrians shared the uneven pathways this night. The air was quiet, the windows all unlit, but Catherine navigated the darkness of the thoroughfare as though it was only yesterday that she had been here.

She came to a halt in front of one of them, its wide black door studded and braced with beaten metal.

"Why are we here?" Antoinette asked behind her.

But Catherine remained silent, distant.

It had been their home during a much better time, an opulent time of banquets and balls, of stealing into the higher circles of society and feeding on both the culture and the aristocracy. Their love had grown, blossomed like night orchids, and they had seen every luxurious corner of Paris.

They had danced to symphonies, they had revelled in wealth, they had partaken in every extravagance they or their mortal counterparts could devise. But then the war had come, and all that they had known and cherished turned to rot and ruin. The symphonies stopped, the money dried up, and the rich went to ground.

Danger came to the streets, even for them, and they had fled too. In the darkness of the Rue du Lac Catherine could see Carlos's ghostly figures writhing amongst the shadows of the house, just as they had writhed amongst the shadows of Jenner Hoard's apartment.

But here they were more real than they had been before. Here they seemed to have weight, seemed to have purpose.

Whether they had come here of their own accord or hitched a ride inside her head, it did not matter, they were still searching for something lost, something unobtainable, lingering in places that brought comfort from another time.

Her husband's ghosts were here, but he was not.

Had he even been here in person? She did not know. But the only thing that was certain was that he was not here now.

She turned away suddenly, and began walking back the way they had come.

"Where are you going?" Antoinette called, hurrying after her.

But Catherine did not answer her. She hurried instead towards the river and the embankment along which she and Carlos had loved to walk. There was no moon tonight to bathe the scene in its silvery wash as it had once done before, shrouded as it was by the heavy rain clouds that were just managing to hold their torrents at bay, but there were still plenty of unnatural shadows to behold.

Carlos's ghosts were here in vast numbers too, hanging from statues, climbing bridges and buildings, black contorting infants swarming stonework and midnight gardens in their relentless search of something long since vanished.

Had he been here, Catherine thought, these unnatural children echoes of his presence?

They seemed not to see her, or if they did made no decision to approach her.

Maybe Carlos had not been here but was still seeing everything. Perhaps these things were his eyes, or maybe manifestations of idle thoughts, whimsies of a life he had once spent. Catherine did not know. The only thing that seemed certain was that Carlos was not here now either.

They went not to the car they had stolen at the coast but to one parked close by, which they broke into and drove south out of the city. Catherine attempted to navigate, not by road signs but by figures that seemed to cling to fragments remembered from a lost time – a farm house, a lamppost, a tree silhouetted upon a jagged crest. Her husband's ghosts had seemingly been dispatched everywhere his mind could remember, routes they had travelled, places they had stopped to wait out the lethal daylight hours. It was not a suitable means of navigation, and surely the slowest. Many times they took wrong turns to find no trace of his presence, and had to turn back in an attempt to pick up the trail once again.

That first night seemed to expire without any conclusion, but Catherine was resolute in how she would search for her husband: she would follow these ghosts that crawled across the landscape like a ship tracking beacons left to burn across a faceless sea.

So that was how they travelled, finding safe haven during the day, pursuing ghostly shadows at night. Across France they journeyed in this way, days passing to weeks, weeks passing to months, all without sign of Carlos, just following his nightly children left to explore half-remembered ground in his wake.

Many times Antoinette urged Catherine to give up her hunt, to see reason and end so fruitless a search. But she would not. And nor could Antoinette leave her. They were all they had in the world now, just each other, and so Antoinette continued to travel with her sire across the murk of the European landscape.

That first year faded into a second, and they ultimately crossed the border into Spain, following Carlos's ghosts towards his birthplace. His minions crawled across the terrain like ants across a mountain of sugar, yet there remained no physical sign of him, no clue that he had even been this way. A further year passed and their search became more and more ragged and desperate as his children thinned and died, until every conceivable route dried up and ended in failure. Then, and only then, after three long years, did Catherine finally relent. And only then did she agree to return to London, and to the only route home to Kar'mi'shah.

PART SIX

ADVENTURES IN A NEW WORLD

## ONE

## UNVEILING

Kensington, London – April 2003: It was indeed a strange sight to behold, a vast swathe of gaudy parkland and glistening steel and glass, forced into a section of London that had been grey for so much of its recent life.

Kensington had been a hectic throng for as long as anyone could remember, and for those that could remember, having this theme park driven right into its heart seemed a pretentious violation, a grand spectacle of tasteless wealth, despite the miraculous wonders that it promised.

Promised not offered, that was the significant difference, because to enter such a place was by invitation only, and for those without a famous face or pockets deep enough to line those of its owners, that invitation was not cheap.

It had been the subject of much debate since the area had first begun to be cleared and levelled, office buildings and hotels stripped and demolished to make way for just one grand temple-like structure, surrounded on all sides by palatial gardens and a tall perimeter fence. It was said that the initial scrabble for ownership over the land had been fierce and bloody, and that those that did not take the highest of offers ended up the target of the most secret of murders. Fortunes had allegedly been made, millionaires fashioned overnight, and dignitaries disgraced at an even swifter pace. Anyone who opposed the ideal fell by the wayside on the way to make this place possible.

It had also been reported that never before had so lucrative an opportunity come along, and yet so secret was the entire project that nobody had even said for sure just what it was that had been causing such monstrous disruption.

A consortium of unheard-of names had risen quickly onto the lips of the media, rising higher than the names of the industrialists and multinationals whose monies fell suddenly and pitifully into shadow, their secret funds buying buildings and the land surrounding the buildings, swallowing a vast section of London whole.

It was rumoured that this consortium had bought the largest and most valuable commodity in all the world, and yet still no one had known just what that commodity was that they had bought. Not until the day their figurehead building had come to be unveiled.

A plaque had been set in the grounds behind the tall steel gates, shielded behind a scarlet curtain that would be drawn at the grandest of ceremonies and in full view of the world's press.

On April 15th 2003, four members of this mysterious consortium addressed those that had been invited to witness the unveiling of what had been dubbed The Eighth Wonder Of The World. And there in front of the world's media they drew back the curtain to reveal the name of the shrine upon which they had spent hundreds of millions of pounds and three years preparing.

Gasps had risen from the gathered crowd as cameras clicked like a swarm of gargantuan locusts. Could any of them dare to believe their eyes now they could all see it for themselves? Could any of them dare to believe it was true?

Engraved upon the stone plaque was just one simple word etched in gold gothic lettering: Eden.

# TWO

## THE BLUE CHAMBER

The populace thronged outside the gates, their glimpse of the spectacle and the ceremony surrounding it more crowded than any other tourist attraction in the capital, and with good reason. What could compare with a glimpse of another land, another city that basked beneath the glow of another sky?

Did the people live in houseboats that sparkled like glittering stars? Were the trees heavy with intelligent monkeys that sang lilting songs? Were the rivers stocked with fish or gold? Were the hills alive with wolves or dragons? So many questions, so many hopes, and all of them fuelled by scraps of nonsense brought back from those few souls who had made the trip back to the world of mundane human existence.

It was the lack of knowledge that aggravated so many people, contrasting accounts that conflicted with each other over and over again.

A number of television crews had been sent from the PaceNet News Group, allowed passage to bring back reports of this magnificent Eighth Wonder. The only problem with the plans laid by news stations and documentary makers was that they seldom returned, and when they did, they came

240

home armed with reels of gibberish, their tapes burned and blurred - interference or radiation, it was claimed - and thus destroying any useful footage.

Some made money from newspaper interviews, others checked themselves into mental institutions where paid staff would listen to anything they had to say. It was a difficult time, those first few months, when news of the revelation came to the masses in desperately short staccato bursts.

Some came to bear witness to this new world, others simply stayed at home and ridiculed such idiocy. But sooner or later, everybody listened, and the truth about another existence took hold.

"We'll never get through this lot," Ben exclaimed, trying to push his way through the crowd that was just as eager to keep him behind them.

"But we've got passes," Annie replied. "They have to let us in."

"I'd keep quiet about that, if I were you, and for Christ's sake put them back in your bag or someone'll grab 'em before we get a chance to say who we are."

Annie Randall clutched the two passes to Eden tightly in her hand. She'd thought they'd only have to get to the main gate and then they'd be whisked inside. It was twenty past eleven in the morning, their departure scheduled for twelve noon, and they had only managed to move about five hundred yards in the last hour, so thick was the crowd.

The gate was just up ahead, a vast elaborate structure of gold-tipped steel that glinted in the summer sunlight. Beyond that, groves of emerald green trees swayed in the light breeze, lining a boulevard that stretched on towards a glorious building of burnished gold and steel and glass that was itself the gateway to Eden.

Everyone knew the name of this place and the wonder that it contained, the biblical reference was immaterial. They were here to report on what lay beyond the threshold, and to bring back drawings and sketches of what they saw. Digital tapes and media could be destroyed. Paper drawings, although crude, were now the best alternative.

"I see a gap," Ben yelled over his shoulder, pushing his way hard between two men in front of him.

Annie looked past him and saw where the crowd had thinned, and followed quickly in his footsteps for fear of losing him altogether.

Guests were led across the portal only at midday, and anyone arriving late simply missed their turn. If you weren't there, you would get no second invitation. It was as simple as that.

They had hoped to be inside the gates of Eden by ten, giving themselves a couple of hours to report on the shrine itself as well as to prepare a few sketches of the grounds and the portal itself. At their present rate they were more concerned about whether or not they would even have someone to show their passes to.

There was a line of security guards in front of the gates, all dressed in black uniforms and peaked caps. They checked Ben and Annie's passes when they finally reached them and allowed both her and Ben entry through the gates, where two more guards checked their pockets and clothes, before going through their bags.

Annie stood back and watched them. There was

nothing in there apart from a few changes of clothes and her art materials. She'd been told to go light, one holdall only, even though the information about what she was to expect on the other side had been vague to say the least.

Ben had a large green rucksack, and the two guards now set their attentions on that, pulling out sweaters and jeans and opening every zipped compartment they could find. Neither Annie nor Ben asked them just what they were looking for, but simply stood and watched quietly as the crowd behind them continued to jostle for the best view of just what might happen next.

With their bags repacked and returned, Annie and Ben hurried along the tree-lined thoroughfare towards the tall entrance to the main building itself. As they stepped through the heavily laminated glass doors, two men dressed in expensive suits came over to greet them.

"Miss Randall and Mr Weaver?" one of the two men asked.

Annie nodded. Ben said yes.

"Come this way, please," he went on, indicating a set of double doors at the back of the foyer. "We don't have much time."

They went with the two men without another word. Everything seemed so formal, so rigid and ceremonial, and it felt almost as though they had arrived late for some royal function.

They walked along a marble corridor until they arrived at an elegant lift which they rode to the fourth floor. Everything was new and manicured to the highest splendour, and Annie could not help thinking that there had been some kind of cruel mix-up and she had come in someone else's place, that sooner or later someone would put their hand on her shoulder and tell her that she'd been found out.

Not even Ben said a word. She glanced across at him and saw the sweat on his face, saw him swallow with anxiety, and guessed he was every bit as nervous as her. She wanted him to look at her, if only to exchange a nervous smile, but he just looked straight ahead, staring at the lift doors.

They stepped out of the lift in silence, and walked briskly to a service desk where a woman in a dark blue dress was busy at a computer terminal. She looked up at them as they approached, and held her hand out for their passes before slipping them into a tray on her desk. The two men waited behind as Annie and Ben now followed this woman deeper into the building.

At a blue glass door, the woman passed a swipe card through a reader, and stepped back to allow them passage through. Only then did Annie and Ben exchange glances, and Annie could see the terror in his eyes, and knew that he did not want to go on.

He lingered momentarily at the doorway, and she saw him swallow hard again, but the weight of where they were and what was expected of them seemed to carry him on, and he stumbled through, glancing back at her over his shoulder as he went.

The blue glass door closed behind them with a heavy metallic click, and they found themselves in a tall circular chamber, domed at the top, and made of the same blue glass panels as the door they had just come through.

The glass imbued the room with a kind of calm luminescence that seemed almost extraterrestrial, as though they had just stepped onto some amazingly expensive film set, suddenly deserted by actors and crew at lunchtime. At the centre of the blue room, however, was a column of nothingness. The room was empty of everything but this ethereal void. And it looked more like a smudge in space than anything else, a blur that remained motionless at the centre of the chamber.

Annie looked across at Ben but he could not take his eyes off it. He was staring wide-eyed at it, his throat bobbing as he swallowed repeatedly, sweat glistening on his skin and running in rivulets at his temple and down across his neck.

He was pale and looked like he was going to pass out. She wanted to put a hand on his, to tell him that it was all okay, but she suspected that he would leap away from her with shock at her proximity. She wasn't even sure if he still knew whether she was even in the same room with him or not.

Annie wondered whether they should have been given more information about all this.

"So this is the hole in the world, is it?" she murmured quietly, her eyes returning to the portal.

Ben didn't reply, or even move, but just stared straight ahead at the blurred smudge that had cost the mysterious consortium so many millions of pounds.

"I'll flip you for who goes first," he said finally, his voice dry and without humour.

"You're coming with me," she told him, and grabbed hold of his arm.

He resisted at first, his eyes still focussed on the gateway. But he ultimately relented, and took the first tentative steps with her towards the portal.

The closer they got, the more they realised that the portal was making a kind of low droning sound, not so much a buzz like an electrical motor, but more like the long drawn-out moaning of something dying. The edges of the column danced like ghostly fronds, fluttering in the air like the fragile tentacles of sea anemones, motes of light flickering along their lengths like tiny fireflies.

The centre of the column was dark and hollow-looking, and seemed to have no visible end. Annie swallowed now as she gazed into it, thinking how prophetic her earlier words had been, for it did indeed look like a hole in the world, an unnatural chasm that had no place being there.

She glanced across at Ben again. He looked nervous, as though he was going to throw up, and she thought that he had no business here either, not anymore. But she also knew that she sure as hell wasn't going in there alone.

She pulled on his sleeve, coaxing him forward, and after a moment's hesitation took another step towards the doorway that would carry her away from the only world she had ever known. They were less than five yards from its gaping mouth now, and Annie could almost feel something against her skin, a breath against her face, a foreign wind that carried mystifying fragrances she had never smelt before. It seemed to reach for her, to entice her closer, but before her mind could even suggest the possibility of this being a trap, Ben had made the decision for them both, and had lurched forward with his eyes clenched shut, his mouth open to inhale whatever winds were coming their way.

Annie felt herself hauled after him into the

blackness, her fingers clenching Ben's shirt in a tightly-balled fist. He wasn't getting away from her easily, and he wasn't going to be leaving her alone in there either.

Her left foot landed on the tiled floor of the chamber as she stumbled forward, but her right foot dropped into nothingness. Panic rose swiftly up into her throat but it was already too late. With nothing to grab hold of to haul herself back, and with Ben already one step ahead of her, the void consumed her quickly, sealing itself behind her until she was encompassed utterly by blackness.

The same winds that had lightly touched her cheek now raged inside the chasm, swirling in dervishes, although she couldn't be sure whether she was falling or not. Her fist still grasped Ben's shirt, but she could no longer see him. She could see nothing around her anymore, not even her own hand. All she was aware of were the hot winds pressing hard against her skin and in her hair, and the darkness that had taken hold of her like a vast caressing hand.

There was only one certainty now.

Eden had them.

# THREE

## A VIEW OF KAR'MI'SHAH

There was no landing or sudden jolt at the end, or if there was she had passed out in the maelstrom and missed it. Annie opened her eyes to a group of people that stood watching her. Ben's shirt was no longer in her fist, but she found him sitting in another chair a few yards away from her, holding his head in one hand and a glass of water in the other.

"How do you feel?" a woman in front of her asked.

She was wearing a white coverall. Annie guessed she must be one of the medical staff. She actually gave the question due thought, mentally feeling around inside her head for damage. Everything seemed to be where it was supposed to be. Her thoughts seemed to work at least.

"Fine," she said at last. "What's wrong with Ben?"

The woman turned to look at him.

"Just a little headache," she said with a caring smile. "We've given him something for it. He should be fine soon."

A man in dark-coloured robes appeared through a glass door at the far end of the room and spoke to two men who stood there. When all three of them looked her way, Annie wondered just what was going on. The new arrival walked towards her, his full-length robes billowing around him, a smile already on his face, and he offered a hand to her as he reached her.

"Annabel Randall?"

"Annie, yes."

"Hello Annie. My name is Marcus Lawson and I will be looking after you while you're here."

"Hello, Mr Lawson," she said to him, taking his hand now and shaking it. "Tell me, is all this really necessary?"

"All what?"

"All these people. I thought we'd just be coming here and doing some investigative work for PaceNet News."

"My dear," he began, "it's not like you've just stepped off a plane and might be suffering a mild bout of jet-lag. You've just stepped across a border into a world few people have ever witnessed. You're a couple of dozen people short of being a pioneer, but this is still something special, and experimental. We're still not quite sure what happens to the human body when it comes through."

"I thought it was safe," Annie protested, starting up out of her chair.

"It seems to be, I'll tell you that much."

"What about Ben? Is he hurt?""

Marcus Lawson glanced at the woman in the white coverall.

"He just has a bit of a headache," she told him.

"There you are, you see?" he told Annie with a glittering grin. "Think of it as a hangover. He's had quite a ride. Both of you have."

Annie let it go and just looked at the pair of them. It was clear that this conversation wasn't going to go anywhere further.

She pushed herself out of her chair and picked up her bag which was sitting on the floor beside her.

"If you're our guide," she said to him, forcing the momentum forward, "where are you going to take us first?"

Lawson smiled at them both now with genuine pride for his new world, and they followed him out of the medical room, Ben still holding his head in one hand, and descended a flight of steps into a long hallway lined with tall gothic windows.

A vast panoramic vista stretched out towards a horizon of jagged black mountains like nothing they had ever seen before. Lush verdant pastures were laid out in irregular patterns, clusters of clay huts nestled amongst them, homes to the workers dotted throughout the fields tending either animals or crops. At the outskirts of a city stood more buildings of a sturdier construction, laid out in conforming districts, beyond which stood vast stone buildings and temples, rising high amid towering columns.

Some areas stood devoted to low buildings, others to higher three or four storey dwellings. Some boulevards ran lined with tall palm trees, others sat on higher ground or raised plateaux. But through it all wound a wide glittering river, boats and barges scattered along its length at full sail. This whole new world looked both alien and yet familiar, yet still as captivatingly wonderful as had been promised.

They descended another flight of steps into a grand hall, with yet more windows that offered an enticing view of the environment they would soon be stepping out into. Two huge doors stood open at the far end of the hall, and already they could feel the dry heat of the wind on their faces, the sweet smell of wild flowers mixed with the salt from the estuary heady on its back.

When they reached the doorway and stepped outside for the first time on a parapet above another flight of stone steps that led down to the street, uninterrupted views spread out before them like some undreamt-of magic carpet, the full heat of the wind lifting Annie's hair as it caressed her face, and bringing with it a myriad of aromatic and sharp smells to her nose.

She breathed them all in as she gazed out over the city she and Ben would be spending the next few weeks in, her eyes hungry to see every new sight, her ears searching out every new sound from the farms and the winding river beyond, her hands desperate to touch every opulent and wondrous surface. She turned to find Marcus Lawson staring at her, a grin of satisfaction upon his face.

"Now you see why I wanted this," he said to her, his smile infectious.

He looked like a child busy with cherished games, and Annie couldn't help but smile back at him. Politics were for another time. Now she was happy to just look out upon a sight unseen by most of her species.

Most would never see it, that was a fact, and others would scrabble like wild dogs for just a glance at something beyond their mundane everyday existence. She was here to look at it all, to draw whatever she could experience, and bring back images of her journey to her tribe.

A distressing thought suddenly reared in her head that her box of artist's tools, her pencils and her paints, her charcoals and her pastels, would be hopelessly insufficient to portray such wonderful sights, and would fail to fully justify her subjects. But perhaps she didn't need to bring back photographic-like evidence. Perhaps just a taster would be enough to entice more people to visit, encourage them to see a sight that needed to be seen. Was that not a greater role? Not just to report, but to be an ambassador, to lure people to see this Eden for themselves?

A horse-drawn carriage waited for them at the bottom of the stone steps, and Annie saw that even the building which housed the portal home was pyramid-like in structure, a temple for a journey that people here might take to another world known only to them as Earth.

Commonplace and familiar to her, it would be a fantasy to any traveller here to see firstly the sights of London, and then the rest of England, and then to explore the differing landscapes of Europe and North America and beyond.

Annie wished, as the carriage started forward, drawn by two huge ebony horses, that she had brought pictures of her homeland with her, so that she could exchange images of London for images of Kar'mi'shah, swap like for like, and spread the world of a new existence for them all.

She realised that her heart was hammering, and she dug out one of her sketch pads from her bag and became busy with it, catching only some of Lawson's commentary as she eagerly made rough pencil outlines of the scenes they passed: men busy with hand tools in the fields or resting beneath the boughs of trees, the species of which she could not recognise; women stepping outside huts to watch the new arrivals, hands up to their eyes to shield them from the fierce sun; children skipping along irrigation trenches, or chasing after dogs in play; horse-drawn wagons laden with crops, jerking along rutted tracks. Every sight was new and needed to be recorded, but as their carriage travelled and clattered along the street, so each one disappeared and became something else, something new to witness, and something that demanded taking back to London.

The pages continued to turn in her sketch book, some sketches little more that a handful of marks achieving notation of something that might be elaborated upon later, or might even make no sense at all. But as they travelled, Annie did not care. She had to draw it all. To miss one sight was not to tell the whole story, and to not do that would break her heart.

She only heard Lawson's words as a distraction, a drone lost somewhere in the background of colour and form. It was not important what he was telling them, they would find it all for themselves in due course when they were both finally let loose to explore the city. For now she was happy with the pencil in her hand. It was both her contribution and her devotion to both worlds.

# FOUR

## BOUNTY FROM THE VIENNE

Ben Weaver, PaceNet News
14th May 2003

I must admit that I was somewhat apprehensive about setting out in such a small fishing boat, but the waters of the glittering Vienne were alluring despite how choppy they seemed, the captain of this one-man trawler allaying my fears at frequent intervals as we stood upon the dock.

I had been told that Meelo Cassadres, fisherman and father of seven, could speak hardly any English, and he offered me little in the way of dialogue except short utterances I could barely understand. Even as he untied the vessel from the dock in the northern part of Kar'mi'shah, aboard which we would spend the next few hours, his face wore a broad smile (at my discomfort or at his vigorous labour I could not tell), but I sat at the back of the boat nevertheless and watched him haul his single sail high to catch the early morning breeze.

The sun had only just crested the mountains as we set out, the boat ducking and rolling as Meelo steered us out into the strong current of the Vienne. But no sooner had the river caught us in its surging grasp, than I began to spot the first of the teeming shoals of fish that we were heading out to catch.

Meelo pointed out the vast shoals of tiny beaded fish that billowed beneath us in great swathes of gold, their backs glinting brightly with the light of this new day as they rose towards the surface. I myself have never been much of a fisherman, but I had never seen fish such as these before.

His English, as I've said, was poor, but he pointed down into the waters to call them Mau, confirming a species that I had never heard of before. They were as beautiful as they were swift, darting in uniform blankets down into the depths one minute, returning to the surface with iridescent brightness the next, but always moving so quickly that I could never get a proper look at them. Further on, we came across a large slow-moving dolphin-like animal, that had squat legs and a series of fins that ran the length of its back. This too I indicated to my captain, and he replied with a series of words I could not disentangle. He smiled at my frown of confusion, and then simply pointed down at the creature, even as it descended into the darkest waters and out of sight, and offered a word that sounded like the French 'mon ami'. I was left with the impression that this was a friendly creature of the river such as our own beloved dolphin.

I could not help my wonder growing as we continued upstream, out of the limits of the city and on into agricultural land. I could still make out the spires and the pyramids of the metropolis that reached out of the lush greenery of the palm tops, but the landscape had shifted irrevocably as I'd studied the waters; scattered farm buildings dotted the ripening fields at frequent intervals, herds of cattle and sheep grazing on wide verdant pastures.

Two children had come to the waters edge to play, and now looked across at us as we sailed by. I waved to them and was pleased when they waved back.

My former anxiety of this trip had disappeared, I realised, and the breeze that lifted the warm scent off the Vienne for me to smell seemed like some wonderful opiate. Glancing across at Meelo, who was now busying himself with his nets, I could see the echoes of the smile that he had first worn at the dock. His hands were rough, no doubt from a lifetime working this stretch of river, but this seemed a good work, a labour that brought its own rewards. I felt the happiness of his being here in this place, bobbing on the surface of the Vienne, the bustle of the city behind us and the crisp warming sunlight that glittered across the rippled waters, while all the time awaiting a catch that would soon feed his family of seven, and bring a handsome price in the markets for whatever was left.

With the nets cast and spanning an arc at least one hundred yards across, we both sat back to watch the day progress. The sun rose steadily, brightening the day yet further, while the boat bobbed effortlessly with a lilting rhythm as the sounds of the cattle and the sheep and the children dappled the background with a dreamy watercolour haze.

Occasionally the river would offer up a hollow plop as a fish broke the surface to catch an insect foolishly trapped by the magnet of the water, or the low boom of a mon-ami would echo around the tall reeds in the shallows, but otherwise the day gave no surprise and no incident.

I could feel my heart beating steadily in the cave of my chest. I could feel my burdens seeping out through my feet, down into the wooden hull and out into the swelling Vienne.

After an hour or so of blissful meditation, Meelo stood up from his calm to begin the process of hauling in his nets. The sudden motion was unexpected, but far from unwelcome, and I stood up also to offer my help. The boat listed dangerously to one side as I did so, and even as I grabbed the small mast to steady myself, he waved me back to my seat with another smile and one of his huge weathered hands, and I was only too glad to oblige.

As I sat and watched this man with a feeling of ineptitude, so came in the nets, one after the other, with surprising swiftness, the cargo of fish and crustacean spilling out across the floor of the boat in long slippery piles, slapping and fighting in an attempt to return to their watery home.

Meelo ignored them all until he had hauled in all of his nets, and then he proceeded to sift through the bulk of his catch. I watched in awe as those two huge hands sifted through this mosaic of thrashing flanks with all the delicacy and efficiency of a seamstress, plucking the small and the thin out of the catch and flicking them over the side of the boat and back into the womb of the Vienne, and sorting the bounteous catches into neat piles.

After perhaps only a few short minutes of skilful labour, his trawl of fat healthy fish lay in order across the wooden boards, the only movement the occasional fin offering one last twitch of life.

Hoisting his sail skyward once more, we turned in a effortless arc, and began our river-bound voyage back to the dock at the northern end of Kar'mi'shah, a bountiful song booming at the back of the fisherman's throat.

The effects of the gateway to this world plays havoc with many of the things I take for granted. My watch had stopped as soon as I had set foot on this wondrous land and therefore offered no guide as to the time, but the sun was close to its zenith and all I could guess was that it was close to midday.

The children who had played at the water's edge had gone, returned home for perhaps either lunch or schoolwork, but the cattle and the sheep remained in their wide pastures, grazing and lowing until the day would edge once more towards dusk.

The breeze filled our small sail overhead and carried us back without incident. We were shortly at dock alongside other similar fishing vessels, most of which were far larger than ours, where Meelo tied up our boat before offering me his hand to help me back onto solid ground.

I stood back a few steps as I watched him unload his hefty bounty, feeling awkward once again because I could offer only hindrance instead of help, and with a feeling of being little more than a reporter in life. Meelo seemed not to care, however, and when he had loaded up his barrow with the fish he had caught, he beckoned for me to follow him along the busy thoroughfare out of the dock and on towards the marketplace.

What happens there I shall chronicle in my next report.

# FIVE

## EXPLORING THE CITY

They travelled through Kar'mi'shah together, Annie and Ben, left alone by Marcus Lawson to explore at their own pace and with their own open agenda. It seemed to work fine. They had approached numerous street traders and city dwellers, to either interview them or simply to exchange words, and Ben had even gotten lucky with a local fisherman who had taken him out on his boat. Despite the fact that the fisherman spoke virtually no English, they had both managed to strike up an agreeable discourse using only hand and facial expressions. For Annie it had been wonderful to watch, and had begun sketching the fisherman in his layers of cloth wrapped around his waist and across his shoulders. It seemed then that a friendship had been struck between them, despite their differences in background and language, and it seemed like one that would pay great dividends for them during their time there.

While some of the people they had met spoke either good English or variants thereof, there were those that could not speak it at all and used a native tongue which they could not decipher. However, they seemed a friendly people, diverse in many respects, and Annie managed several rough portraits of those she came across in a variety of different coloured mediums.

The metropolis, as a whole, was a wonder in itself. Having come from a relatively modern city like London, both Annie and Ben found it both strange and uplifting to walk along cobbled streets lined with clay tenements. There were no glazed windows, only wooden shutters to keep out the dust and bustle of the streets. No homes were fed by electricity, but instead oil lamps burned at night, even oil-burning streetlamps lighting busy open plazas and thoroughfares.

The inhabitants wore no suits but dressed in a variety of robes and gowns, some bedecked with gold and precious jewellery, others with what looked like home-made wooden bangles and neckwear. It reminded Annie in many ways of North African towns from a distant age, more specifically Egypt from centuries long past, and to also see stone pyramids and other temples set in the heart of glorious squares only added to the feeling.

But here and there she found examples of modern infiltration, and saw more of them as they walked through streets and markets, assuming that some people may have been using the portal for commuting between the two worlds and bringing back some of what they found.

Most of the people of Kar'mi'shah wore sandals that looked locally crafted, but occasionally someone would pass wearing highly polished black boots or running shoes. There seemed to be little evidence of an accurate system for measuring time, and yet a richer-looking gent might be seen sporting a wristwatch, perhaps wearing it as just another item of fine jewellery. Where civilian's robes were usually worn simply, she discovered that it was not uncommon to see an item boasting a Lacoste badge or a Calvin Klein logo.

## SIX

## THE PRICE OF FISH

Ben Weaver, PaceNet News
14th May 2003

You may well remember the bountiful catch of fresh fish that the fisherman, Meelo Cassadres, had caught earlier this morning. Well I shall now tell you all about the trading that went on afterwards.

It was only a short walk from the dock to the marketplace, a walk that seemed effortless for the fisherman and his barrow laden with glittering fish straight from the Vienne. So many other traders passed us on this route, other fishermen with similar catches, more still with brown and scarlet lobsters the likes of which Meelo had thrown back, vendors laden with brightly-patterned woven cloths and blankets, livestock on short halters, fruit carriers, basket makers, all either coming in from other places or heading back to boats that would return them. It was such a wonderful sight for me to see all of this, like a snapshot of some ancient way of life before the encroachment of modern ways and monetary greed. As dazzling and exciting as the spectacle of this thoroughfare was, it was nothing compared to the bustle and throng of the marketplace itself when at last I laid my eyes upon it.

I had been to bazaars in Egypt and Israel before,

which would be the nearest likeness I could possibly ascribe to the scene before me, yet even that comparison would fall too far short. I had been brought to a vast courtyard in between two large tenement buildings, before a vast ornate temple and sprawling gardens of rich decorative beauty.

Virtually the entirety of the courtyard was crammed with busy stalls and enclosures, each one of them selling something unique, handmade, farmed or caught. Meelo paused briefly as I stood and gazed in wonder at this spectacle, staring bewildered at everything there was here for people to buy or trade. But we were soon off walking again, heading deep into the market where Meelo hoped to sell his silver-flanked crop, and I followed on, bedazzled by everything that was on offer.

The selection of brightly-coloured weaves that I had seen on my way to this place was only a fraction of what was being offered here for sale. I saw stalls draped in rich silks and the finest of delicate cloths. I came upon vendors walking between these stalls offering gowns and fine clothes made of such exquisite veils that it was possible to see their hands through them. So fine were all these things that I felt as though I had trespassed into some majestic wardrobe, a dressing area inside a palace. Yet these were all for the populace, a myriad of garments available to everyone.

I passed a series of stalls selling musical instruments crafted from wood and glass, some stringed, some not, but as they were picked up for demonstration and played, so they gave off the sweetest of music.

Beyond that, sellers were busy handing out

samples of home-made foodstuffs - cubes of meat that melted before they could be chewed, candies so sweet that they enticed the tongue with a desire for more - and further and further into the market we went, the more the foodstuffs became more varied and less able to be refused.

The air, although heavy with voices and music, vied for dominance with the rich aromas and spices rising up from a multitude of fires, griddles and boiling pots. All around me there came new sights to see, something different I had not yet witnessed, and I am afraid to say that I lost Meelo to the crowd and ended up wandering alone but contentedly so.

I found him probably an hour or so later, and I realised that if I had only followed my nose I would have found him sooner. Fully a quarter of the market was taken over with agricultural produce - fish, fruit and meat - all laid out and being sold by the kilo (or its local equivalent). I went to Meelo, who showed me both a handful of coins (which I presumed by his wide grin was a lot of money), as well as his barrow which was significantly heavier with traded items of bread, meat flanks and apples. His morning's work had been bountiful indeed, and I left him shortly after that, he to return to his family, and myself to investigate more wonders of this wonderful bustling marketplace.

# SEVEN

## THE COST OF PAPER

A nnie continued to draw and paint the scenes and people that she came across, her sketch books filling rapidly with information to collate and expand upon later, her finished works dominating the bag she struggled to carry on her back.

After only one week she had nearly used up the books and pads she had thought would be sufficient for such a trip. Without a precedent – and how could there be one? – she'd had no idea what to expect to find here. The sheer variety before her eyes had dumbfounded her, and she'd worked hard to try and capture it all.

She'd only looked over a handful of her works in rare quiet moments, in the moments before sleep and after waking, and even these became frequently interrupted by further spectacles and events that needed cataloguing, and she wondered just how many of the rough works would prove useful once she had returned to London.

Ben had brought no tape recorder for his interviews or reports, of course, because any recorded media so far had ended up either wiped or burned by the journey between dominions. So he relied on pen and paper the same as Annie, handwritten notes that required little if any elaboration once they were both back safely in the offices of PaceNet. He required, therefore, only a handful of small notepads. Annie, on the other hand, required several pads of varying sizes, as well as an art-box that carried all her many supplies and media.

It seemed certain that their eight week trip would have to be cut short just because of something so ridiculous as a shortage of paper. Annie had discussed it with Ben one evening as they sat at a terraced bar drinking a clear alcoholic beverage with a name that sounded like Yoousta, a local drink that tasted like a kind of spiced vanilla, but was stronger than anything either of them had ever drunk before. They mixed it, therefore, with water from the bar, something which had caused the locals much amusement.

"I don't want to go back," Ben said to her. "Not yet."

"I know," Annie agreed, "and neither do I. But I can't do much else without more paper."

"If we do go back, we don't know even if we'll get another chance to come here again. Not unless we pay for it ourselves, and I don't know about you, but I don't have that kind of money."

"Surely PaceNet will pay for another return ticket. It's in their interests."

"Look in your bag, Annie. You've got images that will last a lifetime. They're not going to need more. At least not for a while, or until someone figures out how to get digital or film footage through without destroying it."

"But we've only just scratched the surface. We haven't even left the city yet. There's a whole world out there," she said, pointing out towards the mountains. "If you'll excuse the pun."

"And what if they agree, but decide to send someone else. What then?"

Annie mused on that for a few seconds, keeping her words. She hadn't thought of that.

"The artwork wouldn't match up if they sent someone else," she said finally, knowing how lame that argument was before she'd even voiced it.

Ben raised an eyebrow at her.

"Okay, you're right," she said. "There'd be backhanders by the thousand for a shot at this. I don't even know how we were chosen."

"Because we're good, that's why."

"Disposable more like. Some people haven't come back, remember?"

It was Ben's turn to muse on Annie's words this time.

"Look around, Annie," he said to her at length. "Think of what we've seen so far, what we've experienced. Would you want to go back to London after seeing all this? They probably just blended in, decided to make a new life here in Kar'mi'shah."

Annie followed his gaze, looking at the pedestrians that strolled past the bar, some laughing, some talking passionately, all of them happy. It was true that what they had seen so far (and it was indeed merely just the surface), had been wonderful, just as it was true that neither of them wanted to return. But to return early was different from not returning at all. Could they even think of doing that? Was that what Ben was intimating?

She looked at him as he took another sip of his Yoousta. It burned as it went down, even with the

267

water, and she stifled a smile as she watched his face crease with discomfort.

She'd known him for many years, and now that she was actually studying him, she realised that she could see a change in him, a kind of peace, a serenity that hadn't been there before. Commuting through London stressed everyone. They'd had just one week away from that and she could already see the difference.

"Would Lawson send a message back to PaceNet asking for more paper?" Ben suggested, after a long thoughtful silence.

Annie shook her head. She didn't like the interruption to her growing fantasies about living permanently in Kar'mi'shah, not now they had started.

"He's not running a postal service up there," she said. "People are paying huge sums of money to come here. A delivery of paper is not exactly going to take up a seat on the train."

Ben shrugged. "It was worth a shot."

"I know," Annie said to him, "and it's my shortfall not yours. I'm not asking you to return with me. You stay here. It's the report of a lifetime for you."

Ben took a deep breath, and smiled as he placed his hand over hers.

"We decided to do this together, remember?" he said to her. "So if we –"

Annie suddenly banged herself on her forehead with an open palm.

"I'm so stupid," she exclaimed, her outburst causing several of the other drinkers seated at adjacent tables to turn their heads. "I can use local paper. It's crude, but it's paper."

"But where –"

"We went in a shop a few days ago selling books and things. I'm sure they had blank paper in there. They write here, for God's sake, they have their own art. How stupid am I for not thinking of that?"

Ben sat there smiling at her and then picked up his glass, holding it out in front of him in order to toast the idea. Annie scooped her glass up with a huge grin on her face, clinking the glasses together before draining the potent clear fluid. It seared like raw chillies as it went down, but the heat from the alcohol spread rapidly out from their bodies, and a heady well-being drifted in through their thoughts.

"To another week in Kar'mi'shah," Ben announced, slumping back in his chair.

"And to a brain that should work better than it does," Annie replied.

## EIGHT

## RELIGIOUS RULE

Ben Weaver, PaceNet News
21st May 2003

It was with extreme reverence that I managed to spend a few moments with one of the priests of the temples of Kar'mi'shah. His name was Rammenen Karee and he suggested that I attend a cleansing ritual that takes place deep in the vaults of the temple.

These sacred temples, some of which bear a striking resemblance to the pyramids found at sites like Giza in Egypt, are home to the Gods to which the populace pray. Vast grand statues dominate their exteriors, carved from monolithic slabs of rock brought back from the mountains so many miles away. Depicting the God of the temple, each statue is different in its design, each deity dedicated to a specific task or order. The temple that I visited today belongs to the God Neeoh, the statue at its threshold that of a crocodile-headed man. Of course there is no real God in either this temple or in any of the other temples littering the city, but the people of Kar'mi'shah are a very religious people and their Gods play a very important, if not an indivisible, part in their lives.

Inside the main chamber stone columns mark

out the areas for prayer and communion. An altar of offering stands at one end, and on the day of my visit a sacrificial lamb had been tied to it, along with offerings of bread and fish.

When I spoke to Rammenen he continued to tell me of the rituals performed upon the most sacred altar in the lower sanctum. The God Neeoh would arise out of the vaults and purify the blood of those people who work with the river or upon its shores.

The ritual obviously involves much prayer, perhaps even the imbibing of animal blood, specifically crocodile blood. Rammenen refused my interpretation, but I fear that it is just a case of confused dialects between us, as it was between myself and Meelo Cassadres. His level of English is good, however, unlike the fisherman's, but it is the only clear explanation I can offer.

Unfortunately our meeting was cut short by a crisis amongst the populace, the reason for which I do not know but will try to find out later. Rammenen has asked me to return at another time,  so I will have to wait until then to report on the temples more fully.

# NINE

## BACK AT THE PORTAL

With her watch and necklace traded for a hundred sheets of paper, Annie was once again able to continue to sketch the world around her. Like Ben's, her watch had ceased to work once they'd stepped through the portal, and her necklace was not as precious as the sights she wished to capture on the paper. They were silver and gold, delicate jewellery for the shopkeeper, but it was the only currency she could barter with.

The act of trading also brought a sense of unburdening, of dispensing with petty possessions in order to fulfil something greater. In a monetary sense, she'd paid well over the odds for just a hundred sheets of paper, but she didn't care. A watch and a necklace came cheap in London and could be easily replaced; a journey back to Kar'mi'shah, and with a record of all its sights and wonders, could not. She did decide, however, to return to the portal to send back the works she had already created. Accumulatively they were heavy and awkward to carry, as well as unnecessary to keep with her all the time while she travelled. She left Ben to revisit a temple he'd been to the previous day, telling him that they didn't both need to go, and took a local version of a rickshaw back to the portal.

She hadn't paid much attention to the structure that housed the gateway home before, but it loomed now out of the desert like a fortress, halfway between one of the pyramid temples that filled the city and a garrison fit to repel invaders. It was several storeys high and built upon layers of solid rock, rising with vast sloping sides and with only one set of steps that led up to two giant doors.

It was a dominating spectacle, of that there was no doubt, and seemed perfectly in-keeping with a building that should house a gateway between worlds. When she at last arrived at the foot of the building and began to climb the stone steps, she became filled with mixed emotions: proud that she had come this far, a life well-lived and worthy to tell her grandchildren; joy that she was part of this whole communion; and dread that this would soon be her last few moments here, fearing (perhaps unnecessarily) that she could have maybe spent what time she'd had here more wisely.

In the chamber beyond the doors she spoke to two officials seated behind an ornate reception area. She asked them if Marcus Lawson was available and waited patiently while one of the two men disappeared through a doorway. The man returned quickly, and guided her through the chamber and up a series of steps, back the way she'd come the day of her arrival. Lawson was waiting for her at the top of a flight of stone steps, his expression halfway between confusion and joy.

"I hadn't expected to see you so soon," he said to her, extending his hand to shake hers. "Is there anything wrong?"

"Far from it," Annie replied, happy to see the

unease lift from his face. "I've found so much to draw and paint that I've used every pad I brought. I was hoping you might be able to send some of it back for me."

"You want to return home?"

"No, not me, just my work. If I go back I'm afraid I won't get another chance to come here again."

Lawson smiled at this.

"This place is pretty special," he said.

Annie smiled back at him, telling him that yes, it was.

"We have some people going back to London tomorrow," Lawson went on. "I'm sure they'd be able to take a package with them. My staff at the other end will be able to forward it to the right people. You're one of Frederick Kramer's freelancers, aren't you?"

Annie nodded.

"He's been back and forth quite a lot in the past few months himself. I'm not quite sure what the frequent hops are for, but he's quite the entrepreneur, isn't he?"

"I've only met him a couple of times, and that was leading up to my visit here. I think he just wanted to make sure I wouldn't screw up."

Lawson tried to offer her a consoling smile, but it just felt odd on his face for some reason.

"He invested significant sums of time and money trying to film this place," Lawson went on. "But I'm sure you heard the stories on that one better than I did."

"Sure."

"Something in the portal doesn't like cameras. I

274

guess it just doesn't want Kar'mi'shah to be filmed, eh?"

"I guess," Annie said, somewhat uneasily.

She pictured a kind of monster sitting in the black ether between the two dominions, a vast guardian that watched those who travelled through it, deciding which ones to devour for violating its rules and which to allow safe passage.

A shiver crept across her bones as she stood there. She was glad that she wouldn't be carrying her sketches past the unseen guardian. It might think they were trying to cheat its system, smuggling drawings and paintings when photographs had been banned. Who knew what consequences it could devise?

"Don't worry about your pictures," Lawson said to her, taking her silence as unease. "We'll make sure they get to where they need to be."

Annie handed over her sketch books and loose pages, hoping that something was not watching her from the shadows, knowing that it was she who had made them, and she who was trying to cheat the monster hiding in the darkness.

She left the building quickly after that, glad to be back outside in the fresh air once again, and hurried down the steps to her rickshaw that would take her back into the city.

She wanted to get back to Ben, her only friend in the busy metropolis, but she did not want to tell him about how she'd felt at the portal. Even as she approached the edge of the road and the rickshaw runner who still waited for her beneath the hot sun, far from any shadow that might be creeping towards her from the tall pyramid-like building at her back, she felt awkward and uncomfortable. There was something about the portal that she just didn't like now, and she tried to keep the dread at the back of her mind, knowing that she would have to step into its void at least one more time, and hoping that there was not something lurking there waiting to devour her.

# TEN

## THE RETURN

When she got back to the room where they had been lodging, Annie found that Ben had not yet returned. She cursed herself for checking her watch, for not only had it not worked since they'd arrived in Kar'mi'shah, but she'd traded it for her paper only a few hours before. She guessed it was somewhere near midday. Her stomach was beginning to growl with hunger, and she went down into the street to find one of the vendors, hoping to pass an hour or so with whatever she could find for lunch until Ben returned from the temple. Then they could go back out into the city once again and explore more safely together.

Night came and Ben had still not returned. Annie tried to reason that maybe he'd simply lost track of time, or that his interview had gone better than he'd expected, or that he'd even been introduced to someone else that could offer him a good story. She waited for him, trying to pass the time sketching the view from their room window. But they'd not been separated for this long since they'd arrived in the city, and her mind refused to stop conjuring unpleasant thoughts.

She finally relented and went to bed when the bustle outside in the street began to quieten, but she slept badly. She tossed and rolled in her bed, unable to pacify the thoughts that just wouldn't leave her, and dreamt ghastly dreams when she did manage sleep.

She rose to an early light, her body aching, and dressed awkwardly before leaving the room, hurrying down into the street to ask passers-by if they'd seen Ben or anyone that matched his description. But one by one they shook their heads, and said that no, that had not seen him.

Annie did no drawing that day, but kept close to the room, venturing out only to find something to eat or drink. Ben had still not returned by nightfall and she began to fear the worst. She went to bed early and slept through, but she did not feel refreshed come morning. Over breakfast she tried to decide what to do. There was no local police organisation as far as she knew, the gods to which the people of Kar'mi'shah prayed having such total control over them that crime seemed to have no presence. Every rational thought ended with the same terrible conclusion, resurrecting the dread that she had felt the previous day. She knew she had to return to Marcus Lawson, explain what had happened, and face the possibility of returning home alone.

The city of Kar'mi'shah suddenly possessed a dark underbelly, tainting what she had thought to be a glorious world with neither problems nor horrors. Her friend was missing, and despite the fact that she had no evidence to the contrary, she could only think that something sinister had happened to him. They were strangers in the city after all, and they were only guessing at its rules.

Did she even want to stay here anymore? That was the question that began to find its way into her head. The opulent city now seemed no different to the one she had left behind, where people could go missing and nobody really cared. On the surface everything seemed fine - people went about their daily business and talked in the street – but what did she know about what lurked in the shadows, the real Kar'mi'shah that glowered beneath the smiles and the sunshine.

Annie gathered up her belongings, as well as those that Ben had not taken with him, and left the room for good. She took a two horse carriage and instructed the driver to take her to the first of the nearest temples. But with no idea which temple Ben had visited, or even in which direction it might lay, she knew she was searching blind. The odds against finding him now would be insurmountable, as fruitless as asking every person she passed if they'd seen the traveller from another world.

After passing through several plazas and enquiring at several temples, Annie clambered back into the carriage disheartened and disconsolate. There was simply no sign of Ben. He had vanished without trace, and all Annie could do was give one final instruction to the driver: to take her back to the portal.

She barely noticed anything of the journey as the horses pulled the carriage through the cobbled streets and back out once again into the rolling green fields. She had both their bags beside her, roughly packed but with nothing left behind. The journey of a lifetime had ended with heartache. She had lost her friend, and with no facts regarding his disappearance it was difficult to know just what to feel.

He might still be alive somewhere, that was all she dared hope to think, but there was no way she could function properly alone in the city. She hoped Lawson would have influence with officials, or perhaps know of people who could scour the city for him. He'd have to know of a way, she thought. He just had to.

She arrived at the foot of the stone steps and climbed them without registering the enormity of the structure or the vista as she had done previously. All she wanted to do now was get home.

Kar'mi'shah had bitten her.

It had sank its fangs into her and shaken her hard.

She'd come off worst, of course, and wanted only to crawl away and lick her wounds. There was nothing she could do for Ben but wait and hope he either arrived back home safely under his own steam, or wait for Lawson to find him and ship him home. Either way she was powerless here, and she knew it. She'd done her job, recording images for PaceNet's many newspapers and TV stations. Now she was done with it.

The same two men greeted her as she entered through the two huge doors, and allowed her through into the chamber where Lawson had met her. He was not there waiting for her this time, however, but Annie spoke to a woman who went to find him, leaving her to stand in front of a line of tall windows that looked out over the dark sprawling metropolis of Kar'mi'shah.

Ben was out there somewhere, that's all she

could think, and hopefully someone would find him and bring him home safely. Farmers still worked in their fields, oblivious to her pain, women tending animals, children playing, while boats continued to sail along the vast flowing river. The city was alive and thronging. Someone, surely, must know what had happened to Ben.

The sound of footsteps snatched her attention, and she turned away from the windows to see Marcus Lawson walking towards her. He still wore his trademark smile, but as he saw the bags at her feet, a frown crept across his brow.

"Not more pictures to be sent home?" he said to her, outstretching his hand to hers.

Annie took it and shook it graciously, but she did not want any formality now. She'd had enough, and wanted only to step back across the threshold and be home again.

"Ben is missing," she began, realising as she said the words that she had to relay the events of the past couple of days more than she wanted to. "He went to visit one of the temples and never came back."

"When was this?" Lawson asked, his face stark now with concern.

"When I came to see you the day before yesterday," she told him. "But I don't know where the temple was, or which God it was for."

Lawson stared at her.

It was clear that he was genuinely shocked.

"I'll do what I can to find him," he said. "I give you my word on that." His eyes dropped to the bags at her feet again. "You're going home?" he asked.

Annie nodded, but Lawson did not press her any further.

"Come with me then," he said, picking up both of her bags and leading her away from the line of tall gothic windows and deeper into the heart of the building to the chamber that housed the portal.

There was less ceremony than there had been at the other end. Annie could see the tall dark tear in the world, smudged at the edges like a watercolour painting, and could not take her eyes off it.

Lawson stood between her and the portal. He was talking to her, no doubt about how he would do his utmost to find the journalist Ben Weaver, but he was saying other things as well - something about the duration of the journey, something else about symptoms - but she was not listening to any of it. She wanted only for him to stop talking, to step aside, and then to allow her passage home. She didn't even care if the monster in the void chose to claim her. What could it take from her that she had not already lost? Sure, there was flesh on her bones and blood in her veins for it to take, but perhaps to die in the void was a way to get rid of all the pain that kept building inside her. Perhaps if she never emerged on the other side she would never feel that pain again. If that was a deal that could be made, she couldn't be sure now that she wouldn't make it. It was crazy for her to think, but there were too many words now, too many thoughts, and too much that tugged at her heart and belly. The city behind her was sinister, that's all she could think now. But was the one she was headed back to any less so?

Finally Lawson stepped to one side, the obstruction to the portal now gone, and Annie started almost immediately towards it. She heard Lawson say one final thing at her back but she didn't catch it. What did it matter now anyway?

The chamber was circular and domed like its counterpart in London, and she crossed the blue tiled floor swiftly, a bag in each hand, stepping into the void without breaking her stride.

Blackness rushed to consume her, and a terror she thought would not trouble her again snatched hold of her. She had made this journey with Ben before, hoping that if she got lost inside the darkness, he would be the one to guide her to safety. Now she was alone, defenceless against the beast that might lurk hidden in the surging blackness.

She wasn't sure if it was her imagination that conjured the growls and snarls inside the portal, or whether the monster that did not want Kar'mi'shah's secrets recorded had called her bluff and desired to show her its face after all.

There was no ground beneath her feet anymore to enable her to flee, and nothing in front of her for her to claw her way through should she need to. She was inside an emptiness that breached two worlds, and it would do with her as it wished.

Her head began to thump with the rapid pounding of her heart, her sight swirling in front of her and making its own visions. She thought she could feel hands taking hold of her, fingers in her hair, claws scraping at her flesh and nerve-endings. Did it want her? Was that its desire? Would it bite her and chew her and then spit her out like so much cheap meat?

But then a rush of light suddenly spewed rapidly towards her, thundering like a brightly-lit locomotive, and she was suddenly ejected back out into the world she had always called home.

Annie stumbled awkwardly as her feet struggled to keep her upright from the momentum she carried. The floor was slick, her feet slip-sliding across it, and she fell hard, her two bags tumbling from her grasp and landing in front of her. She lifted her head in a kind of half-daze but there was no one to receive her, no staff, no medical personnel, no one. The blue chamber was absolutely empty.

She pushed herself to her feet, her knees aching from her fall, her head swirling with black shapes that threatened to push her into a swoon. As she bent to pick up her bags, the shapes bloated and swelled behind her eyes, yet through the murky haze she could make out signs of movement at the far end of the room. Not only was the door to the chamber standing ajar, but there was actually somebody standing there.

She was sure there had been no one there before, but dressed from head to toe in what looked like black sackcloth, the woman seemed only to stand and stare back at her. There was no movement, no sign that the woman had even registered her existence, except for the cold gaze that seemed so threatening to her.

The two of them regarded each other for a few moments, neither of them moving, until Annie started forward towards her and the doorway that lay behind her.

Still the woman remained where she was, just inside the doorway to the chamber, but all the while keeping her gaze fixed firmly on her.

The woman moved only her eyes as Annie walked hesitantly past her. The contempt she felt was overwhelming, but Annie had been through enough already without stopping to answer any questions or queries. It was clear that the woman desired no conversation with her either, and that she did not even work for the organisation. What she was doing alone inside the chamber Annie did not particularly care, but why she should stare at her with such utter loathing made her fear for her safety. Her body ached and her mind still thumped with the echoes of the journey across the void, and she staggered past the stranger and out into the corridor beyond without incident. Outside in the corridor, however, she loosed a short scream as a second figure stared at her from behind a desk, its contents scattered across the floor as though it had been ransacked.

But it was not this offence that terrified her, but the physical appearance of this second woman. So horrifically disfigured was she that she looked more like a monster than a woman, her face laced with white scars, her hair wild and ragged where it had mostly been torn from her skull. Her eyes were sunken, her hands arched like claws, and she wore rags that looked like pale flesh that made her accomplice in the blue chamber seem like a catwalk model.

This second ghostly and ghastly woman made to attempt to stop her, but simply gazed at her as Annie stumbled past the desk behind which she still floated. Hurrying down the stairs that led off from the corridor, Annie hugged her bags to her chest and did not look up again until she found the first of the dead bodies lying gutted and opened on the floor of the main reception area.

285

## ELEVEN

## AFTERMATH

Police officers were already filling the building, Annie could see them through the tall blue-glass windows, paramedics tending to wounded security guards at the main gate. A crowd had gathered, despite the lateness of the night she had returned to, and stood huddled at the perimeter fence like gawking vultures. Lights blazed across the tended lawns from the headlights of cars and ambulances. Sirens wailed.

Two men and one woman lay dead at the main reception desk, their necks opened and raw with blood. Annie pressed a hand to her mouth to stifle her scream as she came to a halt on the last of the stairs, not wanting to breath or inhale any part of their deaths. She'd not seen death before, not really, and never anything like this. This was murder, brutal murder, and it was in the home she'd chosen to come back to.

The main doors were suddenly hammered open and police officers rushed through, approaching her immediately with barked instructions and terrified eyes. She remained where she was, glad that someone had arrived to take charge, and allowed two of the officers to search her and then hurry her out of the building.

They continued their barrage of questions once they were out in the night air, wanting to know just what she was doing in the building, where she was going, and just what she had seen of the dead or injured upstairs. Annie tried her best to answer their questions but her head was reeling. She'd seen only two women, one with black hair and black clothing and a second that looked more like a ghost than a human being. Surely they could not have killed all these people single-handedly. They had no weapons, none that she'd seen anyway.

Annie was introduced to a WPC who led her to a quieter area of the gardens where much of the same questions were asked of her again, only this time she was asked for the first time if she was alright. Her head still pounded with a heavy thud, she felt sick from the journey from Kar'mi'shah, and she had just witnessed several gruesome murders. She shook her head. No, she was not alright.

The WPC guided her along the path towards the front gate, where the crowd had been pushed back to allow for the multitude of ambulances and police cars. The moon was large and full in the clear sky, the air warm and still, and although the wind carried the familiar heady scents of diesel fumes and exhaust gases, it smelt sweeter than the stench of death that had already drenched the Eden building.

They approached a paramedic, busy in the back of one of the ambulances with a security guard with severe head and neck wounds, who instructed Annie and the officer to give him five minutes.

"You'll be alright now," the WPC said to her, attempting to smile.

Annie simply looked at her. She felt tired, too

tired to even speak.

She watched the WPC glance back over her shoulder to where bodies lay scattered across the grass like scarecrows ready for hoisting back up onto their poles.

"You can go back if you want," Annie managed to say.

The WPC turned back to look at her.

"I can stay if you want."

Annie shook her head, the motion causing her head to blacken. The thumping seemed to be getting worse, and a sharp pain was gouging the bone at her temples.

"We'll need to speak to you later, though," the WPC said, "and ask you some more questions."

"Haven't you asked enough?" Annie said, putting her hand across her eyes.

"You seem to be the only person who was left alive inside the building. We'd like to know why."

"You don't think I did all this, do you?"

"Good God, no. The description you gave matches the one that the security guards gave us. We've no doubt that you're innocent. But we will be needing a full statement. Can you tell me your full name and address?"

Annie gave the WPC her details as she requested them and watched as she wrote them all down in her notebook. The pain in her head was excruciating, she felt like throwing up, and she wondered just how long the paramedic was going to be before he gave her something to help with the pain. The WPC asked her a few more questions, noting Annie's brief staccato responses in her notepad, before finally leaving her to return to the bloodbath.

288

Annie was glad of the silence, and leaned against the side of the ambulance as she felt the gentle breeze on her face. It cooled her skin, which now felt hot and prickling, and listened to the incessant drone of the city around her.

Kar'mi'shah had sounded so different at night, still busy and bustling, but different to this, with insects that could be heard, and animals braying in the distant fields.

London sounded like it was grating, an abhorrent never-ending din that predicted its eventual destruction. Kar'mi'shah, however, sounded like it was still growing, as though whatever force was governing it was still very much alive and fighting for survival.

"So what's wrong with you?" came a voice.

She opened her eyes to see the paramedic standing in front of her, his hands on his hips.

"You seem okay to me," he went on. "Do you need any assistance."

"My head's killing me," Annie explained, clutching her head with both hands. Just the simple act of focussing on him brought sharp stabbing pains behind her eyes.

"You interrupted an open neck wound for a couple of aspirin?"

"It's more than just a headache. I've just come back through the portal –"

"You've come back from the other world?"

The paramedic's tone changed in an instant. Enthusiasm surged through him, but Annie did not want to discuss anything now. She just wanted the pain to go.

The paramedic helped her up into the

ambulance, and gave her a seat on the other side of the injured security guard. Annie looked at the guard lying back with his eyes closed, his neck and face bandaged and bloody, and wondered just what that black-haired woman had managed to do to him.

"You sit tight here, okay?" the paramedic said to her. "We're going to the hospital now. You're going to be alright."

"Aren't you going to give me any pills or anything?"

He shook his head.

"I'm not giving you anything, that's for the doctors to decide. As long as you make it to the hospital in one piece, that's all I'm concerned with."

"But I'm in agony," Annie persisted.

"I'm sorry about that," the paramedic went on. "But there might be more going on in that skull of yours than a simple headache. Especially given where you've been tonight."

Annie felt the dread returning to her and an image of the monster in the void flooded back into her head. She knew the sense in his words, of course, but wished that she'd just taken a taxi home and swallowed a couple of aspirin herself. Sitting in the ambulance and waiting to go to the hospital, she figured that she wouldn't even see any sleep for at least a couple of hours. And that was probably the best thing for her right now, better than any pills.

# TWELVE

## THE BITE

Hours had passed. Tests had been done. She'd been placed in an MRI machine and had head scans done. The doctor had sent for a specialist to check the results and then asked for him to come and speak to her, and he had, and had told her how the owner of PaceNet News Group, Frederick Kramer, had been diagnosed with a similar condition to hers after several trips through the infamous portal.

Frederick Kramer had cancer.

Annabel Randall had a brain tumour.

The specialist, although speaking as calmly and rationally as he could, had told her that they would have to drill through her skull and take a tissue sample to find out whether the tumour was malignant. He'd made some notes on a clipboard and went away again.

Annie sat in a small room, staring straight ahead at the plain white wall, as tears tracked down her face. The hospital had used words like cancer and tumour, rational words that everyone knew and understood, but Annie knew that it was the monster in the void. It had taken a bite, and it had taken it deep.

Her head still ached, and she guessed it would

continue to ache until the monster decided otherwise. Her thoughts went suddenly to Ben. He'd suffered from the same headache upon their first arrival. Had the monster bitten him too? Her chest heaved and hurt as more sobs came.

Her skin was freezing cold, and she rocked back and forth in her chair as she stared at the wall, her arms wrapped tightly around herself. Something was inside her head that had not been there before, something potentially fatal. Was this just the price of seeing the sky of another world? Was this the price of trying to escape and leaving the mundane?

She shivered, and hugged herself to keep warm. But the shaking would not stop, and the tears refused to cease.

# THIRTEEN

## BAD BLOOD

Ben's eyes flickered open to an unlit chamber, yet even in the total darkness he could make out the curve of an archway, the texture of the stonework, and the figure of somebody standing close by. The smell of blood came instantly to his nostrils, of an open wound, and he realised swiftly that it was his own.

He tried to recall how he had come to be here, how an attack upon him had taken place, but everything was vague, clouded by uncertainty in his own head. He remembered speaking with the priest and following him down stone steps to an altar. There had been offerings left there of wine and bread. Something had moved in the murky shadows beyond the altar. He could remember something. Red eyes had watched him.

He felt sick.

Something churned in his stomach that wanted to come back up. Ben placed his fingers against his neck and found it was wet. They came away sticky and coated. When he put them to his nose he could smell his own blood. He ran them across his lips and tasted it, to taste his own blood on his tongue. It was involuntary, he didn't know why he did it, yet he found himself licking his fingertips clean with a sickening and ravenous hunger.

His head was buzzing with information, his senses growing more acute as he lay on the stone surface of the altar. Even through his clothes he could feel the coarseness of the stone, but there was so much more to explore than subtle textures, the sounds of spiders and scorpions scuttling throughout the shadows of the temple, the smell of wine and incense heady on the stale air, the taste of hot desert winds blown through the city from hundreds of miles away. All of it came to him in rapid yet intense snatches. But then a motion to his right demanded his attention, and his eyes went once again to the figure standing there.

"Your blood troubles me," the figure said to him, as he approached out of the blackness.

"You did this?" Ben asked. "You cut my neck?"

"Drank from," the man clarified. "I sought to cleanse what was bad in you, but I am not sure that I have succeeded."

Ben tried to sit up but his head suddenly swam with a myriad of thick pulsing shapes. He clamped one hand to his forehead as he sat half upright, and waited for them to clear.

"What have you done to me?" Ben wanted to know.

"I have drunk your blood, and passed my own over your lips, purifying the bad that ran through your veins."

"Bad? What bad?"

The man stared at him for a moment. His body had no movement, his face no life.

"You had a disease," he said at last. "Were you not aware?"

Slowly, Ben shook his head.

"I am not sure whether it still lives inside you or not. That is why it troubles me."

"What is it?" Ben demanded. "What are you talking about?"

The man moved closer to him now, until he was standing at his side.

"You would have died," he told him. "And soon."

It took a few moments for his words to sink in. It was clear that this man was no doctor, and nor did the unlit stone chamber seem like it belonged in any part of a hospital, or at least any hospital he knew about. Yet something told him that what he was being told was true.

Ben tried to sit up again, only this time he moved slowly, swinging his legs round off the altar and slipping his weight down carefully onto his feet. He felt unsteady as he stood upright, and kept one hand on top of the altar, the texture and coldness of the stone still exhilarating his senses with so much information.

"But there is much you need to know," the man said to him, disjointing his thoughts. "You have joined a higher order now, and in payment you have become a servant to me. This temple will be your home, and you will be devoted to me without question. I am your master now, and you will call me Neeoh."

Ben stood in the darkness just staring at the man in front of him, not knowing whether to believe him or not. Had he been kidnapped and press-ganged into a life of slavery, the ignorant stranger, the innocent dragged off the street and now trapped?

Had that been why Rammenen Karee had requested him to return at a later date, when this man Neeoh could perform whatever sick ritual he had just completed?

His fractured thoughts went to Annie. She would come looking for him, perhaps with help from Marcus Lawson. But did she even know where he was?

He stood for a moment, leaning against the stone altar, terror coursing through him as he realised that he had not told her exactly where he was going, just that he was visiting one of the temples; and the city had hundreds.

"Your fears are expected," Neeoh said, as if he had been reading his thoughts. "But you will soon forget them. They are fleeting, as will be everything you once knew. Soon they will be like dust, like the desert that once choked this place. And like the desert, your former life will be beaten back until it will seem like it had never even existed."

Ben revolted at this. He would never forget who he was, or who he had known. Annie was alone in the city, alone with maniacs like this roaming the streets. She had to be warned, and only he could do that.

He started away, his eyes already on the stone archway that led to the stairwell, but he could not remember even placing his first foot before Neeoh had hold of him, his fingertips sharp against his skin like claws that threatened to pierce it.

Neeoh's face was suddenly close to Ben's, his mouth beside his ear, the same mouth that had drunk from him only minutes before.

"Forget her," he hissed, his voice full of venom.

"She is nothing now."

Ben felt Neeoh's hand against his throat, his fingers squeezing, tightening against it. His mind swirled with violent shapes, he heard something creak, and then the chamber and the man who had called himself a God slipped away from him as he slumped onto the ground.

2

He opened his eyes to see Rammenen Karee standing over him, his face creased with disapproval. They were in a different chamber, this one illuminated with indirect natural light, the air less cold and clammy. He realised that they were above ground, he could hear the sounds of the street more clearly that he had in the altar room, and he could smell the aromas that drifted into the temple on the hot desert winds.

"You have displeased Neeoh," the priest said at last. "I thought you would have been more grateful than you have been, and my error in judgement has displeased him also."

"Grateful?" Ben cried, his voice echoing loudly off the stone walls around them. Rammenen hushed him swiftly, holding a hand out over his mouth. Ben relented, and took a deep breath as Rammenen scowled.

"Why should I be grateful?" he hissed. "I don't know what's happened to me, or what this Neeoh has done, but I want out of here. Now."

"You would have died," Rammenen explained

to him, echoing the words that the God had uttered.

"I sensed it that first day you came here."

"What do you mean, died?"

"There is something in you, something bad that I could taste on your breath. It's still there, but less so, and now that you are one of us, even that will diminish and disappear."

"What are you talking about? What was wrong with me?"

"You had a poison inside you that Neeoh has greatly reduced. He drank your bad blood and replaced it with his own. Some of the disease remains, however, but his blood will destroy what is left."

Ben lay for several minutes just trying to cope with what the priest was telling him. Could it be true, that not only had he had some kind of fatal illness without him knowing about it, but that this man who called himself a God could cure it?

His mind returned to the day of their arrival in Kar'mi'shah, and to the crippling headache he'd had for hours afterward. The pain had stayed with him in one form or another for days, reverting to a nagging ache that would not leave him. Had the portal been the cause? Or had there been something else inside him for years? His senses were more alive now than he could ever remember them being. Could that be attributed to new blood, a transfusion of blood perhaps different to his own? Ultimately his thoughts returned to Annie, the woman who had stepped through that portal with him. What of her, he wanted to know, was she suffering the same as he?

Ben lurched suddenly from his bed, Rammenen

immediately reaching to restrain him. The priest's hold was nowhere near as strong as that of Neeoh's, however, and Ben found that he could fend him off more easily.

"What are you doing?" Rammenen demanded to know.

"I have to go."

"You can't."

"I have to," Ben exclaimed. "There's someone here that might be in great danger. I have to tell her, I have to explain everything."

Rammenen attempted to restrain him once again as Ben started for the doorway, but Ben simply pushed him to one side and hurried out of the room, dashing along a corridor that he hoped would lead him outside.

His sense of direction was off, however, the sounds of the streets outside disorientating as they echoed off the stone walls, and it delivered him instead into a vast chamber with a high vaulted ceiling. Daylight was stronger at the far end, and after the dim light of the inner sanctum, it took a while for his eyes to adjust to the brightness.

He hurried towards it regardless, sprinting across the marble floor as the priest shouted at his back. But Ben didn't care. He needed to find Annie and warn her somehow.

The words that might achieve this were not in his head, but he hoped that once he was before her, once he had shown her the wound on his neck, they would come and she would understand, and hopefully she would return home and see a doctor before it was maybe too late.

He dashed out into the bright sunlight, the

sights and sounds of the city violent to his senses after the tranquillity of the temple behind him. The sun was hot, incredibly hot, as he dashed down the stone steps towards the street. He looked for a carriage or a rickshaw as he descended, but his vision began to fail, and he struggled to see through the searing white light of the sun. He lifted his hands to shield the brightness, but still he could not see, his eyes growing as hot as his skin. He smelled the stench of burning meat and it choked him, and he wondered how close to one of the street vendors he must be for it to smell so pungent.

But then smoke began to curl around him, his senses dizzying as his legs threatened to buckle, and all he could think was how blisteringly hot the day had become while he'd been inside. His mind blackened momentarily, and he feared he would collapse in front of everyone. He took another staggering step forward towards the street, distantly thinking now that he needed to find Annie. Then he toppled backwards, and felt the edges of the stone steps hard in his back.

The stench of cooked meat and smoke was acrid in his nostrils now, his sight blinded with fierce white, only now he could hear gasps and shouts from the crowded street below him. He heard the priest's voice loud in his ears, and felt his hands slip beneath him and scoop him up. Then he was being carried, back up the steps and into the darkness of the temple once again.

"That was stupid," he heard Rammenen Karee yelling at him. "If you won't listen, then you'll be dead, and let me tell you now that you won't be going peacefully."

"What... happened?" Ben managed to utter. His whole body was convulsing, shaking violently with livid tremors and tics. His mouth refused to work properly.

"You can't go out in daylight any more, my friend. For you that is now forbidden."

"Why?"

His jaw felt like it would crack.

Ben's sight was still blinded, only now with blackness and a furious pain, but he heard the priest sigh with impatience. His eyes stung as though acid has been sprayed in his face, and he so desperately wanted to look at him.

"Tell me," Ben urged quietly now.

As he lay there, he heard the splashing of water, and then felt the coldness of a damp towel as it was pressed against his flesh. This Rammenen repeated several times before he spoke again.

"You are not who you once were," he began. "You have holy blood flowing through your veins now, a blessing which brings many severe responsibilities. You are immortal, Benjamin. You can live forever without showing signs of age or decay or frailty, but that gift comes with a price."

"Daylight?"

"That is one of them, my friend, as you have painfully found out. Direct sunlight will burn your skin like phosphorus. Night is your only companion now. You will walk only beneath the moon, and use only its silver light to guide you."

"My eyes," Ben said to him. "I cannot see."

"Your sight will return to you," Rammenen explained, "and your burns will heal. That is one of the blessings Neeoh has bestowed upon you, the strength of your body to heal quickly. But that does not give you license to test it. You are immortal, not invincible. Do not try what you just did again."

Ben did not reply, but he knew that he had to think a lot of things through. Rammenen's words were heavy, and they did not sink in readily, but his first lesson had been one hell of an attention-grabber. He would need to take things one step at a time, and learn his other lessons well, but there were things he needed to do, places he needed to visit, people he needed to speak to.

"I need to find a friend of mine," Ben said, attempting to sit up. Rammenen pressed a hand against his chest and urged him to remain lying down.

"Her name is Annie," Ben went on. "She came with me here to Kar'mi'shah through the portal."

There was a pause from Rammenen, and for a while all he did was press the cold damp towel against Ben's burnt flesh. Then the priest spoke again.

"A woman did come asking for you a few days ago," he said to him.

"A woman? Was it Annabel?"

There was another pause.

"I sent her away. I told her I did not know of you."

Ben lay there with anger beginning to rise in him, and he wished that his eyes would work so that he could see the priest's face, could see exactly how he was looking back at him.

"She could be dying," Ben cried. "Just as I was dying."

"I sensed nothing in her that I had sensed in you."

"But you're not a doctor. She needs to get to a hospital to get some tests done. This is fucking serious, do you understand that?"

"What is a hospital?" Rammenen asked.

"What are you talking about?"

"Hospitals, we do not have them here. What are they?"

Ben couldn't decide whether Rammenen was fucking with him or not. The question was idiotic, puerile, something that a child new to the world might ask.

"They're places where people go when they're fucking sick or injured. Doctor's run tests on them, take x-rays, and make them better."

"We do not have them here," Rammenen said again, "unless they are like our temples. The Gods cure people of their ills. They drink bad blood and replace it with good."

Ben said nothing for a while after that, and still couldn't figure out whether Rammenen was fucking with him or not.

"Is that what Neeoh did to me?"

"Yes," Rammenen said.

Ben slumped back and said nothing for another while, and just lay there as the priest continued to bathe his skin. His eyes stung, his flesh felt red-raw, and nothing that Rammenen Karee had told him offered any hope of comfort. He'd been told that he would heal more quickly than if he was still human - or whatever state he had been, if indeed he had become something else now – but he still didn't know how long it would be before he could attempt to find Annie again. But it had to be soon, he knew, before she moved on, or before she left the city altogether.

"Fuck," he said aloud.

# FOURTEEN

## WHAT IT MEANS TO BE A VAMPIRE

B en had felt the hunger for blood growing inside him several times during the wait for his burns to heal, and although he had fought the disgust as much as the hunger by forcing fruit and other foodstuffs down into his stomach – foodstuffs which his belly had forcefully rejected and sent back up - he had at least used these to try and keep track of the passage of time.

With his sight gone, his other senses struggled to tell him whether it was night or day: he could hear the bustle of the street reverberating through the stone chambers, but in a busy plaza it helped little to determine the time of day; he could smell food cooking for the many street vendors, but again with them open for business from the early hours to after dark, it was nigh on impossible to attribute events outside in the city with even an approximate time of day. And when he slept, it erased any passage of time he'd hoped he'd secured.

The priest Rammenen Karee tended to him frequently, bathing his crusted blistered skin and feeding him warm sweetened drinks which strengthened him immensely. His sight returned partially after what he guessed to be a day and a half, but it was nowhere near sufficient to enable him to navigate a city he barely knew. He could make out vague shapes and sources of light, movements in the room that could only be the priest at his labours, but at least it was progress, and as swift as Rammenen had promised.

On what he believed to be the third day, Ben opened his eyes to a near-focussed room. He could make out the shapes of the room, the arches of the vaulted ceiling, the heavy tapestries and scarlet curtains that hung from the walls. He could see the water bowl and towel that the priest had used to bathe him, the candles that sat beside them which lit the room, and another bowl behind them which had held his meals.

His sight was still blurred, and it still hurt his eyes to have them open, but he lay there motionless as he took in the whole of the room around him. A motion at the doorway caught his attention and he could see Rammenen Karee entering, coming towards him with a fresh towel in his hand. The priest was not looking towards him, and showed no sign that he had noticed his patient's return to health. Ben watched him as he approached the table which stood beside his bed, and replaced the soiled towel with the fresh one, placing the former in a brown cloth bag which hung from a belt around his waist.

Ben then watched as Rammenen pulled a knife from inside his robes and drew it without pain or ceremony across his left wrist. Ben jerked with alarm as the priest held his wrist over the bowl to fill it, the same bowl from which he'd drunk. The image of this bloodletting seemed almost to physically slap him, and his stomach convulsed as the reality of his meals struck him like a hammer. But the priest simply stared at him as he continued to squeeze blood from his wrist with his other hand.

Ben tried to retch, to force the priest's blood back out of his body, but he had not drunk for several hours, and with his stomach empty nothing would come up into his mouth, no matter how hard he tried to purge his system. He shook off the priest's touch as he tried to lay a calming hand upon him, and rolled away from him, his body shaking, his stomach still knotting itself from his efforts.

"What the fuck have you done to me?" he gasped, grasping his stomach with both hands.

But the priest just continued to stare at him, his expression one of confusion.

"You've been feeding me your blood?"

"Of course," Rammenen replied. "What else?"

It was Ben's turn to stare in disbelief.

"You are no longer what you once were," Rammenen explained again. "Your body works differently now, it works against how it once performed, as you have seen from venturing out beneath the sunlight. You can try and eat as you remember, vegetables and fruit, but your body will gain virtually no energy from them."

"So I have to drink blood?" Ben stammered, his stomach convulsing involuntarily at the thought. "What am I, some kind of fucking vampire?"

"If that is the word you wish to use, then that is who you are now. But blood is where you get your strength."

Ben stared at him in disbelief, but then collapsed back onto the bed, pushing his hands up over his face and then dragging them back down. He wanted to cry through his fingers. He wanted to scream that this just wasn't true. But he could remember the texture of the priest's blood on his tongue, and remember too how it had slipped down his throat, coating it with a warmth and an energy that seemed to permeate throughout his entire body. He knew what the priest was saying was true, but he couldn't accept it, he just couldn't give in to the truth of what they had made him into. They had made him a vampire.

Ben pulled his hands away from his face and saw the priest still looking at him. There was no expression on his face, no judgement in his eyes. He just stood there looking at him, waiting to accept anything that the man in front of him had to say. But Ben could think of nothing. There was suddenly a great emptiness inside him, a void of pain and hurt and loss that seemed to have no hope of being sated or cured. He'd become a monster, a beast so far removed from the man he had once thought he was that to think about it was to add to the void.

"Just leave me," Ben said at last, and turned his head away.

The priest remained at his side for a few moments longer, but he ultimately turned and departed, and Ben waited until his footsteps had disappeared from the chamber before he let his tears begin to run. They skipped down his nose and cheeks as they came, but he didn't wipe them away. He wanted them on his skin, wanted them to soak his pillow so that he could feel them all over his face. He was a shell, a hollow vessel that felt like it could crack in two. And if that happened, then he would welcome it. He had nothing left now. The man who had once been called Ben Weaver, the journalist who had set foot in another world full of promised wonder, was gone. Left in his place was a monster, a creature that could live only in folklore and shadows, and drink only the blood of the living. He had become what people feared in their nightmares, what people paid good money to see in cinemas or read about in books. He wanted only to die, but where Rammenen had promised Ben's swift healing, so might his other predictions come true: that he would not die soon, or even at all, but live on as a monster, destined to haunt a sunless world forever.

## FIFTEEN

## FOLLOWING IN THE ARTIST'S FOOTSTEPS

He found a reason to live on, if only for a short while, and her name was Annabel Randall. She needed to be told that her health was at risk by being in Kar'mi'shah, and for that matter he needed to spread the word that there were dangers present for anyone who wished to make that journey. How many people had already traversed that bridge? How many of them might already be sick or dying?

By nightfall, Ben was up and dressed and standing at the threshold to the temple. He could see over the roofs some of the low-lying buildings, and he spent time just gazing across the city that still thronged with an energetic people.

He knew that he would be walking amongst them differently now, and feared retribution.

Would they see him as a freak?

Would they run or hide?

Would they batter him with stones or chase him with sticks knowing that he desired to drink their blood?

He tried to reassure himself that he would not do that, that he would plead ignorance to the ways of his condition. And if all else failed he would run away and hide himself.

But his condition was part of their lifestyle, his

mind tried to coax him, their society had made him into what he was. How could they persecute something of their own making? Nevertheless, Ben stood motionless at the gateway to the temple, the building that had become his temple, and watched the still-bustling midnight city for a while.

An hour or more passed before he set foot on the steps and finally began his descent down to the street. The moon was high, the stars bright, their constellations shifting as though the sky was being turned slowly by massive hands. Up in the heavens everything seemed peaceful and eternal.

By contrast, everything in the street below him (that even now seemed to be rushing up as if to grab him), was chaos and noise. People pushed and shouted, bartered and haggled. There were people running, others standing still to talk. There were children who had not yet gone home to bed, and still played with sharp voices. After the silence and tranquillity of the inner chambers of the temple – and he'd heard all these sounds but extraordinarily muted – to be standing in the midst of it threatened to shred his senses. His acute hearing rang to the discordant dirge of a thousand street-walkers, his eyes ached to take in the sight of every colour and every shape imaginable, and his tongue and nostrils tasted every dish the city had to offer as the swirling wind brought their aromas to him from every quarter of the city.

The world outside the temple was brash and horrific to him now, and he fled quickly through the masses in search of quieter back streets in order to make his way back to the lodgings where he hoped Annie would still be waiting for him.

His heart sank, then, when he found the room not only vacated, but emptied of all her things as well as his own. He began to search with an ever-growing panic, to double-check the terrible but certain conclusion, but it was clear that she had gone.

Ben went downstairs to ask of her whereabouts, but nobody knew. Someone had seen her eating and drinking a few days past, but nobody had seen her recently. Annie had gone, but had she returned home to London?

The room had been supplied to them by the Eden Consortium, and it was there that Ben now travelled, taking a carriage to the huge building that housed the portal. He tried to keep his focus on finding the man called Marcus Lawson, their representative in Kar'mi'shah, but his attention kept returning to the driver sitting in front of him.

His eyes would creep back to the man's neck, as the carriage rocked and shuddered over the rough roads once they made their way out of the city, investigating the patterns of fine hairs that grew there, the subtle wrinkles of skin as he turned his head. After a full day's work, the man stank of sweat and horses, but through it Ben could smell something sweeter, something desirable that continued to draw his attention. It mesmerised him, drawing him into an almost trance-like state, and it seemed that he was somehow powerless to sever his attention away from it.

As the carriage passed through farmer's fields and irrigation ditches fed by the river, Ben realised the truth behind his grim fascination, perhaps for the first time. His body was hungry, his stomach the superior of his mind. The monster that the God Neeoh had put inside him demanded sustenance, and Ben fought the urge with everything he had.

He would never kill a man and drink his blood, he demanded of himself. Just the thought of such an act revolted him, and he turned his head away and forced his gaze down to the cultivated land that the carriage rumbled through.

Bright moonlight illuminated the ploughed furrows, casting deep shadows beneath the trees, glinting off the streams like liquid silver.

His hands began to shake, but before he could even look down at them, his eyes had returned once again to the back of the neck of the driver in front of him.

Ben had lunged forward before he was even aware of his own intent. He saw his own actions as though he was another passenger sitting beside him in the carriage, sharing this hellish journey. He saw one hand slide effortlessly across the chest of the driver, saw a second hand grasp the man's hair and yank his skull to one side, and then he saw a taut curve of stretched pale skin just as it opened and spilled its torrent of hot red blood.

Ben felt the thick sweet fluid on the back of his tongue before it surged down his throat. But it was not warm like the priest's blood which he had drunk from a bowl, but hot, fiery hot as he gorged on its richness direct from the source. His eyes rolled up into his head with bliss, his hands crushing the man held restricted and helpless beneath him as he sucked harder and harder, his teeth ripping at the meat of his neck in his frenzy.

The carriage skittered out of control as Ben

hauled the driver back into the main body of the vehicle, the loose reins flapping as the horses began to gallop unchecked. Ben continued to feed, indifferent to any injuries he might suffer if the carriage should run off the road.

As the flow of blood lessened and Ben's eyes rolled back into their sockets, he dropped the corpse onto the hard wooden floor of the carriage and hauled himself forward and into the driver's seat.

The horses still raced madly, but Ben could see everything vividly and clearly now as though he was watching it all play out before him in slow motion. The reins were beyond his reach, whipping amongst the horses' thundering hooves. There was nothing to be gained in risking the reach down for them, but the building that housed the portal was much closer now, an unchallenging walk, and Ben made the decision in a heartbeat. He leapt from the driver's platform and away from the carriage, circling midair before landing on all fours like a cat amongst the tall grasses at the side of the rutted road as the carriage sped on.

Heat and energy buzzed through him like a fierce electrical charge as he made his way towards the portal, and Ben found that he covered the distance much quicker than he had estimated. The uneven ground seemed not to hinder him, and his senses seemed more attuned to everything around him, more focussed and alive than they had ever been before. His memory of what he had done to the carriage driver seemed somehow distant, somehow less important than he had remembered it being at the time. He wanted to feel guilt, to feel anger for what he had done. But his mind just wouldn't give in to his selfish demands, no matter how hard he tried to drag the events as they'd occurred in the carriage back to the forefront of his consciousness.

As he approached the steps of the portal building, however, his priorities skipped once again. He had come here to find Lawson to ask him the whereabouts of Annabel, and he would demand the information he needed or feed from him the same way he had fed from the carriage driver.

The two massive doors at the top of the stone steps were locked, but the mechanisms that held them secure could not withstand his new-found strength. His body felt invigorated, coursing with an energy he could not remember ever having before, and he made his way past the broken locks, stepping into a darkness through which he could see most clearly.

He closed the doors after him in case there were any guards patrolling – he did not need to be disturbed now – and made his way through the first chamber, climbing a flight of steps that led up to a long hallway. Ben waited at the top, listening to the sounds of the building – the beetles in the brickwork, the scorpions in the shadows – until he heard what he had come here to hear: the sound of Lawson's heartbeat reverberating through the wide stone walls.

Ben crept along the corridor, his acute hearing filtering out the many creatures that scuttled across the floors and ceilings, behind walls both inside and out, until he arrived at a door set midway along its length. He pressed his face to it, feeling the texture of the cold timber against his skin, inhaling the scent of sap, before turning the handle and slipping unnoticed into the room.

He found Lawson instantly in the half-light, sitting with his back to him as he gazed out through a wall of windows that stretched the full length of the room, offering a vast panoramic view of Kar'mi'shah, of the mountains beyond and the river due south. Lawson had a drink in one hand, and Ben could smell the heady aroma of alcohol even from the back of the room.

He could hear Lawson's heartbeat more distinctly now, pounding slow and steady, drugged by the alcohol he was just as steadily consuming. Ben made his way further into the room, satisfied that they were alone, before he spoke:

"You think you're the master of this kingdom?"

Lawson jerked violently in his seat, his glass slipping from his hand and rolling across the floor as he spun around to see who had crept up on him.

"Who are you?" he blurted into the half light. "What are you doing here?"

"I'm disappointed that you don't remember, it's only been a week. I'm Ben Weaver, the poor bastard from PaceNet News you had sent here."

"What are you doing here?" Lawson asked again, his eyes flitting to the door behind him as if there might be some paltry security waiting to help him. "The building is closed. You're not supposed to be here."

"Tell me something I don't know," Ben said, walking towards the line of windows to look out over the sprawling city.

Lights burned like glittering embers, moonlight skipping off the surface of the river as it wound its way through the metropolis. It certainly was a view to behold and to savour.

"So are you?" Ben asked.

"Am I what?"

"Are you the master of all this? You seem to be looking out over it all like you own it all. Is this what the whole deal was about?"

"I own nothing but a share in the land upon which the portal in London sits. We own the rights to the portal, and therefore control who can and who can't pass through it."

"Sounds good," Ben said to him, turning round to face him. "Did you do all your own homework?"

"And just what do you mean by that?"

"Did you test your new discovery," Ben explained, "or did you just slap it on the market with a trendy name?"

"I think you should leave," Lawson threatened, getting to his feet and approaching him.

"I wouldn't even try that," Ben warned. "You see, I've become victim myself to this place, in more ways than one."

Lawson narrowed his eyes at him.

"Your portal you've got there -" Ben went on.

"Yes?"

"It did something to me, gave me some kind of condition that would've killed me. I'm not saying I didn't already have something before I stepped into it, but one of your Gods here decided to swap my blood over and make me into some kind of freak. Now I'm asking you, what kind of fucking welcome is that?"

Lawson stared at him dumbfounded.

"You're a vampire?"

He could barely breathe the words, but it was

Ben's turn to stare at him. The V word had been uttered so simply, so matter-of-factly, that it defied all doubt. All Ben could do was stand and stare at the man in front of him as his brain struggled to turn everything over. Was that what he definitely was now? A vampire? He knew the word, of course, just as he'd seen the Hammer films and the low-budget shockers. But to truly be one? Was that even possible?

"I can't believe it," Lawson went on. "How did it happen?"

"In one of your temples," Ben managed to say, his mind still struggling with the name for what he had become. "A God drank from me. He said I had bad blood. Which brings me to the reason I came here tonight to see you."

"What is it that you want?" Lawson said, taking a tentative step back.

"Annie is gone," Ben said. "And I need to find her."

"She returned home."

"What? When?"

"A few days ago. She wasn't -"

"Wasn't what?"

Lawson swallowed. Sweat broke cold on his brow.

"She wasn't what?" Ben asked again.

"She wasn't feeling well," Lawson told him. "She decided to go home for a number of reasons, but there are doctors there, people who can take good care of her. Better than -"

"Better than what they have here?"

Ben swept past him suddenly, but turned to glare back at him as he reached the door.

"I hope you think this was all worth it," he spat. "People are dying because of wanting to come here. Do you tell them what price they're going to have to pay before they set foot in the portal? Do you even mention that possibility? Who knows, you might even have something yourself, wouldn't that be ironic? Maybe you won't even be alive long enough to enjoy all that you think you've got. Your time is fleeting, Lawson. Even without disease your lifespan is short. And your money can't buy you out of that, now can it?"

Ben had tried to be spiteful, to sow the seeds of pain in Lawson's head, and from the expression on his face as he'd left, he knew that he had at least partially succeeded.

Yes, the Eden Consortium had brought the opportunity of a lifetime to the masses, but the cost for some was great, greater than some perhaps would want to pay. Would he himself have come if he'd known the full price? That was a question he wasn't sure he'd like the answer to. For now, though, he only had one thing on his mind, to step back through the portal and return home to find Annabel Randall. After that, he had no idea, and nor did he much care. He was immortal now. He had time to plan his future. Time aplenty.

## SIXTEEN

## LIFE ON THE OTHER SIDE

B en stood in front of the portal for a while just looking at its plainness. The bridge that connected two worlds, blurred at its shifting edges like a bad watercolour painting, showed no outward appearance of what it could do, and offered no threat of the damage that it could inflict.

It stood like a vertical tear, a column of darkness, visible from all sides like a visual conundrum that defied rational logic or scrutiny. But as much as it could transport somebody to a land visited only before in dreams, it also had the power to destroy lives.

As Ben stood in the circular blue chamber, he realised why film and audio footage had been burned or wiped on its journey back through the portal. There were forces inside - call them radioactive, magnetic or evil, were they not all words for the same thing? – and they chose what could and could not travel safely through its void. Those objects were also non-negotiable, and that was the kicker. The traveller stepped through making their own choices, although ignorance had not even placed those choices in front of the traveller. He wondered there and then whether anyone in the Eden Consortium had even done their homework, or whether they had simply not been able to wait to slap a sticker on the side of it, package it neatly, and watch the money roll in. Whatever was the case was irrelevant now to him at least. The damage had been done, and he'd paid the price. His life was irrevocably changed, and now he was only just exploring its capacities and limitations.

He was not dead, which was something, but he had travelled even further to a place beyond death, and where that would lead only time would tell. For now, though, he still had a picture of Annie in his head, and although conflicting thoughts and emotions tried to cloud that picture, he fought to keep it in focus.

He wanted to make sure that she was okay. He remembered wanting that more than anything, but these new thoughts desired that he revisit the boundary that he'd crossed in the carriage, that state of bliss that he'd entered as he'd clasped the driver's head in his hands and opened the flesh around his neck. But it was not easy. Those thoughts were powerful, dominating, but he had so far managed to keep focussed on Annie. He owed her that much at least.

Ben took a step towards the portal, his eyes searching the utter blackness inside, but there was nothing there for him to see, just a hollow empty void that offered destruction on a whim. He was sure it could not hurt him now, not any more than it had, but he closed his eyes as he walked forward, and did not see his transition until his feet swam beneath him, and he fell forward into the abyss.

The journey seemed almost instantaneous. He staggered forward into the chamber on the other side with his head ferocious and blinding. His vision flailed, he was disorientated, and he struggled to make sense of any of the shapes and colours of the blue room in front of him. But then he felt someone take hold of his wrist, hauling him away from the portal. He heard voices too, asking urgent questions, but he didn't care for any of them.

His sight suddenly returned in a rush, as though it had been held back by a trailing wind, and he saw several people surrounding him. Many of them wore black security uniforms, stern faces regarding him beneath peaked caps. Others wore white overalls. Two were police. He hated the scrutiny, loathed their touch upon him, and he yanked his arm free, turning in circles away from them until he found a clear open space.

"There should not be anyone using this facility," one of the women in white overalls said to him, stepping to the front of the assembled crowd but still keeping her distance. "Why were you allowed through."

"No one allowed it. I came because I chose to."

Several of the people exchanged glances. He saw two security guards reaching for something clipped to their belts. As they started towards him, Ben took a step backwards. His eyes searched for an exit from the chamber, and found it on the other side beyond the crowd.

He began circling, attempting to edge round

towards it while still keeping a wide distance between himself and the guards that were now coming after him.

Until they rushed him.

With a shout, the two guards at the front dashed forward. Ben did not wait or try and fight them, but turned and sprinted for the door. He reached it more quickly than he would have thought, his feet swifter than they'd ever been in his life, but as he hauled it open and saw the empty corridor beyond, he felt four hands grab hold of him from behind and attempt to haul him back inside the chamber.

He'd never been much of a fighter, and he'd always done his best to duck into the background in pub brawls and scuffles, so where his defence and subsequent assault came from he had no idea.

The confrontation came in brief snatches: he turned and broke one of the guards wrists with a simple twist of his own, he slashed at the other guard's face with his hand and drew out a crimson fan of blood; as one guard reeled back away from him, he took hold of the other, clasped his head and torso as he had done with the carriage driver, and sank his teeth into the meat of his neck, not to feed – there was no time – but simply to tear it apart. Blood still gushed readily into his mouth, hot and slick and vital, but he pushed the body away from him as he turned and sprinted out of the chamber, blood spilling from his mouth as he fled the length of the corridor and down a flight of stairs and into the main reception area of the Eden building.

More guards and consortium personnel littered the room, and all of them looked up at him as he exited the stairwell. But he had already expected their presence, and moreover possessed the element of surprise, and he dashed past them and out through the heavy glass doors before they could do more than shout after him.

The night sky was clear, the moon full and high above him, illuminating the grounds of the Eden building more than the lamplights that lined the pathway down to the main gate.

He heard the click and crackle of walkie-talkies before he was anywhere even close to the guards at the blocked gate, and heard too the instructions for them to stop the intruder. Rather than face a waiting assault, Ben veered from the path and headed towards the perimeter wall.

Twelve feet tall with a barbed ridge atop it, the wall would have dispirited many potential intruders. But the guard's blood that had found its way down into his belly had invigorated him, just as the carriage driver's had done, and a new-found strength had permeated his muscles.

Ben leapt yards before he reached the wall and soared upward, astonishing even himself as he not only cleared both the wall and the barbs, but landed on his feet on the other side. With one sharp glance over his shoulder, he surveyed the building and its grounds for any sign of pursuit. Then he fled, disappearing swiftly from sight into the blackest shadows of London's streets.

# SEVENTEEN

## AN AGENDA UNMASKED

Lawson had sat for a long time thinking through everything that the reporter-turned-vampire had said to him, about mortality and immortality, and witnessing the passage of time. In a room overlooking the city of Kar'mi'shah, his eyes had seen neither the spread of glittering lights nor the moonlit river that wound its way through the metropolis, but instead focussed only upon images remembered in his mind.

What was the point of owning the greatest wonder in the world if he would be dead within a brief span of human years, a handful of decades at the most? He had set foot upon something grander that he could ever have imagined, and he would be decaying to dust while those that succeeded him explored the places and sights that time refused him. Ben had unwittingly shown him the next adventure that he needed to take, the step that would allow him to experience everything; was that not why he had started on this journey in the first place? That was the key. He needed more time. He needed to see more. He had everything that he had ever wanted, and now all he needed was time to savour it, time to experience it. He needed endurance, longevity, and only one name had come to his lips.

Lawson had left the room before his plan was even half congealed. He did not need to be in Kar'mi'shah, that much was plain to him. The man he needed to see was in London, busy with interests other than this dominion, and Lawson had been sure that only he could help him.

The Eden building had been in disarray when he had emerged from the portal. Two of his senior technicians had run to him when they'd seen him, explaining how somebody had come through earlier that night and had seriously assaulted two of their security guards. Lawson had tried to work his way through quickly. He had no time or interest for such trivial matters. He could have told them exactly who had come through, but what would have been the point?

Police had stood in every chamber of the building, demanding answers from those that ran a project which was slowly but surely racking up quite a lengthy dead and injured list, and when Lawson had appeared, they'd zeroed in on him.

Lawson had found himself resorting to desperation and had taken to his heels, the first time he had actually fled for as long as he could remember, and the movements had come awkwardly. Nevertheless, he knew the layout of the building better than those pursuing him, and he had made his way unhindered out into the night air, haranguing the guards on the gate to let him pass before the police caught up with him. Nobody said no to the boss, and he was soon once again on normal streets.

He'd wanted to put a few streets between himself and the Eden building before trying to find a black cab, and he'd sprinted as best he could. His ankles had ached and sharp pains had pierced his shins, and even after the taxi had dropped him off in front of Sabastine's three storey townhouse, they'd still throbbed from his efforts. But at least he had evaded the police. At least he had made it to the vampire's home intact.

A man who was not Sabastine had answered the door, and had wanted to know exactly who he was and what he wanted. Lawson had told him economically, explaining that it was a matter of some urgency, and the man had asked him inside, explaining that Sabastine was not in at present, but that he could wait downstairs in the drawing room for him if he chose. Lawson had accepted that, had accepted too the brandy that the man had offered him, and had taken a seat in preparation for the vampire's return.

The clock on the mantel had read twelve thirty when Lawson arrived, but by the time he heard low voices in a room at the back of the house, the clock read quarter past two. His eyes were heavy from sitting alone in a warm room at such a late hour, heavy too from the liquor he had been supplied with, but he needed desperately to speak with Sabastine now that Ben had sparked a hunger inside him.

The door to the study suddenly opened and Sabastine stood there alone, his cold eyes regarding the man who had come to his home unannounced and unexpected.

"So it is you," Sabastine said to him, closing the door behind him. "I thought my manservant had made a mistake."

"I understand my coming here is out of the blue, my friend, but I needed to speak to you."

"Of course," Sabastine said, indicating Lawson to retake his seat while he took one opposite him. "What is it that I can do for you?"

Lawson stared at him for a moment, wondering just what labours he might have been interrupting at this hour. Had Sabastine been out on the town, Lawson thought to himself, prowling perhaps for human victims, or merely doing the work of business to which he owed his fortune?

"I don't know quite where to begin."

"Then begin at the beginning," Sabastine said evenly, and crossed his hands in his lap, settling back into his chair as if expecting a long fireside story.

"You were there at the beginning," Lawson started. "In fact it was you who started it all, the quest for another world."

"Go on."

Lawson took a breath and adjusted his weight in his chair.

"That world was found, beyond rational thought or prediction, and I have set foot upon it. I have seen things I would never have thought even existed, experienced wonders and delights that I shouldn't think exist anywhere in this world –"

"And yet?" Sabastine prompted.

Lawson looked into his cold unfaltering eyes. He could see the inhuman in them, the longevity of years spent behind them. Every deed he had ever performed had been well practised, and his eyes were mirrors for every one of them.

"And yet this will all be fleeting for me," Lawson said finally.

328

He half expected the vampire to roll back his head and, with a long drawn-out sigh, tell him how he had anticipated this moment. But Sabastine made no such movement, no physical movement anyway, and no such speech. Yet there was still some hint in his eyes that this was so, Lawson could sense that at least.

The vampire continued to speak without expression or emotion, but used only simple words to the guest in his house, as though he was offering instructions on how to build a model aircraft.

"There are no easy answers, my friend," he said, his words deliberate and measured. "And if anyone offered them, I would call them a fool. You have seen great wonders, greater than most of mankind ever have or ever will. You should be content with that."

"But I am not content," Lawson interjected, rising in his chair. "I've stumbled upon something that would take a hundred lifetimes to explore, and I want to have that time."

"But you are mortal, Lawson. What you ask is impossible."

"Not impossible, Sabastine. You can give me what I want."

Sabastine was silent for a while after that. His cold eyes regarded him as they had when he'd first entered the room. He seemed to know how this game went around, and even though there were no rules to be spied from the hollow pits inside his eyes, Lawson nevertheless tried to bluff his way through.

"I can not give you what you want," Sabastine said at last.

"You can," Lawson persisted. "I know you can."

"Okay then, I will not give you want you want."

It was Lawson's turn to fall silent, and he sat there staring at the vampire with disbelief and a growing sense of rage that he was outwardly attempting to curb.

"I have seen it," Lawson said. "I have seen what can be done."

"Not from me."

"For God's sake, man. Tell me why not?"

Sabastine fell silent again.

His lips seemed to curl as if in a snarl, his patience deteriorating, and he struggled with his outwardly composed manner. His skin was crawling with agitation. His fingers restless.

"I will not give you what you want," he said again. "I refuse to help you."

"Is this how you work your business," Lawson yelled at him. "Through deviousness and deceit?"

"How dare you speak to me that way. I have never given you any cause to doubt my intentions."

"You started me on this road, and I did all I could to find the portal to Kar'mi'shah. Now I know why you refused any dealing with the portal. Everyone else in the consortium is mortal and will die within a short span of years leaving you the sole owner. You will have it all, and to make me like you would ruin everything."

"Tell me how that makes me devious or deceitful?"

Lawson could feel his heart thudding in his chest, could feel the slivers of cracks chasing through it too as though it would break at any moment. His breaths were quick. He could feel himself losing control. He had no answer for the vampire. There had been no deviousness, or deceit, that was the truth of it. Sabastine was rich for a reason. He had done his homework and he had played his games long enough to be their master, and Lawson would be just another man who had fallen by the wayside and left to rot. He understood now that Sabastine saw him as nothing.

"You are not the first man to ask me for a chance at immortality," Sabastine said to him, as if he had been reading his thoughts and pondering them. "Land owners and industry tycoons alike have worn out their knees begging me to help them enjoy their accumulated wealth for longer than their brief span of existence on this earth. And I have refused them all, seeing every one of them into their graves. I acquired their properties and their monies as well as what influence they may have held. I have had devotion pledged by the fathers of wealthy upper-class families. I have brought prosperity to areas of the country where before there had been poverty. I have seen tyrannies crushed and revolutionaries crowned. So many things have I influenced and made possible because of how I choose to shape this land. The Eden Consortium is no different. And neither, my friend, are you."

Lawson sat staring at him dumbfounded.

So here was the confession in all its glory and menace. Here was the vampire's reason for sitting back in the shadows.

Sabastine had played him from the start, used him because of his mortality, knowing that he would ultimately claim it all for himself in due course. He could wait to own it all, and yet here was the dumb mortal, come back to beg for more time to enjoy it, just like all the others. Sabastine had probably expected it all from the start.

Lawson could feel his individuality slipping. He had become just another rich man scrabbling to keep hold of everything they had spent their miserable lives trying to accumulate, desperate to make any deal possible as soon as the shadow of death had fallen upon them.

He wanted to take hold of the vampire and shake him until his fangs rattled in his head, but what strength he did have was fading rapidly, his fight diminishing in the light of Sabastine's words. The vampire would claim it all, there could be no doubting that. And long after every member of the consortium was dead and buried, Sabastine would continue to grow his empire and watch the game develop according to his everlasting rules.

There was so much that Lawson wanted to say to him, but what would be the point? Lawson could feel that he was so far beneath him in his eyes that rational conversation was redundant. It would be like a peasant discussing the workings of a kingdom with its king. There was nothing left to say. Even what had once passed for level ground between them had gone.

With his hands still crossed in his lap, Sabastine watched him as he got to his feet and walked broken towards the study door. Lawson left without another word. His defeat had been explained to him, perhaps as it had been explained to every other land owner and industry tycoon that littered Sabastine's past, and it had left him hollow. Of course he could return to Kar'mi'shah and keep things running until he grew old and maybe died of natural causes, but what would that achieve now? His time had been marked, and would no doubt be monitored by Sabastine until such time as he could come forward and claim the entire project as his own. Lawson knew he still had money and still had power, but all that had somehow been negated in less than one night. He had used his power without guilt or fear of reprisal for as long as he could remember, but for all the murders and briberies that he had had performed, nothing compared to the feat of having it all taken away from him.

As he left Sabastine's townhouse and stepped out once more into the street, for the first time in a very long time, he did not know where he should be going or what he should be doing. He felt like a stranger lost in the world, the path he had been following suddenly covered over and smothered by weeds, and he stood beneath the night sky just staring straight ahead.

He knew he couldn't just stand outside the home of the vampire - and loathed the fact that he might even now be watching him, although he guessed that he would probably not even waste his time on a being so trivial – and forced himself to move along the pavement, but in which direction he didn't really know, and didn't much care.

# EIGHTEEN

## INTO THE ETERNAL FAMILY

Even if it had been a foggy night in old London town, a real pea-souper as it would have been called in the days of Jack The Ripper, Ben Weaver could not have felt more like a killer stalking the ill-lit shadowed streets. Something about that image tickled him, as he made his way through the city towards Annie's flat in Chelsea, of a cloaked murderer flitting from darkness to darkness, and he toyed with the idea of changing his name to something more fear-inducing and infamous. Ben was not the name of a killer, he'd decided, but then he supposed that Jack, on its own, was not one either; it was the Ripper that did it. But to give himself the full Jack The Ripper moniker or at least something similar in time, was to invite such shameless grandeur upon himself that he gave up on the whole notion. But his name would evolve, that much he was clear about, just as he himself had evolved. A name would come, he concluded, and something more fitting to an everlasting soul.

Annie's car was still parked out in the street, and Ben climbed the steps up to the front door of the Victorian terraced house, pressing the buzzer for her flat and waiting for a reply. He had no watch, but he guessed the time to be a few hours past midnight.

Annie would no doubt be in deep sleep, but he had travelled far to see her and his news could not be kept with him while he milled around until dawn, when she might wake peacefully and the messenger burst into flames. He expected the delay to be long, picturing the decision between her staying in bed or crossing a cold flat to answer the intercom. Ben went to press it a second more insistent time, but was surprised when she answered, her voice far from sleepy.

"Who is it?"

"It's me. Ben."

He found his voice lighter than he had thought it would be, and when the lock clicked open and he pushed on the door, he climbed the stairs to the top floor to find her waiting there for him. Her eyes were red with tears and he lingered on the top step for a moment, thinking that she had already learned the news that he had brought, but he went to her anyway with a comforting smile and shared a mutual embraced.

"Where have you been?" she wanted to know. "I've been worried sick about you."

Was this why she had been crying, he thought? Did she not know the true agony that might be coming?

"It's a long story," he told her, following her through into the flat. He had been in her home several times, but now it seemed different for some reason. Was it because he was different? He had no idea, but he struggled to take everything in, the rules of the game constantly shifting and changing.

"I waited for you," Annie said to him, "but you never returned. I thought you were -"

"Dead? No, not quite. But I did come close."

Annie stared at him for a moment, as if trying to see through his inappropriate levity, and then wandered through into the kitchen.

"Would you like a drink?" she asked him, picking up the kettle.

Ben followed her into the kitchen and smiled, but with a humour she would not have understood. He shook his head.

"Oh, I'm so glad you've come back," she cried, wrapping her arms round him again. "I didn't think I was ever going to see you again. Marcus Lawson said he would do all he could –"

"I've already spoken to him."

"So he found you?"

"No, I kind of found him."

Annie took a breath as if to begin a new topic, but Ben silenced her quickly.

"Listen," he began. "I came here because I needed to speak to you. I needed to let you know something, about the portal. You see... Shit, this is difficult."

"Ben –"

"Please, let me go on –"

"I think I know what you're trying to tell me."

"You do?"

Annie tried a smile, and then pressed her hands upon his chest.

"And I want to thank you for your compassion, and for coming here in the middle of the night, but I already know. The doctors have told me. There have been a handful of cases already from people who have stepped across that threshold. The police and the government are investigating all the allegations, and although no one really knows anything about what's going on in there, they're trying to piece together some kind of accountability charge or something."

Ben stood and stared at her. She knew and she seemed to be coping with it better than he had. All he could do was look at her as she smiled wearily at him. Her compassion was astounding. She seemed to have accepted what had happened to her, not happily of course, but with a kind of determination to fight whatever was going on inside her.

"I can help you," Ben finally said to her.

"The doctors said they are doing what they can –"

"They can do nothing," Ben insisted.

Annie stared at him. He could see tears beginning to well in her already red eyes. He did not want to hurt her any more than she was hurting already, and he loathed the fact that she might be thinking that he was trying to crush what little hope she had, but he had to say it, he had to at least give her the option.

"I had the same... condition... as you," he started, "but I was healed in a way that our doctors could never even begin to dream of."

"What are you saying?" Annie wanted to know, taking a step away from him, shaking her head as though she did not want to hear her frail hopes destroyed.

"I can save you," Ben went on, taking hold of her hands. "Just as I was saved."

She wanted to turn away, Ben could see that, and yet he could also see that she wanted to hear more, wanted to hear anything that might get rid of whatever had gotten inside her.

"I can help you," he said again, and that was when she half-stumbled, half-ran, into his arms, and cried like a helpless bawling baby.

2

Ben carried her through into the living room and to the sofa where he gently laid her down. He pressed his lips tenderly against hers and almost immediately felt the sour stench of death curling inside her, the hopelessness and the despair churning like a grim ocean of ruin.

He couldn't stand to see her like that any more, and he moved his head slowly down to the crook of her neck. He could smell the salt of her sweat and her tears, and tasted it as he traced a line along her flesh with the tip of his tongue. His jaws opened to engulf her, and he felt her skin resilient against his lengthening teeth. There was a moment when he paused, when he thought that making her as he had been made might be wrong. But then he decided that he would not lose her to something so hateful as what was hidden in the void, and pressed down hard upon her neck with all his strength.

Her skin broke easily, and he felt her hands grasp him in panic and shock as she began to buck violently beneath him. Ben clasped her hard to him so that she could not break free, and drank from her voraciously as she continued to thrash. Her blood was hot and thick, and he swallowed it all as it gushed from the wound he had opened. In most ways it was no different than the blood of the carriage driver or the security guard, yet he could taste the traces of death concealed within it like bitter acid on the back of his tongue.

He drank until her motions began to slow, her fight draining as her energies were bled from her body. It was then that he pulled away from her, his senses whirling from the meal.

Ben looked down at her with half-lidded eyes, at her body that trembled from massive blood-loss, and delicately pushed her hair from her forehead with his hand. She seemed so fragile, lying there motionless with half open eyes blank and unseeing, splayed across the threshold between the living and the dead, so tenuous, so mortal. Then he opened one of his own veins at the wrist (with teeth still livid and crimson from the wound at her neck), and pressed it to her lips, urging her to feed as his blood pulsed out and over her face, down onto the sofa, staining the fabric swiftly with its deep scarlet.

Her eyes remained closed, however, as his blood ran over her. She seemed almost too far gone, despite the fact that she still possessed a faint echo of a heartbeat, and he became terrified that maybe he had drunk too much from her.

He pushed his wrist harder against her mouth, widening her jaws so that his blood pumped directly into her open mouth. But still her body refused to drink.

With his free hand he forced her head back so that her mouth was uppermost like the neck of a bottle. It began to fill, threatening to drown her if she did not take it down into her stomach. But then her body contorted, blood erupting from her mouth in a thick spurt as she gagged, as her lungs rejected what had begun to fill them. And then her eyes opened wide as she at last began to drink.

Ben pulled her head round so that she could drink at a more natural angle, and cradled her in his arms like an infant as she continued to suckle from the open vein at his wrist, her body drawing life back into itself, fighting for survival.

Ben knew that there would still be a struggle for her to adapt, just as there had been for him in the temple. But he would spend more time with her than Rammenen Karee had. He had learned so much already, but he knew that the rest they could learn together.

There was a chance for them both now, where before there had been nothing but the promise of an early grave. Surely Annie would see that. Surely she would accept the life that he had forced upon her.

She, too, would undoubtedly be repulsed at first, but just like he had done, she would learn the ways of her new life. Then maybe one day they would return to Kar'mi'shah together, and explore the other world they had promised themselves they would do someday.

But who knew what the future held? For now, things would need to be taken one step at a time. Annie was still semi-conscious and feeding almost contentedly now like a baby in his arms. At least he was there to help guide her through it all. At least he was there to cradle her.

# NINETEEN

## THE FINAL DEAL

It hadn't proved difficult to find Annabel Randall's home address. Lawson had walked the streets of London without caring where he might end up, and it had taken a few hours for his situation to really sink in. His options were few, he knew, but as dawn broke over the diesel-blackened buildings of the city, everything seemed to come together with a single name: Ben Weaver.

Perhaps where Sabastine had denied him, so this new vampire might accept. Lawson still had plenty to offer, and whereas Sabastine had so much already, Lawson was sure that Ben had not. There was only one place he was likely to be headed, but Lawson had to wait until 9.00AM for the PaceNet News offices to open.

He called them from a payphone and spoke to a woman in personnel. Reluctant at first, she soon told him Miss Randall's full address once he'd explained who he was and how he might be able to sort out a pass to Kar'mi'shah for her, once he was back in the offices of the Eden building, as a thank you.

By ten thirty he was climbing the steps to Annabel Randall's front door and pressing the buzzer to her flat. When there came no reply he pressed it a second time, allowing it to sound for ten seconds or more before he released it. He tried not to think about the certainty that Ben Weaver had already been here, had already informed Annabel Randall about the threat of illness from the portal, and had subsequently left with her.

He wanted to hammer on the door, to berate it and demand that they let him in, but her flat was on the top floor, and if her flat was indeed vacant it would prove no purpose anyhow.

He was about to leave when the lock suddenly clicked open and the door was pulled wide. A woman who was not Annabel Randall started with surprise when she saw the stranger on her doorstep. Lawson quickly explained that he was waiting for someone upstairs, and would it be okay to quickly dash inside and go up to knock on the door. The woman shrugged, still uncertain, but allowed him entry anyway.

Lawson hurried up the stairs to the top floor where he hesitated momentarily before knocking. He had only partially imagined this meeting in his head, and had no real conversation with the owner of the flat planned. Fragments of deals that he could offer raced through his head as he stood there, his palms clammy, his heart thumping wildly. When there was still no answer, he pressed his head to the door and listened, but the flat was silent.

That Ben Weaver wouldn't be here hadn't really entered his head for more than a passing second. He knew that the vampire was ahead of him, possibly as much as twelve hours ahead of him, but he had expected him to still be here discussing every detail of his condition, as well as her fate, with the artist with whom he had journeyed to Kar'mi'shah.

He paused for a moment, his thoughts still reeling, but realising that he had to know for sure, he put his full weight to the door and shouldered his way inside.

Lawson staggered through the living room and into the kitchen like a desperate and crazed man. The oven was cold, plates sat dirty in the sink, and the kettle was off its base. It looked as though they had left, perhaps in a hurry, but more likely before the onset of dawn, and he slumped against the worktop as he realised that while he had waited for PaceNet's offices to open, Ben might have been leaving this very flat with Annabel in tow.

He clenched his eyes shut as he pushed his hands hard through his hair, wringing it inside his fists with exasperation.

Forcing himself to leave the kitchen, he staggered through into the bedroom just to make sure. Drawers had been left open, and only a scattering of women's clothes hung over the tops, some littering the bed where quick decisions had been made about what to take and what to leave behind.

His despair was complete, his last hope gone. Sabastine would claim everything now, and he was powerless to stop it. There was still the possibility that some of the other consortium members could attain immortality and deny him or even share that ownership, but it somehow all seemed so unlikely. Sabastine had had this planned from the outset, the mortality of the other members surely amusing him like nothing else on Earth.

David Embers had been high on Lawson's list for seeking ultimate control of the Eden Consortium.

A ruthless businessman and entrepreneur, what else other than the acquisition of the greatest 'business' could ever possibly inspire him more? Yet Lawson had seen the man's mental state change within mere seconds of setting foot on new soil, as soon as Embers had first laid eyes upon Kar'mi'shah and the new world beyond. The utter focus behind his eyes had vanished as he'd watched, and he'd almost skipped from the portal building like a schoolchild mesmerised by some fantastic fable come to life. Lawson had not seen him again, but he had heard that Embers had already left the city, hiring a camel train to take him deep into the heart of the desert.

Cecil Lovegrove, on the other hand, had not fared so well. Only days into his new adventures, he had been murdered by locals. Lawson hadn't liked the man, hadn't liked his pursuit of demanded respect, but he hadn't deserved what he'd got. Stabbed repeatedly, his killers had taken whatever valuables he'd had about his person, and knowing Lovegrove there'd probably been plenty, before leaving him for dead in the southern quarter.

Candice Rhodes had not enjoyed her time either, but at least she had left with her life. Kar'mi'shah was not rich with society parties or opulent gatherings. Candice had tired of reality early on, forcing herself to endure the simple pleasures that the working classes enjoyed. But she had ultimately returned to London within two weeks, and to the champagne life she loved so well. Lawson had not seen her either, and hadn't expected to, but he was sure that she was just as unhappy with her life as she had been before. Comfortable, but still unhappy.

But it was Yvette Moore that he felt so bad about. Not because she had failed to love Kar'mi'shah, because she had. Her face had lit up like something wonderful. It had almost made his heart break to see his promises to her fulfilled. But she had wandered into it alone, without waiting for him to share it with her, and that was what pained him so much. All he had wanted was to see this beautiful young woman smile. And he had seen it briefly too. But she had gone on ahead, and he had never seen it again. Word still came back that she still remained in the city, but for how much longer? He wanted to see her again, wanted to press his lips against that smile. He wanted it to be infectious and spend his life enraptured by it. He wanted to be happy for her, and mostly he was, yet a sadness remained inside him that she had refused him the opportunity to share it with her.

He wandered back through into the living room, his hands hanging at his sides, and collapsed into an armchair. He felt hollow inside, and felt an ache inside it that threatened to eat him up. With Yvette gone, and his mortal demise already plotted and swallowed whole, his wealth and power were nothing.

He clenched his head in his hands and cried Ben's name out aloud. His shout reverberated around the small flat, echoing like a voice in a stone chamber, but he didn't care who heard him now.

And then his eyes fell upon the sofa opposite him, his focus settling on the deep scarlet stain that glistened on one of the cushions. He swallowed hard as he stared at it, his hands dropping slowly into his lap as the realisation of what he was looking at dawned on him. Then he heard a footstep behind him.

He half-turned in his chair and saw Ben standing in the doorway to the flat, the artist Annabel Randall standing behind him. Something about her was not right - her eyes were heavy-lidded, her head crooked awkwardly to one side - and it looked as though she was being held up on wires. Ben, on the other hand, was grinning like a madman, and all Lawson could do was look from one to the other in both confusion and fear.

"Whatever it is you're thinking," Lawson said to him, trying to get to his feet, "don't."

"What would I be thinking?" Ben asked, not moving from his spot at the threshold. His voice was level and even, menacing with intent. A suitcase stood beside him, and what looked like a pair of white lace knickers poked untidily out of the side.

Lawson shot a glance to the window, even though he knew he was on the third floor. At best his descent would break both his legs. At worst...

"Don't," he said again, his eyes flickering back towards the woman behind him. "I came here for your help. I can offer you the world. Money. Power."

"Is that stuff so important?" Ben asked him. He still had not moved.

"You know that it is."

"You have it all, and yet you beg from someone who has nothing. Tell me how that works?"

Lawson was breathing hard again. What was it with vampires and logical dialogue? Did their brains figure this shit out quicker than he could?

"You're blood," Ben went on, starting away from the door now towards him. "And that's all you

346

are. A hot meal for the hungry."

Lawson circled the armchair away from him, trying to keep something solid between the two of them. The woman who now occupied the doorway on her own still looked dazed, as though she was drugged or semi-conscious. If he could get to the door before Ben, he might have a shot at the stairs, and if he could make them, he knew that Ben would not be able follow him out into the sunlit street.

"Don't be a fool," Lawson continued. "I could set you up for life. I could give you my stake in the Eden Consortium. You'd be made."

"What else?"

"Money, as much as you want."

"What about your house, your possessions, your car?"

Lawson hesitated. They had turned half a circle around the armchair, as though they were performing some crazed dance, until he was standing between Ben and the woman in the doorway. This was the best shot he had, and yet he lingered for just a few moments more. The words were on his lips, the deal delicate but still there.

"Make me immortal," he whispered.

Ben leaned forward, his crazed grin widening across his face to show his fangs that were already glistening long and white.

"I don't fucking think so."

Lawson pushed himself away from the armchair then and ran as hard as he could for the doorway. The woman still stood dazed, her eyes heavy-lidded and vacant, her head still crooked on her shoulders, and Lawson threw himself at her to force his way past.

The next few seconds came in staggered snatches: he saw her eyes flash open, her jaws gape to expose white teeth pearlescent with saliva; he felt himself be grasped by her thin claw-like fingers and cast down in a dizzying arc where he landed hard on his back; he heard his head hit the floor before he felt the thud; and in the swirling murk that followed, he saw her bending over him with her fangs extended.

As she buried her head into the curve of his neck and he felt the sharp agony of her teeth bursting through his skin like two fat needles, his vision flailed beyond her and settled upon the vampire who stood parentally in the doorway behind her. Pain welled unbelievably in his neck, but he was suddenly powerless now to struggle inside a grip that held him tight. All he could do as the female vampire drank noisily from him, was stare up at her sire through a darkening and dirty haze, and watch as his insane grin spread further across his face.

PART SEVEN


PASSION AND WARFARE

# ONE

## AFTER YEARS AWAY, HOME

It had taken a few days for the vampire Catherine Calleh to realise that the one-time thief Jenner Hoard was not going to return to the flat, and a further couple of days to realise that he had left the city. Whether he had left to go to another part of the country or even to another country altogether, she'd had no idea, and nor had she much cared, but it had left her with what little hope the mortal had given her in tatters.

She'd visited the site of her husband's grave only to find a housing estate built upon it; she'd wandered the streets of London in the hope of finding the vampires who had once lived there, only to find them gone; and then her only contact in England, the mortal who had claimed to be able to help her, had abandoned her also.

For three years she had searched with the tortured wraith-vampire Antoinette for her husband Carlos, but they had failed. They had returned to England with nothing but dejection, but had paid one last visit to the site of his grave in the hope of finding some undiscovered clue as to where he may have gone.

During her first visit over three years ago at the very start of her search for him, she had found the house, beneath which his grave had been dug, the subject of police investigation, the scene taped off to prevent intruders. She had looked around and found the dining room of the house half excavated through its concrete foundation.

She had buried Carlos deep in the earth after she had killed him, and whoever had built that house had presumably never found him. But the question that demanded an answer was just how somebody might dig through a significant depth of concrete and compacted earth using only hand tools, deeper than the people who had laid the foundation with heavy machinery, in order to exhume the body. And more to the point, why they would want to.

The possibility that perhaps the owners of the house had suffered similar dreams and hallucinations to her own had not escaped her, but dreams alone would not necessitate someone taking a pick axe and a shovel to their own home. Something else had gone on there, but with the then owners gone and nothing but an empty grave left behind, there had been few answers available. Nevertheless, Catherine had revisited that same site a while later to discover both the house repaired and a new owner moved in, a slight woman with short dark hair, a woman who had returned her late night scrutiny more than once.

Catherine had surveyed the dining room of that house one night through the downstairs window, and despite there being no new excavation, she had heard what sounded like moans and laments deep beneath the earth. She had not been able to detect whether those sounds belonged to her husband, and indeed had seen none of his shadow children playing at the graveside. So she had left, forced to disregard the sounds as only echoes of his former presence.

When Catherine decided to return home to Kar'mi'shah she had taken the wraith vampire with her. London was dead to both of them, the mortal world hollow and empty of anything that it had once promised. But when she finally returned to the portal and saw the blasphemy that was the Eden Building, she'd become filled with outrage, and a fury had ignited deep inside her. How dare mere mortals claim ownership of the bridge to Kar'mi'shah, and for something so meagre as money?

The two vampires had met resistance at the gates to the building where the Regency Hotel had once stood. Guards had tried to prevent their access, but Catherine would not be denied her passage home, especially by mortals worthy only of dying by her hand.

She'd dispatched them all, every guard who barred their way, every worker who stood in that building, as Antoinette lurked in whatever shadows could be stolen into. There was only one mortal whom Catherine had spared, a woman who had just returned with the smell of the desert on her skin, who desired only her own home, the same as she. This one woman Catherine had left alone. The vampire had felt a sense of loss about her, mirrored only by her own true feelings, and despite her mortality, they had passed each other connected by some unspoken link.

The blasphemy in London had been beyond reprisal. But to see what those mortals had done to her own world had been almost too much to take.

Catherine felt bitter hatred for how they had claimed what was not theirs, disfiguring the landscape as they so chose and creating an abomination inside which they had housed the return portal, a disfigurement of a temple that they dared to call holy. It had angered her beyond words or deeds, but she had stormed from the building without committing any further acts of murder or destruction, desiring only to put the whole place at her back and return to the ice fields with Antoinette where she had previously made her home, away from the distractions and futilities of men and vampires alike.

But her decision became unravelled before it had even started as she and Antoinette passed through the streets of Kar'mi'shah. There she heard the name of the thief spoken in conversation between two women in a market square, his name jarring mid-sentence like a clanging bell. The hour was late, and Catherine faltered in the shadows of an alleyway as she listened to their conversation.

Was this the same Jenner who had left her alone in his flat? Had he returned here of all places?

The women spoke of him as some kind of labourer at a temple near the heart of the city, and although it did not seem likely that it would be the same man, she went there anyway, quickly and with Antoinette in tow.

At a pyramid set in an ornate plaza fronted by two grand columns, Catherine entered the temple of the goddess Arbour alone as Antoinette concealed herself outside, away from the light that spilled like molten gold from the oil lamps within.

The vampire dismissed the welcome of the priestess who approached her, and demanded only information about the labourer. The priestess insisted that this was a place of worship for the goddess, and would not be used for demands or threats. Catherine grew infuriated, and as much as she wanted to tear this woman apart, she remembered how she herself had once been a goddess worshipped by the populace of this city, with her own priestesses devoted to her. Nevertheless, Catherine stormed past her and on into the depths of the temple, crying the name of the thief, her shrieks echoing off the cold stone walls, the priestess chasing after her.

Her voice reverberated throughout the chambers and corridors of the temple ahead of her, but as she turned a corner that led into an altar room, her efforts were rewarded as she came face to face with the thief Jenner Hoard. They stared at each other for a moment, he in shock, she with rage. Then her fury came:

"I waited for you."

"I know," the mortal said. "I'm sorry. But I had nothing to return for."

"You said you would help me."

"I know," Jenner said again. "But –"

"You played me for a fool."

"That was not my intention."

"And yet that is what you achieved."

The priestess hovered behind them, uncertain of her part in all this, and when Jenner nodded to her and told her that everything was okay, she seemed glad to retreat and leave them to it.

Jenner offered the vampire a seat, perhaps to

initiate a conversation that had waited three years to be had, but Catherine simply stood where she was and glared at him. This was no moment to be courteous, and she would not sit and chat like long lost friends when all she wanted was to rip off his head for his dishonesty.

"You are still mortal," she observed at length.

"Yes."

"You return here to devote your time to a goddess and yet you have not been blessed with everlasting life. How is that?"

"I did not want it."

Catherine stared at this creature not knowing whether he was mocking her or not. Why would a devotee not wish a lifetime of devotion? It made no sense to her. And yet despite the many paradoxes and conundrums that encircled this human, she could not ignore his lies or deceits.

He had repeatedly taken back what he had promised, spilling lies from a filthy mouth too profane to tolerate, and now she was here listening to more of the same. But what troubled her most was why she had even come here. Why had she sought him out once again? What was it that she needed from him? The answer came readily to her mind - she needed his help - but to bring that conclusion to her lips and voice it out loud would be like bringing up vile acid.

"Why are you here?" Jenner said to her, prompting the words she loathed to speak.

She stayed silent for a while, just staring at him, just taking in the sight of what he was, what he had been reduced to. The words burned inside her, and she knew that she had to get them out, even if it meant killing herself inside.

"I needed help to find Carlos," she relented, swallowing the agony back down into her belly. "I searched alone but I found nothing, no sign of him, no trace of where he had gone. I was alone in all that."

She could see something change in him as she spoke, something beyond his expression that altered from concern to guilt. She could sense that he hadn't wanted to abandon her, and yet the fact remained that he had.

"I wanted an end to everything," Jenner said at last, visually swallowing pain of his own. "I felt so very tired, so very far removed from everything that was important. All I wanted was to die, but not there, not alone in London. That city cares about nothing."

Catherine stared agog at him. Here was everything that she had felt just a few years ago. But where she had fled to the ice fields in the mountains, he had fled here to this temple. It was not a monastic life like hers, and she wondered why he had chosen to do such a thing. But before she could even question it, he was already supplying answers.

"The woman I loved was killed many years ago," he said, "by one of your own. You saw her in my flat before it was destroyed."

"I remember," Catherine found herself saying.

"She was made into a vampire, made into a goddess, and taken away from me. Here she was given a temple, and prayed to by a people reduced to struggling in an ever-encroaching desert, in exchange for combating whatever hardships the desert could hurl at them. She did her job well, aided by Alexia, the Mistress of all Kar'mi'shah, and fought back the desert sands and its beasts. The city flourished, as did its people, and everything you see here today has been in part because of her. That is why I came back to devote myself to her. To do what little I can for her in my remaining years alive."

"But her name was -"

"Her name was Emma," Jenner explained. "She told me that was no name for a goddess. She took her new name as she saw herself, a sheltered alcove away from the desert where foodstuffs for her people could be grown and tended, and renamed herself Arbour."

"So what have you returned to her as? Her lover? Her labourer?"

Jenner did not reply at first, but after consideration he told her:

"I wanted only to end my days here with her. In what capacity is irrelevant"

Catherine turned away from him, and gazed around the altar room.

"And where is this Arbour? Where is she hiding herself?"

"She spends most of her time in the lower sanctum."

"Not with you?"

"No."

"And what is it that she does down there?"

Jenner shook his head.

"I do not know."

"She does not tell you?"

Jenner shook his head again.

"No."

"Then that hardly seems worth the effort, now

358

does it?" Catherine sneered, feeling her hate for him rising back up into her throat once again.

"What business is this of yours?" Jenner cried. "What do you want?"

"I simply wanted you to know what my loss is like. You have found your love, I have not."

"I could ask Arbour if she knows of his whereabouts."

"Would I see you again if you went?"

"Look," Jenner said. "I'll go and speak with her and see if she knows anything about him, but it can't be now. Come back tomorrow night and I will tell you what I have found out then."

"If you lie to me again," Catherine threatened, "then you will know the true meaning of pain. That I can assure you."

And with that, the vampire turned and swept out of the altar room, leaving Jenner to watch her go.


He was fearful for his life, even though he was in the temple of Arbour, a goddess who had once been a woman called Emma, his once-upon-a-time lover whom he had allowed to drink from his veins in a ruined temple many years ago in order to save her life, when Kar'mi'shah had been little more than rubble. That had been a long time ago, and even though their former lives were so very different to what they had become, Jenner could still remember her as a simple socialite girl who had only been happiest when spending her father's money.

She had been a vampire for many years now, ever since the then Master of Kar'mi'shah, Jackel

El'a'cree, had made her. But where Jenner had aged and grown weary, she looked no different. In fact she looked more radiant and perfect each and every time he laid eyes upon her. Such was the blessing of Godhood, he suspected.

He knew her private sanctum was sacred to her, but she had not risen from it for many days and nights now and he was concerned about her. Now he had a grave reason to speak to her: the vampire Catherine Calleh would be returning the following night, and he had promised her information. If he failed her again, he did not want to think what she might be capable of. She already seemed at the end of her tether, distraught by the continued separation from her husband, and her fury could not be underestimated. He was inside Arbour's temple, under her protection, yet he couldn't be sure of her intervention should Catherine return in a vengeful state. So taking up one of the torches that lit the altar room, Jenner started towards the stone steps that led down into the darkest catacombs of the temple, and down towards the unlit chamber where Arbour lay resting.

# TWO

## BENEATH THE BOUGHS OF THE GODDESS

The flames from the torch he carried flickered eagerly as he descended, the yellow light casting stark shadows across the roughly-hewn surface of the stone, as he made his way down into the long passageway that led to Arbour's sanctum. He had ventured here, to her private resting place, only a handful of times. She did not welcome the intrusion, even from him, but he needed to speak with her, if only to appease Catherine and satisfy the promise he had made to her.

Jenner found her lying on her bed with her head thrown back and her eyes closed. He approached her tentatively, daring to illuminate her an inch at a time with the light thrown by the flickering torch, until he was standing less than five yards from her.

Then he stopped and looked down upon her. He could see her eyes roving beneath her eyelids, her forehead creasing as though she was trapped in the depths of a vivid dream. Her fingers twitched at her sides, clutching and releasing the luxuriant cloth upon which she lay, her lips parting and closing as if speaking to some unseen assembled crowd.

Jenner held back, not sure whether to retreat or to stay until she woke.

He hesitated, hoping that she might open her eyes and look at him. But he simply hovered as he watched her dream, lingering like a schoolboy uncertain before a promised kiss.

When it seemed clear that she would not wake from the light that he had brought into the room, Jenner retreated back a few steps and set the torch into one of the iron holders set upon the wall. Then he took a seat on the hard cold floor, his back to the wall facing her, and settled down to wait.

When they had first met, he had been a petty thief while she had been a wealthy man's socialite daughter. Their backgrounds could not have been more different, and she had only dated him so that her friends might wonder and gasp at her audacity. He'd known this from the start, of course, but the relationship had had its advantages. She was beautiful for a start, and to be seen with her on his arm was enviable. The sex had been amazing, and he had lost track of the amount of times he'd borrowed money from her and not repaid it. But she'd never expected it to be repaid, not really, and that had been part of the fun of her dating a criminal. Her daddy had more than he could keep giving her, and despite the embarrassment caused by his daughter's wilful insolence, it at least made his little girl happy.

But the real kicker – he saw it now – was how often he had shunned her and pushed her away. She would have stayed at his side no matter what, and she had told him that she loved him on so many occasions that he'd lost count. And yet he had repeatedly walked out on her, lied to her about not being able to keep appointments, and used every goddamned excuse he had been able to think of to keep her at arm's length.

Only once she had been killed and turned by the vampire had he realised just what he'd had. Only once she had been taken away from him had he missed her. And that was the shitty fucking story of love in all its glory, the sick joke of only wanting what you can't have.

Now the tables had been reversed. He wanted her more than anything, desired only to be at her side. But she had not only been made a vampire, but had been gifted the role of a goddess; people actually prayed to her and gave her offerings. The very temple he was sitting in had been raised in her name. To want to be the boyfriend of a goddess was so fucking ridiculous that it wasn't even funny.

Sometimes he thought she only allowed him to stay out of pity, he thought as he pushed his hands through his hair. He was still mortal after all, and he had refused immortality because he knew he would never be able to bring himself to drink the blood of the living, and she knew, of course, that one day soon he would reach the end of his span of years and die from old age. All this he was brutally aware of, and it kicked him in the belly every waking moment of his life. And yet it was still favourable to waking up in a cold dark place without her, in a familiar world that was indifferent to whether he lived or died.

The light from the torch guttered as a draught circled the stone chamber, sending flickering shadows dancing around the room. Arbour still moved in her sleep, her hands still clasping the rich cloth upon which she lay, her head turning as if agitated.

He still thought of her as beautiful. She hadn't changed or aged in all the years since she had been a vampire, and he guessed that was one of the states of her being. He felt like he had aged decades in that time, the new life he had led punishing him for all the crimes he had performed in his past. He felt tired all the time, his body aching, and he wanted only for an end to it all, to be at peace beneath Arbour's watchful gaze.

She stirred suddenly, and he wondered if she was waking. He pushed himself upright to try and see her face more clearly, but she didn't raise her head or even open her eyes, but instead fell back to her former state.

It had been hard for him to come to terms with what she had become, he thought to himself as he sat there, and he used the word 'what' rather than 'who'. She'd become a monster in his eyes, a creature that drank the blood of the living, a beast that killed things. Of course that was only part of it in its most primal terms, but she had found shelter beneath the wing of a goddess who was later to become Mistress of all Kar'mi'shah. He remembered even now what Arbour had said to him all those years ago: she saw her Godhood as an honour, while he saw it as a punishment. He'd been narrow-minded back then, he knew that, but then how could he have been otherwise?

It was dark in the sanctum apart from what the frail light of the torch illuminated. His focus struggled with the flickering light, his sight always dancing, and after a while his eyes began to grow heavy. He continued to watch Arbour sleep as he sat on the cold hard floor, but found himself drifting as he thought about the life they could have had. It was melancholy, and it was painful, but he couldn't help his mind invite it all in.

The lure of sleep overtook him finally, and from the blackness of his dream he saw the goddess Arbour emerge to stand before him. She was smiling down upon him, but as her servant or as her once-upon-a-time lover he couldn't tell. Could she even think in terms of their former love anymore? He had no idea. But he got to his feet in his dream state and took her hand when she offered it.

They wandered through a grove of blossoming apple trees, hand in hand, in silence for a while, before the goddess began to speak.

"What is it that brings you to me?" she asked him, her voice gentle and lilting.

"I have a favour to ask," Jenner began, "a request, really, from an acquaintance."

"And what is this request that your acquaintance cannot ask me personally?"

Jenner hesitated for a moment.

"Her name is Catherine Calleh," was all he said.

"The goddess?" Arbour said, astonished. "She came to you rather than me directly?"

"She's confused about a great many things. She wants help to find her husband, but doesn't seem to recognise the world any more."

"I've heard a great many things about her, and it surprises me why she has requested help from you."

Jenner looked at her.

"I think it was more out of desperation than desire," he said. "I don't think she would ever have chosen to deal with me on any terms other than hostile, but I don't think she has any choice in the matter. Everyone she has ever known has gone."

Arbour nodded solemnly as she walked.

"There have been many gods returning, but not to the high positions they'd once held. I think they have needed to find themselves and their place amongst things anew."

They walked in silence again for a while after that, the delicate smell of the apple blossom around them almost physical on the air. Their perfume caressed him in his dream, drawing him deeper into his sleep, carrying him along until Arbour spoke once more.

"What is the name of Catherine's husband?" she asked.

"Carlos," Jenner told her, and as soon as he mentioned his name, a tremor of agitation rumbled throughout his dream.

Arbour turned and stared at him, her face stark against the soft blossoms around them.

"You are sure of this?" she asked him.

"Of course. Do you know something about him?"

Arbour kept her silence for a few moments more, as though unsure whether she should reveal the knowledge she obviously held about him.

"There have been great disturbances out in the desert. My people despair about a force that has been darkening their lands?"

"What kind of disturbances? What force?"

"Ghosts haunting their homes and fields, animal mutilations and deaths, deformed births, crops burned and withered, earth tremors and cracks. I have been doing all I can to locate the cause of it all, but whatever it is refuses to be seen and denies my every effort. I have tried to contact Alexia, but not even she responds to my pleas. I'm not sure what I can do about any of it, but the name Carlos has been on more than one person's lips."

"And this is out in the desert?"

"To the north. Three days travel from here."

Jenner paused for a few moments, as though the only words he could possibly say now were too obvious to utter. In the end, it was only he who could speak, and it was only those words he could voice. It came as a statement more than a question.

"You want me to go there?"

The goddess Arbour turned to look at him, and cupped his coarse face inside the cradle of her delicate hands.

"I would not order you to travel there for either myself or my people, but if you should go there for your own reasons and for the assistance of your acquaintance, I would deem it a personal courtesy to me."

Jenner nodded briefly and then said that he would go.

Arbour returned his smile, and then bent towards him and placed a kiss gently upon his lips. His eyes closed as the delicate contact enraptured him, but then as he opened them once more, he found himself no longer in the grove of blossomed trees, but back once again in the flame-lit sanctum of the goddess. She still slept atop her bed, her hands still clutching and releasing the luxuriant cloth upon which she lay. And very slowly he pushed himself to his feet, looked down at her for a few moments more, and then retrieved the torch from where he had set it on the wall. Then he turned his back on her, and climbed the steps back up towards the main body of her temple.

# THREE

## INTO THE DESERT LANDS

Jenner anxiously awaited Catherine's return. She appeared before him an hour after nightfall in the halls of the temple, out of the shadows and without announcement, in her usual black swathe of robes that covered every part of her but the bone-white skin of her face.

She glared at him from the blackness, yet she said nothing to him. It seemed that she would wait for him to reveal to her whatever he had learned from Arbour, and that nothing else would keep them in the same company. Indeed, when Jenner informed her how the goddess had told him in a dream that the name Carlos had been uttered in a small town three days travel into the arid northern desert, and that he was to go there to see for himself what disturbances had occurred, Catherine seemed taken aback, unsure about whether his unexpected charity was for her benefit or as a gesture towards Arbour. Whichever it was, Catherine was vehement that he would not be going alone. She would travel with him.

When the two of them stepped out into the night, however, their travelling companion approached for the first time out of the dark. So wretched was her appearance that Jenner started with alarm, thinking this to be a ghost and not a physical being at all, a phantom risen up out of the darkness of the city. Her name was Antoinette, Catherine told him, and that, it seemed, was to be the poor creature's only introduction. It was also to serve as an explanation.

Guides had already been assigned by Arbour for the journey ahead, along with a sturdy two horse carriage fashioned with heavy shades to protect against the harsh desert sun. There were four guides in total, two to drive the carriage, and two escorts on horseback.

Catherine was very much aware and suspicious when the carriage left the temple of the goddess Arbour, its roof laden with food and water for those creatures that needed such things. It was only Catherine, Jenner and the wraith-vampire who occupied the interior of the carriage, but they exchanged little in the way of conversation as they travelled. The air between them, despite, or perhaps in spite of, the history they shared, had become something far beyond tense. The ghost vampire said and did nothing, but remained silent and motionless in the corner of the carriage, her eyes vacant and unfocussed and as dead as the heart in her cloaked chest.

Jenner slept as well as he could those first few hours, as they made their way out of the city and through the foothills of the mountains, hesitant about lowering his guard to the vampire who'd promised his death so many times (but knowing that he must find some sleep during the nights ahead).

When he woke to the carriage bucking over rocky terrain he found Catherine gazing out through the opened shutters at distant wastes of desert, its featureless barren vista stretching unhindered to the horizon in every direction and illuminated only a sallow moon. He wasn't sure whether she even noticed his scrutiny or not, and perhaps she didn't care, but she seemed somehow melancholy to him, and he felt some kind of empathy with her, just watching her lonely vigil.

She would never concede such feelings to him, he knew that, and perhaps he was simply projecting his own feelings of loss for Emma onto her, but there was a kind of bond between them that seemed somehow forbidden ever to admit to and certainly never to be spoken.

Whether the ghostly Antoinette paid either of them any attention, Jenner had no idea. He turned his eyes her way several times as they travelled, but he could read nothing upon what features he could discern. Her face concealed almost always by shadow, she kept it hidden from view. But he had seen it that first time on the steps of Arbour's temple, a grotesquery of old scar tissue fused with the echo of deep wounds, and despite her being a vampire, he pitied her.

He continued to drift in and out of sleep as the carriage continued to rock over the hard baked floor. Recollections of his dream with Arbour filtered in and out of his head. She'd been preoccupied for some time about these disturbances that had destroyed crops and livestock for her people in Olin, disturbances so bad that it had even been troubling Alexia, the Mistress of all Kar'mi'shah. And what of her? She hadn't answered any of Arbour's pleas. What trouble might be going on there?

Jenner knew that Alexia had taken up residence in The Curbane shortly after becoming Mistress. He also knew that it was the source of The Blood Of The Ancients, the most hallowed and holy place to the BloodGods, and the location where she might fully experience the desires of the land she had inherited control over.

The Curbane was situated high in the mountains through which their guides were currently taking them. That proximity troubled Jenner as he sat in the uneasy darkness of the carriage. Arbour had instructed him to go directly to Olin. She had not instructed him to drop in on Alexia along the way. Such sacrilege would surely cost him his life before he had even set foot in the halls of The Curbane. Such things happened. They were not just idle threats.

But the hope that he might succeed where Arbour had failed, in having his questions answered directly by Alexia, lingered in his mind like a nagging itch and were not quick to dispel.

He glanced across again at Catherine still gazing out through the small carriage window at the blank desert landscape ahead of them, and wondered how much he really owed her.

Jenner shifted his weight in his seat and eased the shutter back from the window on his side, gazing up at the vast mountains that dominated the horizon to the east. How much of a detour would it be to travel there? How much of a blasphemy to seek out Alexia and ask Catherine's questions in her place?

The carriage bucked and shuddered over the rough rocky road as the questions went round and round again.

He finally decided that they needed to take the risk. Much to Catherine's agitation, Jenner hauled himself out of his seat and hammered on the carriage ceiling, yelling up to the driver to stop. Clambering out into the night air as the carriage staggered to a halt on the uneven surface, its horses snorting with disgust, Jenner approached Marius Dee perched high up on his seat to ask how long a diversion it would be. But the driver seemed wary about making such a journey to The Curbane at all.

"We would not be welcome there," Marius explained. "The Curbane has its guardians, and they would not allow us entry."

"But if we explained -"

"They would not listen."

"What if I entered and you remained outside."

Marius stared down at him from his seat atop the carriage. His indecisiveness was carved upon his face.

"You do not understand," he went on. "It is a holy place, the most sacred shrine of all our Gods, the essence and spirit of our entire culture. There is nothing there for you."

"Alexia is there," Jenner said.

Marius almost toppled backwards at the mention of her name, especially in so informal and disrespectful a fashion.

Jenner apologised quickly.

"You do know why you are taking us to Olin?" he asked Marius.

"Because Arbour desires it."

"Yes, but why?"

"Because its people are blighted by a mysterious curse."

"Exactly. Arbour doesn't know what has happened, and she can't get anything from Alexia, but I think it would be a good idea if we could shed some light on just what it is we're going to find when we get there. We're right here, for God's sake. The Curbane is up there in those mountains."

Marius pondered this for a moment, and then turned and had a brief but heated debate with Lo who sat beside him (who had heard every word), before turning back to look down at Jenner once again.

"If it is for the benefit of Arbour and the people of Olin, then we will take you there. But on your head be it if we displease Alexia or her guardians. And we will not be held responsible if they tear your head off either."

## FOUR

## WHAT HAPPENED AT THE CURBANE

It was a rugged trek for a horse-drawn carriage to make. The two escorts, Samuel and MeySeh, rode ahead on horseback up through the twisty ravines, their bodies appearing and disappearing between the vast hulking rocks of the mountain, while the carriage made its way more slowly across the uneven terrain.

"Why are you taking us there?" Catherine demanded.

"Because Alexia knows everything," Jenner told her.

"Alexia? Don't tell me she's still alive."

And the carriage continued in silence again after that.

Higher and higher they travelled, on and up the narrow twisting ravines towards the plateau where the entrance to The Curbane lay. Dread soured the interior of the carriage, but the real horror came when Marius finally managed to coax the horses up onto a flat stretch set into the gorge. Jenner heard the driver yell out, Lo echoing his alarm moments later.

As the vehicle shuddered to a halt Jenner clambered out, demanding to know what the problem was. But they did not respond. They just stared directly ahead.

He followed their line of sight, and less than thirty yards from where they stood, the bloody remains of MeySeh and Samuel (or what was left of them) lay scattered across a scarlet radius some twenty metres wide.

Blood painted the grey rock. Bones shards and torn clothing blemished the livid crimson like dull daubs of paint. Their horses were nowhere to be seen, vanished into safer crags elsewhere on the mountain.

"What the -"

"The guardians..." Marius whispered, his trembling voice barely audible. "I told you..."

"You said they'd be displeased," Jenner replied, unable to take his eyes away from the hideous slaughter.

The air was soured with the heady stench of death. The wind seemed to make no attempt to cleanse the warning to them.

"We should go," Lo muttered.

"I have to see Alexia -" Jenner declared.

"No."

Jenner cast one swift glance up at Marius and Lo, and then started forward, on towards the fresh wet remains that had once been their two scouts.

Almost immediately, before Marius or Lo had even had a chance to yell after him, the very rock beneath his feet began to groan and creak. Jenner halted as the ground shifted, threatening to take his balance as the groaning intensified.

The rock suddenly split apart between his feet and he toppled, his arms flailing as he failed to keep himself upright. He landed hard as a shower of rock shards blew from the ground, soaring high into the air before raining back down on him. He clamped his arms over his head as they peppered the ground around him, and he gazed up through the settling dust as the ground rumbled afresh, shaking and contorting as though the whole mountain was coming apart. And it was then that he saw the hulking face of living rock split apart as the emerging guardian spoke:

"You will come no further."

Its voice boomed like a hammer beating on stone, dull and grinding. Jenner lowered his arms fro his head to see this thing better as it hauled its massive frame up out of the granite.

"I came to see Alexia," Jenner cried. "I need to speak with her."

"You will come no further," the monster boomed again.

It stood up to its full height now, towering over him by some twenty feet. Its stone-cracked eyes gaped down at him, its ghastly maw hanging open. It was a beast made of living rock, yet it defied all laws of nature and heaved massive breaths deep into its cavernous body.

"I will crush you," it roared now, "and make pulp of your blood and bones."

"Alexia will want to speak with me. I was sent to the town of Olin by the goddess Arbour because of the disturbances there. I wanted Alexia's help -"

The guardian suddenly rolled its immense head to one side, as though some other voice was inside there and giving it staggered instruction. It opened its mouth as if to speak again, but then it slammed shut again before any words were ground out.

"What do you know about these disturbances," the guardian uttered finally, the words coming awkwardly, more awkwardly than they had done before.

"Very little," Jenner said. "Arbour doesn't know what's been causing them."

The guardian of stone rolled its head again, twisting and grinding on its granite neck as though its mind was struggling to fight off a bout of schizophrenia.

It staggered back a step, the first time it had shown any behaviour other than offensive.

"Come with me," it said, and took another step back as it turned.

2

"My name is Nomad," it said, as it thundered its way up and through the ravine, Jenner cradled inside one of its massive hands like a bird in a cage, carried on this journey alone.

The guardian had demanded that the carriage return back down the mountain along with all its passengers, which Marius had only been too glad to accommodate. Catherine had kept her silence inside, clearly content to stay well hidden from the Mistress of Kar'mi'shah. So Jenner travelled alone with the guardian of living rock, climbing steadily-worsening terrain, until finally they arrived at a plateau, and a gaping entranceway into the very heart of the mountain.

Steam and smoke curled at the threshold as

they approached, and only once Jenner had stepped out of Nomad's fist and into the shadows of the carved halls did he fully see the source of both. Fire guttered inside fissures in the very walls like veins, hissing to steam where it met the ice that penetrated every crack in the cold stone floor. The entire mountain seemed to be alive, watching him, crawling after him in his wake, and only when Nomad explained to him why did he fully realise just where he had demanded to be taken.

Two more guardians, one of fire and one of ice, respectively named Rail and Vessel, held station in the rock all around him. The Curbane was the holiest of places and therefore commanded the most formidable of protectors. And here it had it aplenty in the form of three elemental brothers forged by The Curbane itself.

Nomad led the mortal through the vast halls until they emerged into a monstrous cavern, its vastness illuminated by what seemed to be the very walls themselves, filaments of flame and luminescent ice shedding light like millions of tiny stars.

At the heart of the cavern rose a monolith of stone, rising to the full height of the ceiling. At its base, and fused into the tower as though she had been part swallowed by molten rock, lay a human figure, a woman half-consumed by The Curbane. But there was agitation here, and Jenner now saw the figure consumed by crawling shapes. At first he thought this part of her unification with The Curbane, but after seeing her three guardians' trepidation and their unwillingness to approach any closer, fearful of the faceless beasts that sought to smother her like a plague, he realised that these things were not a part of her, but of a different order entirely.

Jenner approached cautiously. Alexia's head hung back, her hair knitted with rock that seemed to have once seeped into her skull. That same story was repeated across the whole of her body, flesh and stone melded and fused so many times so that it seemed impossible to separate where one state stopped and the other began.

Her arms and feet disappeared into the stone seat upon which she sat just as that same stone found its way in through every orifice, her mouth and nostrils, her anus and vagina. Jenner found himself looking down upon her with pity, as though this place mastered her and not the other way around. But before he could even speak, she was answering him from beneath the scourge of black faceless forms that swarmed across her, her voice shifting and contorting as it seemed to emerge from all around him at once, echoing around the vast chamber like spiralling coils.

"The darkness watches and breathes," she told him. "So many eyes blinking and studying, returning my gaze. It writhes like a pit of snakes. It wants to consume me."

Jenner stood motionless before her. He didn't know what to say or do now that he was here. He let her continue, staring down at her naked disfigured body as the midnight demons roved across it with hands oblivious to her nakedness or her womanhood, even though she did not move or speak or breathe. Jenner thought her body dead, her words filtering out of the very rock around him, but still he could not take his eyes away from where she lay.

"It does not speak," she went on, as though ignorant of the creatures that sought to consume her, sought to find some way in where the rock had not. "It brings death to the earth, to all living things. It poisons the ground, suffocates the hearts of newborns. I can not appease it. I can not talk to it."

"What can I do?" he yearned.

Her eyes shot open for the first time, and found and focussed instantly upon him. Almost immediately the tiny black monsters surged forward towards the exposure of her opened eyes, and as her mouth snapped open to speak from her own two lips, cracking the rock that had flowed in boiling and hardened to stone, so they sought out that new breach too.

But her words came from her own tongue before the hands of the creatures sealed her throat, her warning finding him before it was smothered and extinguished:

"You will suffer this same black fate."

# FIVE

## CAMEL TRAIN

Jenner had returned to the carriage alone, allowed to descend the mountain with neither assistance nor intervention from either Nomad or the other guardians. The carriage stood waiting for him on the hardpan road, Marius and Lo busy with their agitated horses. As he approached out of the darkness he noticed that they had found Samuel and MeySeh's horses and had tethered them to the back of the carriage.

The two remaining guides looked up at Jenner as he approached, startled by his sudden appearance and seemingly both surprised that he had made it back alive at all. They said little in response to his arrival, and asked nothing of what had transpired, but seemed grateful that they were at last able to pack up and be away.

Neither Catherine nor Antoinette said a word either as Jenner climbed back into the carriage. There was something unutterably disturbing in what Alexia had said to him - as the swarm of ghastly creatures had rushed in to further their attempts at smothering her - prophesising his doom at the conclusion of their journey, and he was in no mood to discuss it with anyone, especially Catherine.

With the horses pulling the carriage once more

and the vehicle bucking from side to side again, Jenner wanted only to gaze out through the window at the scenery rolling by and let his mind drift to blankness. But then a sudden declaration from Catherine, indicating a lightening sky and an imminent dawn, shook him from the darkness behind his eyes all too soon. He opened them to see that she had refastened the shutters back over the windows, and now acknowledged him with only the briefest of curt utterances.

It was to be a straight journey, directly north to the horizon, but with only a tentative road to follow. The baked ground was hard, rocks giving way to dust that swirled inside eddies created by winds that gusted from the east, but it made for more comfortable travelling as they continued their journey towards the desert town.

Arbour's high priestess had confirmed many of the details about their journey, primarily because the goddess herself had remained in her dream state since Jenner had visited her. The name of the town was Olin and was home to approximately four hundred people, mostly farmers and traders. The land was arid and dry, but Arbour's intervention had brought water to a serviceable level and a welcome acreage of verdant pastures and orchards. Crops grew in abundance where her power could hold back the vicious grip of the desert, and her people praised her well for the prosperity her benevolence gave them.

Jenner could only visualise the oasis that was awaiting them, and he imagined a circle of deep green surrounded by the same baked earth across which they were currently travelling. What he couldn't imagine, however, was why the townspeople would even choose to exist in such a harsh climate. The high priestess had not been able to answer that question, but had offered him only one of her own for which he'd had no answer: why shouldn't they choose to live in such a place instead of a constricted city choked by too many citizens and with too little space? He'd abandoned his enquiry with that, and had thanked her for the information she had given him. Yet now he could not help but return to such fancies, with nothing else to distract him but the perpetual gaze of the two vampires who undoubtedly scrutinised his every breath and movement in the blackness of the sealed carriage.

Hours later, when finally the horses were brought to a halt once again, and Marius called down that it was close to dusk, Jenner hauled himself out to stretch his legs. The horses needed to be fed and rested after the long day's travel, and he watched as Marius and Lo began hauling down bladders of water and bushels of feed from the top of the carriage, his arms and legs cramped and awkward after being confined for so long.

When the huge baking sun finally dipped below the featureless horizon, and it was safe for the carriage door to be opened for the two occupants, only Catherine emerged from the shuttered vehicle. The sky was still illuminated with a bright orange glow, but the vampire was not interested in seeing it, and simply stared straight ahead at the point on the horizon towards which they were travelling.

Jenner strolled into the desert a little way to bring some life back to his legs, stretching the muscles of his arms and back as he walked, the heat of the desert turning rapidly to cold around him.

His thoughts turned once again to what he was actually doing, helping a vampire who had threatened to take his life more times than he could remember. It occurred to him that perhaps she was incapable of showing any kind of compassion towards him, and perhaps was not even capable of uttering a single kind word, yet so bitterly had she treated him that he refused to defend her.

She knew her own mind, he told himself. She could thank him or speak decently to him if she wanted. She just chose not to, that was the truth of it. Which brought him back full circle to the question of why was he helping her at all?

It wasn't because he feared for his safety. He'd dealt with vampires before, had killed some too, and besides, Arbour would offer him a place of refuge away from her if necessary.

No, it was something else.

He just didn't know what it was.

As he stood in the desert, some hundred yards or so away from where she had emerged, he glanced over his shoulder to look for her. But he could not see her, only the carriage and the two men busy with their horses.

Jenner continued to walk, but circled the carriage so as not to take the direct route back. He knew it would be awkward to sit inside the carriage with her if she chose not to speak again (and it would be with hostility if she did), and more so if he could not sleep any more.

The sky had darkened almost totally by the time he eventually returned. The guide and the driver were busy building a fire, snapping sparks onto dried kindling. They had pouches of meat and fish beside them ready to be cooked, and bedrolls already laid out for them to sleep through the night. They spoke little as they worked, and Jenner was content to just sit and watch them as they prepared a simple feast for the three of them that would eat such things.

The meal was good, the heat from the fire blissful as the freezing desert winds sought to find its way inside his clothing and blankets. Sleep did not come readily, and he watched the patterns of the stars shift almost imperceptibly across the vast blue-black heavens above him for a few hours as he dozed and lost himself to idle thoughts.

So peaceful was it out in the desert that a decadent feeling of calm stole over him. He found himself grinning up at the stars like a lunatic, and he chastened himself more than once for doing so. His whole adventure was ridiculous. He tried to rekindle the severity of what he was doing as he lay there, but it seemed almost impossible. Even Alexia's warning of doom seemed ludicrous.

The icy wind swirled dust around his bedroll as he lay listening to the silence of the night broken only by snores and snorts from either the two guides or the horses still tethered to the carriage, he didn't know which. No sound came from inside the carriage, however, the two vampires clearly satisfied to sit like chastened children, making no contribution to the journey.

Only when morning came, with the bedrolls packed away and the horses harnessed and ready to go, did the tension break.

Jenner had climbed back inside and secured the door behind him - the shuttered windows still secured and severing the burning light of dawn outside - and found himself in an utter blackness that his eyes struggled to penetrate. Catherine kept quiet for a while, he could hear neither breath nor any sound of movement, and with only his hands to find his way, he located his seat and settled himself in for another lengthy journey of awkward silence. When the carriage finally started away, that was when her voice came as sharp as acid.

"You know you have me at a disadvantage," Catherine said to him at last.

Jenner wanted to keep his silence, to play no more of this ridiculous game, but he had to concede finally. There was no other choice.

"How's that?" he said, his words cradled on the back of an irritated sigh.

"Out here, in the middle of nowhere, no shade or shelter except for this tiny carriage."

"I don't get you."

"Don't treat me like an idiot. There's a lot of unprotected sun out there. If you thought to try and kill me, you'd be wise to disregard all notions of it."

Jenner took a frustrated breath and shifted in his seat.

Then he exploded.

"You're fucked, you know that?"

"How dare –"

"No, you fucking listen to me for a change. I've put up with a lot of shit from you and for no good reason. I know you've got your problems, but let me tell you that you ain't the only one. I've wanted death for myself more times than I care to think about, and most of the time I'm awake I wonder why I'm even bothering. I'm out here to help you, though

387

God knows why. So don't lay your all-important shit on me, or your paranoid schizophrenia for that matter. If you've got any more bullshit like that, you can keep it to your fucking self."

He found he was shaking after his outburst, his hands tense and trembling, and he was glad of the darkness for concealing it from her. His heart was hammering, his chest wound tight and knotted like the rope of an old fishing boat, and yet he felt better for having unloaded it all. He was surprised that the vampire sitting opposite him in the darkness did nothing, indeed said nothing, and for quite some time afterwards continued to keep her silence. But then she spoke, quietly and evenly, and her words shocked him more than any other she had ever uttered.

"I'm sorry," she said.

Jenner, in turn, said nothing to this.

He didn't really want to accept her apology, so her words were left floating uncomfortably in the blackness of the carriage in the space between them. He guessed that she could detect his features plainly, more plainly than he could detect hers, but he didn't care. He'd said what had needed to be said, and that was the end of it.

His heart had begun to slow after his outburst, his eyes beginning to grow heavy, and in the shattered darkness of the carriage he began to drift into sleep despite the hours he'd had beside the fire.

Shapes began to spiral around him like blossoms, apple blossoms from the grove of trees he now found himself wandering between, and for a handful of moments he wondered if somehow they had blown in through the door of the carriage.

Then a figure emerged from the dappled shade of the orchard, the interior of the carriage now gone, and he saw the goddess Arbour moving effortlessly towards him as though she was gliding across the soft carpet of grass beneath her feet.

A smile coloured her face, and she held out one hand for Jenner to take and press his lips against. She cupped his face in her other delicate hand, lifting it from his kiss against her flesh. Then she bent towards him to speak quietly in a lilting whisper.

"The disturbances in Olin have begun to worsen," she said to him. "Tremors shake the earth, and my people beg me to help them more than ever. I am glad you are making this journey, for myself as well as for Catherine Calleh."

"I would do anything you asked of me," Jenner said to her in his dream.

The goddess smiled at this, and together they walked through the orchard, petals of delicate apple blossom drifting around them on the circling fragrant breeze.

"There is so much you need to know about where you are headed, but I cannot furnish you with any more information than I already have. There is some kind of barrier that prevents me from seeing what is in the ground at Olin, an obstruction that resists my efforts. I keep trying to see. Every moment of the day and night I explore the earth, but there is something that does not want to be seen."

"I went to see Alexia," he admitted.

"I know," Arbour said to him.

"She seemed so utterly consumed by the mountain. Is she... I mean, are you sure that she's -"

"She is everything and more," Arbour said with

a glorious smile. "Have faith in her because she belongs in everything around us."

"But there were things writhing over her -"

"I know," she said again, "and I am sure they are nothing that she cannot cope with."

Jenner tried to be comforted by her commitment to the Mistress of Kar'mi'shah, but he had seen Alexia, he had laid eyes upon what had seemed to be a wreck of a body consumed by both a living mountain and a plague of black demons. Had that really been her? Had that been the legend that was keeping everything together?

The calm that he had felt beneath the stars the previous night had all but evaporated. His previous fears had taken up residence in his heart once again, and were slowly twisting knives into it.

"It is wonderful that you are even doing this at all," Arbour said to him, as she cupped his face in her slender pale hands, "to show your physical presence as my envoy to a people that still worship me even though I fail them."

"But you are trying to help them," Jenner persisted.

"Trying, yes, but my powers are insufficient. I have summoned Alexia many times to assist me, to discover what this terrible force is. But the longer this continues, and the longer Alexia fails to respond to my pleas, the more my people will suffer."

Jenner could say nothing after that, and indeed wondered just how he was likely to achieve anything if two goddesses with the power to move heaven and earth could not.

Yes, he could show his face, and say that he had come to try and find out what their goddess perhaps could not. But if they were expecting miracles, then he knew they'd be so far beyond disappointed that they'd probably just lynch him as a fraud and a blasphemer.

"Just do what you can," she said to him, as though she was reading his thoughts as they came. "Try to bide some time until I'm able to penetrate the dire murk that exists beneath their lands. That will help me immeasurably."

The image of Arbour, and indeed the whole orchard, shuddered suddenly as though the earthquakes of Olin had found their way somehow into his dream. His eyes flickered momentarily between waking and sleeping, petals of apple blossom dancing across the divide as though they were now falling inside the carriage.

Then he started as he heard his name cried from somewhere outside. His eyes were now fully open, his dream utterly severed.

He reached for the carriage door, turning the handle before he had even checked whether there was sunlight on the other side or not, and clambered out as the harsh early morning light rushed in. Catherine hissed with fury behind him, and he heard her flail to cover herself with her robes as what partial direct light there was found its way into the carriage to kiss her skin. But he was half outside already, and had no time to apologise to her as he struggled to take in the sight of a vast camel train stretching out before them, its line meandering like some vast black desert viper, its riders armed heavily with rifles and unsheathed daggers.

# SIX

## BEDOUINS

There were raised voices outside, fused with the dirge of braying animals. Jenner staggered out of the carriage and into the angry dispute with a head still blessed with images of Arbour and her groves of apple trees. There were perhaps some fifty or sixty camels in total, each with deep brown shaggy fur, and grossly over-laden with either armed Bedouins or bulging crates and packs.

Jenner was hesitant about approaching the quarrel, a heated exchange in a language he could not understand, and hung back beside the carriage. Several members of the camel train had already approached them, some still astride their beasts, to investigate and look down at these trespassers in their desert, perhaps wondering just how many more might still be inside the carriage. Jenner kept his silence, and simply stood and watched with a barely-concealed anxiety at just what might be going to happen.

They were virtually defenceless, he knew, and with so many armed riders around them, he knew they had little or no chance of resisting anything they wanted.

He tried to keep a steady watchful gaze upon Marius and Lo, but only when two of the camel riders urged their beasts towards the carriage and began to scrutinise the load more closely, tugging at the ropes that held them, did Jenner realise just what the riders wanted. It was clear they wanted everything.

Marius lurched forward to protect their only supplies, despite how outnumbered they were, his voice raised in a tongue Jenner had never even heard before. A gunshot rang out almost immediately from the crowd behind them, and Lo clasped his head and shrieked with horror as Marius staggered sideways, a lethal hole puncturing his skull, before doubling in two and toppling to the dirt. Shrill cries ignited the air from the Bedouins closest to them, the hooves of their startled camels stamping dust clouds up and around the carriage. Jenner caught sight of Lo reaching for something at his belt, but a series of gunshots penetrated the confusion and he was dead before the resistance had even started.

Two more camel riders urged their mounts forward and worked quickly to untie the bonds that held the possessions and supplies to the roof of the carriage, hauling the packs down to other members of their train who now hurried greedily to receive them. Jenner could do nothing but watch, and felt the weight of the rifles that had now been levelled at him like a colossal hand upon his back. The sun was still edging slowly over the horizon, so he knew that the two vampires that were still hidden away inside the carriage would not appear to help them. He wasn't sure whether even they could defeat the dozens of armed riders that surrounded them, and was even less sure that they would even choose to.

The two vampires needed nothing of what the

Bedouins were taking, so to them, Jenner guessed, there was nothing of any value being stolen.

He even suspected, as he thought of her sitting in the back of the carriage, that Catherine was probably even wearing a smile, knowing the dire predicament that the three remaining mortals of her party would now face, to cover the rest of the distance across the desert to Olin without supplies of any kind. And she would piss herself laughing if she knew that those three had now become one.

The armed riders did at least leave them the horses and carriage, even the two steeds that still remained tethered at the rear of the vehicle, but out of necessity or kindness Jenner had no idea. Horses might be good for a desert journey of a few days, but useless to a nomadic life in the desert. Jenner guessed that the riders valued camels higher than anything, higher surely than the lives of the people they had just robbed and left without supplies in a featureless and burning terrain.

With the last of their supplies unloaded and packed upon the already over-laden camels, the Bedouins ultimately started to move away, and all Jenner could do was watch with helplessness and despair. He knew they could have all been murdered if they had tried to prevent the theft to the end, but that didn't help the knowledge that they were still at least a day away from the town of Olin. Even with a guide.

The sun was setting, the heat of the day dissipating towards the threat of another bitter cold night, and every last scrap of food and pouch of water was slowly making its way into the depths of the desert, along with the firewood and the bedrolls that he'd need to survive. All he and Catherine and the ghost could do now was travel through the night without any kind of break, and hope their bodies would sustain them through the cold night and the blistering heat of the following day without supplies.

Jenner climbed up onto the driver's platform and took up the reins, snapping them hard and urging the horses to get them the hell away from there before the Bedouins, already noisy and jubilant in their departure, changed their minds and came back.

He thought of Catherine again as the carriage bucked and rocked over the hard baked ground, and was still sure that she would not risk her own safety for the sake of his. So he decided to leave her where she was, he thought as the carriage rolled on, and not open the door again to let her out until the town of Olin was in sight.

He drove all night with only a brief respite for the horses and himself. There was no longer any water for them anyway, and the harsh desert cold was taking its toll on them all.

Dawn approached quickly and brought with it a furious sun that would beat down upon them with neither remorse nor mercy for the duration of the long day ahead. Jenner shielded his head with whatever he could find, driving blind as he clasped the reins with dull hands. The horses dragged their hooves as dusk came again, their heads bobbing low from relentless effort, yet still they walked on.

The day ultimately drifted into another cold night, and although the moonlight and the stars illuminated the desert with a cool brightness, it remained impossible to discern anything or anyone they might be approaching.

Jenner's mind began to play tricks on him as tiredness and sunstroke fought for control in equal measure. His sanity threatened rebellion, his eyes conjuring images at random out of the murk. Where there was featureless desert, there suddenly rose a shanty of billowing black tents. Where there was endless blackness, there was suddenly as oasis of cool water and verdant grass. A stand of palms would wave and bow one moment, only to disappear into a chaos of dark nonsense the next. On and on it went, towns and waterholes appearing from nowhere, enticing him with welcome comforts, only to confuse his senses and destroy them when they receded back into the uncertain folds of night.

His head grew thick with the effort of fighting what he saw, his eyes aching in a skull too numb to function properly as they lost the knack of deciphering the endless reaches of the black night. Before long he slumped into a heavy sleep, his body bent double at the reins, not to reawaken until the sounds of shrieking pierced the air behind him.

Jenner snapped forward, gazing out into the night, straining to discern just what it was that had produced such a shrill animal cry. In the dust thrown up by the carriage behind them it was difficult to make anything out. Had it been a desert rodent crushed by the wheels of the carriage? Or one of the horses? Or maybe one of the Bedouins come back to slit their throats?

Then he caught sight of a figure running through the drifting dust cloud that trailed the carriage, a human form shrouded in black, and he recognised it instantly as the vampire whom he'd thought still occupied the carriage.

Snatching up the reins, Jenner yanked the staggering horses to a complete halt. Dust swirled in thick clouds as the horses snorted their pain and weariness, but he ignored them as he clambered down and hurried back to intercept the vampire.

As Catherine got within twenty yards of him, he could see by the pale starlight overhead that she was covered with something that glistened. Only when she reached him and collapsed into his arms did he realise that it was blood, and that not all of it was hers. Of Antoinette, however, there was no sign. Had she remained in the carriage? Was she still out there?

"Help me," Catherine gasped, clutching his clothes in her fists in order to keep herself upright. She may have been severely injured but her strength was still considerable.

"Where's Antoinette?"

"Never mind her, get me back to the carriage."

"What happened?" Jenner wanted to know, as he helped support her weight back towards the carriage. "Where have you been?"

"The Bedouins," she explained. "I followed them on foot after the sun went down. I killed and fed upon six of their number before I was seen. Including an Englishman called Embers who dined with them upon your supplies."

"They did this to you?"

"With their rifles. I killed two more as I tried to flee their camp, but I could not escape all their gunfire. Even now they pursue me. We must be away."

"How could you be so stupid?"

"I needed to feed."

Jenner gazed back into the night the way they'd come, his eyes failing to make out any sign of the camel riders. Then from out of the desert, Jenner could make out the distant rumble of camel hooves and the Bedouins' shouts and cries on the still air.

Over the uneven ground they hobbled like a wounded four-legged animal. Jenner glanced over his shoulder repeatedly but he could still not locate them in the gloom of the night.

When they reached the carriage and he helped the vampire up and inside, he caught sight of the figure of the ghost vampire still occupying the exact same space she had taken at the beginning of their journey. She had not moved, had not followed Catherine on her quest for either vengeance or food, but had remained behind alone. Jenner caught the briefest of glimpses of her face as he helped Catherine up into the carriage - a snatch of an eye brightened by starlight, a flash of skin once torn by fury and rage - and it was as indifferent as it was scarred. He had no time to question either her loyalty or history, but slammed the carriage door shut and clambered back up to take hold of the reins once again, charging the horses as hard as he could and cracking the reins across their backs, yelling at them to go.

The carriage lurched dangerously as it raced headlong across the uneven desert floor. Jenner was forced to grasp the reins in two white-knuckled fists and anchor himself into the driver's seat as best he could in order to steer the horses on as straight a course as possible that would not see them destroyed. Yet even over the din of the horses hooves and the wheels thundering over the rutted track, he could hear the shouts and rifle-shots of the Bedouins growing ever louder behind them.

He cried out in alarm as a bullet ricocheted off the carriage to his right, and hunching down as low as he dared to avoid any further assault, he struggled even more to keep the carriage pointed in a straight line.

But the desert floor was too furrowed with parched-earth cracks and uneven rock to allow such speed from a wheeled vehicle, and as the carriage clipped the edge of a deep fissure concealed by the darkness of the night, a wheel caught and twisted, yanking it from its hub, and sent the entire carriage careening sideways and then over onto its roof.

Jenner was hurled from the top of the carriage as it rolled and he hit the ground hard. He tumbled awkwardly, he heard and felt something give inside his body, but he managed to snatch a single look up through the glutinous haze of pain to witness the carriage destroying itself, the horses continuing to gallop hard and dragging the wreckage behind them. The remaining two horses lurched free as their tethers either snapped or were yanked loose, and raced kicking like unbroken stallions off into the darkness.

Jenner struggled to find his feet, his legs refusing to support him and bear him up, and all he could do was lay on one throbbing arm and watch his only means of escape disappear inside a billowing cloud of swirling dust.

The shouts and rifle-shots of the camel riders, however, suddenly erupted loud in his ears, and he glanced painfully behind him, spears of sharp agony coming to his neck and back, as a dozen or more of them skidded to a halt around him.

The Bedouins jumped down to take hold of him and dragged him roughly across the ground. Jenner cried out in agony, yelping as he was kicked and punched, struck with rifle-butts and spat upon. There was shouting in a language he could not understand, but he kept his head covered with his arms as best he could, and waited for it all to be over. His mind conjured an image of the goddess Arbour as their blows came and came, and he remembered how he had wanted to die, but in her arms, for it all to be over with her lips upon his. Not like this. Not to be butchered by a furious mob intent only on murderous and bloody revenge.

# SEVEN

## BLACK DOG OF THE DESERT

Before their assault had even really started, the Bedouins' hands suddenly lifted from their hold upon the outsider. Their shouts changed from anger to confusion, and then to fear. Jenner still had no idea what they were saying but it was clear that something had happened.

He dared a look between his bloodied clenched hands, and saw that most of the Bedouins had turned their backs on him and were now in chaos, shouting and pointing out into the depths of the desert.

Then one of their number screamed, a shrill shriek of terror slashed with agony, and a streak of black, blacker than the night, snaked between them like a razor.

He flailed in front of them, dead legs somehow buoying him up, his neck suddenly opened in a spray of rich scarlet. The Bedouins all screamed in unison as his head hit the ground with a dull thump and rolled at their feet, wide eyes still staring.

Some rushed in an attempt to remount their camels, whilst others pulled their rifles from their backs and began to fire wildly into the night.

Then another of their number fell, his robes slashed with red, blood gargling up out of his mouth as he continued to scream.

Jenner caught sight of it, a huge black dog with fangs slick with freshly-drawn blood. Turning to face them in the cloak of darkness, its eyes burned with the ferocity of the midday sun, its hackles raised like poisonous quills, and from deep within its chest there rumbled a deep and forbidding growl.

The Bedouins saw it too and fired at it, all of them screaming and shouting. Jenner clawed a broken route away from the gunfight as the huge black dog pounced once more into the group of Bedouins.

He glanced back only once to see the beast's head buried in the meat of one of the men's stomachs, blood erupting from the wound like a fountain, but Jenner did not look back again. Rifle-shots continued to ring out, but they seemed to have no effect upon the black dog of the desert, and indeed only lessened in frequency as one by one the Bedouins were gored and silenced.

Only when he was a hundred yards or more away did Jenner dare look round again. The shouting had ceased, the moans of death died to nothing, and it was clear that the lives of all the Bedouins had been extinguished. His eyes searched the night desperately for the black dog, the beast that had slipped unseen out of the blackness of the night in order to kill thirty or more men, but there was simply no sign of it.

Swallowing hard, he repeated the sweep of the area, his eyes attempting to make sense of the butchered bodies of the riders. The camels had taken flight, braying into the desert, and there was now no sign of any of them, not as though he could have hauled himself up onto one of their backs to escape anyway.

The desert had fallen eerily silent once again but for the rasp of the dust-laden winds skittering across the ground. The cold was biting at his hands and feet, and the great dog that had killed those that would have murdered him had seemingly vanished.

But then he heard the sound of breathing behind him. He lifted his head only marginally in the direction of the sound, and his heart sank as he looked straight into the eyes of the black beast as it bore down upon him. But its eyes were no longer feral and burning, its maw no longer dripping with foam and drawn blood. But as he watched, so the creature began to change – its snout shortening, its weight transferring so that it stood upon its hind legs – until it was no longer a dog that stood before him, but the figure of the goddess Arbour, the vampire who had been sired by Jackel El'a'cree, the original black dog of the desert.

Jenner gasped with utter disbelief, his voice barely audible.

"You did this?" he uttered.

The goddess nodded.

"You were in trouble, so I came," she said.

"How?"

"It is the gift of my sire," she explained, although he already knew the heritage of the vampire clan to which she had become a part, the power of the shape-changer.

"The carriage," Jenner told her. "It's gone. Catherine was inside."

"We'll find it."

"But when the sun comes up, which will be

403

soon, she'll be in danger."

"We'll find it," she said again. "I'm sure she can look after herself. You, on the other hand, need time to heal."

Jenner watched as Arbour took a few steps back away from him and then knelt down, pressing the palms of her hands delicately against the hard earth. At first Jenner wondered what she was doing, but then the motes of dust began to move as he watched, skipping over themselves like pebbles on a shoreline, spiralling around her as though she was the centre of this vortex as the shape of the earth began to change and transform.

The ground began to fall away from her touch, deepening and widening, as other areas began to creak and groan and contort from the forces being applied to it. Tendrils and roots suddenly erupted from her touch and broke the surface, twisting and cavorting across the earth like blind snakes searching for sustenance, before burrowing swiftly down to where water seeped from nowhere to soften the sun-baked crust.

The hole she had made suddenly began to fill with water, thick and laden with silt at first but rapidly clearing into a crystalline pool fit for drinking. Grass broke the surface and covered an area of several square yards, lush and wide enough for a welcome bed. But over the top of it all, and providing significant shelter from the sun that would soon be high and ferocious, grew half a dozen palm trees, sprouting rapidly out of the earth with enormous fronds that unfurled blissfully like vast green sails.

The transformation from desert to oasis

happened as he watched, and Jenner could do nothing but stare at her, the provider of this miracle, with unprecedented awe. This was the woman he had shunned so many times when she had still been human. How could he have known that this was her potential, this was what she would one day become. And how shameful he felt that he had wanted her to deny all this, deny all that she could be. It was in that moment that he realised just why the people of Olin chose to live the way they did, why they chose to worship such a benevolent and nurturing goddess that was their Arbour.

"Take my hand," she said to him suddenly, easing him from his base of rocky earth and helping him to the oasis she had made for him from nothing.

The grass was more wonderful than any mattress he had ever laid upon, the cooling touch of their blades caressing the cuts and bruises he had sustained from his fall from the carriage, as well as the blows he had received from the Bedouins. Even as he glanced behind him to where their bodies still lay, he could see that the desert was already busy covering their corpses, burying them where they had fallen with sand eager to have their bones. Whether this was Arbour's doing or simply the will of the desert he didn't know, and he chose not to ask. Instead, he lay back amongst the soft blanket of grass and closed his eyes.

He heard Arbour telling him to wait until she returned, that he would be safe with her protection around him until that time came. But he heard little of her words, the oasis around him already working hard to comfort and heal him, and sleep pulled him quickly into its welcome embrace.

# EIGHT

## OLIN

A series of carriages and riders on horseback had come for him during the second day of his rest at the oasis. Jenner had survived well in the magical haven, a respite from the furious heat of the desert that burned every inch of sand and rock around the circular island of rich greenery and verdant palms. Fruit had ripened on vines that grew around him, their taste more wonderful than anything he had ever passed across his lips before. The water in the pool was cool and clean, and refreshed him fully. Arbour had cared for him well, and his body had healed miraculously.

It had been hard for him to leave his own private refuge, so extraordinary and incredible had it been, but he'd known that it wasn't real, and that it had been created only for the purpose of providing him shelter against the harm that the desert could do him. Nevertheless, when the carriages had come to collect him and he'd climbed up into one of them when it had been offered, his heart sank, when he looked back, to see that as soon as the oasis had been vacated, the desert had already begun working quickly to reclaim what had once belonged to it. The lush green grass and palms were already withering beneath the hot sun, sand billowing across their retreating blades and fronds in great sheets blown by a wind obscene in its desire to smother this transitory miracle, and he could only imagine the refreshing clean water receding down into opening fissures even before the blazing sun had a chance to turn it to unsheltered substance to steam.

But all that had been the day before. For the remainder of that day and the resulting night, and on through the next dawn, the carriage in which he'd sat alone had rocked and bucked across the desert without stopping. Now, however, as he climbed down out of the carriage, he was overwhelmed to see the town that he had travelled so very far across the baking desert to see.

The oasis that Arbour had made for him was only a microcosm for what she had achieved here. Nestled in the heart of such an arid dry land was a town rich with lush vegetation and greenery. Tall palms lined the main street, their huge fronds shading the walkways and shop fronts. Fruit trees grew in colourful groves, their boughs weighed down with bountiful crops. Flowers grew between every kerbstone and every gap that wasn't occupied by any other wonder. And even the people, from simple pedestrians to the carriage drivers to the farmers that laboured in the fields beyond the town, looked happy and well-fed, blissful in their haven hidden away inside the lethal expanses of the desert. This was what Arbour had made for them. This was why they stayed and praised her.

But everything he saw and witnessed possessed a barely-concealed dark side. The closer he got the more he noticed the cracks and the fissures that ran across the walls of the buildings, rutting the roads and disjointing the lands where the earthquakes of which Arbour had spoken had taken their incessant toll. Crops in fields lay flattened or blighted. The people that laboured in them wore expressions not of joy, as he had previously thought as he'd been driven past them, but grimaces worn by hardiness and a determination to survive. And beneath the noise of the desert winds that howled across the desert floor around the town, echoed a constant low lament of sorrow for those that had died here and for those resigned to the inevitable.

"Do you need help?" the carriage driver asked, looking down from his seat as Jenner remained motionless on the running board.

"No," Jenner called up. "I'm fine. I was just looking."

He wanted to say something more, but instead climbed down onto the hard surface of the main boulevard, and looked around a little more closely as the driver reached down to close the carriage door behind him.

Children were playing a game with sticks and a ball in a small park across the street. A few parents were stood close by, watching their offspring. Some held parasols, others wore large broad-brimmed hats to keep off the hot sun where the numerous palms failed to shade them. But they all wore the same mask of weariness, a dark sadness that cast its shadows across their eyes.

Jenner heard a polite cough behind him and turned to see a small thin man in a long white robe.

"Excuse me, Mr Hoard," the man said, leaning towards him and looking up. "My name is Feral Keema, and I have been instructed by our goddess to bring you to her temple."

Despite the sadness which had overtaken him, Jenner smiled, and wanted to say that he and the goddess had shared quite a past the two of them, but decided better of it. These people didn't need to know a down-to-earth version of the deity who had brought forth prosperity out of a dry hard land.

"Thank you," he said to the man instead, and walked with him off the street and onto the cracked and uneven pavement.

"I'm afraid our goddess has told us little about you, my friend, and I was hoping you would forgive my impertinence if I asked you a little about yourself."

"About me?"

"Certainly. It's not every day that a shaman is brought to us out of the wastelands."

"A shaman?"

Feral Keema nodded enthusiastically, a wide smile slicing his narrow face in two.

"You are here to help resolve our terrible misfortunes, I believe?"

"Arbour told you this?"

"No, but why else would she protect your passage through the desert if not to help us? You are her mortal hands, no?"

Jenner wanted to tell the man that he was no shaman, no religious man of any order. Hell, he'd been a liar and a thief, a guy that had traded stolen blood and information with vampires, and a guy that had seen men butchered. He sure as hell wasn't the saviour that this man obviously thought he was, and he was hoping that if this man wanted to know the truth about him then Arbour should be the one to tell him. So he kept his credentials to himself as he walked, and prayed that the temple was not too far away.

Feral Keema, however, was not to be assuaged so easily, and continued with his questions about the stranger delivered like a prophesy into his town.

"If you are not a shaman," he went on, "then perhaps you are some kind of engineer? A scientist who understands earthquakes and what goes on beneath the ground we walk upon?"

"I'm neither an engineer nor a scientist."

"An archaeologist then?"

"No."

"A water diviner? A soothsayer?"

"No."

Feral conjured a frown.

"Then why is it that our goddess brings you here?"

"You know what, I'm starting to wonder that myself. I came here with someone else, another goddess who sought something she'd once lost."

"Another goddess? Here? But who?"

"Catherine Calleh."

Feral Keema stopped instantly in his tracks, his face visibly bleached at the sound of her name. He winced, as though something bitter had found its way past his lips and onto his tongue.

"You are sure that is her name?" Feral asked.

Jenner nodded and said:

"You know of her?"

"I know of her name. It is the sound the ground makes when it rumbles and shakes. It is the cry on the wind when it roars through our town. It is the utterance that makes our children cry in their beds

410

and makes adults huddle together in the darkness."

The man's dread infected Jenner quickly, and made him wonder just how much he actually knew about the vampire Catherine Calleh? Was it possible that she was destroying this place? And if so, why? What did she want here?

He'd travelled with her not knowing how powerful she must be in order to shake this town until it rattled, to cause misery and death from hundreds of miles away. He knew she'd once been worshipped as a goddess, the same as Arbour, but what he didn't know was what her real abilities were or the true extent of her hatred for life. He'd seen Arbour's capabilities. Now, it seemed, Catherine's secrets had been spilled and he'd seen a little of hers.

Feral Keema stared long and hard into Jenner's eyes.

"I feel you have brought a final death to our town by bringing her here," he said gravely. "Whatever has been plaguing us has been waiting for this goddess to arrive. You must tell me, where is she now?"

"I don't know," Jenner explained. "We were separated. Out in the desert."

Feral turned to stare out past the cracked houses and failing crops to where the pale burning sands of the desert shimmered and reached out as if to choke the horizon.

"A goddess could not survive out there alone with no protection against the day," Keema said. "I hope the desert destroys her, and everything she has done here."

"She was inside a carriage, its windows sealed with shutters and black cloth."

"You did that to protect her?"

"No."

"Then what of her driver?"

"There was no driver. He was killed."

"By her?"

"No."

"And where was this carriage headed?"

"Wherever the horses chose to gallop."

Feral Keema's face grew sterner still. Panic and fear crept into his eyes as a hundred thoughts flickered there, his mind visibly racing.

"I hope that she is dead," he said at last. "If she is still alive somewhere near the outskirts of our town, we are finished." Then he turned back to look at Jenner. "I hope you have not finished us all," he said.

He started away then, continuing towards the temple of the goddess Arbour. Indeed, he said nothing for a while after that, and Jenner could only wonder about the darker sides of the vampire Catherine Calleh, the sides he knew nothing about. He recalled how Montague had referred to her as the most vicious vampire he had ever met, and what few dealings he'd had with her certainly seemed to confirm some of that feeling. But for her to bring death to an entire town? That didn't seem to fit at all. She'd desired nothing but to find her husband, and he'd believed her. Could it be true, he began to think, that she'd deceived him so cleverly and so utterly, whilst also using the help of Arbour to bring her here to this place? Was that her plan finally revealed, to destroy this simple town?

"We are here."

Jenner looked up to find a modest white-painted building, jagged fissures tracking up its sides like vines. Feral Keema stood at its threshold and held open the door for him. The temple was nothing of the scale or opulence of Arbour's temple in Kar'mi'shah, and yet somehow it defined her, revered yet humble.

Stepping through the tall oak door, Jenner found himself in a long windowless nave flanked on both sides with candles, the gentle light from their flames flickering across the bare walls. At the far end stood a wide brightly-lit chancel, and in front of the stone altar stood a figure with her back to them. As they approached the figure turned to face them, and Jenner saw that it was Arbour. Beside him, Feral Keema fumbled to proffer his greeting before descending quickly to his knees in a penitent gesture. Jenner hovered, however, uncertain whether to do likewise and honour the town's respectful posture in the presence of their goddess, or remain standing as he usually did. But Arbour left her place at her altar and came to greet him with a smile on her face, and all traces of doubt left him.

"It's good that you came," she said. "You have seen some of the troubles already?"

"Some," Jenner said.

She indicated for Feral Keema to rise, and then thanked him for bringing Jenner to her, before dismissing him from her temple. He went gladly, content with his duties as errand boy for a deity, and Jenner watched him go before turning back towards Arbour.

"What is it that has done all this? Feral said that it was Catherine's doing, but I don't see any evidence of that."

413

"It is true that her name has been heard on the backs of the storms that have blown through here, rattling around the doorways of houses and shaking tiles from roofs. But there is so much I don't know, Jenner, so much I cannot fathom. Something is down in the ground, deep down where I cannot see, and it continues to resist my every scrutiny."

## NINE

## THE VALUE OF OTHERS

The horses had dragged the carriage for what seemed like miles before they'd eventually slowed and then halted altogether. Catherine had sat with Antoinette in the darkness of the overturned carriage, listening to the sound of the horses' harried breathing, their hooves stamping in agitation upon the baked earth. She'd called out several times to the thief who had brought them here, demanding his return to them, but he had not answered. Just where the horses had dragged them she had no idea, but burning slivers of sunlight pierced the carriage where its carcass had cracked and splintered, imprisoning both her and the wraith until either somebody offered them shelter and escape, or nightfall visited them once again.

Apart from the sound of the horses and the wind gusting across the desert floor, everything else outside the carriage was sheathed in lonely silence. While Antoinette sat motionless and quiet, unwilling or unable to participate in their own salvation, Catherine strained to pick up the most minute sounds of civilisation that she could. But there was none.

At least the cries of the camel riders had gone, that was something at least to be thankful for. She'd killed a fair number of their tribe, in both revenge and to feed, but she had been discovered, putting herself in grave jeopardy, outnumbered and with an ever-growing distance back to the carriage away from which she had slipped unnoticed.

Now the two vampires were alone, and for beings with such strength and power, it infuriated Catherine to be left so helpless. With the narrow shafts of sunlight filtering in through the splintered cracks of the carriage, she could not afford to fail in her vigilance as the sun made its way across the sky and tracked those shafts from one side of the interior to the other. Her body had already begun to heal itself from where the bullets had found her, but to be burned due to negligence on her part would only slow the restoration of her body.

They still needed to reach the town of Olin, if that was where her husband had indeed chosen to dwell, and if they left what safety the carriage offered, they would have to find either the town or some other shelter during the night and before the next sunrise. Their only other option, she knew, was to wait and be rescued, but without knowing where they were it was impossible to know whether it was likely for anybody to even pass by that day, that week, or indeed ever.

So she sat and watched the dust dancing in the shafts of brilliant light as it filtered in through the breaches of the carriage, as Antoinette continued to sit in silent contemplation, and turned over the frailty of immortality in her head.

Mortals were stronger in so many ways, Catherine thought to herself, the reality of such words paining her even as they came into her head.

They could survive in so many more extremes of temperature, climate and condition. The vampire was supremely dominant in the states in which it could exist, but to put one in an opposing state reduced them to little more than animals bound and gagged and ready for slaughter.

She hated being forced into a position where she could not control her own movements, and she had known the predicament into which she would be placing herself before she had even set off into the desert. Now her worst fears had come true, and she was stranded at the mercy of whomever came along, and that eventuality brought with it a fury matched only by her own sense of terror.

Her life was on the edge of an abyss. Hundreds of years of existence balanced on whoever opened that carriage door and at what time of day.

She would have to keep her senses sharp for the entire duration of each day, listening for approaching footsteps, straining to filter out every sound that she heard or her encroaching madness conjured.

Antoinette just sat in the shadows of the carriage, seemingly oblivious to their peril, her face concealed by the ragged hood that shrouded her. She offered no help, no comment, and indeed seemed the epitome of worthless death itself.

Catherine estimated midday when the shafts of sunlight became vertical, and she continued to study them as their angles decreased, tracking the motion of the sun in its arc across the sky.

As the strength of the sunlight began to fade with the approach of dusk, Catherine began to ready herself for their departure from the wrecked carriage. The horses were still tethered, which was something, although she had never even ridden a horse, even as a mortal, or ever been allowed near one without their terror overtaking them at her proximity. But she had very little choice but to at least attempt to mount one of them. She'd healed very little throughout the duration of the day, unable to rest because of her ceaseless vigil of studying the lethal rays from the sun, and she was not as strong as she might otherwise have been, or indeed hoped she should have been. So when the last of the faltering shafts of horizontal sunlight had disappeared from the cracks in the sides of the carriage, the vampire dared hold her head near the largest of them to look out.

Dusk had indeed taken over the desert, colouring everything with colours from livid oranges to cool blues. An already chill wind swirled along the desert floor, carrying sheets of dust and a barrenness out of the wasteland, and as she looked all around her, she saw nothing else but the empty void that they had ventured uninterrupted through for the past three days.

The horses snorted and glared white-eyed at her, stamping their hooves with distress, as she climbed out of the overturned carriage. She ignored them, checking to see if the vehicle was still serviceable. But one of the wheels was smashed, another missing altogether, and it was clear the vehicle would never roll again without serious repairs.

Her attention returned to the horses, still watching her with terror in their eyes. Still restrained by their harnesses, and after a restricted wait beneath a burning sun, Catherine was surprised at the strength they still possessed even now as they began to panic, jerking the weight of the carriage around as they tried to get away from the unnatural passenger they had not seen until now.

Catherine knew she could not risk being kicked by either of them, not with her condition already weakened and her senses slack, and in a mood of charity she went to the front of the carriage and began to unbuckle their harnesses. The straps snatched in her hands as the horses turned and fought to be away, and as the final clasp came free and their moment of release came, the two beasts thundered away in a billowing cloud of dust.

She stood for a few moments just studying the wake of their dust as they raced off into the desert. They knew the way to Olin just as well as she, but at least they'd be covering the distance to nowhere more quickly.

"Our only means of transport," Antoinette said behind her, "and you let it go."

"I thought you were already dead, sitting in there like a pitiful corpse."

"And what would you have me do? Search on my hands and knees like a dog for your husband?"

"Anything but this indifference, this sullenness."

"What do you expect? I may as well be in the grave. You've made me a slave again, just as you did when you first took me and made me what I was. This is no existence. Look at me. At least the dead have mourners, at least they are loved after the night steals their breath. No one will look at me again without revulsion. I am nothing but a monster."

Catherine stared at her for a moment, and then

she turned without another word and set off in the direction of the horses, without another look back at either Antoinette or the broken carriage that had brought them here.

She expected a further outburst from Antoinette at her back but there was none. Indeed, after she had taken only a handful of steps, she heard the scraping sound of the wraith vampire's bare feet across the cooling sand as she began to shuffle after her.

They had been together for the last few years, the two of them, misfits in a world that had rejected them as they in turn had rejected it, with only each other to cling to. It wasn't a perfect existence, but it was all they possessed.

With her body still pierced from where the Bedouins' bullets had found her, and from the further battering it had taken when the carriage had overturned and been dragged for many miles, Catherine was surprised at how much the cold of the wind affected her. Wrapping her arms around herself prevented some of it getting in, but with little protection against the rapidly freezing night, she hoped that what strength she did possess would keep her walking throughout the night. What happened then she did not want to think about, but prayed that oblivion would at least be swift in its despatch of her.

On she walked with the cold wind swirling and gusting around her, the sound of Antoinette's feet still shuffling some distance behind her, as if it was trying to force her in every direction at once. It was clear that they were lost, with no idea in which direction lay the small town of Olin, or any other town come to that. They were prey to the desert, insects lost in a void of open wasteland, and it was certain that sooner or later they would succumb to its desire to make them part of its dust.

Catherine tried to keep her thoughts coherent, but time and again they drifted into an inky limbo where blackness ruled. Her eyes were heavy-lidded against the stinging weight of sand on the back of the wind, and several times she found herself walking with them clenched altogether. What did it matter anyway if her eyes were open? There was nothing to see in any direction. So she walked, without direction or hope, with Antoinette in tow, into a featureless void that offered no other outcome but an inevitable death. Either the night and its sandstorm would claim them, or else leave them to the deadly promise of the ever-approaching dawn.

When Catherine collapsed and struck the ground hard, she knew she had been asleep, or at least in some state of semi-consciousness. She put her hand to her head and found it came away bloody, congealed with the dirt and sand that coated her exposed face. She looked up to see the figure of Antoinette looming over her. But as she tried to push herself back to her feet, she discovered that her limbs refused her order and would not bear her up. And Antoinette offered her no assistance in helping her find them either, but simply stood and stared down at her.

So weak was she that she could not even manage the simple task of standing. She wanted to be angry at that, infuriated that her vessel of bones and blood were so desperately weak, but she was too exhausted, her whole body wracked with pains and aches that simply could not heal while she tortured

421

it further with a trek on foot across a freezing moonlit desert.

Catherine slumped back onto her knees and rocked gently for a while, just staring up into the heavens above their heads. But the stars simply returned her gaze with indifference, and offered neither help nor hope.

She had no idea how long they had been walking for, or indeed how many hours sunrise was away. She could still make out no shelter in sight, no farms or cottages with lamps lit, not even any vegetation beneath which they could shelter. There was nothing. When the sun eventually broke the distant horizon they would be dead, burned into unnatural dust which the desert wind would eagerly claim and scatter across its endless plains for all eternity.

So she rocked back and forth with her aching arms wrapped around herself, listening to the sound of the wind scattering age-old dust across the hard desert floor, and feeling the cold penetrate beneath the layers of her robes, as Antoinette stood above her like a sentinel guarding a fallen angel.

When her eyes rolled back up into her head once more, she fell backwards onto the ground and tumbled into a limbo blackened by her own mind. The wind snaked her hair across her face and created drifts of sand around her body.

She didn't move again, not even as the first colours of the new day began to brighten the horizon with shades of burnt orange and yellow, not even as her skin began to smoulder and char as the first shafts of sunlight spilled across the baked earth, not even as that very ground began to suddenly groan and tremble with its imminent earthquake, cracking and shaking as it buckled and began to split apart.

Antoinette cried out. Catherine heard her scream through the black haze inside her head as something came up through the crumbling earth towards them, up from below. Fissures tracked rapidly across the dirt like jagged snakes, splitting it wide as the great booming thunder grew louder, shaking the very air itself with its shrieking wail, until a huge hideous monstrosity broke the surface and hauled its vast ugly bulk from the chasm it had made for itself and stood looking down at the slowly smouldering bodies of the two vampires.

The beast's head and torso were mostly devoid of much of its natural flesh, and great livid wounds covered what was left. Yet it reached down and plucked up the bodies of the vampires in its massive spade-like hands, scooping them up inside its ragged arms as if to smother them. Antoinette resisted, Catherine hanging like a cadaver, but they were both claimed utterly as the monster enveloped them and retreated down into the chasm of the earth, stealing them away from the rapidly approaching dawn and the lethal rays the sunrise was bringing with it, before sealing the ground after them like a vast ungodly trapdoor.

## TEN

## INTO THE ABYSS

The darkness was almost total when Catherine eventually opened her eyes again. Knowing that the approaching day had been swift in its greed to claim her, she wondered if this was the oblivion she had often wondered about. It was cold, chillingly cold, and the tang of ancient sweat and decay filled the abyss around her. Her flesh was hard and painful from where the sun's first rays had seared and blackened it, and it crackled like roasted hog fat as she tried to move. Her mind struggled to make sense of all that she knew, and second guessed all that she didn't. Her eyes fought to make sense of the patterns and the shapes that began to form around her - they looked like formations of rock, intricate stalactites hanging from the ceilings and walls of what now appeared to be some vast cavern. She lifted her head to scrutinise this realisation further, but a shock of pain sliced through her neck and shoulders as her scorched flesh was ripped apart, forcing her to cry out in agony.

Catherine collapsed back onto the ground, her eyes clenched. From out of the darkness came a sound, a muted almost retracted whimper, and when she realised that it was not Antoinette who had uttered it, she froze all her other senses as she strained her hearing to locate it again.

But the cavern had fallen into silence once again, except for the workings that made its structure – the dripping of water, the creaking of suspended rock – and it remained so until she shut off her inquiry and relaxed once more.

Then the sound came again, a low sound halfway between a howl and a moan.

"Show yourself," she demanded into the darkness.

But no reply came, at least not one that carried words.

A strange unworldly whine, like that of some demonic dog chastened by God into submission, rolled around the cavern, echoing off the craggy walls so that she could not tell from which direction it had even come.

"Who's there?" Catherine called, but as she did so she thought that it was probably just some scavenging animal, curious about the new creature that now shared its lair. Another thought came rapidly on its back that so defenceless was she in her current state, that to such a scavenging animal she would be little more than an easy meal.

She tried to haul herself up, despite the agony that seared like fire through her body as her flesh cracked and tore open from the movement. Instantly, however, the whine changed to a puny gasp, and then a hush descended over the entire cavern once again.

Catherine, still half sitting and with a pain that almost blinded her so fierce did it grip her, searched the jagged misshapen shadows for anything that might be watching her. But so dark was it, and so deceptive the echoing whimpers, that she could locate nothing of its position. She wanted to call out to Antoinette, but remembering how she had screamed at the sight of this now unseen beast, suspected that she would not show herself now, and had probably found somewhere cowardly to hide anyway. Yet when a series of clicks came, like the percussive chatter of cold teeth, she caught sight of a glint of feral white, and finally observed the maniacal face grinning out at her from the darkness. No wonder Antoinette had screamed.

She froze as she watched this hellish face regard her from halfway behind a huge stalagmite. Its eyes were wide, its face ragged, and its grin faltered now as a look of disgust and fear broke over Catherine's face.

The creature was less than fifty yards from her, and she could barely sit up let alone make any kind of escape. She tried to push herself away as she saw it stand, even though she had thought that the beast was already standing, but the agony that came was wonderfully tolerable as she at least managed to increase the distance between herself and something so grotesque, even if it was only by a few inches.

"What are you?" she managed to breathe.

The monster did not reply this time, but instead cocked its head as a look of such utter sadness washed over its hideous features.

Catherine ceased any further escape she might have managed, and indeed could not bring herself to say anything further. This creature, whatever it was, had been wounded by her words. It understood her, it seemed, and even now was staring at her, its eyes ringed with wet as though tears were welling. Such a scene was ridiculous, Catherine knew, and what both astonished and angered her more was that she had no alternative but to witness such a pathetic scene.

But then a realisation crept slowly over her, as she looked at both it and their surroundings, and then her lips parted to speak once again.

"Did you save me from the sun?" she asked quietly.

The monster said nothing at first, but then very slowly it began to nod.

When it took a step out from behind the rock formation, Catherine forced herself to remain where she was, to not attempt to recoil any further from its hideous appearance or its approach. It seemed to acknowledge this, and to be genuinely grateful to her for that, yet as it took another few tentative steps towards her, Catherine managed to examine more of its face.

It was still almost totally dark inside the cavern, but her sight explored the creature more fully now until she was sure that this had somehow once been a man. A few more steps and she could make out where his jawbone had once been, and where his skull had grown as nature had intended. But as he got to within ten yards of her, she could not help but let out a gasp of both horror and revulsion, as she realised that this had once been the same face that she had kissed and loved for over a hundred years. The familiarity was as sudden as it was horrifying. This was her husband that she had come to find. This was her Carlos.

He seemed to understand her final recognition of him now, and he stopped that short distance from her. Neither of them said anything for a while, both of them searching each other's eyes, each other's faces.

It was Carlos who ultimately broke the silence, perhaps knowing that his wife could not bring herself to say anything that could contradict her expression of utter disgust.

"I had to... remake... myself," was all he said, his declaration both pathetic and disjointed.

His voice was as ragged as his flesh, distorted and awkward, and it seemed that it was something that he could only barely manage to do. Catherine wanted to go to him now that she had found him, but she could do nothing but stare at him.

His frame was almost twice that of what she remembered, and his limbs hung from his body at irregular angles, like tools tossed idly into a cupboard. She had destroyed him many years ago for what he had done to her, but he had somehow managed to rebuild himself. But without the aid of a mirror, he had done a very poor job of it.

"I'm sorry," was all she could say.

"I've been... alive... all this time," he said to her, but without any tone of malice or resentment in his fractured voice. "Alive... inside my own head. And alone."

"But I buried you in London. On waste ground. How did you manage to get here?"

Carlos stared at her, and for a moment Catherine wasn't sure whether he was even going to answer her, if indeed he was even able to. But then he spoke, drawing breath as though this was a story that had been waiting a long time to be told. His bones creaked as he moved, his flesh sliding across them as he pushed his great hands up and over his face.

"You never killed me," he began slowly and simply. "I remember knowing that the pain was beyond measure, but I cannot recollect that now. Those agonies are long ago in the past, along with so many others. I think the pain of being without you has been worse."

"Carlos –" Catherine started, but he waved her back with one hand.

"My body was broken when you dropped me into the hole," he went on. "It would not work, and I could say nothing to stop you covering me over with that cold damp earth. But all the time my mind worked, alone in the grave you had dug for me, making thoughts for which I had no outlet. I heard the years trudge slowly past, yet still you did not return for me. I heard the sounds of the living walk the ground over me. I heard them build roads and houses above me. Yet still you did not return to save me. Your punishment was severe, and deservedly so, yet I remained in my lonely prison without reprieve."

Carlos shifted his weight, his joints cracking awkwardly, and he made himself a seat out of one of the rock formations. His eyes were huge and wet when he looked down at her, but still he did not want any comment from her. Not yet.

"The years were long and I was very weak. With so much weight of soil above me I couldn't dig myself out. With concrete and houses built, my fate was sealed. But my mind began to wander, out of my head and up through the earth. I could see the tiny creatures with whom I shared a world, and I took some partial peace in watching them. Their development was slow, but it at least marked some minor passages of time. It was only when my mind broke the surface that I began to explore the world above me."

Catherine listened to her husband's story spellbound, the history of the only man she had ever loved, risen from the grave she had dug for him, not realising the horror she had put him through, thinking that all this time he had simply been rotting in the ground.

She took a seat opposite him, watching the contortions of the meat he had made to cover his bones, studying the multitude of tics that twitched like maddened insects throughout his roughly-fleshed body.

"I followed the comings and goings of a young family," Carlos went on, "but it was only in a kind of fractured isolated state. Perhaps a better way of putting it is that I knew of their existence. I had no physical form, at least not at that time, and I took whatever comforts I could in not being alone for the first time in many years. They felt like my family, even though I lay many yards below their feet. Their son grew, and I listened to him. My pleasures were simple, but they were all that I had."

"But that doesn't explain how you got here," Catherine said, her thoughts racing ahead of her tongue.

"So much of that was out of my hands," Carlos explained solemnly. "You see, the more I yearned to spend time with them, the more my manifestation was growing. I had no idea what they could or couldn't see, until one day I saw the boy looking directly at me. The look of terror he had on his face still haunts me today. This was a child I had somehow grown to love, even though I had never met him or spoken to him."

"You found love for a mortal?"

"At first, yes. I was so utterly alone, and the more the boy saw me, and the more horrified he became, the harder it was for me to continue with the overwhelming pain of rejection. It hurt me immeasurably, and it began to consume me. The more he rejected me, the angrier I became. I only wanted to watch over him, while he slept or while he played, but he wouldn't even let me do that. It was all I had, damn it, and I was refused it."

"It was not his fault, Carlos. He was scared. He was just a mortal child."

"I couldn't have it though. I couldn't let him, or the rest of his family, treat me like that."

"It wasn't their fault, Carlos," Catherine said again, but she had already seen the glimmer of madness creep into his eyes.

"I couldn't have it..." he murmured once more, and he turned away from her to stare into the darkness of the cavern.

Catherine moved as if to go after him, but the pain in her charred flesh ceased her motions. She winced as the fire burned beneath it.

"What did you do?" she breathed at last.

But Carlos did not reply. He just stared into the darkness of the cavern, his eyes lost to distant regrets.

And then very slowly Catherine followed his gaze, realising he was not staring into middle distance, as she had at first thought, but at something

431

hidden in the depths of the shadows.

Her head turned, her eyes trying to locate just what it was that had so suddenly consumed her husband's attention. But the blackness was nearly utter, and she was still weak from where the first of the sun's rays had licked her. Then she saw three forms standing motionless amongst the irregular patterns of the rock.

It seemed as though they were looking at her, as if waiting for her to come and save them. But she was far too late for that.

As she focussed on them, she saw the hollowness of their eyes, the vacant dead stares of the murdered family, and she turned away almost immediately to look back at Carlos.

"I couldn't let them do it," he explained pitifully. "To look at me with fear and loathing when all I wanted was to love them. They were all I had, and they treated me like something that would do them harm."

"But how did you get here?" Catherine wanted to know. "You've told me nothing of that."

"I took them," he said simply, continuing with his story. "I gathered the boy, then the mother, then the father, and dragged them down into the depths of the darkness that swelled below me."

"But that still doesn't explain –"

"My mind continued to work furiously," he went on. "I wanted to go to the deepest and darkest depths imaginable. You had torn me apart but I was still alive inside my own head. Only now I had passengers. Rafaela, Sebastian and David had been my only distractions from the grave you had dug for me, and I wasn't about to let them go. When I came here I built thrones for them where they could live like kings with me. They sit there still, yet even now they refuse to talk to me."

Then he turned back to the darkness in which they lay frozen and cried out:

"You'll talk to me one day. I promise that you will."

Carlos slumped back against the wall of rock at his back and pushed his great hands up and over his face. Catherine could see his vast chest heave, his clumsily-made ribs groaning from the exertion, and she wondered just how he was managing to keep his body together. As his wide fingers parted across his face and she saw the glimmer of the whites of his eyes peer out, she feared for her own life for the first time since he had claimed her from the desert.

In the few moments that those two maniacal eyes stared down at her, she wondered just what kind of vengeance he could have nurtured in his mind for her should they ever meet again, or indeed how he might keep her for the rest of eternity here in his kingdom beneath the earth.

Whatever he was going to do was inevitable. She knew she could never escape him, not down here, not where he knew every crack and crevice, or where he had already sealed up every exit. But it surprised even her when the next few words left his lips.

"I love you, Catherine," he said, "and I want us to be as we once were, together again. Just the two of us. I've been so alone, without you, without anyone."

Catherine just stared at him, unable to comprehend just what he had said to her. Yes, she had wanted that more than anything, but how would that now be possible? Carlos was so very different, almost twice her size and livid with deformations. She could barely recognise in him the man she had watched breaking horses in Spain all those many years ago, nor the man to whom she'd been devoted for the many decades that had followed. Could she ever love him again now that he looked like this? Did she even want to?

Carlos stared at her as though he was reading her mind, and with his statement left unanswered he came to only one conclusion.

Pushing his vast weight out of his seat of rock, he towered above her like one of the monstrous stalagmites that grew from the cavern floor. He gazed down at her with eyes that glimmered with his former lunacy and anger, but rather than strike her down or berate her for her cruelty to him, he retreated back into the blackest depths of his kingdom without another word, his footfalls thudding and echoing throughout the vast chamber after him.

Catherine watched his retreat until her eyes could no longer permeate the darkness. She felt ashamed for what she had done, or rather what she had failed to do. She had come here to the desert to find him, and by some miracle she had achieved that desire, realising that if she had made it all the way to Olin she would not have found him at all.

And yet she had rejected him - not by her words, but by her inaction.

She guessed he would return to her, after a time. He would not have saved her from the desert sun only to let her die down here alone. He just needed time. And so did she. And that was something that they both had in abundance.

She lay back against a slab of curved rock and closed her eyes, her fingers gently examining the worst of her wounds, the burns and the places where her flesh had been turned hard and black. Her skin was already healing, her strength returning, but slowly, almost imperceptibly, and she would still need to rest for a couple of days at least before she attempted to leave this place, either with or without Carlos.

She needed to think things through. She had been unprepared for finding him this way. How could she not have done? Maybe their restored companionship might calm the agony and torments of his mind, and hers along with it. Or maybe not. Maybe it was all for nothing, and she should just leave all the mistakes of the past buried where they belonged.

# ELEVEN

## ESCAPE

Antoinette had fallen from the giant's claw and scurried to find her shelter in whatever narrow recess she could find. She had escaped its attention, of that she was certain, at least for now. But loose in its lair, she was certain that it would not take it long to find her and destroy her.

With no light in the cavern it was difficult to negotiate her route across the uneven floor. Her senses were sharp yet the darkness confused them readily, but she made steady progress away from where the beast had delivered them. She could still hear the beast at intervals, always at her back, moaning and wailing like a monstrous banshee. It had not noticed her escape at least. It had not come looking for her yet.

Catherine was still behind her, left to fend for herself. It occurred to her, as she stumbled over the rocks and boulders, that maybe this was her revenge on her sire at last, to leave her to fight alone with something that would bash in her skull with one single blow from its vast fist. There was no guilt in her leaving. She wanted only to find her way to the surface once again.

Only when the cries of the beast faded and the cavern fell into silence, did Antoinette's other senses begin to prickle. She dismissed her initial worries as paranoia, but gradually those concerns took on more weight as the evidence grew. She'd felt something brush against her hands and feet, delicate like the strands of a web, yet almost clutching like hands made of soft wet tissue. Movements skipped tiny stones around her as she made her progress. But she also felt as though her flight was being monitored from eyes hidden amongst the rocks and from the ceilings high above her head. Yet nothing stopped her, nothing took hold of her with force enough to stop her.

Still she clambered across the surface of the cavern as it rose and dipped, sometimes coming to deeper fissures that needed to be circumnavigated, other times coming to huge pillars that blocked the route ahead. But all the time she heard nothing more of the beast that had dragged her and Catherine down into its pit.

When a pale luminescence lit the end of the vast chamber, Antoinette almost cried out at the sight. She stumbled headlong towards it, not noticing the midnight children that had been following her progress, touching her and watching as she'd made her way. Their black ethereal forms had been concealed by the blackness of the cave, but now that natural light had managed to enter the cavern, they were there to be seen.

Antoinette saw them now, and a scream almost slipped from her throat as she saw how they carpeted the floor of the cavern in their thousands, their dull eyeless sockets somehow all regarding her without exception. She'd halted beside a rock as she'd finally seen them, and they in turn had halted to sit and watch her with utter scrutiny. They had made no attempt to either stop her or harm her as she'd stumbled through the absolute darkness, and she had nothing to confirm that they might do so now. Yet she remained where she was as she looked all around her. They waited upon every surface, clinging to the rocks on all fours, hanging from hand and foot holds in the ceiling, their forms knitted from blackness, their eyeless sockets trained upon her.

Then she continued forward towards the shaft of light that spilled down into the darkness of the cavern. As one single mass the night children suddenly shifted their positions and followed, crawling over the rocks and fissures with hands and feet that negotiated the myriad of awkward surfaces with all the ease of spiders. As more and more light dispelled the darkness of the cavern, so it seemed that the walls were alive, every surface moving with the teeming legions that followed the wraith-vampire's exit.

Just short of the shaft of natural light, Antoinette halted once again. The sun would burn her on contact, yet she witnessed the night children crawling beneath it without peril, up and over the rocks that led up towards the day, swarming ahead of her now and out into the day.

She hesitated, wondering how they managed to survive the sunlight, and again about their intentions, but most of all about the beast that still remained silent and ignorant of her escape now some considerable distance behind her.

She was frozen to the spot. How could she hide with so many sentient creatures watching her, waiting on her every movement? She felt as though she couldn't delay her ascent to the surface any longer, despite how it would surely destroy her, yet she knew that she had little choice but to try. Dawn had only just broken when the beast had taken them. It had not taken long to get here. Dusk would be hours away.

The midnight children waited and watched with patience and almost knowing nods between themselves as they awaited her next move. But when the howling of the great beast suddenly started up again behind her, its horrific echo resounding along the cavern like a locomotive thundering towards her, they grew agitated and began screaming themselves, hopping from rock to rock and crawling over each other like insane shrieking monkeys. That was when Antoinette hauled her rags up over her head (for what tiny protection they offered), and ran headlong for the opening above her and the sunlight that seemed almost grinning with a gleeful anticipation of her fate.

# TWELVE

## THE BEGINNING OF THE END

Jenner had visited several of the families, who had heard and seen what Olin now called 'desert devils', with Feral Keema. Unearthly creatures made from the night itself, they had invaded homes and farm buildings, butchered animals and attacked infants, crawled across walls and ceilings, and gotten into every parlour and storeroom - sometimes with no intentions, other times with blood and murder on their minds.

They possessed no discernible features such as eyes or hair or genitalia, and were as black and faceless as shadows. Some of the families had lost livestock, others their children, while others had lost nothing at all. Some devils were silent, others howled and shrieked. Some bore livid arsenals of teeth and claws, while others had the bloated physiology of overfed slugs. It seemed there was no pattern to their invasion, yet they all came crawling inside the dust clouds of the storms that blew in from the desert, and all with an undoubted malevolence.

Arbour had done what she could, patrolling the streets of Olin in her form of the savage black dog, but she could not be everywhere. The devils had gotten past her, around her, skirting her patrols, and they had continued to bring death and despair.

Then shouts out in the street had brought everyone from their houses.

A cloth-covered wagon was already shrouded by people as it skidded to a halt, the townsfolk all fighting to get a look at whatever it was the farmer had caught. Feral hurried into the heart of the riot, Jenner just behind him, where he was hastened to the rear of the wagon. But it was not a desert devil that had been caught, no, but something far larger, and it came bundled inside a swathe of charred and blackened sackcloth.

"It came running up out of the ground," the farmer cried over the shouts of the crowd, all of them pushing to see the creature in the wagon. "All aflame and screaming it was, like a demon out of the bowels of Hell."

His horse was stamping at the head of the wagon, white-eyed with terror and desperate to be away.

"Where?" Feral wanted to know.

"The caves," the farmer said pointing.

There was no need to follow his finger, but many did anyway. What they saw was not just the rocky foothills that led up towards the mountains, but what looked to be a black tide spilling up out of the ground and across the desert floor like a massive surge of crude oil.

The crowd quietened as they tried to deduce just what it was they were looking at. But it was certain that there was going to be more than just a single flaming figure being spewed from the caves.

Then one of the townspeople muttered what they were all thinking:

"The devils are coming..."

441

And then the panic really set in.

It didn't take long for the terror to rip through the crowd. Screams rose from all sides as women hoisted children from the ground, men gathering their families together in jostling bundles. The crowd dispersed and scattered towards their homes, and Jenner stood with Feral Keema as the crowd separated. Only the farmer hesitated with them.

"What am I supposed to do with it?" he wanted to know, staring at the motionless figure still smouldering in his covered wagon.

"Take it to Arbour's temple."

"Not me," he cried. "You know how to drive a wagon? You take it yourself."

Then he was off and running, away from the tide of devils that was rapidly advancing on the town, and towards whatever shelter he had time to find.

# THIRTEEN

## AND SO THEY CAME

Like locusts they approached at supernatural speed, consuming the distance between them as though it did not even exist at all. Some came upright, some on all fours, but the night children came running like an all-consuming tide, smothering the earth whole.

The sun still burned bright and hot overhead, creating heat snakes where the land had been turned black with the multitude of their writhing bodies. The townspeople had scattered, making for any shelter they could reach in the moments before the desert devils invaded their homes.

Jenner clambered up into the farmer's wagon, snatching up the reins and snapping them across the back of the horse, urging it forward towards the temple of Arbour with its cargo of the burned body behind him.

Feral returned to the cracked whitewashed building on foot, and helped Jenner to haul the charred remains of the body off the wagon. As the fierce sunlight touched what little exposed flesh there was of the corpse, smoke curled almost immediately in rivulets, blistering the already seared surface.

Jenner had assumed the person dead or close

to, but a low moan escaped her as they lifted her over the edge of the wagon and into daylight, followed by a shriek as the smoke trail suddenly ignited into a lick of yellow flame.

"Quick," Jenner yelled. "Into the temple."

With his hands clasping the near-dead woman's shoulders, and avoiding a head that was already jerking back and forth in livid agony, he ran-stumbled with her as Feral struggled to keep hold of her thrashing legs.

Into the building they cajoled her burning body as the woman's shrieks and screams tore the air. Only once they were inside and out of the day's heat and light could they usher her to the floor and attempt to smother the fire.

Molten flesh burned Jenner's hands as he grappled with the blaze, but the short distance between the wagon and the doorway to Arbour's temple had mercifully been short, and the fire had been given little opportunity to grow. Even so, the woman still lived, in rags burned as black as her own destroyed flesh. How she still existed Jenner had no idea, but her moans and sobs proved her vigour to remain alive.

"The devils are coming," Feral insisted, tugging at Jenner's arm, urging him to cut short his inspection of her. "We must secure the building."

A heavy length of timber stood against the wall, which they used to bar the main doorway, using a smaller length to seal the door at the back of the temple. There were no windows along the temple's length, and no other ways in. For now they were safe, as was the woman born of fire from out of the desert. They returned to her now, kneeling at her side, but there was little they could do for her.

Jenner lifted the remains of her cowl, and recognised the furrows of scarred wounds beneath the blackened crusts of where her remade flesh had been. She had been a terrible sight before, but the sun's rays had performed worse atrocities upon her. He pressed a gentle hand to her brow and the skin crackled there. Her eyes seemed melted shut for they did not open. Indeed there was little movement from her altogether, just a series of tics that accompanied the sobs that slipped from her throat.

Then from outside in the street there came a rumble that sounded like a thousand hooves thundering across the earth. Feral and Jenner both turned towards the barricaded doorway, their breaths held, and waited for what would happen next.

The building seemed to reverberate around them as the stampede hit town, timbers rattling, beams creaking and groaning.

And then something slammed hard against the door.

WHAM, it went, but the door stood firm.

The sound of claws scratching at its perimeter echoed along the hallway towards them, followed by further thumps and bangs as individuals attempted to pound their way through.

Howls of frustration rocked the air as the timber continued to resist the intruders, until the scratching died and the thumping ceased and the stampede continued on its way.

There was a moment of relative calm after the devils had passed them before a series of screams - human screams - rose up from further down the street.

"This is the end," Feral sobbed, hanging his head in his hands.

"What can we do?" Jenner demanded.

"There is nothing. We'd be torn apart as soon as we stepped outside."

"But we can't just sit here."

Feral said nothing, and just sat and wrung his hands. Below them, Antoinette groaned and lifted her useless burned hands skyward as if to pray for someone to snuff out her life.

Outside the screaming continued, but now they could hear timbers crashing, the destruction of the town of Olin muffled from inside the barricaded temple. Hideous shrieks slashed the din of breaking buildings as the night children found their entry, feasting on the living in whatever unspeakable ways they could. Jenner paced the aisle with frustration, mimicking Feral Keema by wringing his own hands.

"We have to go out of here," he cried.

"No, we stay where we'll be alive."

"But people are dying."

"And you would have us join them?"

Then a new creaking stole their attention, this one far closer and uncomfortably louder, and they froze and stared at one another quickly as it shattered the comparative quiet of the temple. It was a short sound, over before it had even really begun, but it had already set their hearts racing with dread.

A spiral of dust circled down from above them, and in unison they lifted their heads skyward to the ceiling. The creaking came again, and this time they could see a shaft of daylight penetrate the darkness of the temple as another tile was suddenly ripped from the roof.

Dark fingers stole in through the breach as they sought a third tile, the nails giving way like tired fingers on a cliff edge. The shaft of light grew brighter as the opening widened another couple of inches, and Jenner waited only a few moments before shaking Feral out of his stupor.

"Take hold of her," he yelled, grabbing two fistfuls of Antoinette's sackcloth clothing and hauling her up.

Feral's eyes flashed white with terror. A roof tile dropped into the building and smashed on the ornate floor at their feet.

"Do it," Jenner yelled. "Pick her up."

But Feral bolted for the door instead, his feet slip-sliding with panic.

Jenner shot looks at the ceiling, through which the night children were already forcing themselves, then at the back of the departing priest, and finally down at the helpless crust of the vampire in his grasp. Then with a cry in his throat he ran, dragging her down the nave towards the sanctum at the back of the chancel.

The night children came tumbling through the breach in the roof and hit the temple floor with loud slaps, their shrieks reverberating throughout the narrow temple as they came running in pursuit of them, some over the tops of the pews in their haste to tear them apart. Jenner reached the doorway to the sanctum as Feral loosed a scream of his own, but Jenner had no time to turn and look for him in the tide of black devils.

Once inside the sanctum, Jenner dropped the vampire to the ground before turning and kicking out at the door, slamming it shut against the approaching hoard of barely-made creatures as they reached for him. This was the first time he had actually seen them up close, and it chilled his skin as he now forced all his weight against the door.

Some possessed bulging pupil-less eyes, others gaping maws lined with lethal needle-teeth. Some snarled and dripped saliva, while others came blind with no features at all. Some clawed with talons, others with hooks and barbs. But like nightmares they writhed over one another in competition to be the first one to draw human blood. But Jenner had managed another small reprieve. The door came furnished with a steel bolt, the room's only defence, and he had slid it home.

The devils banged and thumped upon the heavy timber door, berating it and the surrounding walls with whatever claws and fists they possessed. Jenner allowed himself an anxious step away from it and watched as it shuddered inside its jamb. But the timbers, he knew, could not last forever.

2

Catherine could not bear to look at her husband. For years she had searched for him, her former dreams rekindling the desire she'd once held for him, and now his visage only served to repulse her. She'd wanted him to be at her side again, but it now seemed clear that her desire was only for the handsome man he had once been, before his wounds, before she had unmade him, and before he had fashioned himself into some gruesome hellish monster. He stood before her even now like some vast chastened puppy, innocent and pathetic, damaged by ancient wounds and her more recent rejection of him. And she despised him even more for that.

"What am I without you?" he asked her pitifully.

He held his awful hands out to her, palms up, in supplication.

Catherine said nothing. Her eyes still studied the rocks of the cavern floor.

"I have no purpose," Carlos said, "no life. What can I ever be again if I remain alone?"

"I loathe what you have become," Catherine said at length. "Darkness should remain your closet companion, just as you have already chosen. Stay here, that is what's best."

"No," Carlos exclaimed. "I have existed with my own horror for years. I am sick of it. I want my loneliness to be over."

"But I do not want you."

The expression upon his discordant features shifted beneath her perception, pain slipping out, anger slipping readily in. Teeth glared suddenly between slashed lips. His eyes narrowed and burned. All this she missed in the unlit cavern.

"Then I will make you want me."

Her body, still slowed by a suit of melted flesh, denied her quick movement. Her husband's massive hands, that had once cherished and caressed her soft white skin, now clasped her wrists inside a coarse grip and tugged her from her seat. She resisted with a force that speared jags of pain beneath the plates of melted flesh. Her screams pierced the blackness and echoed off the unseen formations of rock. His grip slackened momentarily as indecision crept in. Then he tightened it once again until she heard her bones creak.

"You will stay at my side," he roared. "I will not be alone again for another hundred years."

Despite the agonies that seared through her, Catherine doubled in half so that she could sink her teeth into the gnarled muscle of her husband's arms. His skin tasted rank, like putrid meat left to rot in a cold dank cellar, but she clamped her jaws around it, bit deep, and yanked with all her strength. His flesh was tough, and clung to his bones surprisingly well. But blood welled swiftly into her mouth, sour and acrid, and Carlos howled like a baying wolf caught in a steel trap.

"Release me," Catherine demanded, as his blood coursed from her mouth and ran down over her throat and chest. But his hands remained firm, his might still grinding her bones.

"I will not be alone another hundred years," he cried again, and hung onto her with all his strength as she struggled to shake herself free.

"Then you will need to kill me as you killed your mortal family," Catherine gasped.

His grasp stayed firm a moment longer, but then he relented. He shrank back like a wounded beast, waited a moment, and then slipped away from her altogether. She could no longer see him in the darkness but she heard his sob, followed by the sounds of his body slinking away like a snake slithering across a cold dank floor.

Antoinette lay useless behind him. Jenner stood between the vampire and the door as the midnight children hammered and beat upon the timbers, their teeth, claws and bodies berating the entrance as they shrieked for bloody murder. There was no other way out, not even a window in this sanctified chamber, and he could not be expected to scale the smooth rendered walls to reach the ceiling as those creatures had done - he was just not built that way.

A dervish rose suddenly in the air, the dirt of the floor whipped up into a whirlwind as the very air folded before his sight. A form blossomed inside that vortex, a human figure that stepped from the vortex where before had been nothing. Jenner staggered as the goddess arrived inside her own temple.

He took a step towards her, but halted as soon as he saw the blood that ran wet and fresh from her face and throat. It was her own blood, and her stark eyes confirmed the severity of her injuries.

"They're everywhere," Arbour murmured. "My people are dying. My town is being destroyed."

The door shook in its jamb. Claws skipped between the gaps like knives, looking for a way in.

"There's no way out," Jenner told her. "We're trapped."

"I know," Arbour said. "But I cannot get you out. I can only help you fend them off. Until -"

"Until what?"

"Until the inevitable."

The door was thumping now, banging against the bolt that was tearing itself away from the wall.

Arbour faced it now, blood tracking from wounds slashed across her once-unblemished face in a dozen or more places. When she took a step towards the door, Jenner reached out to take hold of her.

"What are you doing?"

She flinched from the contact, and he realised that it was probably the first time she had been touched in years. She was cold – he had forgotten that – but he kept his hold upon her.

"You can't," he said.

"I have no choice. It is my responsibility. It is what I do. Maybe you can escape while I divert them from the door."

"My life means nothing without you."

"Your life means everything without me. Now let me go."

"But they'll smother you before you can even step outside."

"I will kill some."

"But not all," Jenner declared. "This is pointless. It solves nothing."

"It is what I do," she said again, and slipped out of his grasp.

Even as he watched her lay her hand on the shuddering bolt, ready to draw it aside and force herself out into the maelstrom, he saw her body deform. Her mouth and nose elongated into an angular muzzle, her head drawing long and sharp into that of a dog. Her skin darkened as coarse black hair sprouted and grew to thick fur. Her limbs contorted, her knees snapping backward into those of an animal, a long tail erupting from the base of her spine.

As she slid the bolt open with a hand that was

neither human nor animal, the door pounded forward, and Jenner saw her hackles rise and her jaws spring open to a lethal array of sharp savage teeth. Then the tide of clamouring half-made bodies washed in, smothering her whole, and he lost sight of her altogether in the sea of death.

4

"You are more cruel than I remember," Carlos said from out of the darkness.

"And you more pathetic. You whimper like a dog, sob like a widow. Even if you had not made yourself into this monster I would pray to see through your appearance and see the worthless wretch beneath."

"Your words have changed little. I must have heard something else before."

"That is your failing, not mine."

Carlos paused a moment.

"Why are you doing this?"

"Doing what?"

"This. Trying to hurt me, always delivering pain."

It was Catherine's turn to fall silent. It was just her way, that's all.

Her mind had been keeping something back, something that felt awkward, uneasy, crawling inside her head like something that didn't fit. She wanted to see her husband's face in the gloom, now that he had returned from the darkness, but there was nothing, no scrap of light that would illuminate him.

She wanted to see his expression to watch if it changed. The awkwardness was for him, for the words she had been keeping back.

In a way they were both her children, that was the truth of it. She had sired them both, but taken one as her lover, the other as their servant, and had ultimately destroyed them both for how they had returned what she had begifted them.

Was it right for her to put her two children together, to sanctify the hurt they had both done to her so they could find contented union once again?

Her eyes searched the blackness but failed to find his face.

"The other I came here with," she began.

"Yes?"

"You did not recognise her?"

"No. Should I have?"

"In more ways than one, yes. Ignore what she now is, and see who looks back at you from beneath."

Carlos seemed to stare at her from the darkness, but it was clear that he didn't know what she was talking about.

"You loved her once," Catherine told him, "just as you had loved me once. You did not recognise her because I did to her what I had done to you."

Carlos still did not speak.

"It was Antoinette," Catherine prompted.

"Antoinette?" Carlos breathed, his voice barely audible. "That was her?"

"Yes," Catherine told him. "You brought us both down here."

"No," Carlos said. "She left. I saw her go."

"What?"

"I didn't know who she was," he stammered. "She went to the surface. I didn't know."

"Go to her," Catherine told him, the words coming awkwardly. "Take her and go away somewhere, far away where no one will care for your grotesquery."

"I didn't know," Carlos murmured again.

But then he left, and began to claw his way upward towards the ceiling.

5

Jenner charged after her, despite the fan of blood that sprayed up and out of the mass of clawing bodies. He heard Arbour howl with pain over the din of the night children's shrieks, and heard some of their number savaged too. Most of their barely-made heads had turned towards the black dog of the desert as she'd leapt into their horde, but some still gaped towards him, and it was these that he now kicked out at.

The first two or three went down swiftly, dropping from the strength of his initial attack. But where he was one, they were many, and they reached and took hold of him with long bony fingers before he could regain his balance or strength enough to kick out again.

Teeth sank into the meat of his calf and thighs. He felt flesh break, tendons snap. The chamber lurched before him as his legs buckled beneath him.

He dropped immediately and hit the ground hard. Before his attack had ever really started, and before he could punch or destroy anything that sprawled in front of him, the tide swept over him and stole any further retaliation from him.

Their teeth were in his arms and chest, tearing and ripping. Bony hands probed and groped, snaking and clutching, seizing any human prize that might be of some worth later on when the spoils of war were piled and distributed. They were in his mouth too, sour fingers, pulpy with blisters, searching out his teeth, a tongue that made language. His bones were creaking, his flesh snagged and being coaxed from them, and all the time he felt himself expanding, two dozen or more creatures tugging him in all directions at once.

It felt like the earth was shuddering beneath him, so hard was their assault upon him. He could not move, except from where their jagged labours jerked his limbs and torso. Yet it still felt like an earthquake so brutally did they bounce him off the ground.

He barely noticed the first of their teeth slip from his flesh, just as he barely noticed the first shards of the floor rocket into the air. More and more of their number shrank back from his bloody and torn body, just as the fissure in the floor split and cracked apart and crumbled in upon itself with a deafening boom.

Jenner's vision came in blurred snatches between blinks filled with blood. His arms failed to bear him up, and all he could do was lay staring up at a ceiling mired by chastened devils and spiralling dust. Something was in the room with him, something vast that had terrified the night children, holding them momentarily at bay. Was it their master? Was it their enemy? He had no idea, and he could no longer move his body to see.

His muscles throbbed, his chest stricken by whatever injuries the creatures had already performed. It hurt to breathe. Pain stabbed him in a hundred different ways.

Then he lifted his eyes through the scarlet mush.

It hurt to swallow.

His tongue tasted blood.

Then he made out the shoulders of something hunched.

Within seconds of the monster clambering out of the chasm through which it had made its entrance, the horde of desert devils released a shriek of attack once again, and swarmed upon this new beast with renewed vehemence.

Jenner watched with utter helplessness as they surged upon the massive form of Nomad, the stone guardian who had led him through the chambers of The Curbane to meet with the goddess Alexia.

The guardian flailed with disorientation as twenty or more beings, a mere fraction of its domineering size, set upon it with claws and teeth ineffectual against the substance which made up its form. But the word seemed to spread quickly, and dozens more of their number left the battle with Arbour, some even flooding in from elsewhere on the battlefield, in order to come and assist in the destruction of this interloper.

Jenner struggled to haul himself away from the assault and crawled towards a corner of the room. Blood washed over him from wounds that lacerated every part of his body. Blood gurgled at the back of his throat, rising up like vomit even as he tried to swallow it back down.

He watched as Nomad staggered back a step as the tide of black bodies swelled massively, crawling up and over the guardian's body like an inky black soup. Jenner watched helplessly as he tried to pull them off him, but there were simply too many of them. As he took hold of one and crushed it in his mighty hands, so five more took its place, clawing and snapping at the living rock that was surely beyond their means to destroy. But what could not be broken could be smothered, and it seemed certain, as Jenner lay helpless, that Nomad lived and breathed just as any other natural creature.

The guardian staggered back another step, and then another, until it was forced down onto one knee. Jenner could no longer see any part of its body, so utterly had the night children smothered him. Still they swarmed into the chamber, crawling across walls and ceilings in their lust for his defeat.

The mass thronged for only a handful of heartbeats more, as they found their way inside his mouth and down into his throat, choking him as their filled what cavities he possessed.

Jenner slumped back against the wall as Nomad finally slumped down onto the ground, dead from the incessant onslaught of these tiniest of assassins. Some of their number became trapped by his fall, crushed by the guardian's colossal weight, but those that survived seemed not to care, or even to attempt to rescue their siblings trapped but still alive and thrashing.

As their bulbous black eyeless sockets lifted back up to Jenner once again, he closed his eyes and waited for the inevitable. If a massive unnatural creature constructed from living stone could not prove victorious, then the chances of his escape were surely nil. Yet once again he was to be saved.

Just as the majority of the horde of devils that now turned their attentions on him had been summoned by those inside, so they in turn were summoned back outside. As a series of screams lit the air outside, the crowd of bloodied night children all lifted their heads to listen. Still laying prone and slumped against the rendered wall of the sanctum, Jenner could only watch as they suddenly turned and fled back out of the chamber, fresh shrieks of fury already livid in their throats.

A movement to his right caught his attention, and he rolled his head to one side to see the fire-burned vampire struggling to find her feet. He watched with utter disbelief as she fought the wounds that cracked and split apart, her face neither wincing with pain nor wet with anguished tears, but as blank and indifferent as a mask.

When finally she managed to stand upright, she gazed around the room, taking in the sights of the dead stone guardian, the crushed bodies of the night children, and those that still thrashed beneath the immense weight of their victim, until her eyes came full circle to look down upon Jenner.

Her head cocked to one side, and in what was left of her eyes Jenner could see her misery. It pained him to see it, to return a broken gaze so burdened with wretchedness and despair. He went to speak but she stopped him with a shallow movement of her hand.

"It was you who saved me," she managed to say.

Jenner stared at her. Was she implying that his deed had been good or bad? The sadness in her eyes confirmed neither.

Then she took a step towards him.

Jenner watched as Antoinette reached out her hands as if to help him up. He shook his head, telling her that he was in no condition to stand. And besides, what possible place of refuge could he be taken to?

The night children swarmed throughout the town of Olin. Surely everything was either dead or dying. They would find their way in everywhere. He had already seen the dominant guardian Nomad overpowered and destroyed by their numbers.

But Antoinette would not have it.

"Take my hand," she said. "I am not going out there alone."


6


Arbour had made it as far as the threshold to her own temple. The view outside was fit only for apocalypse. Every building burned, the air itself on fire and thick with black smoke. Night children crawled over every surface, devouring every living thing they came across, some dragging screaming trophies out into the open where more would arrive to help tear them apart. She had despatched those creatures that had defiled her temple, tearing their filthy bodies apart until she was doused with their blood. But her victory had not been without injury to herself.

There was not an inch of her body that did not seep blood. Her flank was opened, raw meat exposed to anyone curious enough to look. One of her front legs was broken, useless and hanging crooked. Claws and teeth had been lost, left behind in bodies that now lay dead behind her. She would heal if she survived, but as she hauled her body out of her temple, she saw that what she had killed was only a paltry fraction of the entire army that swarmed outside.

While she still had life in her body she would not quit in her defence of her town. Yet the sight outside in the main street was almost enough to smother that life with one single look.

Olin was almost utterly destroyed. There seemed no part left to save. Yet something in the din surrounding her grabbed at her attention, urging her to filter it out of the bloody raging maelstrom. And it was in this process of filtering that she made out forms of fire and ice, two guardians defending the goddess Alexia from the teeming hordes of the nightmare children.

Alexia had come, that was all Arbour could think as she raced across the main street towards her, still in her form of the crippled black dog of the desert. Alexia had come to save her town.

As she neared her, however, it seemed clear that her two guardians were not enough. Even as their fire burned the nightmare children almost immediately into blackened husks, and their ice froze solid those that came within reach, the creatures that had swarmed and grown strong beneath the surface of the world overcame the deaths of their siblings, and turned the battle to their favour.

Arbour had halved the distance between them when the fire guardian fell. Searing flames leapt skyward, only to be smothered and extinguished almost immediately by the hundreds of bodies that clambered relentlessly over his burning form.

Smoke billowed and flesh hissed as he was extinguished, his life claimed by the multitude. No one could have helped him. Everyone stood to suffer the same unrelenting death.

Arbour tore at those midnight children too sluggish to find Alexia's flesh. The Mistress of Kar'mi'shah could no longer be seen now. She stood somewhere inside a vast shoal of writhing bodies, all of them shrieking and clawing at each other, so desperate were they to taste the blood of the most hallowed of all goddesses. The ice guardian had given up all hope of defending his mistress, toppling backwards under the weight of the unnatural army, his body cracking and shattering into shards as they broke him apart.

His screams died swiftly, however, swallowed whole by the din of his butchers, yet Arbour persisted in her effort to find Alexia's side.

But the dark children had grown wise to her intervention, some of them diverting their frenzy away from Alexia and setting it instead upon the savage black dog that was tearing at their backs.

Their retaliation was merciless, and Arbour felt her wounds reopened and forced deeper by the multitude of needle teeth that were now set upon her, ripping and rending, devouring her more swiftly than she could devour them. The tide of darkness washed over her, stealing what little light remained of the day, and she fell beneath their insurmountable number as they claimed yet another victim.

7

They made it as far as the door to Arbour's temple, Jenner and Antoinette, human and vampire both hand in hand and ready to witness the end of it all.

They had barely said more than a dozen words to each other, as they'd staggered the length of the nave across the corpses of the midnight children left scattered in Arbour's wake - including the shredded remains of Feral Keema - yet they stood before the bloodshed and the screams on the main street of Olin like voyeurs on Judgement Day.

Sunlight no longer penetrated the billowing clouds of burning smoke that choked the small town. Night had come early. The town of Olin was darker than anyone had ever seen it. But most of the population of Olin was no longer alive to see it anyway. The invading army had been as swift as it had been merciless.

Antoinette stepped forward, out into the day, Jenner still holding what was left of her hand. Her skin hung from her bones like roasted beef left forgotten in a scorched oven, but there was no more harm the day could possibly do to her. She walked out with her head high, indifferent to the monsters that ran across the main street looking for anyone they had overlooked, feeling the heat of the air against the hard crust of her face.

Jenner said nothing as they walked. He looked for Arbour, but there was now no sign. She must be dead, he thought, just as he and Antoinette would soon be dead. But still they walked through the turmoil, ambling like foreign tourists come to witness the grisly sights.

The air was thick with the stench of death and fire, but Antoinette seemed to breathe it all in as though it was fragranced with delicate flowers. She seemed almost happy, this unfortunate woman that should have been made a corpse many times over, yet she walked like someone consumed with bliss, and he trailing after like some unlikely lover.

So when the booming cry rose up out of the ground, the earth shuddering as though it had finally decided to open wide and swallow the whole pitiful town, it came as a surprise that the shrieks of death and frenzy died almost immediately to a whisper, rather than raised to a crescendo.

Antoinette halted beside him.

She turned her head, her melted eyes searching blindly for something at the far end of the main street. Jenner followed the direction in which she now began to step, her hand slipping from his. Whatever had made the first thundering noise now made it again, and he watched anxiously as she began to quicken her pace towards it.

The desert devils had stopped in all their movements, and stood motionless in whatever activity they had been busy in. It was as though they had been frozen in time, halted by a clock that would not be wound again.

Then from out of the billowing smoke clouds came a giant, a hideous creature seemingly fashioned

464

from spare parts that refused to go together, yet somehow their maker had achieved his foul task.

The monster boomed again, the ground shuddering with his lamenting howl, and Jenner watched helplessly as he now lumbered forward towards them, and to the ever nearer form of Antoinette.

Jenner watched with disbelief as the two unlikely figures reached one another and embraced, she standing almost a third of his height. The booming howl died as the smoke clouds billowed along the main street towards them, until they at last reached out for them and consumed them utterly, wrapping around their forms like some kind of enveloping blanket, the sight of the two of them stolen from view while still locked in their grim embrace.

The thick choking smoke clouds continued through the town, swallowing buildings whole before ejecting them once more into view. But as Jenner watched, so they seemed to collect the midnight children inside them. The beast had gone, taking Antoinette with him, his horde of night children following in their wake like the long silken train of a burial gown.

# FOURTEEN

## AN ENDING, A BEGINNING

Catherine watched Carlos return with Antoinette in his arms. From the light that spilled down from the chasm he had made, she could finally see the hideous proportions to which he had refashioned himself. He would be better off with someone his equal, she thought, better off not being alone, for both of them.

They went, too, along with his army of ghosts, but where they were headed she did not know. The awkward place in her head had gone as well, and although there existed a word for it, Catherine Calleh would not be the one to label it as kindness.

She climbed up out of the chasm after nightfall. The thief Jenner Hoard was still alive, bloodied and torn but being tended to by what few lamenting mortals there were left breathing, those that had hidden from or survived the assault of her husband's hideous offspring. But the goddesses Arbour and Alexia lay dead from wounds too severe to survive.

Catherine did not stop to offer her assistance to either those that tended Jenner Hoard, or to those mourning or preparing burial for the two slain goddesses, but instead wandered to the edge of town to look out across the vast expanse of desert.

It had a beauty all its own, she thought, a cruel

wasteland that stretched to a hard unwavering horizon. Even the mountains at her back had a mystery in their desolation. Maybe the town would need another goddess to help rebuild it, someone to help bring rebirth and prosperity back to the town Arbour had already once blessed. Even Kar'mi'shah would need a new angel of salvation if it was to survive.

The moon was high above the horizon, bathing everything in a cool blue light that cast rich shadows that did not move with any ghostly ambition. It was quiet except for the activity of the injured being tended.

Maybe she should help, Catherine thought.

Maybe that was what came next.

# EPILOGUE

# THRESHOLD

When the gateway had ruptured, the dining room floor had been sucked down, and the weight of the desert that replaced it had destroyed most of the house.

Romy had returned home from work to find dunes of burning white sand spilling across the driveway and out into the street. The insurance company hadn't known quite what to do, not at first, but when the media had ultimately discovered this second portal to Eden, and the word had gotten out more quickly than anyone could have thought possible, people came from around the world to witness the spectacle, the desert heat and landscape that had come in torrents from a house in an urban development on the outskirts of London.

A new threshold had been made, a gateway that would allow visitors from both sides free access to a world so very different from their own, nomads and explorers rubbing shoulders with the brave and the adventurous. When word spread that this journey was safe, yet more would make that trip, the timid and the shy, the disbelievers and the wary.

But the truth was undeniable.

Eden had become a brave new world.

The word was out.

The portal was open.

And it was free to whoever chose to step forward.

# The Business Of Fear

## Paul Stuart Kemp

A young thief steals a mystical deck of cards, only to incur the wrath of their unnatural owner.

A mother is tormented by forms that seem to move within the shadows of her house.

A man stops at midnight to fix a flat tyre and sees eyes watching him from the blackness of the woods.

From malevolent ghosts to carnivorous cats, from street-walking angels to life-loving zombies, The Business Of Fear is a collection of twenty four dark tales that unravels the mind and makes us face our most primal nightmares.

Paul Stuart Kemp is one of England's darkest writers, and with this book, his first collection of short stories, he takes us on an exploration of the human capacity for fear, playing on our emotions, and exploring what it means to be afraid.

ISBN 0 9538215 6 0

# The Unholy

## Paul Stuart Kemp

In an old forester's cottage in rural southern England, Irene and Michael Rider, a young married couple, decide one night to 'play the ouija'. What they invite into their new home begins to take its toll not only on their lives, but also on the lives of those around them, and the lives of their, as yet, unborn children.

Trapped in a world in which they no longer have choices, they struggle to raise the idyllic family of which they've always dreamed.

The birds in the trees are watching them, waiting for some eternal event, but the ancient evil that sits behind their eyes has time on its hands, time enough to wait forever.

Paul Stuart Kemp is one of England's darkest writers. The Unholy takes the reader into his darkest world yet; a place of demonic possession, of nightmarish visions and creatures, and the destruction of an entire family. But only at the heart of this world can true values be found: the resilience of love, the sanctity of marriage, and what it means to be human.

ISBN 0 9538215 4 4

# Bloodgod

## Paul Stuart Kemp

An archaeological expedition to a desert region uncovers both an ancient temple with strange hieroglyphics as well as an old man with a story to tell. Merricah speaks of a creature that decimated most of two tribes, and relays the whereabouts of a magical box that contains the Master of Kar'mi'shah. He has remained in isolation inside the buried temple for hundreds of years, waiting for the tribes to return, and for someone to release his Master.

Jenner Hoard is a thief recently released from prison. Montague, his benefactor, does not want him to quit working for him, and already has two lucrative jobs lined up for an anonymous customer, a deal involving the Blood Of The Ancients, and the theft of a mysterious box from an apartment building in London.

Times have never been more desperate for the vampire community living in the darkest depths of London. Alexia is one such vampire who has a brutal encounter with The Howler of Westminster after a butchered corpse is found floating in the Thames.

Human vampire hunters, known as Skulkers, have become more skillful and connected over the years, and find easy prey in those demons who are too careless about their actions. Join Alexia as she struggles to survive in a dark and foreboding world, where even demons suffer anguish, and in death there is still a fight.

ISBN 0 9538215 2 8

# Ascension

## Paul Stuart Kemp

Hampton, England 1172: After witnessing the death of her family in a frenzied witch-drowning ritual, Gaia, an eight year old girl, flees for her life. Alone and afraid, she stumbles upon a magical young boy who takes her on a journey to meet Calista, a spirit capable of harnessing both dreams and time, with promises of so much more.

Makara, Kenya 2589: There are desperate times at the end of the human race. Kiala is a man living at one of the last stations on Earth, a planet where all life has been eradicated by snow and ice. With his future hinted at, could he hold the key to preserving what little life remains, and if so, why is Calista intent on stopping him?

London, England 1994: When Carly Maddison's fiance is suddenly abducted under very strange circumstances and her fleeing brother is accused of his demise, she finds herself trapped in the depths of a dark and secret world. Her love for them both draws her deeper into that world, and if she is to discover both its rules and, ultimately, its solution, then she must face the past as well as the future, in order to learn truths that she would previously have thought unimaginable.

Witchcraft, alien abduction, ritual murders; all unfathomable mysteries, all with a human heart. Paul Stuart Kemp's science fiction horror fantasy takes the reader on an extraordinary journey, where such mysteries are found to be sown into the human soul, unable to be removed, and unable to be revoked.

ISBN 0 9538215 0 1

# Natura

## Paul Stuart Kemp

In the heart of the Jume mountains live Orkhas, creatures who it is believed guard and keep rule over Natura - the city of the dead. A war between two factions has raged for centuries, one side worshipping them as divinities, the other demanding their extinction.

Finding herself caught between both, Jessie McHard - a disillusioned scientist - stumbles upon a bridge spanning worlds to face a battle not only of blood but also of love, on a journey where she will have to make decisions she'd never believed possible. But only at its end can she rest, where mysteries can be unveiled and secrets be made known.

Paul Stuart Kemp's science fiction horror fantasy takes the reader on an extraordinary journey through space and time. Join Jessie as she embarks upon an experience that will lead her, ultimately, into the dangerous and unknown realms of self-knowledge.

ISBN 1 86106 499 3